'Lest We Forget.'

A SACRIFICE OF INNOCENTS

Best Wishes!
Alan Barker

Tommies Guides
Menin House
13 Hunloke Avenue
Eastbourne
East Sussex
BN22 8UL

www.tommiesguides.co.uk

First published in Great Britain by Tommies Guides, 2009

ISBN 978-0-9555698-7-6

Cover design by Tommies Guides
Typeset by Graham Hales, Derby
Printed and bound in Great Britain by CPI Antony Rowe, Chippenham and Eastbourne

A SACRIFICE OF INNOCENTS

by

Alan Barker

TOMMIES GUIDES

1

Grey, wet, Romford. It was raining. The interminable sort of wetness that finds its way under all the openings of your clothing and changes your outlook in an instant before you know it, making your mood match the dullness of the day. I crossed the road at a run, dodging the puddles and cars that seemed intent on splashing me with the contents of the gutter as they ran close to the kerb, making all of the pedestrians on the pavement duck involuntarily. Boy-racers, aiming deliberately in their souped-up, asthmatically-wheezing, crappy Corsas, as they tried to gain maximum points by soaking the unwary. Romford on a rainy day, God help us all. Not the best, but who makes beggars out of choosers? The High Street was surprisingly full of people, swathed in raincoats or sporting drab umbrellas in a vain attempt to keep the wet from seeping into every pore of their bodies. I weaved in among them, walking fast as I always did, a habit my wife was never slow to pick up on.

'Slow down!' she'd cry plaintively, 'Where's the fire?'

I purchased my paper, my 'drug' as my father called it, though it was he who had first introduced me to *The Daily Telegraph*. Leaving the newsagent I bumped into a fat woman who cursed me roundly as I tried, vainly, by stuffing the paper into my own raincoat, to protect the newsprint from the predations of the wet. She ignored my good-intentioned apologies and spat her obvious voluble annoyance at me before sweeping on down the street with the smug attitude of the righteous, no doubt pleased at having put me firmly in my place, as she saw it. You meet them all the time. Cursing her retreating back – it was my wet paper after all – I made my way slowly down the street, peering into each window through the raindrops coursing down them in a vain attempt to discover their contents.

Not a good way to spend a day off work you might think, but my wife had a cake to bake and I hated the thought of feeling I was in the way by sitting in front of the television. The house was reasonably tidy, housework never being a good trait of mine, and, besides, I needed the freedom of several hours spent wandering round the streets free from any schedule or timetable. Free to indulge my every whim without a raised eyebrow or question. Free time just for me.

I turned left off the High Street into South Street, heading towards the railway station. The bookshop occupied a corner of one of the drab buildings, one of those nondescript premises that are passed by every day without people ever being aware of their existence. An off-white, peeling front door and a single filthy window filled with adverts was hardly the way to advertise your presence, nor the best way to entice punters inside. Mind you, some people turn their noses up at the thought of buying second-hand books, but not me. Books were treasured in our house from an early age, taking us as children to places and countries we'd never visit as adults, filling our minds with adventures and characters and colours. I love the smell of old bookshops, that damp, musty smell of old books and papers that belies the treasures within. Phil's was no different to all the others I'd visited in my travels, and pushing the door open I stepped inside and stood awhile, taking in the familiar musty smell of the hundreds of careworn volumes lining the shelves and piled up in stacked rows on the dirty floor.

He appeared suddenly. There was no bell on the door but Phil had a nose for a customer, a rather large nose it must be said. It was that cultivated, innate sense that here was another lamb to be fleeced. He was of nondescript appearance and if pushed I would have struggled to describe him. He was, well, just Phil. Age? I couldn't say, but he talked now and then of his children which made me think he was younger than he looked. His hair wasn't that grey, though mine is and I'm only 53. That and the big nose I've already mentioned, together with the same old black woollen cardigan he always wore with his felt slippers, made up the man. He always made me think of Armenia for some reason but I never dared ask him where his origins lay. You have to be so careful these days...

I didn't even know if Phil was his real name, just that it was what he'd called himself when we first met as he was trying to add a few quid onto a rather nondescript first edition I'd taken a fancy to. His prices were always fair, don't get me wrong, it was just that he seemed to stretch the buying of a single edition into three times as long as it should have taken and slip in a price increase when he thought you hadn't noticed.

I didn't mind, here was manna to my soul, mountains of books and miles of print, and we'd talk endlessly about the redeeming features, or otherwise, of this book or that, each of us trying to outdo the other in our own way in showing what we knew. To an outsider we must have sounded peculiar, but over the months I'd been going there we'd evolved our own sort of language. Both of us knew what we were trying to say to the other, although I never left the shop without the feeling of somehow having been thoroughly diddled after a particular choice turn of phrase of his.

'Oh, it's you!'

With that he turned around and began studying his reflection in the mirror by the entrance that led to his den at the back of the shop. Now he'd recognised me he had lost interest, quite content for me to rummage around unattended and see if I could find something worthwhile. That way he could go back into the den and do whatever it was he found solace in until I came up with something I fancied or, as was often the case, left empty-handed.

It was the usual rubbish again. Half the contents of the dusty shelves came from house-clearances, gathered up and offered to Phil in response to the peeling advertisement in his shop window. I never ceased to be amazed at the steady stream of people who staggered through the doorway under the weight of boxes of books brought from God knows where, their relatives' history of a lifetime's reading habits contained within the cardboard interiors. These would be dumped smartly on the floor by the till and after picking through them in a bored manner, Phil would murmur an offer and they would leave smartly, the derogatory sums he shelled out in such cases burning a hole in their pockets. It was all so sad, goodbye Mum, so long Dad. Debenhams or McDonalds, The Black Lion, wherever, here I come.

I wandered around for ten minutes or so, picking up and discarding books at random. For some, the titles are what catches their eye, for others it's the book cover and the often lurid scenes on the front of the dust jacket. I must confess to having a foot in both camps. I would pick a book up and read the description inside only if I'd never heard of the author before, and if it sounded good I'd take a detailed, closer, look. Or a particular vivid dust jacket would stand out and I'd make a beeline for it, only to be just as quickly disappointed once I'd examined it. Phil knew which of the books were likely to be of most value and so they were placed nearer his perch by the till where he could keep an eagle eye on them.

I'd had my obligatory rummage round and was making my way back to the front of the shop. Nothing had caught my eye – it was one of those days I suppose. I was trying to squeeze past a large, heavily-bearded weirdo in a duffel coat (I had murmured 'Excuse me,' but he'd ignored me and continued to block my path) when my arm knocked a box full of musty-smelling books from one of the shelves. The weirdo took off quickly – probably thought Phil would accuse him of paying too much notice to the 'adult' books he hid from younger eyes at the back of the shop – leaving me to pick up the debris. Of course Phil was round in a shot. He must have ears like a bat in flight.

'Oi! Watch what you're doing, you clumsy bugger!' he shouted. 'Mess up any of those books and you'll be paying for them. D'ye hear me?' Before I could answer he was gone again. Cursing softly under my breath I bent down to gather them up. Yeah, right, Phil. Give me a hand, why don't you! It is *your* shop, isn't it? Something on the floor caught my eye and I stretched down and came back up with a battered, nondescript volume of nearly A4 size. Colour? Hard to say. Greenish-brown? I couldn't make it out. Dirty, that's for sure. There was an official-looking number up in the right-hand corner and a title in the middle of the front cover, but owing to its filthy state I couldn't quite make it out. Opening the cover, the first muddied page revealed a title in faded ink: *War Diary of 19th (Service Battalion) King's Own Lancashire Rifles 1915–16.*

Aha. My curiosity aroused, I turned it over. I'd heard of battalion war diaries, read about them, but never seen or handled one, until now. Putting on an innocent expression I shouted, 'Phil?'

Reluctantly he appeared again, wiping what looked like greasy breadcrumbs (I didn't want to ask) from his moustache. 'What?' he whined, 'Can't a man get something to eat without being disturbed, for Chrissakes!'

'What's this?' I said, proffering the book in my outstretched hand. 'Where did this come from?'

'I dunno,' he grumbled. 'Maybe it was in a lot I got from a house-clearance. I get a lot of stuff coming in from that sort of thing, you know that.'

I did know that, and not wanting to antagonise him further or spoil the remainder of his lunch I ignored him and turned back to the book I was holding. Flicking through the pages I could make out entries in different handwriting, in pencil as well as ink. Some were smudged and barely readable, in others the handwriting was legible with a clarity the years had done little to diminish. Names jumped out of the pages at me, names from nearly a century before. Cuthbert Snaith, Charteris and Ludlow. It all added up to whetting my curiosity. My mind made up, I turned back to the waiting Phil, trying hard to look disinterested. If he knew that I was really interested the price was going to rocket, make no bones about that.

'What would you be wanting for me to take this off your hands?' I asked. 'It's a bit battered and you can hardly read what's inside. It's the sort of thing I read though, so I'll give you a couple of quid for it, how's that?'

Mistake. Big mistake.

'Gimme it here, let's have another look,' he responded slyly. I handed the book over, reluctantly, and he turned it over once or twice before looking up at me. 'It looks important to me; I've never seen anything like this before. Looks official, like. Must be worth a few bob. Two quid? Nah. I'd want more than that, mate.'

The gloves were off. Now it was a battle of wits between us. I *was* going to have the book. I airily brushed some more dust off its cover and tried again.

'Look, Phil, this will go great with my other First World War stuff. Give me a break. It's not that much of a rarity; you get these at car-boot sales all the time. Two quid's not a bad price.'

Car-boot sales. Another mistake.

His eyes flashed dangerously. It's that Mediterranean thing, I'm reliably informed. Phil hated car-boot sales with a vengeance. They cut down dramatically on his income, he said, and he was always ranting on about them. I should have kept my big mouth shut.

'Seeing how its you and we've done a fair bit of business before I'll do you a deal. Gimme, oh, twenty quid.' He raised his arms dramatically at my horrified expression. 'That's gonna be my final offer, so take it or leave it. 'Ow about it?'

What did I want to say about 'it'? Plenty, but I could see by his set expression that it would get me nowhere. Still, I just had to try.

'C'mon, Phil. Don't be so hard on me...' I wheedled.

'What, you still standing here? Open your wallet, my friend. Pay the price or bugger off.'

'Don't be so heartless! Come on, haven't I always paid you up front, with no messing?' I entreated. 'Gimme a break, eh? Ten quid, that's a fairer price and you know it, mate!'

He looked down his nose at me, lips curled. Mate? Mate? Friendship didn't mean a thing here, we were talking about money. That equated to a serious subject in Phil's eyes.

'Put the book down and get out if you don't like,' he snarled. 'What did I say? Twenty quid? That's the price! Take it or leave it.'

'*C'mon!* Ten quid, that's fair enough.'

'Forget it! '

'Your funeral. Keep it. I'm off then, I'll go up the road in future.' Now *I* was annoyed.

'Wait! OK, OK! Don't get mad at me. It's only business, mate. Look, I'll do a special just for you. One time only. Fifteen pounds, my last offer.' The change in him was immediate. Funny how that happens when people see a sale slipping away.

'Meet me half way, come on, how's about we split the difference?' We were just getting warmed up.

He next tried the 'tugging at my heart's strings' scenario. 'Meet you halfway? I've already come all the way down, and all on your side! I've got a business to run here. Do you want to come home with me and tell Mrs Phil and the little ones that we can't afford to eat this week 'cos Daddy is giving books away now?'

'Look, I'd like the book but can't you see you're having a laugh with your price? Talk sensible. What will you take for it?'

He swallowed hard. 'My absolute bottom price, twelve quid.'

Something in his eyes told me I was going to lose this one. Thinking of what the wife would have to say if she found out how much of our hard-earned cash I was willing to part with, for what she'd regard as a tatty book, I reached into my back pocket for my wallet.

I left the shop feeling cheated. Damn and double damn! So much for my good intentions. Who was going to show who, eh? I walked off, shaking my head, annoyed for having capitulated so easily.

When I got home I carefully parked the car in the garage and walked through the connecting door into the kitchen, surprising my wife, Dawn, as she was mixing her Christmas cake on the table.

'Oh, hi darling, you're home early; did you find what you were looking for? Pass me the brandy could you? No, it's for the cake, not me. What's that?' She pointed an elbow in the direction of the Co-op bag Phil had wrapped the book in.

'Oh, just a book I conned Phil out of,' I replied brightly, hoping she wouldn't ask how much I'd had to fork out for said pleasure. My luck held. Not for long though. She turned back to battering the goo once more.

'Oh,' she pronounced sarcastically, staring fixedly at the mix in the bowl, 'that'll be another of those 'bargains' you keep filling my bookshelves with, then!'

Five minutes and lots of Brownie points later, having made Dawn a welcome cup of tea, I was sat in my comfy armchair, steaming mug of tea in one hand and the book in the other. I turned it over in my hand and looked hard at the cover. I could now make out some of the writing on the front of the book. It read, as far as I could see: 'Army Form C. 2118'. Looking inside I was confronted by a mass of pages, beginning with the main headings and instructions:

War Diary
or
~~Intelligence Summary~~
(Erase heading not required)

Someone had very carefully and neatly ruled the Intelligence Summary line through with a bold hand. Below each of these two headings was a page divided into various other headings: *Place, Date, Hour, Summary of Events and Information.*

At the back of the book were a number of dates in the same handwriting. Alongside these were a number of names, filed under headings of *Killed in Action, Wounded, Missing, Other.* There were a lot of names written here on certain dates, giving me some inkling of what could be gleaned from reading through the diary. There were also some other jumbled comments and numbers on the back pages, written in a different hand to the two styles I had made out so far. Turning to the front of the book and flicking swiftly through the faded pages, names and dates leapt out with a better clarity than I had seen in the shop. I could see some entries were short ones, as if the person writing them had become bored: *Saturday 9th October. Working parties out wiring trenches in battalion area.*

Those entries I ignored somewhat – it was the longer ones that attracted my attention and brought my imagination to light. *Tuesday 28th September 1915.* That had a longer entry. What had happened that day? Who'd done what? The pale, sepia photographs I'd pored over in other books, together with this diary and my passion for and knowledge of all things to do with the Great War could bring it all to life. Sad, but what else is a man supposed to do when he's got a ruddy great mortgage, a wife who bakes innumerable rock-hard cakes and a library filled with stories of the Great War just five minutes down the road?

My slight interest in the Great War had taken off with the discovery of my grand-father's army records in the National Archives in London. Through them I found that he'd served in the Royal Garrison Artillery as a Gunner/Driver, caring for the horses that pulled the big guns around the battlefields. The sense of outrage I'd always felt at the shocking waste of life in the four years between 1914-18 had been further fuelled by reading those records.

At a time when a casualty occurred every 15 seconds in every minute, every hour and every day for four long years, he'd been sentenced to seven days Field Punishment No.1 for "Urinating in the line at 7.30 am." All those deaths, the carnage, the sheer horror of it all, had paled into insignificance when a pompous, uncaring Commanding Officer sentenced him to being lashed to the wheel of a supply wagon for hours each day for the simple act of taking a pee in the trenches! Unbelievable!

His records had whetted my appetite and from then on I had read avidly, from the Western front to the Dardanelles, each book I devoured strengthening my belief in the contempt the generals commanding the huge armies had for the common soldier. The lives they had squandered recklessly on grandiose schemes had brought nothing but pain and terror to the men charged with carrying out their fantasies, together with untold miseries for the families of the men back in Britain who added to their grief a future of poverty and uncertainty.

The diary looked as if it held the promise of some serious reading so I approached it with a feeling of intense anticipation. It wasn't heavy – a warm, comfortable weight – so settling it down across my knees I reached over for a digestive biscuit and took a large bite, tossed back a quick slurp of tea and concentrated on the book. Opening the cover at the first entry I inhaled its warm, musty smell, a smell that stretched back over the years, and began to read.

I'd only just begun to eagerly devour the contents when Dawn popped her head round the door. 'Oh, there you are, John. I'm away out, I promised Marge and the girls I'd meet them at Susan's for a look at her Virgin Vie stuff. Sorry I've not had time to do you any tea; if you're starving when I get back I'll rustle something up.' More sterner now. 'And don't touch that cake I've just completed. It's not for you so keep your hands off, you hear?'

Seconds later the front door slammed. Sighing gratefully I subsided back into the chair, picked up *two* digestives and swiftly demolished them. I strolled over to the drinks cabinet and reaching for the Macallan poured myself a generous three fingers and sat the glass on the edge of the table next to my chair.

Lounging openly now, I finished off my tea with a final swallow and picked up the diary. Casting my eyes quickly over the stained, careworn cover I opened it carefully at the first page with a mounting sense of anticipation.

2

This being the War Diary of the 19th (Service Battalion) King's Own Lancashire Rifles, September 1915–March 1916

Monday 13th September 1915

Ten months of hard, solid training since the formation of the battalion came to an end last night. The battalion marched to the train station through the town and after a rousing send-off from a regimental band and the townspeople of Liverpool, entrained for overnight journey to Folkestone on Sunday. Battalion was to be transported to Boulogne, France, by SS Invicta'. Owing to suddenness of departure, Rear Party under Major Redford to follow later with men's kit and effects. Men very tired. Suffered our first casualty on quayside at Folkestone. 213389 Corporal F. Hackett B. Coy died of wounds.

R.D. Sprightly, Major, C Company

The train rocked, its wheels squealing, and after several longer, shuddering, shunting noises came to a stop having reversed for what had seemed a life-time. The sound of seagulls wheeling high, and the soft hissing of damp steam broke the silence. Half-cocking one eye open he looked around in an effort to establish his bearings. He'd been asleep but for how long he couldn't tell. It had been a long night. After the march through the gathered crowd at the train station the previous evening they had stood ramrod-straight on the platform as their colonel had arrived to join them. The cheers when the CO had presented Private Ludlow of A Company with a silver cup for musketry had reverberated off the iron ceiling of the platform. Bertie Ludlow had easily been the best shot in the battalion. They had cheered even louder at their CO's words before they boarded.

'Men,' he had somewhat pompously addressed them, accompanied by Captain Dundas, one of the battalion chaplains. 'When the War Office brought me out of retirement I was a trifle sceptical at their faith in the likes of you. When Lord Kitchener personally asked me to command one of his New Army battalions I became troubled at the great responsibility this would bring. I was wrong on both counts. You have fulfilled all your country's expectations.' He had cleared his throat noisily before continuing.

'We stand on the brink of a great adventure in our leaving these shores to take up arms against an implacable foe! Our training has been cut short and so we travel tonight to join our comrades in France, to shoulder some of the burden they already bear in the solemn defence of this great Empire. The Hun will rue the day they started this war and we will be there to play our part in their downfall. We shall chase the Kaiser and his Boche gang all the way back to Berlin! Be proud of the uniform you wear, be proud of the great Commonwealth of countries you go to defend and above all, be as proud of yourselves and the 19th Battalion as I am. Do not let me or your king down. May God be with us all!'

The regimental band that had been waiting then struck up several martial airs and at that point the crowd of civilians who were not supposed to have been present but who had patiently waited behind the barriers had joined in the rousing cheers and swarmed through, sweeping the barriers aside in their eager haste to embrace their loved ones one last time. He had looked for a glimpse of his fiancée, Lizzie, or his mother, but in the great crush surrounding them all had seen no one familiar and had boarded the train feeling slightly depressed. The months of rushed training near Morecambe had ill-prepared them all for the practicalities of parting and amongst the cheers he had seen many of the women, and it must be said, several of the men too, quietly dabbing wet eyes with coloured flannel.

The choice of travelling companions had been left up to Regimental Sergeant Major Findlay's lists, and Findlay had beckoned him over at the entrance to the platform where the train stood waiting patiently. 'Lance-corporal Simpson,' he had hissed menacingly. 'You will take charge of those misfits in your carriage and they *will* behave. Get me?' He had then swept off down the platform to bawl out some other misfortunate, leaving a slightly bemused NCO looking after him, shaking his head at the humour of it all before turning his attention to the slightly brassed-off waiting figures who represented part of the section he commanded.

The battalion had boarded the long line of carriages and eventually set off, leaving the crowds and waving handkerchiefs far behind in minutes. There had been no need for threats; after the novelty of speeding through the darkening countryside had worn off, they had arranged themselves as best they could in what little space they could find there was and tried to sleep as night approached, each of the eight men in the compartment lost in his own private thoughts.

Of the journey itself, he remembered little. Suffice to say that he had become bored too quickly and tried to make the most of a poor bargain. His chosen seat was against the far window and early on he had pummelled his knapsack into a semblance of a pillow. Resting it on the cold glass he had tried to sleep away the long, uncomfortable journey. He faintly recalled that they had stopped, possibly twice, but nothing had been visible through the glass and he had slid back into sleep again, trying to find some warmth from the crumpled, snoring body pressed into him on his right.

The days that had stretched into long months in the bleak, windswept camp outside Morecambe were a fading memory, the hours spent drilling, being taught the intricacies of modern weapons of war, and the hours spent on the rifle-ranges putting those lessons into practice were now gone. In their place was a feeling of being complete, part of the whole machine of war, and as he had turned restlessly, he had been made aware of another, more pressing recognition of his present military situation. The serge of his uniform tunic was grinding every fibre of its itchy coarseness into his tender neck. With a groan, he had writhed restlessly and scratched fruitlessly as the train had pursued its remorseless way towards their destination.

The dawn was a dim glow on the horizon outside the window to his left, and from where he was slumped, crushed into the body of the man to his right he could make nothing out of the dim shapes seen through the glass. The air in the compartment was heavy with the smell of sweating bodies, the foul, fetid air of body odours and sleep. As he continued to stretch his neck he could see across from him four khaki-clad shapes still sprawled in a deep slumber, their limbs intertwined in a welter of puttees, scuffed boots and creased uniforms. As he watched, one of the inert trio opened his mouth to emit a deep snore and he gazed, fascinated, as a perfect bubble emerged. It burst with a soft plop!, waking its owner up with a start.

'Wassa...?'

He got no further, as the door of the compartment was thrown open and the icy morning air rushed in, rousing them all with its cold touch.

'Right you lot, outside on the double! Come on! Let's be having you. Show a leg! Out. Now! Get them out Simpson. Move it! Move it!' The owner of the voice, a similarly clad giant with three stripes on his arms glared in as he barked his commands. Grumbling and groaning the occupants struggled to untangle themselves and stand up, unconsciously pulling their uniform tunics into place and vainly attempting to refasten their puttees that streamed across the compartment like rolls of khaki bandages. With a disgusted final glare the sergeant left them, to repeat his commands in the compartment next door.

'Bloody typical, all he can do is shout. Don't he know there's a war on?' This from the bubble-blower of minutes earlier had them all laughing at his choice Liverpudlian accent. 'Christ, I could murder a cuppa,' another rejoined, 'after all this bloody travelling I've a mouth like a gypsy's armpit! 'An I'm itchin' like a dockside whore! Anyone gorra fag?'

'Corp, are we getting fed today or what? '

'Hey you lot, are we there yet?' This quip never failed to raise a laugh.

'Right lads, you heard the man, let's get ourselves out of here,' Bob snapped grumpily as he pulled himself up and wrestled with his tunic, unconsciously rubbing his neck where the rough serge had lacerated his skin. His unshaven face itched, too, and he scratched it hard as he finished straightening his uniform. He tucked his short blonde hair firmly inside his cap and looked down searchingly. The single stripe on each arm gleamed whitely, mute evidence to having been hastily stitched there only two days previously. The men were comfortable with his lofty elevation and so far he had not had to raise his voice to obtain the correct response to his orders. It would probably come later, but for now they were content to be led.

Within the confines of the compartment the men finally struggled into some semblance of order. Caps were retrieved from the overhead shelves and jammed firmly on heads, webbing pouches were donned and straightened, and packs were grasped firmly as they prepared to disembark into the fast approaching dawn. At the last moment, one of the group remembered the rifles on the floor under the seat and, pulling them out, each man hefted his own brand new SMLE: the short-magazined Lee-Enfield .303 calibre rifle, newly issued prior to boarding. A trifle self-consciously, each of them took his place at the door before climbing gingerly down onto the platform.

Looking around, Bob saw the carriages and in the distance the locomotive, stretching back almost to infinity as a tide of khaki disgorged. The platform streamed with men all shaking the vestiges of sleep from their eyes, peering every which way to catch a glimpse of their immediate surroundings. Comrades were recognised and roundly abused in a friendly manner.

'God, my arse is sore. Another hour in that compartment an' I'd 'ave needed surgery to separate me from the seat! Hey, Cookie! Look at you, a bloody sight and no mistake!'

'Jim! Keep us a seat on the boat, next to the lifeboat! An' watch them fuckin' sailors, yer know what our mam says about them randy buggers!'

It had the appearance of a works outing, a day by the sea, but the clatter of arms and the long, deadly bayonets securely fixed in their webbing scabbards told a different story. Over 800 men were rapidly filling the platform with a heaving throng. NCOs scuttled everywhere, barking orders, pulling and pushing at the men and knapsacks in their charge, swapping men about to keep the platoons together, trying to make some semblance of order out of the chaos.

'Wadley, where the bloody 'ell do you think yer going'? Here, you daft twat, over here! Now, man, not when you bleedin' well fancy! Jesus Christ an' Holy Mother of Saints!'

The morning was now a bright glow around them, a stiffish breeze bringing to their nostrils the smell of seaweed, iodine-sharp, together with the oil and steamy smells of the carriages and engine that had brought them to this place. After reversing across the inner harbour the train had stopped on a long curved platform, from which the rails carried onto a jetty that jutted out into the sea. Eager to make sense of their surroundings the men looked around them with growing interest. A filthy, unpolished brass plaque bore the name FOLKESTONE HAR-

BOUR attached to one of the platform railings; the only clue to their whereabouts. Further down the platform Bob could see a small tea trolley, the uniforms of the women tending it proclaiming them to be members of the Red Cross. A canteen on the platform beckoned and already the women who manned it were being mobbed, each man endeavouring to relieve these angels of a mug of hot, steaming tea and a free bun or cake.

'Watch it lads, here comes the Old Man!' At the hurried warning Bob turned from his vain attempts to straighten the tunic of the baby of the company, Ben 'Boy' Godley, to see their commanding officer, Lieutenant-Colonel James Cuthbert Snaith, DSO, surrounded by his company commanders, bearing down on them. Never one to use his first name, and always being addressed by his good lady wife as 'Cuthbert', the colonel looked as fresh as the moment they had boarded the night before, with no trace of the overnight journey apparent in his immaculate appearance. Recalled from retirement to take command – a 'dugout' as such men were known – he had set to work with a vengeance. As he approached, Bob could see he was clean-shaven and wearing a fresh shirt sporting a silver tiepin stuck through the collar. His uniform was spotless, tunic and riding breeches topped with gleaming brown boots laced to just below the knee. The small greying moustache he sported on his upper lip had the appearance of being freshly clipped that day and he smelt reassuringly of fresh cologne. His turnout was completed by a bamboo cane tucked under his right arm.

'Good morning lance-corporal!' he spoke heartily, making firm eye contact. 'A good day for travelling over the water, would you agree? That's assuming, of course, that we don't have to swim for it. '

'Yes sir!'

'At ease lance-corporal' the colonel chided him gently. 'We'll be here for a while until our friends from the Navy arrive, so until then you and the men fall out and relax for an hour or two. Let them grab a cuppa and a bun from the ladies for now. Major Ramsbottom will be sorting out some breakfast for you all, once we find out where those dammed cooks have loafed off to!' He turned irritably to the sanguine figure behind him.

'Damn it, Walter, another foul-up. We did so well being allowed to detrain here instead of in the town and having to march down that ruddy great hill over there. I suppose being met was too much to hope for, despite all the promises we were given prior to leaving Liverpool. I was assured Shorncliffe would have a meal waiting for us when we arrived. And no sign of the Navy either. A shambles! Can you see anyone that looks vaguely official? No, neither can I. All right, make sure no one leaves the platform until we sort ourselves out and someone tells us what the bally heck it is we're to do. Got that? See what you can find out and let's get these men fed. God knows, it'll be a while before we see another good, hot meal if the stories from over the water are true.'

'Righto, sir.' Major Ramsbottom sighed, looking down his long, aquiline nose with a bored expression. He wore the medals of the South African war on his tunic. He swept his hand wearily through his silver-flecked hair. 'I'll send one of the NCOs up to the barracks and see where the hell those cooks have got to.' He strode off, shouting, 'Sergeant Willox! A word if you don't mind...'

The colonel turned and pointed his cane in Bob's direction. 'Fall your men out, lance-corporal, let them smoke by all means but be ready to move smartly when you're needed.' He swept by, acknowledging Bob's weak salute, and was gone, pointing out this and that to his following staff, all scurrying behind trying to keep up. 'C'mon, c'mon! Keep up. Must see about some breakfast ourselves.'

Bob wheeled round to find he was too late. The smell of tobacco wafted over to him as the men took their CO at his word and lit up, taking huge drags into their lungs as they stamped around on the platform, trying to ease some feeling into feet that were still suffering the effects of the journey. Others had already fallen out and were shoving their way eagerly down the platform towards the tea trolley.

'Oi, Jonesy, is it true all them Frenchie girls have the hots for a man in uniform?'

'Wadley, all it would take is one look at that ugly mug of yours and any bint worth her salt would pull 'er draws up an' run screaming to her mum!'

'Up yours, Jones!'

Bob grinned at the soldiers' ready lapse into old habits and walked to the end of the platform where he stood, staring back down the tracks across the grey, listless body of water that comprised the marina. The town was a black smudge across the inner harbour and he soon lost interest in trying to spot any signs of life, preferring to turn and gaze out at the white-tipped waves that broke against the outer harbour wall. Somewhere over there lay France and their destiny, but for the moment he was content to gaze silently and ponder.

A shadow fell over him and he half-turned to see who was disturbing his moment of peace.

'Look at them, the bloody fools!' The newcomer hissed his objections at the men's antics. 'Christ, if they knew what was waiting for them they'd soon bloody well stop pissing about and start praying! Ten minutes in the line and they'll all wish they were back here. Stupid bastards. Can't you see? Are you all so fucking stupid?'

'Come on Ferdy, they're only having a bit of a lark!' Bob protested, 'We've been cooped up all night in that train and it's the first opportunity they've had to relax. Are you all right?' He stared with concern at the slight figure before him. Corporal Ferdinand Hackett, 'Ferdy' to them all, was definitely not all right, his normally ruddy complexion as white as if the battalion cooks had rubbed flour into it. His paleness matched perfectly the pipe-clayed whiteness of the wound stripe on the lower left arm of his tunic. The tunic itself was crumpled and blotched, his flies gaped openly where he'd forgotten to do his trousers up properly and his ragged puttees trailed untidily down his legs. From where he stood Bob could also see that he was unshaven and sweating profusely.

'Go to blazes!' he snarled, savagely throwing off the hand Bob put out to steady him with and looking fixedly out to sea, his eyes red. His wan face assumed a haunted, hunted look.

After a long silence he spoke. 'I thought I was fine you know, I thought I could... but, I don't...I can't. I don't sleep at nights now, not since I came back from...all I see are ghosts, the faces of my dead chums. I don't think I can go back. The smell, that damn smell. The thought of it makes me feel fucking sick. You don't know what we're bloody well in for over there!' He gestured wildly in the direction of the sea. 'None of you. None.' He lurched off down the platform and came to a stop by the footbridge which stood by the harbour wall, leaving Bob staring after him. Looking round he caught the watchful eyes of his platoon commander Marching over to the young officer, Bob threw his arm up in salute.

'Sir, did you see that? It's Corporal Hackett. He's not well, there's something wrong, sir. He's not quite right. What should we do?'

Twenty-year-old Second Lieutenant Richard Arnold Whiting had frowned as he'd watched Hackett push his way through the densely packed throng, knocking protesting men aside in his agitated desire to be by himself. A university student only ten months before, Whiting's rushed training and brand new uniform resplendent with gleaming pips and Sam Browne belt had not prepared him for this. Unconsciously he straightened his khaki tie and cleared his throat.

'Thank you Simpson, yes, I did see it. Do you know where the MO is? He might have an idea. You know, have a look at him or something...' He spoke lamely, conscious of how weak his reply sounded to the anxious soldier standing in front of him.

Frowning, Bob replied, 'All right, sir, I'll go and find Doc Hughes and let him know.' He saluted and wheeled around to walk to where he had seen the officers aimlessly milling minutes earlier.

'Keep me informed, Simpson.' This was to Bob's departing back, but already he had moved out of earshot. The men moved readily out of his way, something in Bob's face alerting them to the urgency with which he pushed and shoved his way through them. Ben Godley, still trying to straighten his tunic, smiled as he saw Bob approach. 'Look Bob, I've almost...' The words died on his lips at the sight of his friend's grim visage.

Just as Bob was beginning to lose hope of ever spotting the officers, he saw the rising plume of smoke from a pipe. Simultaneously he saw the square, lantern-jawed face of the battalion medical officer, Captain Bevan Hughes, pipe firmly grasped between his teeth as he conversed laughingly with several of his fellow officers.

'No, no, seriously, I told her. You jolly well nip off and bring your mother back with you and then we can...' He stopped abruptly, staring inquisitively at the anxious face in front of him.

'Well? What? What is it, young fellow?' This despite the fact Hughes was only thirty-two himself.

'Sir, could you come with me now, it's rather urgent. It's Corporal Hackett sir, he's gone, well...sort of peculiar.'

'And you are?' The question came laconically as the MO stared enquiringly at him. Bob felt his face redden as those around the doctor also stared.

'Beg your pardon sir, Lance Corporal Simpson, second platoon, 'B' Company. Second Lieutenant Whiting requests your attendance, sir.'

'He does, does he , laddie? Then why didn't you say so in the first place? Righto, lead the way Macduff.' The MO grinned, to put the serious young man before him at his ease. 'Shall I bring my bag? No, don't answer that one, how are you to know? This shouldn't take long Roddy, so don't, I repeat don't, have any thoughts about pinching my breakfast when the order comes to join the CO.' They made their way back in seconds this time to where Whiting stood, staring at the lonely figure by the footbridge, gazing morosely over the harbour.

'What-ho, Richard,' the MO enjoined, 'I hear you have a problem with one of your men? Where is the blighter? Not wanting to cancel his ticket for the trip is he? All this fuss because breakfast isn't here waiting!'

Whiting raised a hand in greeting and pointed down the platform. 'Not one of mine I'm afraid, sir. That's him over there. Corporal Hackett. Lance Corporal Simpson here will tell you what's going on. There's something not quite right with the man.'

Bob spoke quickly. Bevan Hughes listened in silence, and then spoke quietly.

'Hmm. I see what you mean, but it doesn't mean anything, could be just a show of nerves you know. Has he been like this before?'

Whiting answered him. 'He's not in my platoon sir, but I do know a bit of his background. Hackett's a replacement, been with B Company a month now, to bring them up to full strength. I do know from a conversation with Major Redford, his company commander a week or so ago, that he's a bit of a dour cove. He's the only one of us who's seen action so far, been out to France before with the Buffs earlier this year. Was slightly wounded in a show near Neuve Chappelle. Apparently everyone else in his section was killed and Hackett was the only survivor. He spent three days lying in front of the enemy wire before a raiding party found him and brought him in. Doesn't speak much of his experiences. Won't talk about it. Tends to keep to himself a lot. That's about all I can tell you.'

'All right, let's have a look at him.' Hughes looked round at Bob. 'You come with me.' He turned to Whiting. 'All this over nothing. We're missing a good brekkers you know, the Old Man has ordered breakfast for all the officers in the

Pavilion Hotel over there on the other side of the harbour. He'll be there already with his cronies. Looks like you and I will just get the leftovers, Richard. Right, Simpson, walk with me, there's a good fellow. Let's go and have a look at your man!'

They walked slowly down to the footbridge to where Hackett stood. At their approach he turned to watch them, his right hand stuffed inside his greatcoat. 'Hello, old man, I understand you're not feeling so good. How can I help?' Hughes enquired solicitously. Hackett brought his head round slowly to stare blankly at his enquirer, his eyes focusing from their previous far-away gaze. The morning shadows cloaked his face in dark lines as he looked at first the captain and then Bob before answering slowly, pronouncing each word emphatically as if in some form of a trance.

'Help? Help me? No. I'm sorry, sir, I think it's far too late for that.'

'Why don't you let me be the judge of that,' replied the MO easily, 'I'm supposed to be a doctor.' He started forward but as he stepped close to him, Hackett suddenly moved sideways, away from the railway tracks. He drew his right hand smoothly from inside his greatcoat and pulled the hammer rearwards of the service revolver that had magically appeared in his hand until it locked into the cocked position with a loud *click!* Waving the revolver nervously in the direction of the MO as he continued his approach, Hackett then placed the blued barrel of the gleaming revolver to his right temple. The gun wavered loosely as he sought to keep its heavy weight pressed against his head. It's khaki lanyard flapped incongruously from its butt, the free end trailing over Hackett's right shoulder.

'Please sir...don't...no,' he pleaded. 'Please. I can't. Don't you see! I can't! I'm sorry, sir. *Don't!*' His left arm rose up pleadingly, the outstretched hand and the loudness of his voice stopping the MO in his tracks, pulling him up in shock and amazement. Hughes took an involuntary step forward and mouth opened as if to speak, but this only galvanised Hackett into action. His body stiffened and his gaze hardened. He took a further step backwards and sighed, a long, drawn out sigh, transfixed the MO with a penetrating stare and, keeping his eyes firmly locked on the officer in front of him, pulled back hard on the trigger.

The report, shockingly loud in the still morning air, jerked heads round frantically in an attempt to ascertain the location of the sound. The gulls, quiet of late, rose shrieking into the air once more, wheeling around in large numbers, adding their vocal presence to the scene of horror as the sound of the shot echoed and re-echoed around the harbour. Bob's left hand jerked involuntarily at the sound of the gunshot, grabbing the MO's tunic sleeve.

The impact of the shot snapped Hackett's head back violently, his body following suit before collapsing and slumping down tiredly against the footbridge steps in a vivid spray of bright red blood that lashed at the MO's tunic and face. A wisp of blue-white smoke slowly uncurled, surrounding the corporal's head like a halo. The revolver fell with a thud out of a limp hand and rested against Hackett's right boot, the blood slowly seeping into the khaki lanyard as it lay immersed in a pool of spreading crimson. A uniform cap rolled along the track and fell over at Bob Simpson's feet. He looked down uncomprehendingly. A brass badge shone dully up at him and he concentrated on it, frowning, recognising the battalion's badge. A Lancashire rose, with two crossed Lee-Enfields behind and the number '19' in front, picked out in silver. The cap was spattered with fresh blood and what looked like bits of brain matter.

Hughes reached out and caught Bob as he retched violently, tottering on the edge of falling. 'Oh God! The poor, poor blighter. Look, I'll deal with this, Simpson. You go back and stop anyone approaching. Got that? Send someone for the CO. He'll need to know straightaway. And God help the poor chap who's going to catch it when he finds his pistol missing from his kit. Go on then, man, do as I say. Are you all right?'

Bob nodded numbly as he fought to contain the nausea that queasily threatened to overwhelm him, his mind still unable to take in what had happened in front of them moments before. The MO gave him a shove and he stumbled back up the platform to where the massed ranks waited for him, their faces shocked and stunned. White-faced and open-mouthed they watched as he sped past.

Behind him, slowly pulling a snow-white handkerchief from his breeches pocket, the MO approached the inert figure lying slumped where he had fallen. His racing mind identified the gun as a .455 Smith and Wesson revolver. A service revolver, an officer's side-arm, no doubt about that. The left side of the man's head where the bullet had exited was a shattered, bloody mess of white bone fragments and pulped grey brain matter, the face almost unrecognisable. Testimony indeed to the destructive power at close range of such a large calibre bullet. He reached over and closed the dead man's fixed, staring eyes in a gesture of pity.

On the other side of the harbour, in the well-appointed Pavilion Hotel dining room, Cuthbert Snaith DSO was holding court among his gathered officers. As he had swept down the railway platform on his way to the hotel he had been addressed by one of the volunteer ladies from the canteen who had flourished a large book under his nose and implored him to sign it. A visitors record of all who passed through, she explained. Graciously he had taken the pen from her and scrawled both his and the battalion's names in his neat copperplate handwriting on the page she had indicated. An idea had taken hold as he'd handed the book back and he now gave vent to his thinking.

'This War Diary matter. I don't want it handled by one of the junior officers. It will be the record of our service wherever they're going to send us and by God I want it done properly. Mark my words well, gentlemen, when we get over there I shall expect nothing but the best from all of you. Therefore, I propose to put our war diary in the hands of a more senior chap. Ronald!'

Further down the table, Major Ronald Sprightly started guiltily at the sound of his name, his head jerking round in the direction of the CO.

'Ronald? I'm talking about the battalion's war diary. Looking for a first-rate chap to take it on. Think you can make a good job of keeping it in good order? Good man, knew you would.' He nodded kindly in the major's direction and was in the process of lifting a forkful of superbly-scrambled egg to his appreciative, waiting lips when the sound of the gunshot echoed and re-echoed through the still, morning air. With a start he dropped his fork and looked round apprehensively as several of his officers rushed outside in order to ascertain the cause of the noise.

Back on the platform, the MO remained crouching for several, long moments, before the loud blasts of a whistle rent the air and he looked up to see appearing around the headland the silhouette of a large steamer. Wreathed in clouds of coal-black smoke that trailed far downwind behind her as she headed for the harbour and the quayside, flanked by the sleek, sinister-looking greyhounds that passed for her destroyer escorts, the transport for France had arrived.

'Whey, lads, look at that! All aboard the flippin' *Skylark*! Tickets 3d a throw. C'mon, don't 'old back. Oo's goin' ter be first?' a wag from the crowd shouted but no one from the watching, sombre group answered. The reality of where they were heading had hit home with Hackett's death. The 19th were finally on their way to the war.

3

Tuesday 14th September 1915

Transport delayed leaving Folkestone until after enquiry into 213389 Cpl Hackett's death.
2/Lt. Wordsley, A Company, severely censured for loss of service pistol from his belongings.
Captain of Invicta *then refused to leave until nine o'clock that night, citing enemy subma-*
rine danger. Battalion remained on quayside for rest of the day. On arrival in Boulogne after
midnight, Battalion marched to camp outside the town to rest before marching to train
station at 0:600 ack emma for onward travel to Bethune. Poor travelling conditions left
many men tired. Battalion billeted in and around Bethune for the night.

R.D. Sprightly, Major, C Company

They awoke tired and depressed. The shocking events of the day before had left the scene indelibly etched on their minds. A hastily-convened enquiry into the events on the quayside had taken up much of the morning before the captain of the *Invicta* had flatly refused to sail after lunch, citing the low state of the tide and the danger lurking on a flooding tide of enemy submarines. When at last they had boarded the ship they were too tired to take in much of their surroundings. Consequently, the time it took them to cross the Channel, escorted by the now blacked-out warships, was passed by many in a thoughtful silence.

On arrival in France they had been met by a bored, yawning transport officer who, after giving them desultory instructions on how to reach their resting place for what remained of the night, had disappeared like a wraith as quickly as he had arrived. Once safely disembarked in Boulogne – no small matter given their state of mind and physical and mental tiredness – they had sleepily formed up in a light drizzle and marched through the deserted streets of the town, their boots slipping on the wet stone cobbles. It didn't feel as if they were overseas – for all the strange architecture they might well have been back in England.

No one had peeped out from behind the wooden-shuttered windows, the deserted streets and the haze from the drizzle giving an eerie effect of wandering through a ghost town. No conquering heroes here, no cheering crowds with pretty girls laying flowers at their feet with warm, welcoming smiles. Nothing but rain and a deathly stillness, broken only by the ringing of their boots. Grimly, they had tramped on in a sullen silence.

The camp was a few miles outside the town. An orderly officer had also fleetingly welcomed them with callous indifference and shown them where they would be resting for the remaining few hours of the night. When at last they had reached the leaking, draughty bell tents he had indicated they had flung themselves down, officers and men alike, on the muddied floors that had awaited them and tried to catch a few hours of broken, disturbed sleep. Reveille had been at 04:30 and after it was obvious that no breakfast would be forthcoming, they had morosely donned their packs, webbing and weapons once more. Feeling damp, hungry and exhausted they had marched back to the town.

The colonel strode purposefully ahead of the main body, tunelessly whistling as he swung his bamboo cane in time to the measured tramp of boots behind him. The overnight drizzle had cleared away and though it was not quite light yet, the prospects were looking good for a fine day.

'Look at 'im!' whispered 'Titch' Magilton to his mate Alfie Parkes, shuffling along next to him. 'Where the bleedin' 'eck does he think we're goin'? To the park for a fuckin' stroll?'

'Magilton! Shut it!'

'Yes sarge,' he wearily responded, and looked sideways at his mate to see a sly grin spreading across Alfie's face. That was him told and no mistake!

They skirted the grey buildings of the town and approached a large, dilapidated building that shielded the railway tracks they were seeking. A long column of dirty grey smoke rose lazily into the air above the building, indicating the whereabouts of the marshalling yards and the transport that would take them onwards to the Front. On the corner, an old woman and a young girl, both dressed in patched, drab black dresses, watched their marching with an air of resigned indifference. The old woman, her hair drawn back into a severe bun, scowled as they drew nearer, but the girl eagerly scanned the mass of men as if looking for someone she recognised. Alfie Parkes grew emboldened enough to give her a huge salacious wink as they passed. He was rewarded by her letting forth a giggle from behind a dainty hand pressed to her mouth. The old woman rounded on her furiously, and snarling in a high falsetto that no one could understand, pulled the young girl by her shoulder backwards through the doorway into the building. Several of the men who had witnessed the incident laughed uproariously.

'Parkes!'

'Yes, company sergeant-major?'

'I saw that! Report to me when we gets off the bleedin' train an' I'll give you something to occupy your time!'

'Yes company sergeant-major.'

Now it was Titch's turn to grin.

They swept into the marshalling yards and came to a straggling halt, the rear files colliding with the men in front of them as the colonel raised his cane to the sky.

'Battalion, halt!' he shouted, but it was too late. What space there was in the entrance to the yard was now filled with a mass of struggling, interlinked humanity. In front of them, seeming to stretch forever, was a mass of railway tracks branching off in all directions. Some bore wagons and tired-looking locomotives astride them, others were empty.

No one was in sight, the yards seemingly devoid of life. Angrily, Lieutenant-Colonel Snaith whirled round and collided with a flustered lieutenant, his red armband bearing the legend 'RTO' in white on his right tunic sleeve, who seemed to have materialised out of nowhere. The clipboard the lieutenant was holding in his right hand caught the colonel a stinging blow to his face and he reeled back as the young officer advanced remorselessly on him, oblivious to the pain he had just inflicted.

'Are you the 19th Battalion? You're late!' he said angrily. 'You were supposed to be here twenty minutes ago.'

'Who the hell are you?' Snaith shouted, rubbing his reddening face vigorously in a vain attempt to take the pain away.

'Oh, sorry, sir. The train needs to be away shortly or it'll mess the whole schedule up for the day. Calais is bunged up solid so I've a hospital train coming in from Rouen, and...'

'I asked who the hell you were, not what games you were playing with your damned train set, laddie!' the colonel curtly interjected.

'Oh, right, er, sir.' The lieutenant stepped back and threw a parade ground salute. 'Lieutenant Williamson, deputy rail transport officer for Boulogne. Sir!'

'Good. At ease lieutenant. Now that we've got the social niceties out of the way let me introduce myself. Lieutenant-Colonel Snaith, commanding officer of the 19th Service Battalion King's Own Lancashire Rifles, on our way to God knows where. As you can no doubt see, my men are exhausted, hungry and in no way fit to travel anywhere.' He looked Williamson up and down, keenly aware of the other's immaculate appearance. An early call with a cup of tea in a comfortable bed from his batman, no doubt, before catching the official transport down to the railway yards to intimidate some poor hapless beings.

'Now let me tell you what's going to happen, Williamson. You, sir, are going to make arrangements for my men and myself to be fed. After we have had some decent food and a hot drink we will allow ourselves to be transported to wherever it is our High Command sees fit to send us. My men are tired, hungry and thoroughly fed up. We've been travelling for almost two days.

'My machine-gun section has no machine-guns owing to our failure to receive them prior to leaving Liverpool. My stretcher-bearers have no stretchers. We have very little in the way of small-arms ammunition so God help us if we do meet the Boche on the way. We shall have to fight to the last man using only our bayonets and rifle-butts, if the enemy is stupid enough to come that close.

'We are, no, I am, starting to get severely annoyed. Do I make myself understood?' His voice rose by several decibels as he delivered this impassioned speech in the direction of the by now thoroughly discomfited man in front of him.

'Ah, perfectly, sir.' The poor lieutenant was only too eager to ease his way out of the confrontation that was threatening to develop. 'If you would just give me a moment I'll see what can be done. I'll be back shortly, sir.'

Snaith turned. 'Walter? Walter! Ah, there you are. D'ye see what happens when one shouts? Damn base wallah! Tell the men to fall out and take their packs and equipment off, there's a good fellow. All we've done so far on this damned journey is wait for someone else to pull their finger out. Hopefully that fellow will rustle up some hot food for us all and a cup of tea. Then we'll think about boarding his damn train, but not before.'

'Roger, sir.' Major Ramsbottom laughed as he turned to carry out the Old Man's request. That should stir them up. Snaith might look an old codger but he let no one browbeat him.

It took a while but within thirty minutes a series of motor lorries arrived, carrying a contingent of sleepy-eyed, grumbling cooks who quickly erected a field kitchen under the watchful eyes of the colonel. Before long, a queue formed and the men peeled away from the urns and cooking ranges bearing a hot, greasy, bacon sandwich and a mug of steaming, sweetened tea. The colonel looked on with satisfaction as his men were finally fed and only after the last one had moved away from the makeshift kitchen did he allow himself to be led over to where the cooks had prepared him a hot meal.

'Ahh! That's better, doncha' just love a good feed?

I was beginning to think we'd never get fed again. Bring on those filthy Boche, I feel like a fight right now!' exclaimed Private Bill Godsman of D Company, cap pushed back on his head as he leant squatting against a storeroom wall. He pulled his rifle to his shoulder and, peering along the barrel, took aim at the neighbouring group of men over the open sights. Working the bolt back and forth he pretended to fire.

'*Bang! Bang! Bang-bang!* Yer all dead, you miserable bunch of Hun bastards! Ouch! Wharra...?'

He was rewarded for his gallantry with a swift kick in the shins and jumped round to see the angry figure of his platoon sergeant looming over him.

'Godsman, you stupid turd!' spluttered Sergeant Leonard Jeffries. He looked mad, his face puffed up as he squinted down at the unfortunate object of his considerable wrath. 'What have you been told about pointing guns at people? Do you want to kill someone? Put that bloody rifle down and get back with the others. Seein' as how there's no Boche within miles for you to work all that energy off on, why don't you take hold of that large dustbin over there and walk round collecting up all the shite? Now! At the double!'

'Right-ho sarge.' Godsman scrambled quickly to his feet, taking care to keep out of range of the sergeant's rather large boots as he peered round to see where the dustbin lay. It was quite heavy but he bore it like a feather duster as under the watchful eyes of the still-wrathful sergeant, and moved around the small groups of men stuffing the remains of the leftover sandwiches in it.

While still sitting and waiting they were visited by the RSM. Standing over them and putting on his sternest face, RSM Findlay addressed them in a loud voice.

'Men,' he intoned bleakly, 'we are now in France. This country is not Blighty and has some peculiar habits and customs that you will all too soon become aware of. Did I not promise your mothers I'd look after you? So pay attention. One, leave the bints alone; you'll be too busy killing the Boche to want to dally with members of the fairer sex. Two, the strong drink you will encounter roundabouts is called "vangt blonc". It is foul and tastes worse than vinegar, so best leave it be. Three, read the cards issued to you in your pay-books and inwardly digest. See what your country, king and commander-in-chief demands of you. Your best behaviour, men. You won't be told twice, I can assure you.

'We will shortly be boarding the transport to the Front, if these lazy base wallahs can get their fingers out. You have all been issued with iron rations so if you get hungry during the journey, break into them. But be warned, there might not be anything waiting for you when we finally arrive. Do I make myself clear?'

A voice from the back innocently piped up, 'Oi, sir, isn't there a brothel around here where a man can get a drink an' a good feed then?'

'Who said that?' the RSM screamed wrathfully as the men exploded into laughter. He raced around the crowd of guffawing, mirthful khaki in a vain attempt to find the culprit but the sea of innocent upturned faces gave away no clue as to the wag in their midst and he gave it up as a bad job. After the laughter died away, they stared at him in solemn silence and realising the futility of trying to find his man, Findlay gave them his most ferocious look and moved on to the next group.

Meanwhile, the RTO moved gingerly over to where the colonel sat wiping his lips as he chewed on the last morsel of a rather fine piece of cheddar.

'Er, I wonder if I could impose upon you, sir.'

'Yes? What is it?

'We really must start getting your fellows loaded sir, there isn't much time left and if we don't get you away on time there'll be hell to pay at headquarters.'

'My dear chap, we mustn't upset HQ must we? Let's see. Walter! Get the company commanders to get their chaps together and see if we can't get a move on to help this fine fellow out. There, you see? All taken care of. Now, just one more thing before we do move off.'

'Yes sir?'

'My orders,' the colonel informed him bluntly. 'Haven't the faintest idea where the hell it is we're supposed to be heading. We left in too much of a hurry for anyone to tell us anything, other than to get ourselves to Boulogne and join up with the 15th Division. Said we'd find out on the other side. Don't suppose you have an earthly, do you?'

With a sense of relief Williamson pulled an envelope off the front of his clipboard.

'My adjutant gave me this last night to give to you, sir. I think you'll find your orders in there'

The colonel took the envelope from him and tore it open impatiently. He scanned the lines typed on the single piece of paper inside and looked around exasperatedly.

'Ah, I see. Or, rather, I don't see. We're to join up with 15th Division in 4 Corps area it says. We're to be part of 45 Brigade at Bethune. Divisions, corps, brigades, what a carry-on. How the dickens do they expect me to know where Bethune is? We've no maps.'

The RTO spoke soothingly. 'It's all right sir, I'll get one of my men to bring a map down to you. You can keep it, although you should get supplied with everything when you arrive. The train we've commandeered is to drop you off in Bethune and you'll find further orders awaiting you there. Now, sir, do you think we could make a start loading your chaps? According to my paperwork here, you should have thirty-two officers and 834 other ranks and NCOs. Would that be right?'

'If you say so,' the colonel laughed, feeling more cheerful with each passing minute, especially after the food he'd just consumed. 'I think we left Liverpool with that number.' The events of the previous day hit him like a thunderbolt and he frowned. 'No, make it 833 ORs. We'll be leaving here one short so best you amend your ticket. Right my man, come along; let's see where you're going to put us.'

Obediently, the RTO fell in behind him as he strode off, surrounded by his now alert officers, stopping to converse and share a few words with his men as they waited patiently in the small groups they'd gathered into. He finally reached the last group and looked past them at the waiting train. Several of the men followed his gaze.

The locomotive away in the distance belched its smoke to the sky, the sound of quietly hissing, wet steam filling their ears as they gazed in amazement at the long collection of carriages that snaked seemingly forever behind it towards them. At the front, immediately behind the tender, a long, brown carriage with dark, grimy windows running the length of it could dimly be made out. Behind that were approximately twenty-five dirty, wooden-slatted, covered wagons, none of which carried a single window but all of which were equipped with a solid sliding door on each side. These bore the legend *Hommes 40, Chevaux 8* along their sides in big white letters.

'*Cheveox? Sheveyox?* What the bleeding 'eck does that mean, our kid?' Hands on hips, Private Reggie Pilling gestured towards his pal next to him as he unconsciously mangled the French words.

'It's actually pronounced *shevaux*, Reggie,' explained Henry Watson solicitously, polishing his spectacles on his sleeve as he gazed at the wagons' doors. 'It means horses. And *ommes* means men. Eight horses or forty men. I reckon that must come to mean how many of us each can hold,' he finished thoughtfully.

'Get a load of him!' exclaimed Reggie. 'Welcome to bleedin' France, courtesy of Henry, fuckin' know-it-all Watson! Right then, show me which one of these 'orses I get to ride.'

Hurriedly the RTO explained as the colonel continued to stare in silence. 'We'll get you going as soon as you're loaded sir. You'll be travelling on a branch line to Bethune, via Hazebrouck. It'll take some time I'm afraid. These Frog trains don't travel that quickly and you might be shunted in to sidings at any time to allow more priority traffic through. The carriage at the front is for you and your chaps with your kit, the other carriages are for the men. Looks lousy but I'm told they're quite comfortable.'

The colonel gestured disdainfully at the wagons. 'Have you journeyed in one of those yourself?'

'Well no sir, I haven't been out of Boulogne yet. I mean...' He reddened and looked down at his immaculately polished boots.

'No. Quite. I don't expect you have,' the colonel answered coldly. 'It'll have to do, although this is not what I wanted for my men. For now, kindly get your chaps to assist and let's get a move on. We don't want to miss the war, do we?'

The loading of the train got under way. Men were detailed off to carry the officers' luggage into the compartments of the single carriage, an act they carried out with ill grace.

'Oi, Reggie,' Sid Bates, a lean, leathery-faced private asked his chum, 'what 'ave you got there?' He pointed towards the bundle Reggie Pilling was struggling with.

'Don't ask, pal,' Reggie replied, puffing under the weight of his burden. 'It's Second-Lieutenant Hanson's extra kit. I think his mummy must have bought him it in London. There's a folding canvas chair, a wash-stand of the same stuff and a waterproof bucket, would you believe. Its fair knackered me trying to carry it.'

'Give it here, you berk. I'll show you where to put it.' Before he could react, Reggie found his bundle torn roughly from his grasp. As he looked on, open-mouthed, Sid Bates spun round and casually tossed it behind a large pile of packing crates in an alleyway between two shunting sheds. 'There, you go, me old mucker, lost in transit! Ain't his mummy going to be sore!' Laughing loudly, the two men rejoined their comrades and boarded the train.

Elsewhere, other officers found their luggage tossed willy-nilly into the overhead netting provided in the compartments, as the soldiers worked in pairs, impervious to the hostile stares of the owners of the said luggage. Once done the men stumbled back along the railway lines to where their own packs, weapons and accoutrements were waiting and joined the queue as their comrades waited to board.

'Christ! Can you smell that?' Private Luke Woodham recoiled at the acrid stink of urine and something else more unpleasant that wafted out as the sliding door was slid back with a rusty, squealing noise to reveal the dim interior of the waggon before him. 'Corp? Corp? There's no bloody way I'm getting in there!'

'Now what the fucking hell are you playing at, Woodham!' snarled his section corporal, Harry Sheldon. 'Get in there or I'll move you in at the point of my bloody bayonet. Move it!'

'It's full of shit, corp!'

'Get out of the way, man! Get out of the way damn you, let me have a look.'

Corporal Sheldon jumped into the open doorway and inhaled deeply. He bent down inside the carriage and examined the deep, filthy straw that lined the floor, waving his boot among it and looking intently down to see what he had disturbed. Finally he straightened up and turned to face the expectant, waiting troops.

'Well,' he said finally, 'I've some good and some bad news for you lads. The bad news is you're right, Woodham, it's full of shit. The good news is that if you're in here for some time and if you get hungry you'll be fine 'cos there's plenty of it. The French have a word for it I'm told. They call it *"orses doovers"*.' He chuckled at his own wit, then his face changed abruptly. 'Now get in here! All of you.'

'Hang on corp. Watson from A Company says there should only be eight of us in each wagon. Ain't that right, Henry?'

'Listen you soddin' little barrack-room lawyer! I said all of you get in here now. The bleedin' number eight refers to the horses, not you, you stupid bunch of God-forsaken shirkers! And if I have any more crap from you, Woodham, I shall explain further with the toe of my boot. Now move your arses! And no smoking while you're in here either, we don't want to have to stop in the middle of France to throw precious water over you 'cos one of you fancied a crafty drag. Got that? Right, now git inside, all of you. Move it!' As they threw their rifles and packs into the carriage and began to board, he exploded again. 'No, you soddin' arseholes! What've you been told? Keep your rifles clean, for Chrissakes! If we have to charge into action when we get there, what are you going to fight Fritz with? Not with those bloody things bunged up with crap, you won't! Clean them now. Go on then, do it, don't just fuckin' stare at me like that, laddie!' With a snort he moved on.

Gingerly the men climbed inside the gloom of the carriage and tried to find a place among the straw that was uncontaminated from the depravations of the previous, equine, occupants. It took a while but eventually they were all on board. Along the length of the train similar scenes were taking place and it took over an hour before the battalion was ready for departure. Snaith and the RTO indulged in idle chit-chat while waiting for the train driver and his assistant to board the locomotive. One officer stood by the open door of a carriage, peering inside.

'Just a moment there! It's Watson, isn't it?'

Henry Watson turned at the mention of his name and squinted myopically at his questioner, to be confronted by the enquiring gaze of Major Roberts, the battalion adjutant.

'Yes, sir?'

'Ah, Watson, Did I hear you telling the others the meaning of the phrases on the doors just now? Speak the lingo do you?'

'Well, sir,' Henry replied wistfully, 'my wife and I were in the habit of taking our holidays in France. During the school holidays, you understand. She's a school teacher. I picked up quite a bit. Sort of a hobby of mine. Languages and all that.'

'Yes, yes. Quite. Look here, man, the colonel could do with someone like you to help translate for him. Avoid any unpleasantness. We were supposed to get a Froggie liaison chap but the blighter's never turned up. Typical shambles. Not to worry, you bring your kit along and come with me. You'll be travelling with the colonel and me in our compartment from now on. Close at hand, you see? Come along. Come along!' With that he spun around and hurried away, not waiting for Watson to follow.

The smile on Henry's face stretched from ear to ear. With an affected air he picked up his rifle and knapsack and turned to go. As his mates watched, openmouthed, he pushed his spectacles back on his nose and turning back quipped, 'Now then lads, you heard the officer. I'll see if I can survive the comforts of home, me and my mucker the Old Man. Take it easy now. Ta-ta, or should I say, *au revoir*.'

Already on board at the back of the waggon, Sean Murgatroyd, eyes narrowed, opened his mouth to snarl something choice at his friend's departing back but before he could utter a word a piercing whistle rent the air. The sound was the catalyst for the yards before them to suddenly fill with scores of uniformed men, all wearing Red Cross brassards on their right arms. Slowly, around the side of the buildings, the outline of a train hove into sight, travelling infinitesimally slowly before their inquisitive gaze. Long carriages with white-blanked windows filled the yard as the train came to a smooth, practiced, squealing stop opposite them.

'Jesus and Mother of God! Would you look at that!' Murgatroyd gasped audibly.

No one answered him; they were all too busy looking past him through the open doors, watching the waiting men fall on the train as it stopped and, opening the carriage doors, dive inside. Moments later the first pair arrived outside, carefully carrying a stretcher between them. The watching men took in the whiteswathed, inert figure lying on the stretcher as the bearers carefully carried him over towards a waiting ambulance. It was too easy to see the crimson bloodstains leaking through the bandages as an officer wearing the same brassard as his men strode over and peered down at the still figure. Gesturing purposefully, he walked over to the next stretcher to approach as the two men behind him walked over and deposited their load into the ambulance.

Within a few minutes this scene was enacted several times over as more and more stretchers were unloaded from the train, all carrying their precious burdens of humanity.

Eventually the stretchers stopped coming and several figures now emerged, some hobbling with crutches, others slowly limping down the platform. One of the walking wounded hobbling along became aware of the crowded train opposite and stopped to gaze back at them. He painfully straightened his bent back and took a long, hard stare at the soldiers. After a while, he leant on one crutch and lifting the other with an effort pointed it at the silent, watching crowd.

'You're next!' he shouted.

The sigh from them was a great collective one, as men exhaled noisily.

The colonel took charge.

'Williamson,' he shouted, 'get us moving. *Now*, damn you!'

Williamson sprang into action. He dived into his office, where he'd been relaxing as the men embarked, and reappeared holding a red flag in his hands and a whistle clamped firmly between his teeth. Frantically he waved the flag in the direction of the locomotive and blew hard on the whistle. He was rewarded by an answering blast from the locomotive's steam whistle. Seconds later, with a loud, reluctant, squealing noise, the train lurched forward, hard. Slowly it began to move, inching along the rails at first, picking up speed as the huge steel wheels gained a purchase on the rails below.

Those still waiting to board had only time to throw their rifles and packs inside and then themselves as the train began to move faster and faster. Through the open carriage doors, those that still could, watched intently. Keeping their eyes on the ambulance train and its human cargo still being unloaded they gradually drew away from the yards and began to move out into the sunshine that had burst through the clouds.

Long, long after they had rattled into open country they continued to sit in silence, each man contemplating the sights they had left behind. The war which had seemed so far away had been brought closer, and in a manner that was both frightening and disturbing. What they had just witnessed was the ugly face of war, one where pain, death and disfigurement came all too easily, and for many it had touched a cold spot in their inner beings.

The train's pace was a sedate one, almost that of a man walking, and before long the soporific swaying and the noise of the clacking, clanking wheels beneath relaxed enough of the still-exhausted ones among them to try and curl down into the straw and, carefully avoiding its contents, reach a troubled sleep. A few brave souls trotted alongside until angry shouts from their NCOs made them dive hurriedly inside again. Those who were lucky enough not to have a watching NCO in among them soon had the ubiquitous Crown and Anchor boards out to try and relieve as many unlucky 'pigeons' as they could of their last remaining money. One or two tried to get a sing-song going but their hearts weren't in it and after several attempts the singing died down, leaving each man with his own thoughts as the train unhurriedly drew them closer and closer to the front line.

The day stretched out before them as the train slowly clattered its way through the lush, green fields. The countryside seemed almost devoid of humans, and what people they saw gazed solemnly after them without an expression on their blank faces. No one waved or acknowledged their passage.

As they rattled slowly through one small collection of dirty, green-shuttered low houses, a horde of small children appeared from nowhere. Sprinting furiously alongside the train they raised grimy hands upwards in an imploring gesture of entreaty. '*Breetish Tommy! Hallo! Bullee Bif? Biskit?*'

'Christ, quick, get the quartermaster sergeant!' one of the men exclaimed. 'There's a few young shavers here who'd really appreciate that rubbish he feeds us.'

His words drew a round of laughter and in a trice a hail of tins and packets of tea sailed through the air, to be furiously fought over as the train drew away from the squabbling youngsters.

'D'you know,' remarked Ernie Wadley to anyone listening as he lay reclining on a soft bed of straw, digging his fingers into a cold tin of McConnachie's stew, 'we've been in this bleedin' country, what, coming up two days, an' I've yet ter hear a single word of Froggie being spoken. Kinda spooky don't you think?'

'Nah!' answered his pal Arwyn Jones from the other side of the carriage. 'What's the point of listening out for a language if you can't bloody well understand it? Daft I call that, boyo!'

'Oi, Jonesy, 'ave you noticed owt else?' Wadley posed the question as he stuffed more of the cold, greasy stew into his maw.

'No, Wadley. But I figures as 'ow you're goin' ter tell us, then.'

'Well, there's no blokes in France either, my little Welsh rarebit. They've all gone to the war. All I've seen is bleedin' women and kids so far 'an I'll bet all those lonely ladies are just lusting after some hot action from someone o' the likes of me.'

Private Jones raised himself disgustedly up onto his elbow and looked over at his friend.

'Christ, Wadley boyo, is sex all you ever bloody well think about? Disgustin' I calls it!' Ignoring the indignant upraised two fingers of Wadley's outstretched hand he lowered himself down into the thick straw and returned to his thoughts. The shadows would be falling in the valley back home and he pictured his wife getting the little ones ready for bed. Sighing, he turned over and tried to make himself comfortable. It was beginning to turn colder now even though the day was still young, and what breeze there was streaming in through the open doors and between the slats had lowered the temperature within the carriage. After a while he was grateful for the insulating properties of the straw, and slipped into a light, troubled sleep.

Shortly after midday they slowly steamed to a halt. The men filled the doorways to gaze around in wonder. The train had halted in a siding, alongside a huge dump of army materiel.

The siding bore the slogan: ARMY SERVICE CORPS DEPOT HAZE-BROUCK. Piles of artillery shells, wooden ration boxes, tarpaulins and lines and lines of horse-drawn service wagons filled their view. Within a short time a small army of men appeared, bearing steaming urns and hunks of bread. Gratefully the train's occupants disembarked, stretching their stiff limbs to accept the hot drinks and food awaiting them. RSM Findlay took charge, encouraging them all to fill their knapsacks with any spare bread.

'Go on lads, eat up. Take as much as you can off these beggars from 'Ally Sloper's Cavalry. And don't forget to fill your water bottles. We're going to be halted for a while, the colonel says.'

'RSM, sir?'

'Yes, what is it Parker?'

'Sir, could you tell me where the toilets are?'

The RSM snorted. 'Just you jump down from that wagon now lad and I'll show you where the toilets are! See that patch of France at the side of the track, Parker? Help yourself, lad, because that's the only toilet you're going to see.' Within seconds Parker was joined at the trackside by a crowd of men all blissfully relieving their aching bladders.

'Psst.'

'Pssst!' This time the sound was more persistent. Puzzled, Bob Simpson looked round to see where it was coming from. In the shadow between the carriages he was standing next to he made out a dim figure.

'What is it?' he enquired, bending forward to see who it was.

'Quick. Help me throw this into the wagon,' the voice implored. 'It's too heavy for me.'

Bob recognised the voice of Fred Maitland, the battalion scrounger. Slowly strolling over so as not to attract attention, he peered at the soldier opposite him. His dark foxy features screwed into a scowl from exertion, Maitland was pulling a large, rectangular wooden box with rope handles at each end. It looked heavy and Bob reached under the carriage coupling mechanism to grab hold. He recoiled when he made out the writing beneath the large, bold black arrow painted on the lid of the box: WD BALL AMMUNITION. .303 CALIBRE. 1000 RDS.

'Jesus!' he gasped. 'Where did you get that from, Maitland?'

'Over there,' said Maitland, gesturing vaguely over his shoulder, 'There's loads more where that came from, corp, so stop buggering about an' give us a hand. I can't manage it meself, I told you, it's bleedin' heavy.'

Bob opened his mouth to speak but before he could do so another quiet voice made its presence felt.

'May I ask what you two are up to? No, Simpson, let him answer.' The calm voice was full of sinister menace and Bob cringed as RSM Findlay stepped into sight, inches from the coupling.

'Ah, well, you see sir, I, this box. It was, well, sort of. Er...just lying there...and I...'

'Did I hear you right, Maitland, lad? Did you say there was plenty more where that came from?'

Maitland gulped audibly and replied. 'Yes RSM, loads of it, under a tarpaulin over there. I thought, ah, well, seein' as how we've not got...' His voice trailed off in silence as he caught the full effect of RSM Findlay's parade-ground stare. After several thoughtful, long seconds Findlay turned to Bob, his head cocked suggestively to one side.

'You heard the man, Simpson. Some careless base wallah has obviously left *our* ammunition under a tarpaulin. Now, get a few more of the men, quietly, and see how many more of these boxes we can load without being seen before we get going from here. No need to upset anyone, just taking what's ours. Move it, laddie.' With that he was gone as quickly as he had arrived, without a sound.

Within minutes Bob collected a small group of fellow travellers from his waggon. Under Maitland's directions they quietly sneaked over to where the boxes of ammunition lay stacked under a tarpaulin. Keeping a sharp lookout and with two to each box they struggled over to the train. A whistle shrieked. Quickly they returned to their own waggon and were hoisted back aboard. Seconds later, the now-familiar shunting movements told them they were under way again.

Once clear of the siding and the cheers and waves of the soldiers manning it, those carriages lucky to have received one broke open the box using their bayonets. The gleaming clips of rifle ammunition, swathed in their cloth bandoliers, were soon dispersed, each man cramming as many of the clips as he could manage into his webbing pouches and knapsack. A trail of hastily discarded boxes and bandoliers soon told of the train's passing, the detritus littering the track far behind them.

'Eh, Fred, what do you think it's going to be like when we get there? Will we be going into action straightaway do you think? What do the Jerries look like? Are they as big as they say they are? Will we get to see the trenches soon?' Boy Godley leaned over the mound of webbing and weapons in the middle of the carriage they were travelling in to gaze over at Fred Maitland who was busy with his bayonet trying to hack open a large tin of bully beef.

'So sorry to disappoint you Godley but me an' the Old Man don't exactly meet for breakfast these days, so stop asking all those bloody useless questions!' snapped Maitland, throwing the bayonet aside with a pleased grunt and peeling back the ragged edge of the tin. 'In fact, the bastard 'ardly speaks to me at all these days. Something I did at dinner in the officers' mess obviously upset him. An' me with impeccable table manners too! How the bloody hell do you think I know or care where we're fucking going or who we're going to meet when we get there. Which judging by the speed of this load of old bollocks is going will be well into next week!'

He continued. 'All I do know my little bantam cock is that when we do finally arrive it's going to mean one heap of trouble. It ain't going ter be like we was in Morecambe, charging round with some poncy officer shouting orders at us from a book. Nah! This is for real and a lot of us ain't gonna be coming back. Why do you think that poor sod Hackett didn't fancy accompanying us? He'd already been out here and look what it did for 'im! Now sod off an' let me get me teeth into this choice piece of Army grub.'

Up front in the carriage carrying the battalion officers it was a similar story of boredom and ennui. The pecking order had swiftly been established according to rank and everyone had settled down into their allotted seats to eat a packed lunch. Snaith was positively glowing with good humour. His seat faced forward next to the window immediately behind the locomotive's tender, according him splendid views of the countryside as they passed through. Walter Ramsbottom sat opposite him and together with the adjutant, Major Roberts, they pored eagerly over the map that had been provided for them back in Boulogne.

'At this rate we'll be all day travelling, eh? The men looked ready for anything, though, don't you think? Bags of pluck there, I'll wager,' Snaith enquired of Roberts, sitting back in sated ease. He pointed at the map with a piece of chicken bone. 'Is that Bethune there?' Hastily swallowing a piece of chicken, Roberts nodded in agreement. 'Spot on sir. I've marked it in pencil for you. As to the men I fully agree, they seem terribly keen to get to grips with the Hun.'

'Quite so!' Snaith ended this short conversation by lowering himself back into the cushioning of the seat and promptly falling asleep. Not wishing to seem impolite the rest of his compartment followed suit. Henry Watson glanced at the sleeping officers before resuming the letter he had started shortly after leaving Boulogne. He tried to write twice a week at least and travelling in comfort like this allowed him the luxury of putting his thoughts down without one of his pals reading it over his shoulder.

'*Dear Beth*', he wrote, '*We are now leaving for the front...*'

On they passed through France, drawing ever nearer to Bethune. On the long, slow bends it was possible for those in the front wagons to stare back and see their pals waving twenty-odd wagons behind as the immense length of the train became apparent. The novelty soon wore off however, and they returned to their reverie. The train stopped again, twice more, in open country for an hour at a time with no explanation before just as suddenly moving on again. Darkness began to fall and still they moved along at the same sedate pace. For many, their iron rations had long been consumed apart from the left-over packets of tea, and hunger pangs were making them feel decidedly wretched.

After the last stop, while lying recumbent in the straw, Ernie Wadley languidly stretched out a leg and kicked 'Boy' Godley, as he'd come to be known, on the shin.

'Ouch! Shit! What did you do that for, Ernie?' Godley rubbed his aching shin painfully and looked indignantly over to where Ernie lay, a large straw stalk hanging limply from his mouth as he watched Godley glare at him.

'Eh, Boy, tell us again why you wanted to come here with us real soldiers,' Ernie said. 'I reckon as how you should still be sucking on yer mum's tit not lying in a train to God knows where with a heap of Fritzes to fight at the other end.'

'Yeah, well, that's what you know then, clever-dick!' Boy answered him heatedly. 'I was just like you lot, I volunteered didn't I? Yer always picking on me, Wadley. I'm old enough to fight like the rest of you.'

'Garn, sonny. Old enough, my arse! You look like my nephew an' he's only fourteen! What did you tell the recruiting sergeant yer age was, then?'

'Mind your own bloody business, nosey bugger. D'you hear me?' Boy threatened.

'Oh right sir, at your command sir! Or what?' Annoyed now, Wadley heaved himself upright and glared fiercely at the young man opposite, who glared back with just as fierce an expression. Wadley opened his mouth to let fly an avalanche of expletives but as he did so Godley's expression changed to one of puzzlement and he bent forward, concentrating intensely.

'Shh! Eh, Fred, can you hear that?'

'Hear what? I can't hear a thing with all these bloody wheels clacking an' you two babbies arguing!' replied Fred Maitland from the other side of the waggon. He had satisfied his hunger and was now trying to jam another five or six clips of rifle ammunition into his already bulging knapsack.

'No, I mean it, listen. There! There it is again. Don't tell me you can't hear that!' Godley bounded up and pushing aside one of the men lounging in the doorway listened intently in the direction they were travelling.

Maitland was about to answer him with a rude retort when his eyes narrowed as his keen ears picked up a different noise to that of the train.

''Ere, get out of the way, blast you!' He pushed his way to the open door and joined Godley in listening to the faint sound they were both now picking up. Above the noise of the train's wheels both men could make out a dim, distant, ragged muttering sound, rising and falling in the far distance.

Puzzled, his brow creased, Maitland turned to the waiting others. 'That's weird,' he enjoined, 'I've never heard anything like that before. It sounds like, well, it's like...'

'It's shellfire.' The voice pronounced this calmly and succinctly. 'We're nearing the Front. What did you think it was, a welcoming band?' Maitland wheeled round and glared at the informant, who sat slowly drawing his bayonet through a piece of wet cloth as he frankly returned Maitland's stare .

'What the fuck d'you know about shellfire, Bates? The only bangs you'll 'ave 'eard before would've been the rozzers bouncing their truncheons off that thick skull of yours when you was lying sozzled in the gutter on a Friday night, like!'

Ignoring the hoots of laughter at his intended humiliation, Bates calmly continued wiping his bayonet.

'Oh aye? That so? We'll soon see then, Maitland, who's right and who's wrong, won't we? Very shortly too, I'd opine. Or do you know any better?'

Maitland scowled and opened his mouth to retort but the quiet truth of what Bates had imparted had an effect on him. Glaring at the impassive figure opposite him he returned to his place on the floor and flung himself angrily down, leaving the other occupants of the carriage, Bates excepted, looking round anxiously. A few more hardy souls pushed their way to the open carriage doors and listened intently. The distant muttering rose and fell as before and after a while, gradually, reluctantly, one by one, the men resumed their positions in the warmth of the straw.

The sound stayed with them for the rest of their journey until it ceased abruptly when Bethune was reached late into the night. Here, the appearance of the war was more apparent. Even at this late hour uniforms of all colours scurried around them as they stiffly disembarked under the yellowish glare of gas lamps and formed up outside a railway station for the second time in as many days, looking around them curiously. Bethune was a comparatively large town, the buildings densely packed and bearing evidence of the war in several buildings marked by what could only be shellfire. The air smelled different, too, a burnt smell of desolation. As they bemusedly stared about them, an RTO, an older, weary-looking man this time, strode over to the waiting officers. Saluting the colonel he addressed him directly.

'Nineteenth Battalion? Lieutenant-Colonel Snaith, I presume. Lieutenant Germaine, sir, RTO for Bethune. Welcome to Bethune sir, I trust the journey up from the coast didn't trouble you too much. Some regiments have taken two days to do that journey. If you'd like to follow me I'll show you and your officers where you're being billeted for tonight. Tomorrow I'm informed, you'll be on your way up to the Front. Of course that could all change but for now you'll be tired and no doubt in need of a hot meal. My men will deal with the ORs so if you gentlemen would accompany me I'll lead the way. Please feel free to ask any questions. Sergeant Hobson? Macaulay will take care of the NCOs. Take care of the others, there's a good chap.'

He acknowledged his sergeant's salute and strode off confidently towards the main entrance of the station.

'Wait, wait!' Snaith stopped the RTO in his tracks. 'Look here, Germaine, its good of you to take care of us this way but do you have any idea where we're going tomorrow, because I'm damned if I or my men do. I've had no other orders except these, telling us to make our way here.' He brandished the papers given to him at Boulogne.

'Oh, sorry, sir, my apologies. As far as I know, you and your men will be moving up to the Front, opposite Loos, and your battalion HQ will be in Hepernay-le-Petite. That's about seven miles from here, south-east as the crow flies, on the Bethune-Lens road. It's no secret there's going to be a stunt pulled over there shortly. You may have heard the artillery softening up the Huns as you approached Bethune. The word is there aren't enough shells to go round so the firing doesn't go on all day. Pity. They could do with some softening up, you mark my words. You'll be seeing the brigade commander before you leave tomorrow, sir, that's the rest of what I do know. Now if you don't mind sir, I've got a lot on so the sooner we get you men billeted the better.'

Obediently they tucked in behind him as Germaine strode off again purpose-fully, only stopping every now and again to point vigorously at a building or local object of interest. Behind him his provost sergeant, Hobson, beamed benevolently at the expectant, slightly fearful-looking men gathered around him. The battalion NCOs had disappeared with a different provost sergeant, leaving Hobson in sole command of the remainder.

His features now twisted into a scowl, Provost Sergeant Hobson surveyed his charges.

'Right you lucky lads,' he boomed, 'we're going to take a little walk to the out-skirts of the town to your billets. Pick up your rifles and your kit and walk this way. Hang on, hang on a sec! Well I'll be damned! Is that my old pal, Maitland I see? Fred? Fred Maitland lad, where the hell have you come from?'

Maitland looked bitterly down at the ground. 'Jesus Christ! And I thought my luck had changed!'

'Well, well, long time no see, Fred.' Hobson raised his voice further, looking round at the assembled men. 'Mark me well, lads, me and this specimen go back a ways. So when I tells you to keep a close eye on yer kit when this sly dog is around sniffing at what he thinks you've got, you'd better bloody believe me.' He grinned savagely at Maitland's obvious discomfiture.

'Come on Fred, don't take it to heart, you know what I'm getting at. Now then, forget all you've been told, this here's the start of yer education. Keep close together, look after yer pals, Maitland excepted, and keep yer wits about you. The Front ain't that far away, as you can hear. The Boche will try and kill you in as many different ways as you can think of, so if you want to get home again to see your mummy once more, keep yer bloody heads down! Right?

'Now, follow me. I've reserved some nice, clean pigsties for the discerning gen-tlemen amongst you. The rest of you gets to sleep in the cellars. Don't you lot worry, though, we cleared all the Huns out of them before we got them ready for you.'

Several of the men laughed at his attempt at humour. They shouldered their arms and hefted their knapsacks. Thirty minutes later the smiles were gone. Ser-geant Hobson had not been lying.

4

Wednesday 15th September 1915

Battalion is to remain in billets at Bethune and surrounding areas for a few days yet, for acclimatisation. We have been promised to be re-equipped during our stay. Men marched to firing-ranges for weapons instruction and firing practice with the new Lewis guns, and our rifles. Our Vickers machine-guns have not been issued yet. Close Order drill later in the day for all ranks. Colonel Snaith at Div HQ all day, obtaining our orders for the front line.

R.D. Sprightly, Major, C Company

After a good night's rest Colonel Snaith felt refreshed. He stood on the steps of the house he'd spent the night in and reflected on their fortunes so far. The old woman whose house he had so pleasantly occupied for the night had cooked him some eggs for his breakfast. Not a word had passed between them, neither understanding the other's language, but by signs he had been able to tell her how much he had appreciated her hospitality.

It had been a messy business back at Folkestone but that was behind them now. The men had soon recovered their good humour and on the journey across the Channel he had even heard some coarse jokes being told about the unfortunate Hackett's death. It was a pity for young Wordsley but to be fair, he had been careless, damnably careless, in leaving his valise open as he had. Anyone could have removed the pistol from it. The main thing was to move on and concentrate on the job in hand. Quite.

As he stood enjoying the warmth of the morning sun the faint noise of artillery guns reached his ears. He was still frowning at this interruption to his reverie when a staff motor car puttered up to the front door and a smartly-dressed corporal dismounted from the driver's side and approached him.

'Lieutenant-Colonel Snaith, 19th Battalion?' he enquired, with an equally smart salute. 'Corporal Shankly, sir, I've orders to take you to Brigade headquarters. That's of course if you're ready, sir.'

Thank you, corporal,' returned the colonel, 'yes, thank you, I'm quite, quite ready.' Moving round to the passenger side of the car he allowed himself to be seated. Throwing the car into gear, the corporal drove off.

On arrival at a large, stately-looking building in the centre of the town, on the corner of a large square, two NCOs assisted him out of the car before carefully shepherding him into the building's interior. In a long, cool corridor one of the NCOs knocked on a door bearing the legend: 'Brigadier-Gen Wilson GOC 45 BDE'. After a brief conversation as the door was opened he turned and ushered Snaith inside.

A large, heavy-set man with a florid face and full moustache sat at the desk opposite the door, wearing the uniform and red shoulder tabs of a Brigadier-General. He gestured to the officer standing by the door as Snaith entered. 'Fine, Geoffrey, if you'll see to that I'd be obliged. Could you leave us now?' He rose as Snaith approached him and offered an outstretched hand as the other officer exited the room.

'Cuthbert, good to see you. How was the journey? I'm sorry you were pulled out of your training regime so suddenly but the boss has an urgent need for troops and I was ordered to fill the coffers, so to speak. We have a need for numbers, not necessarily fully-trained you understand, and your battalion fits that criteria exactly. It's common practice for a newly-arrived battalion to spend some time in readjusting and re-equipping but in your case, Cuthbert, I'm afraid you'll be going straight into the line in a day or so.

'I'm attaching you for the time being to the Scottish part of the line, with 15th Division. The boss wanted to put you in straightaway but I managed to change his mind this morning and give you a few more days grace. It can't be helped old man; I need three of your companies in the line by Sunday and the other close by your HQ in reserve.'

Snaith opened his mouth to speak but fell silent as the brigadier moved over to a large map on the wall. The walls were covered in maps and large, official forms, but the Brigadier tapped his fingers on the nearest map as he addressed him.

'In the next few days, Cuthbert, we're going to give the Boche hell, down here at Loos.' He gestured at a point on the map. 'Your men will not be taking part, in so many words, but will remain in reserve on the far right of the intended action until we break through the enemy lines. I intend to move you up through the gap our troops create and the 19th will then be used against the Boche in mopping-up operations. We're shelling the enemy lines daily now, no foul-ups as happened at Aubers Ridge earlier this year you know, and in addition when the time comes we also have a nasty surprise for Fritz up our sleeves. Field-Marshal French is assured of a breakthrough once we utilise all the weapons at our disposal and he wishes to use all the manpower we can put together. It should keep those armchair generals in their bally clubs in Whitehall off his back for a while. Lord knows he could do with a free hand after all the reverses we've suffered this year. Enough of that for now, any questions?'

Snaith thought hard and then spoke. 'I've no machine-guns, sir, my men are short of everything from blankets to rifle ammunition and we're short of rations. In short, it will take some time before we can be used in a tactical role I'm afraid.'

The brigadier spoke soothingly. 'I fully understand your predicament, Cuthbert. Make a list of all your deficiencies and give it to my staff officer as we go out. I intend keeping you here until you have all we can spare and you have some firm idea of what is expected of you. You'll be attending me here over the next few days to be brought into the full picture but for now I fancy a spot of early lunch. There's a jolly quiet restaurant reserved for staff officers a short walk down the road, so why don't you join me for a bite to eat and a glass of the local plonk, eh?'

At the mention of food, Cuthbert Snaith's face lit up. 'That's jolly decent of you sir, I'd love to.'

He was answered by a broad beam from the brigadier and a shout of, "Geoffrey!"'

* * * *

The men saw Bethune through different eyes. Having mustered and finished a hasty breakfast of greasy stew and bread they were marched with their NCOs to the firing-ranges on the outskirts. Here they were split into smaller groups under the command of armourer and drill instructors to zero their rifles, and the machine-gun sections were singled out to be taught the intricacies of the Lewis machine-gun.

'No, no, you dozy beggar! Tuck the bleedin' thing into your shoulder; hold it tight to your cheek like you were dancing with your young lady. Christ, no! Not like that, like this! What did they teach you back in Blighty?'

Private Godley was not having much luck. Being of a slighter frame than the rest of his section, the instructor had singled him out as the one to be taught while his pals looked on.

'Pull the trigger gently; hold your breath before squeezing. Look down the bloody range, dammit, not at me!'

'I tried corporal but it hurts me shoulder every time I pull the trigger,' Godley whined, trying to pull the heavy rifle into his shoulder as had been demonstrated.

'That's 'cos you're holding it too damn loosely, you berk!' The instructor was getting annoyed. Godley had only managed to fire fifteen rounds in ten minutes and there were still another forty men to get through yet.

'Right, last time. Look through the sights at the target, hold that breath, concentrate on the bull and slowly squeeze the trigger.'

Bang!

'Jesus, you nearly put one through the range flag! All right, son, you've done for me. Apply the safety catch and get out of my sight. If Fritz attacks, just you fix your bayonet and charge them 'cos you ain't gonna do any damage firing at him. You might even kill more of your chums than Fritz. Right, you lot, who's next?'

Further down the machine-gun section was being shown the Lewis gun.

'All right lads, here she is. The Lewis gun. Fairly new which is why you lot 'aven't seen one up to now. Don't worry, the battalion will be getting a few of them before you goes up to the Front. Now, pay attention. Air-cooled, not water-cooled like the Vickers gun. Weight approximately twenty-five pounds, circular drum magazine as you can see. Holds forty-seven rounds, so easy on the trigger finger. Fire short bursts at a time. She'll spew out 600 rounds a minute so don't try and empty it in a one-er or you'll run out of ammo very quickly. Which will make you very popular with your pals if Fritz has a bit of a charge on. Same calibre as your rifles, .303, so if you gets short, nick your mates' ammo. It's a bit of a sod to reload the drums that way, especially if it's raining at the time and the Boche are getting closer and closer, but believe me, when you has to, you bleeding well will do. Just takes a bit of time that's all. There'll be six of you in a team, one to fire the gun, one to reload, the others carrying the spare magazines and looking after the cove what fires it. You'll all change round so each one of you gets a go on the gun. Be careful, she's very temperamental. Hates the mud almost as much as she hates Fritz.'

The men grinned. This was more like it. This was what they had volunteered for, to give Fritz a bloody nose. They set themselves down with a renewed will and soon the ranges rang to the sound of the guns firing in staccato bursts.

It was a tired battalion that marched back to their billets that evening, tired but well satisfied with the day's proceedings. In the daylight they were now able to discern in the distance the low, dark smudge of higher ground and all around them in the countryside were the pitheads and slagheaps of the French coalfields. The rumble of renewed artillery fire followed them all the way back to the town, but most of them ignored it. They were becoming accustomed to the war on a daily basis now and marched back like veterans.

Provost Sergeant Hobson was waiting for them as they marched into the town.

'Well lads, don't you look the picture of health,' he called. 'I'm glad to see so many smiling faces. The colonel was telling my boss how pleased he was with you today. So pleased he's agreed to release all of you to me in the morning for some vital war work. Gentlemen, tomorrow, apart from the chaps what is going back to the ranges to play with the Vickers, we're all going to fill sandbags. Especially you, Maitland! Oh, yes, I've got something really good lined up for you, me old mate.' With that he was off. A collective groan went up. The war had caught up with them after all.

'God blast 'im,' Fred Maitland complained bitterly, throwing his webbing pouches down. 'That bastard ain't goin' ter let up on me, I know he ain't. Well, that's it, I'm off!'

'Where you going to Fred, you know we was told to stay in billets.'

'You can bloody well stay there if yous wants. As for me, I'm off to lay me 'ands on some real grub. No bloody bully beef stew for me tonight, I can tell you!'

His rifle crashed down onto his webbing and with a quick look round, Maitland disappeared into the next street.

When later that night they lay exhausted after the day's toil, Jim Shaw watched curiously as Henry Watson began writing by the light of a guttering candle on a postcard-sized piece of buff-coloured card.

'Hey up, lad, our Henry,' he enquired, 'what's that you've got?'

'It's a Field Service postcard, Jim,' Henry patiently answered him. 'I scrounged some from one of the chaps in the stores back there. You just put the address on one side and cross out the lines on the other to leave what you want to say. Things like: *I'm well*, you know, that sort of thing. It's just to let Beth know I'm all right. She worries so, poor girl. And the good thing is, they're free.'

'D'you have a spare one there, then?' Jim asked.

'Well, I just have one more and I was keeping that until...oh, go on then, here you are.' Sighing, Henry dug into his pack and pulled out the card. Jim Shaw thought quickly. Reading and writing had never been his strong point, being barely able to write his name, so he quickly interjected as Henry held out the card.

'Tell you what, Henry, seeing as how you've got it in your hands already, if you write my old woman's address on the other side I'll just do the crossing out on the other. How's that?'

Henry sighed again. 'Righto then Jim, sing out your address then. Let's have it quickly so's I can get on with mine.' He wrote quickly as Jim recited his address and on finishing passed the card over and bent back to his own writing.

Jim Shaw turned the card over in his hands. The words leapt out at him, lines of them on one side, making as much sense as hieroglyphics. He delved into his own pack and after rummaging round found the blunt stub of a pencil and took another cursory glance at the card. Taking a guess he began drawing a line through the printed lines on the card until he was left with just the one.

'There, that ought to do it. I'll just nip off now and see if I can find where to post this. Do you want yours doing too, Henry?'

'No, it's all right, Jim, I'll take a walk out myself later. Be careful, you heard Sergeant Hobson. Don't get yourself into trouble like Maitland will if he gets caught.' Henry's reply was absentminded as he looked down at the card in his hands, his thoughts miles away.

'Suit yourself, chum.' Jim heaved himself up and walked out. The onlooker watching him go might have expressed mild amusement to see the card held loosely in his left hand. Being unable to read the card's contents, and not wanting to ask in case he was laughed at for his illiteracy, Jim's remaining line, to inform his wife of his welfare, read:

I have been admitted into hospital (wounded) and hope to be discharged soon.

5

Monday 20th September 1915

Rear party under Major Redford finally arrived at 07:00 ack emma yesterday. Battalion moved by motor bus up to the Front. Drew iron rations. Entered the trenches at Hepernay-le-Petite, relieving 12th Worcestershire's around 19:00 pip emma last night. A, B and C Companies moved up to the front line, leaving D held in reserve in billets near battalion HQ. Heavy shelling around battalion area as all companies arrived at the Front. Suffered our first war casualty in France when 2/Lt Hanson, B Coy killed by sniper fire this morning, soon after our arrival in the Front.

R.D. Sprightly, Major, C Company

'Whee!' Archie Higgins of A Company sang as the open-topped omnibus rattled and swayed along the poplar-lined road. The wind whistled through what was left of his hair and he clasped his hat tightly to stop it blowing away. After three days of small arms instruction and working parties they had reassembled in the town centre and were now on their way to the disembarkation point, at which they would enter the trench system. The rear party had arrived that morning, exhausted by an overnight train journey and been soundly ragged for missing all the fun so far. The newcomers had swiftly rejoined their various companies and made ready.

The word was that A, B and C Companies would be going up to the front line with D Company staying in the area of the battalion HQ, in reserve. The normal method of reaching the front line was by route marches but as time was pressing the town major had agreed that the battalion should be transported by bus. 'Quite rightly so!' Cuthbert Snaith had snorted.

The routine would be four days in the line followed by two in reserve, forming work parties as required when in reserve. All the companies destined for the line were issued with two days' rations to last them until the battalion's chefs could start supporting them in the trenches.

'This bully beef smells rancid,' grumbled Private Hartson, but a warning look from Sergeant Willox soon quelled any further mutterings.

Owing to the limited number of buses available ('Another shambles!' Snaith had mumbled under his breath) it had been decided to take the companies up to the line one at a time starting with A Company. Hence, Archie's exuberance at being told to sit upstairs with his pals. Beneath them, Snaith and some of HQ staff sat inside and pored over their newly-issued maps, trying to understand the marked lines of trenches that snaked their way over and around the papers in front of them. The engine stuttered and roared as the driver contrived to keep their speed up, overladen as he was. Every now and then the gears crashed and crunched noisily as he tried to find the right one to match the speed he was endeavouring to stick to.

The journey didn't take too long and as soon as the men had climbed out of the convoy of vehicles the buses promptly about-turned and headed back to Bethune for their next pick-up of human cargo. The men had been dropped off on the outskirts of a small village. From a distance came the sound of mutterings and grumblings and several faces became anxious as they peered round to ascertain the origins of the artillery fire.

Large water-filled craters were everywhere and from the edge of the village the mouldering smell of a decomposing horse wafted over their nostrils. As they gazed in wonderment at the destruction before them, two figures approached from the ruins of the nearest house. The first wore the uniform of an officer in the Royal Engineers, with captain's insignia. A tall moustachioed officer accompanied him.

'Good morning, gentlemen,' the engineer officer greeted them, coming to attention and saluting. 'Captain Robert Jordan of 3 Company, Royal Engineers. Let me introduce you to my friend here, Lieutenant Henry Bartholomew of the Worcesters, the chaps you'll be relieving. He's to be your guide and as we'll be staying here awhile before making the journey up to the front line. Please feel free to ask him any questions you might have. We'll leave as evening begins to fall, that way we'll avoid the Boche strafing us as we go up.'

'At ease captain, and thank you,' Snaith enjoined. 'We're only too pleased to see you both.' Bartholomew grinned in reply.

'Good morning sir, We'll have to wait not far from here and then go quickly before the Boche see us. I'll now take you now to where we can wait. Please follow closely.' He spun round and marched off, back towards the building he had appeared from, leaving a puzzled CO staring after him.

'It's all right, sir,' Jordan called out, 'Henry here will take your men up to the support trenches. Your battalion HQ is situated over there. You'll be billeted in the lower storey of the cottage sir.' He gestured in the direction of the ruins behind him, 'We've built a fine HQ dugout and series of shelters for you. We've also run a telephone wire up to your positions. Saves your runners charging up and down for the present. I'll take you over there shortly, and then we'll see to getting your chaps up in the support lines. Henry will take care of that, for the main part.'

As Colonel Snaith and his staff complied with Jordan's request, the rest of the men and their officers followed Bartholomew to the far side of the cottage. There they gratefully eased their packs and firearms down onto the soft earth and subsided into a sitting or lying position as the fancy took them, looking around them curiously. The cratered ground stretched before them to the horizon, a churned-up vision of shattered tree stumps gazing forlornly at the heavy skies and water-filled holes as far as the eye could see. Dimly on the horizon loomed some large, strange-looking hills, almost like volcanoes. The knowledgeable among the men recognised them for what they were – slag-heaps from the myriad coal mines that dotted the area.

They sat or lay in this manner, some sleeping with their caps over their faces, others listening to the ever-present distant noise as the day drew on, until the late afternoon. It was then that their guide reappeared, waving his arms about excitably as he gathered up the first group to make their way forward. A Company prepared for their journey up to the front line. Slinging their weapons the men followed Bartholomew. He stopped every few yards to look behind and wave furiously at them to close up. Behind the house they made out a sign with a large arrow on it pointing to their right. The sign read: 'Commonwealth Avenue'. Wondering, they walked a few more steps and soon came across the broad entry to a large, deep trench dug out of the chalk. As they milled around the entrance, uncertain now, the sound of shellfire, louder and not so distant this time, reached their ears. Bartholomew didn't hesitate.

'Colonel. Quick! We must leave now.' He turned back into the trench and gestured frantically for them to follow him. Snaith didn't waver. 'Come on you men, you heard our friend here. Get moving, Walter, and see everyone moves pretty sharply, will you! Go up there with the first lot.'

Major Ramsbottom waved his hand in reply and moved towards the trench entrance as several of the men started up the trench after Bartholomew. There were over 200 men to sort out and he looked around for help. Thankfully, A Company's commander, Captain Charles Brasher, was close to hand, so between them they started feeding the men in, by sections and platoons. The trench snaked away into the distance, turning a sharp corner eighty or so yards up its length and surprisingly soon swallowed up the mass of men who had filled its entranceway.

The trench was wide enough to take two men marching abreast and the men had time to look inquisitively round as they stumbled along. Surprisingly, after all they had heard, there was very little mud beneath their feet and they made good progress along the duckboard floor. Never staying in a straight line for very long, twisting and turning, they followed the half-crouched figure of the officer leading them. Half an hour followed in this fashion, the men bumping into each other and losing their balance occasionally as the hard-packed floor beneath them suddenly dropped in height. The trench gradually widened and the men could see several holes burrowed out of the walls around them. Gesturing to the men nearest him Bartholomew urged them to take cover there and after a short conversation with Major Ramsbottom he turned and was lost from sight as he hurried back for his next party of men.

Stretching their legs and making themselves as comfortable as possible, A Company hunkered down on its haunches and waited for the rest of the battalion to join them. The minutes stretched on and as more men arrived the space available to accommodate them became more and more cramped. It was a relief to all when the lieutenant at last marched to the head of the trench and raised his arm aloft. Rising to their feet, the hundreds of men filling the support trench system gladly followed him up and out of the trench and into a smaller, darker branch of the system. Darkness was growing and in the distance they could make out the sound of artillery fire.

The noise to their front grew in volume as they stumbled their way along and several men ducked involuntarily as loud bangs and thumps made their presence felt. Abruptly, the column came to a halt as Bartholomew raised his hand. They all stopped and watched him intently. The men in front could see they had reached a fork in the trench and after a quick look at the map that he now held in his hand Bartholomew motioned for them to follow him as he entered the right-hand section. The trench now narrowed considerably, the open top of the previous, wide section being replaced by an uneven sandbagged parapet. Some of the bags had split and the coarse earth in them oozed out, trickling down on them as they passed beneath.

More and more branches of the trench system appeared now but with only a cursory glance at his map the lieutenant strode confidently on, taking them into this entrance then that one, stopping every now and then to encourage his band of followers with yet more vigorous hand-waving. More signs appeared out of the gloom. 'The Strand', 'Kensington Walk'. There was no time to stop and admire them as Bartholomew set a fast pace. This led to their being spaced out as those in front started to open up a long gap between themselves and the rest of the column following behind.

The shellfire was a fierce drumming noise now, assailing their eardrums from every direction. Sometimes, as they crouched there, fearfully darting glances at each other's scared faces, they could make out the individual shriek of a particular shell but were unable to ascertain whether it was an incoming shell or one winging its way outbound from them. Meanwhile, Bartholomew walked steadily on in his half-crouched manner as if out for a stroll.

'Come on, come on!' he encouraged them.

'Bloody 'ell,' panted Archie Higgins, sweating furiously as he tried to keep up with the man in front of him. 'Trust my luck, come all the way to France and the first real soldier I meet wants to win a bloody medal in the next Olympics!' He pushed his rifle back up onto his right shoulder and tried to keep hold of its webbing strap with a wet, sweaty palm. The rifle was growing heavier by the minute and if they didn't stop soon he was sure he was going to collapse in a heap on the floor, just what he didn't want with his platoon sergeant two men back behind him.

'Shit!' he exclaimed as he collided with the man in front. They had stopped again and this time they didn't start off again immediately. Gratefully he eased the rifle from his aching shoulder and leaned against the trench wall for support. Not for long.

'Higgins! Straighten up you dozy clod!'

'Yes, Sergeant Clark.' he answered and hefted the rifle once more. Just his bloody luck!

'Hey, Higgy, can you smell that? What the hell is it?' A strangled question came over his shoulder from the man in front. Archie had been too engrossed in his struggle to keep up to notice any gradual changes in the trench's atmosphere, but in answer to the questions he arched his head and took a deep breath. He gagged immediately and almost fell, putting a hand on the trench wall to hold himself up. The smell that filled his mouth and nostrils was indescribable, a dry malodorous composition of faeces and rotting tissue. It reeked of something far worse than he had ever smelled before. An abattoir smell, it had the tang of death about it and he recoiled from its cloying embrace. It was making him feel decidedly nauseous but he found that if he breathed carefully through his mouth he could bear it. Just.

He was aware of whispering along the trench and a few seconds later his companion in front of him bent his head. 'We're here,' he whispered, 'Tell the man behind you we're going to move up a few at a time to let the first company of the chaps we're relieving pass. Pass it on.'

Archie nodded his head to acknowledge the information the man had imparted and turned aside to relay what had been said to the soldier behind him. He became aware of loud shuffling noises to his front and a moment or so later the trench was filled with the sight and sounds of men moving towards them in the failing light. As the first soldier filled his sight he took a sharp, inward breath. The man, and those following, was gaunt and haggard, his face lined with tiredness, eyes red-raw. His uniform was torn and covered in patches of dirt and what looked like chalk; the brass of his cap and shoulder-badges was a dull, mouldy green colour. Only his shouldered rifle seemed clean, gleaming with fresh oil. He pushed closely by with a wan smile and Archie became aware of another smell this time, the smell of men whose personal hygiene had become a forgotten ideal. Each passing soldier stank deeply of sweat and something else besides. Deep, ingrained fear.

A few muttered, 'Thanks,' and 'Take care up there chums,' as they pushed past and stumbled gratefully down the trench and out of sight. All of this took several long minutes to accomplish and during that time Archie had noticed another phenomenon. None of the men passing them had ducked during the barrage going on around them.

At long last they were gone and the men were able to resume their journey. Another half hour or so it seemed, and the soldier in front waved his hand backwards. Archie slowed his pace and eventually came to a stop as they rounded another turn in the trench. The noise from overhead was almost deafening as shells screamed and shrieked through the air. It was obvious some counter-battery fire was occurring too, as loud explosions were heard and felt nearby. Peeping overhead as they struggled along the trench some men were disturbed to observe large black clouds as shells burst above them. They were all nearly bent double by now, panting with their exertions and the gut-wrenching fear each loud *bang* and shower of earth brought.

Archie became aware of several dugouts in the trench wall as they slowly picked up pace again. This trench had a firestep built under the parapet to their left and as he came level with one of the dugouts he was roughly bundled into it by the soldier to his front, almost falling full length as his rifle dug into the wall of the trench.

'Sarge says we're to share this one for now. Sorry about the shove, Archie.' His erstwhile companion, Bill Thomson, stated by way of explanation as he helped him up, offering his hand for Archie to shake. Archie responded by taking the proffered hand and nodding his head vigorously. In front and behind them, similar noises told of their companions also being detailed off into openings on either side of the trench.

The dugout was filthy and smelled as foully as the men who had recently passed them. It was just large enough for the two men to crouch in and take stock of their surroundings. Lined with old planks of wood, it held some belongings from the previous occupants towards the back of its interior, but for now neither man was inclined to explore. Archie pushed his face past his neighbour and took an inquisitive peek down the now-deserted section of the trench.

It was quite narrow, and only deep enough to take a man of average height standing up. Any tall men would be severely disadvantaged. Both the firestep and the wall on the other side of it, the parados, were reinforced by some form of planks and wattled panels made of branches, and he was gratified to see that both the parapet and parados were heavily packed with sandbags. Thirty or so yards down, the trench disappeared from view into the deepening gloom as it wound its way through the traverses and firebays. Now and again he could make out bits of wood panelling forming part of the walls, no doubt robbed from the houses in the surrounding area, and further to his right a bright sheet of rippled metal further strengthened the wall. The chalk floor was dry for now; hard-packed, with no duckboards and none of the mud they had all come to believe was ever-present.

The shelling had stopped abruptly and as he looked skywards he could make out dark clouds scudding across the visible sky. It looked cold but promised better for the morning and his spirits rose. A noise came from outside and their opening was suddenly filled with the face and shoulders of Sergeant Bill Clark.

'Right you two!' he exclaimed, 'we need sentries out here and you fit the bill. Get yourselves out here my lucky lads an' I'll fill you in as to what's goin' to happen.'

He waited patiently for them to struggle out and stand before him. Getting out of the dugout in a hurry was not as easy as it looked.

'Righto lads, now you two are to hop up onto the firestep and take guard. Load yer rifles. Not now you dozy clods! D'ye want to shoot my foot off? Do it when you stand on this 'ere firestep. Stay there until I come back and tell you to stand down. Keep yer heads down and for God's sake don't try and take a peep over the top. Fritz snipers is fairly active I'm told an' you two have the size of heads even he couldn't miss. And keep awake. I don't want to come here in an hour or so an' find you kipping! If you hear anything, holler. Got all that? Right then, up you go!'

With that he helped them take their place on the firestep. With a reassuring pat on Archie's lower leg he was off, leaving them crouched nervously at their new-found post. Archie concentrated on keeping as low as possible, holding his rifle pointing at the trench floor. He carefully worked the bolt and slid home the cartridge from the five-shot magazine of his SMLE. Automatically his finger pushed the safety-catch on. He thought briefly of fixing the bayonet onto the rifle but dismissed the thought as quickly as it had come. In the confined area of the trench any lengthy item of weaponry would be a hindrance. No, he'd just have to shoot Fritz should he appear.

His new friend, Bob, was occupying himself in a similar manner and soon they were both armed and ready, crouching low below the parapet.

'Here we are then, Bob, in the war at last. God! What a smell. If only my old mum back in Liverpool could see me now, our kid. She'd have kittens! What are we supposed to do now?'

'I dunno. He said to just stay here and listen out. I say, you don't fancy a look over the top, do you Archie?'

'What, and get me soddin' head shot off!' Archie replied. 'Don't be bloody stupid. You heard Sergeant Clark, he said there's snipers over there just waiting for some stupid berk to lift his head.'

'I should cocoa! I'll bet he was just messing us about!' Bob replied, but it was noticeable he crouched a trifle lower after that. In front of his questioning gaze an inch or so over the parapet was an object whose shape puzzled him and after looking at it for a long while and keeping his head low he tentatively stretched out a hand and felt it. Still puzzled, unable to identify it, he grabbed the object and brought it swiftly into the trench where he could peer more closely at it. It was the remains of a leather boot and as he stared he became aware that it contained a gleaming, white length of what looked to be bone, with scraps of uniform still sticking to it. Gagging, he threw the object back over the parapet and knelt down as he tried to regain control of his heaving stomach.

Further down the trench in B Company's area, shivering as he sat huddled against the chalk wall, Fred Maitland stared morosely at his rifle. Through clenched teeth he muttered snatches of words as he ceaselessly worked the bolt to and fro, causing Ernie Wadley to look sideways at him in alarm.

'Hey up , Fred, all right are you?'

'No I'm fuckin' well not all right!' Maitland hissed, the bolt moving faster in his hands.

'What's upset yer, lad?'

'That bastard, Hobson, that's who!' Maitland spoke savagely. 'I thought I'd left him miles behind me and now he's here, in me face, mocking me!'

Wadley looked on uncomprehendingly. 'Do you know him, then?'

'Know him? Course I do! He's the bastard that put me here, damn his eyes!'

As Ernie shook his head in puzzlement, Maitland leaned forward and began to speak animatedly.

'I were doin' this posh house in Bury, like, at the start of all this shite. I'd got a good haul for the night and was just shinnin' down the drainpipe to make me getaway when Hobson appears out of nowhere, gives me a good kicking, steals half my stash and then hauls me off to the clink. Constable Hobson he was then, and a right miserable sod to boot!

'Gets me banged up in court for burglary, the tosser of a judge believed Hobson when he told him how he found me, calls me a liar for accusing Hobson of knocking me about and then the old sod gives me a choice. Join up and fight for me king and country or rot on dry bread and water for the next few years. Some choice, eh? That's how I got here with you lot, you don't think I swallowed all that pathetic, patriotic crap like you lot, did you?

'I heard later that Hobson was found with too many fingers in too many pies and that he'd been given the same choice I got. Look at him though, he's a bloody sergeant and I'm here, stuck in the same old shite! Don't it make you sick!' He bent over and spat ferociously at the dirt floor.

After a minute or so he broke the silence again. Speaking in a low, bitter voice he went on, 'When I were under training I got a letter from my missus. She wrote sayin' she'd 'ad enough and was going ter live with her sister, like. Took the two kids 'n all. Said she'd get more of a handout from the parish council than she'd ever had off me. Cow!'

He pointed the Lee-Enfield's muzzle at the sky. 'See if that bastard Hobson ever walks past the end of this rifle, there's goin' ter be a loud noise an' he'll never know what hit him!'

Ernie looked at him, startled. 'You can't do that, Fred, they'll shoot you, you know!'

'Shoot me? Shoot me? You daft bugger, Wadley, what do you think Fritz is 'ere for!'

The night passed slowly, the men becoming extremely tired and bored. After several hours Archie and Bob were relieved and tried to sleep in the confines of their funkhole. Sleep did not come easily, each man lying awake, lost in his own thoughts and the strangeness of the surroundings. Just before dawn they were kicked awake and resumed their place on the firestep. Further down the trench other men were manning the firestep in a similar fashion and after bobbing up and down and waving to them the novelty soon wore off and they remained crouched there, becoming stiff and tired.

'When are we going to get fed, I ask you!' Archie grumbled, kicking at the loose earth in his annoyance. His stomach was making growling noises in protest at the length of time that has elapsed since its last intake of food. A shout of 'Stand-to! Stand-to!' interrupted his reverie and he hurriedly stood up with the rest of his companions as the cry was taken up all along the trench by the battalion NCOs.

'Watch it, Archie, here comes Lieutenants Charteris and Hanson!' Bob alerted his friend.

Stopping to speak with the men in his path, Neville Charteris, one of the more popular officers, exchanged a smile and a word with those men he recognised. Charteris had endeared himself to his men by standing up for them when they had fallen foul of the many petty Army rules and regulations. He brooked no misdoings or malingering but was human enough to realise that these young men, like himself, had been thrown into a strange, alien way of life unassisted. His humanity manifested itself in the calm way he cared for them and they responded to him in a way that they did with no other of the battalion's officers.

Behind him, Second-Lieutenant William Hanson moved slowly along the trench. A slightly supercilious twenty-year-old platoon commander, Hanson had never become used to commanding men and while the men in his platoon obeyed his orders they had all become nettled in the preceding months at his failure to involve himself more in their lives and well-being.

Hanson was talking heatedly to his superior. 'Now look here, sir, those items of my kit were definitely there at the station before we embarked. Those damn Froggies! One of them has lifted my kit. How am I to get it back?' Charteris answered him soothingly in a low voice before passing by and disappearing round the next corner as Hanson drew abreast of Bob and Archie and nodded at them.

His earlier annoyance was still apparent as he sized them up and gestured impatiently for Archie to straighten his cap. He made to pass by but then stopped and returned.

'How are you chaps doing, anything to report?'

Bob looked over at Archie in exasperation before answering.

'No, sir, Sergeant Clark said to holler if we heard anything but it's been as quiet as a mouse since we got back up here this morning, sir.'

Hanson flushed. 'Yes, well keep me informed, not Sergeant Clark. And get those bayonets fixed on your rifles. Simpson isn't it?'

Bob nodded in assent. 'Sir.' They both slid their bayonets from the scabbards and prepared to click them into place.

Hanson was about to walk on when he stopped and fumbled with the small, leather side-pouch he was wearing. After a while he produced a small pair of battered, black binoculars and proffered them towards Bob.

'Do you see these, Simpson? My grandfather carried these round with him in the Boer War. Actually they're Boche glasses, made by Zeiss. Supposed to be jolly good glasses. My father gave them to me before we left for France. Sort of a good-luck gift, what!'

Bob laid his bayonet aside and took hold of the glasses, turning them over in his hand. They looked solidly built and the lenses shone brightly in the early dawn. He handed them back.

'Very nice sir, it's just a pity you'll not have much chance to use them here.'

'Oh, I don't know. The chaps who just left told us there wasn't too much action around here, sort of a quiet sector. Mind you, that was before those recent whizz-bangs started up. That just might have annoyed Herr Fritz. The Boche trenches are over two hundred yards away so they'll not see much from there. About as much as we can.' As he spoke Hanson heaved himself up onto the firestep alongside the two men.

'Come to think of it, I'll just take a quick peep with these glasses; see if I can spot anything useful.' He shifted his weight and began to haul himself upright. Alarmed now, Bob tugged at his officer's sleeve.

'Sir! Sir!' he exclaimed anxiously, 'Sergeant Clark said to keep our heads down. There's snipers out there sir!'

'Get off me, man!' Hanson snapped testily, 'I'm just going to take a quick look. They'll have their heads down and besides, no one will see me in this light.' Shrugging off Bob's restraining hand he lifted his head over the top of the parapet and brought the glasses to his eyes. He slowly swept his gaze from left to right, concentrating hard. Bringing the glasses back to his side he looked laughingly down at the two crouching men.

'As I thought, not much at all to s—'

Crack!

The binoculars spun up through the air as Hanson's body was flung violently off the firestep to land in a crumpled heap below them. They stared down in shocked disbelief as he thrashed convulsively on the ground, both hands clutching his throat, eyes wide, staring, his back arched in a paroxysm of agony as his heels drummed madly on the bare, earthen floor. Bright red blood sprayed in thin streams from between his whitened fingers as he sought to cover the massive tear in his throat. Bob found his voice as he jumped down to land alongside the stricken man.

'Oh Christ! Oh God! Quick! Stretcher-bearers! Stretcher-bearers!' He bent over the subaltern, frantically tearing at the wound dressing he carried in his pouch.

Archie joined him but it was to no avail. Within seconds, without uttering a sound other than a tortured gargling noise, the young officer's quivering body relaxed. His hands dropped away from his throat revealing the gaping, hideous wound the bullet had made as it had torn through the vulnerable flesh. Beneath his still body the blood slowly seeped into the floor of the trench in a spreading pool, caking the soles of their boots.

'Come on, move out of the way, blast you!' The stentorian roar told of Sergeant Clark's appearance on the scene as he shouldered his way through the small crowd of men who had now collected to gape at the stricken man before them. He stopped to take a long, hard look before pushing the crowd aside and grabbing hold of Archie's uniform tunic.

'What did I tell you, God damn you? What did I bloody well tell you?'

'Sarge, we told him not to take a look but he insisted. A sniper got him.' Archie wiped his bloodstained hands down his trousers and gestured at the officer's body. Clark squatted down and closely examined the crumpled form beneath him, belatedly recognising the rank badges he had missed in his earlier, wrathful appearance onto the scene. He looked up disgustedly at the men around him.

'You'd think he of all people would've known what not to do. Five fuckin' minutes it seems we've been here and already we've lost someone! All right, back to your posts everyone. Show's over. Well, it is for him anyway. And remember, as if you need it pointing out now, this is not a bloody game we're playing here!' He pointed at Archie and Bob. 'You two! Go and get us a blanket. We'll get him taken away. Oi, Smith, you go and find the doc, he might need to see him too. Last I saw of Mr Hughes he was in the regimental aid station! Down there, on your right.' He looked reflectively up at the parapet and wondered, musingly. 'Over two hundred yards they reckon to the nearest Fritz trenches. That was some shot in this light, straight through the neck. Shows you what we're up against.'

Bob rescued a dirty blanket previously left behind in their dugout and between him and Archie they wrapped the body in it under the watchful gaze of Sergeant Clark. When they had finished, at a nod from the NCO, they hoisted the inert form up and stooping low under the weight carried the body awkwardly down the trench. Charteris appeared suddenly and they left him to speak with the sergeant.

Behind them, unnoticed by any of the men who gazed out inquisitively from their dugouts to watch their passage, Fred Maitland, far from where he ought to be with his own B Company compatriots, had appeared. Casually picking up the recently-deceased officer's binoculars, unseen by anyone, he surreptitiously tucked them inside his tunic before just as casually making his way around the next firebay to his own dugout, whistling tunelessly.

Above him, etched against the sky, a skylark, its progeny long-departed, hovered briefly before diving into the unseen grass on the other side of the parapet.

6

Tuesday 21st September 1915

Opening bombardment of enemy lines opposite us began in earnest. Companies in line required for work parties, engaged in digging jumping-off trenches ahead of front line. Men spent this time adjusting to trench warfare. Bombing instruction carried out for all companies.

R.D. Sprightly, Major, C Company

Wednesday 22nd September 1915

Bombardment of enemy trenches increased. Big guns joined in at midday. No casualties from shells dropping short. Enemy trench-line covered in a pall of dust and debris. Hard to make out any damage inflicted. D Company into front line. A Company to reserve. Ration parties out in the afternoon.

R.D. Sprightly, Major, C Company

Thursday 23rd September 1915

Bombardment of enemy trenches still in progress. Heavy thunderstorm over our trenches. Periscopes issued to ascertain damage to enemy front line and reports sent to Brigade HQ. More work parties for trench-work in no man's land. Two Os wounded from B Coy, one severely, during night work in no man's land. Cpl Simpson, B Coy, one of the wounded, commended for his gallantry during the action.

R.D. Sprightly, Major, C Company

The long-handled spades and picks were stacked in a pile against the wall of the parapet, waiting to be picked up. Bob Simpson, a corporal now since their arrival in Bethune, turned round in the gloom and automatically counted the men as they passed him and hefted a spade apiece. Fourteen and himself from the number one and two platoons of B Company. That made fifteen. He frowned. He looked the waiting men over. Maitland. That's who was missing. He might have known. That shitty little shirker, always absent from where he was supposed to be. He opened his mouth to pose an angry question but shut it once more as round the nearest corner, adjusting his tunic, a nonchalant figure wandered. He recognised

Maitland, the object of his wrath, and gestured fiercely. Seeing the waving arms Maitland insolently made his way over to where Bob waited and peered through the dim light at the wrathful figure before him.

'What's up, corp?'

'What's up? I'll give you bloody what's up! It's nearly midnight. You're five minutes late and we're waiting! Where the hell have you been this time, Maitland?'

'Been for a shit, corp, only the latrine pit was crowded with bods so I had to go further down.'

Bob glared at him but Maitland's dark, saturnine face stared back steadily. He had an answer for everything and by now knew just what he could get away with without being cited for defaulters' parade. Clever so-and-so. It made Bob's blood boil but there was a job to do and there was always later.

'Right then, smart-arse, just you go and pick yourself a nice spade from over there and then you come back next to me, where I want you to stay, so's I can keep a good eye on you. Got that?'

'Righto, corp.' Maitland moved easily over to the waiting men and pushed his way through. They parted to let him pass and he picked up a spade, made an ostentatious show of examining it and slowly walked back to stand by Bob's side. Curbing his anger Bob gestured to the others.

'Let's get on with it then. We've a fair bit to do tonight. Watch me and do as I told you in the briefing this afternoon. We'll get going now so pick your gear up and follow me. And remember, keep the blinkin' noise down.'

In the days following their arrival in the front line the men had slowly adjusted to the unnatural life they had encountered. The previous occupants of the dugouts they now inhabited had left one legacy behind to which they were all swiftly introduced. *Pediculus humanus humanus*, the common louse. Lice. Millions of them, living in all the rags and blankets. In a day or so they were all infested, making sleep almost unbearable as the creatures nestled into the warmth of their hosts' bodies, causing the most unimaginable itching that no end of frantic scratching could relieve. There was no escape from the misery although night working parties such as tonight's, out in the cold, brought some relief as the parasites' movements quietened with the drop in temperature.

Bob turned and walked down the trench and after a moment's hesitation the others lifted their spades and followed meekly behind. Maitland brought up the rear with an amused smirk on his ferret-like face. They were adorned with a variety of headgear, some wearing comforters, others with dark balaclavas pulled down over their faces. Other than the borrowed service pistol in a holster on Bob's waist none of them were carrying firearms but the pockets of some bulged with coshes and knobkerries fashioned out of pick handles. A few carried a stock of bombs in their tunic pockets.

After several twists and turns they arrived at a section of the trench where some ladders lay against the sides, leaning against the parapet. The glow of a sneaky cigarette told of the position of the sentry and he half-stood to watch them ascend the ladders carefully and ease their way over the parapet into no man's land. Once clear of the trench and safely through the gap left for them in the barbed wire they spread out and slowly moved forward, trying to put each foot down without a sound and all the while contriving to keep in close contact with the man on either side. It was inky black, the total darkness making it difficult to navigate. As they worked their way deeper into no man's land it began to drizzle again, a cold, wet, miserable feeling that together with the smell of unseen death soaked down into their inner spirits.

Bob stumbled along out in front, his unwary feet catching in the myriad ruts and runnels that thronged no man's land. The ground was littered with all sorts of debris, tins, bottles, the odd bloated, foul-smelling corpse and broken and discarded equipment that had either been thrown or dropped there. A squeal under his foot told of a rat's presence but he smothered his revulsion with a silent curse and grimly strode on.

At last Bob held a hand up and his immediate followers stopped, bringing the rest of the group to a halt. He looked round carefully and then spied what he was seeking. Lying a few yards away to their left lay the gleam of white tape on the surface. Turning his back on where he thought the German trenches lay he withdrew a shaded electric torch from a tunic pocket and leant down. Quickly he switched the torch on, swept the ground beneath him and grunted in acknowledgement of what he could see. A shallow scrape had been made in the ground beneath the tape and the spoil dumped on the ground in front.

'This is it, I reckon, boys,' he whispered. 'Get down into there and start deepening this one. Keep as quiet as you can. I'll move over there.' He gestured, forgetting some of them would fail to see his signals in the dark. 'And if I see or hear anything I'll give a sharp whistle. We've a lot to do so let's get on with it.'

They needed no further bidding, even Maitland, and all save Bob carefully eased down into the shallow trench and just as carefully started to dig into the ground using the picks to dig with and the spades to shift the spoil. From where he was crouching it sounded to Bob like a giant scrubbing board being scratched and his anxiety level climbed steeply. He stared intently in the direction of the German trenches but could discern no movement or sounds other than the rain drumming down, and he gradually relaxed again. Once, he caught the sound of a man coughing hard from over to his right but it stopped as abruptly as it had started and there was no further noise to disturb his party's exertions.

Whoosh! A blinding light held them all in its sudden brightness, piercing the darkness savagely and catching them all remorselessly in its merciless glare. All movement stopped and the men froze in their respective poses, everyone standing stock still as they'd been instructed to do. The night was turned into bright daylight, freezing the retinal images in front of them like a black and white photograph. For long seconds they stood there, frozen in time, until the light slowly descended and darkness once again enveloped them. The blinding light had destroyed their night vision so they crouched down and concentrated hard until shapes and outlines once more became apparent.

Two hours passed in this way, the only sound being stifled grunts as they threw the spoil out over the lip of the trench. Now and again, more flares lit up the sky but none were near enough to cause them to stop their work. The trench was now almost deep enough to stand half-upright in and after a careful look over it Bob concluded they had done enough. A relief party would be out soon to finish the work. The shallow scrapes would be linked up by their reliefs in the early hours to form the jumping-off trenches the assaulting infantry would use on the Saturday morning, not many hours away now. Satisfied, Bob quietly crawled round and touching each man on the shoulder indicated to him that it was time to retire. One by one they slipped away.

Looking round for the last time Bob was about to follow when a stealthy sound reached his heightened sense of hearing. A chink of metal, followed by a guttural curse, sounded from what seemed to be only a few yards away. Ducking down, nerves stretched tight, his heart hammering in his chest, he silently drew his pistol from its holster and peered into the darkness. Gradually he made out the shape of a crouching figure, bent over, creeping towards where he sat hidden behind the spoil heap of their recent excavations.

He forced his breathing to remain steady as his heart threatened to accelerate its beating, a sweat appearing on his brow even though the night air was cold. As he watched he began to make out more figures following the first, all of them carrying weapons and heading in his general direction. By now the approaching men had cut off his route back so he forced his mind to concentrate on working out an alternative path as he tried to count the numbers in front of him. He had counted five when the leading figure stopped suddenly.

'Willi, hier. Schnell. Mach schnell, aber rühig, neh?' The sentence confirmed their identity so easing the hammer back on the pistol Bob pressed deeper into the spoil heap in the hope they would pass by without spotting him. A second soldier wormed his way forward to join the one who had spoken earlier and as he drew level with the leader he turned and looked directly at Bob.

'Ach. Was ist...?'

Without thinking, Bob pointed the pistol at him and pulled the trigger. As the sound of the shot shattered the darkness several things happened. The German he had shot at point-blank range collapsed limply without a sound into the trench, sliding down in an untidy tangle of limbs. The leader of his party brought his rifle up and fired in Bob's direction, aiming for the sound of the shot. The flash lit up the night and the bullet hummed over Bob's shoulder. He rolled sideways, heart thudding madly now as he aimed a shot at the other soldiers. It missed and as he squinted to fire again the Germans bunched together and charged in his direction, shouting hoarsely.

Bob leapt to his feet and collided with the first soldier as he lunged at him, the man's bayonet passing under his armpit with inches to spare. The force of their collision winded him and as he fell to his knees as the soldier drew back his rifle for another attempt. Dark as it was Bob could see the fiercely exultant expression on the man's face and he tried to raise his pistol, sensing as the other man did that it would be to no avail. As the German stepped forward to plunge his bayonet deep into Bob's body a dim figure reared up behind him and a spade smashed down with great force onto the enemy soldier's head. With a loud groan the soldier flopped down and whirling round, Bob's rescuer slammed his spade with equal force into the face of the German nearest to him.

With a crunching noise he too collapsed wordlessly. The remaining two enemy soldiers turned and fled, their lethal intentions forgotten as they sought to escape the demonic figure that had attacked their comrades with such deadly, savage force.

Bob stared in amazement at the panting figure that loomed over him and his eyes opened wider still as his racing mind recognised his saviour.

'Maitland!' he breathed. 'Where the hell did you come from?'

Fred Maitland bent over the nearest recumbent German before answering. 'Back there,' he said, controlling his breathing and pointing casually. 'I heard a noise an' figured there might be some action goin' on.'

'Jesus! Well, you saved me and that's a fact. I owe you for this one, Maitland!'

'Its all right, corp, you don't owe me a thing,' Fred Maitland replied nonchalantly as he began rifling through the dead man's pockets. He began stuffing the contents into his own pockets without examining them. 'I've always fancied getting hold of one of these Pickelhaube helmets an' now I've got the pick of three. Ain't life good at times, eh, corp?'

The darkness was rent by the *whoosh!* and brightness of another flare but Maitland continued unhurriedly his scavenging of the German's belongings. The sight of the flare galvanised Bob into action. Reaching over he grabbed Maitland's shoulder. 'Come on man, quickly,' he urged, 'Fritz will be hopping mad when he finds out what's gone on here. Those two men will let them know we're here. We have to go. Now!' He pulled at Maitland's shoulder again more urgently this time but the man just shrugged him off.

'Be with you in a second,' he grunted testily as he lifted two of the enemy's helmets up eagerly.

The bullets came swishing out of the gloom a split second before the sound of the machine-gun reached them. *Zzzzzzt! Zzzzzzt!* The enemy gunner was firing blindly but the bullets landed uncomfortably close to the two men as he traversed from right to left across no man's land. Another flare rose up from the German lines, bathing them once more in brilliant light, followed by another and then yet another. As Bob looked over to Maitland his ears caught the dull, faraway bark of a field gun firing.

The shell screeched over and landed a hundred yards or so away, showering them with earth as it exploded with a huge metallic *bang!* Another swiftly followed and soon the air was filled with the sound of incoming shells. They ran, all pretence of keeping quiet abandoned as they fled in the face of the barrage that sought them out. Bob overtook Maitland and led the way back as they sprinted hard for their own trenches.

Above the screeching and the sound of exploding shells he heard a shrill cry and looking back saw a shadow crumple to the ground. He stopped and peered back, trying to make out the shape on the floor. 'Maitland?' he enquired loudly and was rewarded by a faint groan. Doubling back he ran to where his companion lay writhing, grunting in agony, his recently-won trophies scattered around him in the dirt. Bending over the recumbent figure Bob grabbed his arm and turned him over.

Maitland was mumbling incoherently and Bob bent closer to make out the jumbled speech. 'Where's my fuckin' helmets, corp?' Without answering Bob roughly heaved him up, causing Maitland to moan in pain. Leaning him against his own body, Bob anxiously peered at him to ascertain the extent of his injuries. Apart from the tears in his uniform Bob could see no other wounds so he tried to wrap the injured man's arm around his shoulder with the intent of dragging him.

As he tried to move off Maitland screamed in agony as his broken ribs grated noisily, and collapsed back onto the ground before Bob could catch him. The shells were falling thickly now and the air was filled with the wicked hum of splinters and clods of dirt as each explosion drowned out the previous one. Bullets kicked up the dirt near them as the enemy gunner retraced his movements across the broken ground. Desperately Bob leaned over again and pulled Maitland upright for the second time. The injured man screamed again but his voice was lost in the sound of more shells exploding violently nearby.

Bent double under Maitland's weight, Bob staggered towards the point where he judged their own trenches to be. His breathing was laboured now as he gulped in huge quantities of air with each step. Maitland was a pressing weight on his back and shoulders, pulling him lower and slowing his progress as each second passed. His vision was filled with a red mist and he briefly thought of letting the burden across his back slide down to give him some relief, but as quickly as the thought entered his head he dismissed it and staggered gamely on.

Just as he sensed himself reaching the limit of his endurance he heard voices roaring at him and weakly raising his head made out the dim shape of a trench looming out of the darkness. Willing himself on he headed towards the parapet. A hammer blow smashed into his right hip and he gasped aloud with the pain, spun, and fell headlong with the sudden impact of the bullet, spilling Maitland from his grasp as he sprawled helplessly onto the ground. Willing hands reached out over the parapet and dragged the two men over the covering sandbags and down to lie on the floor of the trench. Bob tried to speak but the words would not come and, giving up, he lay inert in a sea of pain.

His nose caught the sour taste of smelling salts and he jerked awake.

'Its all right, old man, lie there still and let me have a look at you.' Dimly he recognised the soothing voice of the battalion MO and he tried to look up at Captain Hughes. It seemed so long ago since they had knelt over Corporal Hackett on the Folkestone quayside and he tried to speak to remind the MO of who he was. The prick of a hypodermic needle entering his arm caused him to jump suddenly and before he could protest he felt himself drifting off in a warm cocoon. He was unconscious long before the platoon stretcher-bearers carried him and Maitland down the trench to the battalion aid post.

The shelling carried on in a desultory manner for another forty minutes before gradually dying down. The reliefs were stood down for fear of attracting more fire down on them if they went out. Before dawn slowly broke the British guns started again in earnest. As the light improved, one of the watching sentries awaiting the order to stand-to yawned and blearily peeped through his periscope. What he saw made his eyes bulge and he shouted for an NCO. CSM Frank Mason was first to reach him and wordlessly the soldier handed him the periscope.

On the far side of no man's land a large white board had been hoisted over the parapet of the German trench. Written on it in large black paint was the message:

See you on the 25th Tommy

7

Friday 24th September 1915

Heavy bombardment of enemy trenches continues. No opposition is to be expected when battalions to our left go over the top tomorrow. Battalion still held in reserve. Thunderstorm in the evening brought heavy rain which left many men soaked. Fresh rations and ammunition issued, for emergency use if battalion called on. Work parties finished the jumping-off trenches at 23:00 ack emma under sporadic enemy fire. No casualties. Line companies issued with gas masks. A Company recalled from reserve. All save HQ holding front line trenches.

R.D. Sprightly, Major, C Company

Saturday 25th September 1915

Opening day of Loos offensive. Huge explosion in early hours of morning as mine under enemy trenches exploded. Troops sent over at 06:30 ack emma. Battalion held in reserve. Enemy shellfire increased and several casualties in battalion trenches. Major Sprightly and eight ORs killed. Fifteen ORs wounded. A and D Companies called up later in day at 11:30 ack emma to support Highlanders. Capt Brasher and Lt Charteris did sterling work in enemy trenches opposite. No gains obtained and both Coy's forced to retire later in day. 2/Lt Wordsley and nine ORs killed, eight ORs wounded, five ORs missing.

L. Carey, Captain, D Company

'Stand-to! Stand-to! Come on, come on! Get up there you lot! Keep your eyes to your front and a sharp lookout. Godley, get up there! Help him for Chrissakes, someone.'

Wearily they responded to the sergeant's shouts. The last four days of heavy shelling had left nearly all of them with a lingering, nagging headache and it took an effort to mount the firestep and peer into the growing daylight beyond. One welcome respite was that the rats, the thousands of them that inhabited the trenches and no man's land, had disappeared during the shelling and so far were still absent.

Above them the shells screeched and screamed, making the air sing with their passage, the pressure waves battering at the eardrums of the men below. The siege howitzers and 18-pounders were adding their fire to the bigger 'heavies'. In the direction of the enemy trenches they could see huge gouts of multi-coloured flames twinkling and flickering along the enemy's front line as the shells exploded.

It was both exhilarating and horrifying. Their own guns had been firing all night and the noise of the explosions deafened them. Orders had been issued that everyone would stand-to wearing gas masks but as they were not to be involved in the initial assault it had been left to the individual company commanders discretion whether to enforce this. Not surprisingly, they had all chosen to ignore it given the claustrophobic time the men would have faced had they been made to comply, so a compromise had been reached. Everyone on the firestep had his flannelette gas mask within easy reach, ready to don it at a moment's notice should the need arise.

'What time is it, sir, please?' Sidney Bates turned and looked down at Lieutenant Neville Charteris crouching below him. Twenty-eight years old, a native of Peckham, London, Charteris had been an office manager for an insurance company in civilian life. In his new role he let nothing faze him and his affable manner and common decency had won him many admirers. Of average height, he sported a thin moustache that he hoped, unsuccessfully, would help disguise his boyish good looks.

'Look to your front, man!' he replied curtly, then glanced at his watch instinctively. The luminous hands glowed dully as he peered at them. 'It's just coming up to 06:30 ack emma,' he said automatically, noting the time with some surprise. He would have sworn they had been standing there for a lot longer than an hour. He removed his hat and absentmindedly ran his fingers through his thick, dark hair. Dickens, his batman, had shaken him awake at half-past four with a hot, sweet cup of tea and that now seemed in the distant past. He felt tired, still not having shaken off the effects of the long march up with the rest of the company from the reserve trenches the night before. The lack of sleep and thundering crescendo of the overhead barrage was making his head ache severely. Jamming his hat back on his head he eased his pistol from its leather holster and after checking all the chambers were filled, spoke again.

'Keep a good watch now you chaps, this is it. It's nearly time for our men to go over, so keep your eyes peeled. Any minute now and you should see movement.' As he spoke he became aware that their own guns had fallen silent for the first time in days.

'Sir, can you hear that?' The voice from the firing-line spoke and he strained to listen. In the distance, faintly rising and falling on the early morning air, he could make out the keening noise of a set of bagpipes. Just as faint to begin with, then growing louder, he heard the sound of whistles. Above the German trenches the sky was filled with red and white distress flares as the beleaguered defenders called for help from their own gunners.

'They're going, they're going! God! Look at them! All of them, they're going!' Charteris jumped up onto the firestep and peered to his front, following the out-stretched hand as the man to his right pointed excitedly. In the growing daylight his immediate view was of a stream of kilted men, clambering over the top of the para-pets of the jumping-off trenches he and his men had dug over the past few days, with rifles held rigidly in front of them. As he watched, more and more men appeared from the trenches behind them, checking their dressing before quickly breaking into a run as they advanced over the open ground towards the enemy front line. Further to his left he could see great rolling clouds of what appeared to be greenish-yellow smoke enshrouding their own trenches.

'Give them hell, chums, stick a Boche for me!' Henry Watson, his normal quiet air of reserve gone, had heaved himself over the parapet and was capering around shouting and shrieking at the distant waves as they formed up. Charteris vaulted up and roughly grabbed him, pulling him back into the shelter of the trench.

'You bloody fool; do you want to get us killed? Get back up there and stay down!' he raged.

'Sorry, sir,' Watson shame-facedly acknowledged before picking up his rifle and taking his place alongside his companions. Charteris joined them and looked back out to his front. The ground seemed to be full of troops moving rapidly. A veritable tide of khaki-clad men thronged no man's land as they surged forwards. Gazing at them he became aware of several of the men throwing up their arms and collapsing.

With daylight breaking fully now he could see explosions bursting with black-tinged fire among them and his ears picked up the low stuttering rattle of the German machine-guns. Groups of huddled figures lay prone and while he stared in horror the noise of the German gunners reached an ear-shattering peak, the full weight of the defenders lashing at the waves of assaulting infantry. Flame-edged puffs of grey smoke in the sky told of shrapnel bursting overhead, catching many in the open. Faintly to their ears came the screams of dying and wounded men as the machine-guns searched them out in earnest, cutting huge swathes out of the darting, dashing figures.

Further along the trench, the men from C Company were watching the same scenes. Before their horror-filled eyes they could see the waves of men cut down in the open. Several wept impotent tears as they continued to watch in silence. Shells began falling near their trench and they ducked as the gunners opposite ranged their shells down on them, filling the air with the wicked, whining hum of shrapnel and huge clods of earth and chalk. Bernie Millard watched with awe as several large puffs of black smoke appeared overhead, announcing their presence with a loud *whoof!* Absentmindedly he reached a hand up as if to catch one. An sharp excla-mation of pain was wrung from his lips as he stared down at the bloody mess the shrapnel balls from the enemy shell had made of his left hand. Clutching his shat-tered hand under his right armpit, he fainted.

After he had been carried away their Major Ronald Sprightly walked below them, encouraging and reassuring them.

'Keep to your fronts lads,' he shouted hoarsely, 'it's only a bit of dirt from the whizz-bangs. It'll soon pass.'

One of the privates nudged his neighbour and grinned, gesturing over his shoulder at the major as he darted up and down the trench. He opened his mouth to laugh but the breath was dashed from his lips as a shell burst alongside them in an incandescent blast of white-hot colour and overwhelming sound. In an instant, living flesh was turned to raw, pulped meat as the hot, jagged steel tore through unresisting bodies, flinging limbs and pieces of what had once been men in all directions.

Major Sprightly was flung with enormous force to the floor, smashing into the far wall of the trench. His eyes were filled with dirt and he thrashed convulsively as he tried to draw a breath into his aching lungs. There was no sound of battle now, his ears were filled with a loud ringing tone and in his mouth was the acrid tang of blood and cordite. He tried to rise but his legs would not support him and he slid down to lie half-supported by a baulk of timber on the floor of the trench.

He became aware of voices yelling for the company stretcher-bearers and hands grabbing at him but he screamed in agony as they moved him and they released their grip to let him resume his former position. Blearily he looked up to see the shocked, concerned face of his company sergeant-major. As he lay there his hearing began to return and he was annoyed to hear at close hand a high screaming noise. His hands fluttered uselessly as he felt something tear deep within his body and he slumped over, coughing up great gouts of bright, arterial blood. His eyes rolled upwards and his breathing stopped abruptly.

'Jesus!' breathed CSM Hornby. He leant over his company commander again but it was obvious it was too late. The officer's pallid expression and fixed stare told him he would be wasting his time, so he straightened up and looked around. He stared into a scene of utter carnage. Bodies, parts of bodies and equipment lay everywhere in a macabre parody of a butcher's shop. Blood filled the trench, running down its walls and forming large puddles on the floor, intermingled with rain water. The trench wall had collapsed and he could see a pair of legs, ominously still, sticking out from underneath the mound of dirt now obstructing the way. A rifle, splashed with its owner's blood, stuck out from the parados, buried in a sandbag up to the hilt of its bayonet. Unthinkingly he reached over and pulled it free, flinging it high over the parapet.

The screaming in his ears came from his right and he scrambled along the trench to find a huddled figure lying prone, hands clasped to his abdomen. From where he stood Hornby could see the purplish-blue coil of the man's intestines glistening in the rags of his uniform as he vainly tried to hold them in place. He slid down alongside the man and tried to move his hands away from the gaping wound, but the soldier beneath him clung rigidly to his stomach.

'Tell her, I...My mum, tell her...' He screamed again, a loud agonising wail of pain and terror.

'Stretcher-bearers! Where the hell are those bloody stretcher-bearers!' Hornby jumped to his feet and shouted frantically but when he looked down again the man's hands had relaxed and he lay silent, the rain from the night before mingling with the bloody wound, causing it to spill out of the shattered body and lap up against his feet. Another shell landed alongside the first and its hot breath flung Hornby sideways, filling the air once more with deadly shards of whining, hot, jagged metal. He could hear more shouts and screams but for the moment he was unable to move. Rubbing his hands through his hair he felt wetness but in his stunned state of mind he was unable to make out if it was water or blood. He hauled himself upright, retrieved his battered hat from where it lay and, after slapping it firmly on his head, strode grimly towards the sound of the shouting.

Charteris heard the shells striking the trench line to his right but for the moment he was too engrossed in what was happening in front of him to take any notice. From where he stood, half-crouching, he could see in the distance the tall, steel towers of the Loos pithead, nicknamed 'Tower Bridge', brooding over the valley. Behind it, half in shadows but still visible, rose the pit spoil heap known as the Crassier. The men he could see away in the distance seemed to have traversed the front line and appeared to be making their way towards the German second line, their original objective.

A movement to his right caught his eye and he looked round to see a bedraggled bird painfully, drunkenly, staggering along the parapet. It's eyes were glazed and he could see it's beak was wide open. The concussion of the shells passing overhead must have traumatised the bird, by it's looks a blackbird, and as he watched it fell out of sight over the parapet.

The morning passed slowly for them. Heavy firing could be heard in the distance but even with the aid of binoculars it was hard to make anything out in the smoke wreathing the ground to their front. Around eleven o'clock the men started to unpack the rations issued the previous day and just when Charteris was thinking about joining them in having some breakfast his company commander, Captain Charles Brasher, appeared. An Old Etonian, Brasher was only two years or so older than Charteris and his easy, friendly manner had impressed from the start.

'Neville, old man,' he spoke quickly, 'I've just been given our orders. The company is to go up in support of the Jocks. The Jocks've reached Loos but are being picked off from the rear by small pockets of Huns dug in among the ruins. The reserves under General Haig will be coming up shortly but for now we're to be committed. Can you get your chaps together as quickly as you can? We'll be going over in about ten minutes, on the half hour, with D Company. Take your men and dig in on the Boche first line. Wait there for further orders. And make sure you take plenty of bombs and extra ammunition. Good luck.' They shook hands heartily and with that he was gone.

Calling for his CSM, Frank Mason, to follow him, Neville busied himself making sure the men under his command received the news, swaddled themselves in extra bandoliers of ammunition, and readied themselves for the off. With every third man carrying a cloth bag of Mills bombs in addition to his other accoutrements they made ready below the parapet. For himself he donned a webbing map case and stuffed a prismatic compass into one of the voluminous pockets of his tunic. Promptly on the half hour they heard several loud blasts of a whistle and the hoarse shouts as Brasher and his platoon went over the top, followed closely by the men of D Company.

'Come on then first platoon, follow me!' Charteris shouted at the top of his voice, waving his now-drawn revolver in his hand as he leapt up over the parapet for the second time that morning and began to half-run into the churned-up ground immediately in front of the trench. Answering shouts told him his men were following him. 'Chaaaarrge!' he shouted, and picked up his pace, zig-zagging to and fro as they had been instructed all those months ago back in the safety of Morecambe camp. He could see the white, chalk-tipped jumping-off trenches ahead and, his heart pounding wildly in his chest, he aimed for a gap between the nearest two.

The ground he was running over was a mess of splinters, shell-craters and discarded equipment, and as he neared the jumping-off trenches he began encountering bodies. Lots of them, in all manner of disarray, lying in swathes where the machine-guns had caught them. The trenches themselves were full of inert figures, mostly wearing kilts he noticed, many lying on the parapet where the enemy fire had swept through them as they emerged. The pale-white thighs and lower limbs twisted askew stood out starkly against the rich earth.

Some looked to be lying there as if asleep while others bore horrific wounds, their bodies torn asunder by high explosives, shrapnel and the effects of the German bullets and shell splinters that had torn into them. He noted with surprise that many of them were wearing the same type of gas masks he and his men had been issued days before. The faces he could discern looked ghastly, pale bluish-white in many cases, screwed up and contorted in their final death agonies. Blood, lay everywhere, filling the shell holes and running in rivulets around the stiffening corpses. His gorge rose in his throat at the awful stench of so much violent death and he swallowed hard before running on.

The wounded, too, lay everywhere, raising their bodies and imploring hands, crying piteously for aid or water as he passed. The lightly wounded among them sat head in hands as if dazed by their experiences while others, more seriously injured, crawled aimlessly around, unconsciously seeking shelter from the firestorm that had been unleashed upon them. He could do nothing to help and moved swiftly passed them, keeping his eyes on the approaching enemy trenches as he ran.

It took scant seconds, a minute or so, and as he neared the wreckage of what he saw to be the enemy's first line of defence and their belts of barbed wire he noticed another phenomenon. The ground was strewn with thousands of round, spherical shrapnel bullets and shells, littering the wire entanglements and surrounding areas. 'Duds!' he exclaimed as he ran on. The sight of all those unexploded shells filled him with fury and he forgot his present circumstances for a while as he tried to take in their meaning. The British guns had fired thousands of shells of all calibres in their efforts to destroy the German front line and its protective wire. Many lives had been lost by the abject failure of those worn-out guns utilised to try and destroy the German's means of defence at long and short range.

A stuttering noise woke him to the sound of danger and he leapt instinctively sideways into a shallow crater as machine-gun bullets kicked up the earth where he had been running seconds before. As he lay there, half-winded, another figure dived in and landed on top of him, forcing him down into the growing puddle at the bottom, making him grunt in pain. The soldier's rifle caught him a painful blow on the ankle and he grimaced as they both lay there panting. Faintly, as he lay there clutching his ankle, he caught a whiff of lilac and he struggled strenuously to sit up and ascertain whether or not he could see any trace of the chlorine gas that had been loosed off that morning from the British trenches.

'Beg your pardon sir, but that Boche bullet thought it had my number on it!' Reggie Pilling exclaimed in fright. His cap had fallen several feet away and he automatically reached for it and placed it back on his head.

'Keep your head down, man,' Charteris grunted as he squirmed from underneath the private. Both men spotted a third occupant of the shell hole at the same time but a quick glance at his shredded torso told them their companion was beyond any help. The smell of gas was just a memory now, so slowly Charteris edged his way to the top of the shell hole and began to rise up.

Spang! Spang! A shower of bullets whined off a metal barbed-wire support directly in front of his face and he slid hurriedly down again.

'That Hun knows his business!' he exclaimed loudly as he crawled over to the left-hand side and tried again. Another shower of bullets told him the enemy machine-gunner had that direction covered also and he rejoined Pilling once more in the protection of the bottom of the hole, discarding his map case as he did so. Holstering his revolver he took stock quickly.

As a nearby explosion spattered them with dirt Charteris sprang to his feet and jumped up onto the lip of the crater. 'Come on Pilling,' he shouted. 'That machine-gunner won't be able to spot us in this. Run man, follow me. Quickly now!' Pilling needed no urging and quickly followed his officer, hefting his bag of bombs as he did so. In his haste his rifle lay where he had dropped it but in the tension of the moment neither man noticed.

They ran forward, hunched against the hail of shells dropping around them. To their left and right loud explosions told of the shells finding their mark but they ran through the firestorm miraculously untouched. As he ran Charteris tried to work out in which direction the machine-gun fire had come from. His instincts told him it was from his left so he ran at an oblique angle to where he thought the gun might be sited. Just as quickly as it had started the salvo of shells ceased, and spotting another fresh crater Charteris motioned to Pilling and they both dived over its lip into its comparative safety.

They were now both soaked through from their dousing at the bottom of the shell hole and their clothing clung stiffly and uncomfortably to them, covered in mud and thick, white chalk. He could hear gunfire all around them, together with shouts and screams, but from where they lay he could not ascertain where they came from. He and Pilling seemed to be all alone on the battlefield for the time being.

'I have an idea. Give me your rifle,' he asked. Pilling looked round aghast and for the first time noticed he was not carrying it. 'I must have dropped it back there sir,' he gasped.

'Damn!' Charteris grunted in annoyance and then noticed for the first time the cloth bag Pilling was carrying. 'Are they bombs, Pilling?' he enquired and was heartened to see the private nod vigorously in answer to his question. 'Good man. Pass me a couple over here, carefully, and we'll see what we can do with these little beauties, eh?'

Pilling passed him a handful of the Mills bombs. After checking the safety pins were firmly in place Charteris placed them in his tunic pockets and crawled up to the lip of the shell hole. No fire answered his movement, so growing bolder he drew himself up onto his elbows and carefully scanned the surrounding area. Looking back he could see the prone figures of several of his men firing rapidly at something or someone he was unable to see. He also saw dirt kicking up among them as the machine-gunner who had tried so hard to knock him and Pilling out of the game concentrated on these fresh targets.

Still lying on his elbows he began a slow sweep to his left. A movement in a jumbled heap of earth and chalk behind an enemy trench caught his eye and as he concentrated on it he began to make out the camouflaged barrel of a Maxim-type machine-gun. A German Model 08, no doubt of it. It covered a large gap in the belts of barbed wire around whose entrance huddled bodies lay prone in large numbers. Several had yellow divisional marker flags on long poles lying next to them.

He turned to Pilling and motioned him closer. 'Those Boche have been left behind to hold up any support. See that gap in the wire over there?' As Pilling nodded he continued, 'When I shout *when!* chuck one of your bombs over there and then get down. Understand?' Pilling nodded again and Charteris patted him encouragingly on the shoulder as he squirmed over to the other side of the shell hole.

'*When!*' he shouted.

Obligingly, Pilling pulled the pin from his Mills bomb, counted three as he had been taught and lobbed it hard in the direction his officer had indicated. It burst against the barbed wire with a dull *thud!* and he ducked swiftly down. As Charteris had anticipated, on hearing the noise of the explosion the machine-gun barrel swung towards the direction of the sound, away from him. Smoothly he rose to his feet and pulled two bombs from his pocket. Pulling the pins out he ran forward and threw them at the protruding barrel, drawing his revolver swiftly from its holster as he did so.

The bombs burst one after another in rapid succession. Loud screams emanated from the machine-gun's position and the barrel lurched drunkenly, to point uselessly skywards. Three of the gun crew lay inert by their weapon, helmets askew, but a fourth member, bloodied but still alive, was crawling weakly over to where a group of Mauser rifles lay stacked. Without hesitation Charteris shot him twice at close range and the German slumped down and remained still. The gun looked intact so he drew another bomb, pulled the pin and threw that under the breech before running back to where Pilling still cowered. As the resulting explosion told of the gun's destruction he gestured urgently to the other man.

'Come on Pilling, on your feet, man. We need to keep moving!'

They moved forward to spot in front of them a small group of soldiers crouched down among the dead bodies of the defenders, taking cover from the drizzle by the open German trenches. Recognising him, one of the men came over and saluted.

'Private Allinson, sir, three platoon. Captain Brasher's orders, sir, we was told to stay here and hold these trenches until relieved. We thought all the officers had gone west, beggin' your pardon, sir, so we stayed here as we were told. We was pinned down until you come along. Some of the lads got into a scrap further to our left but we couldn't get to them because of the shelling, sir.'

Charteris spoke soothingly. 'Are there any more of our chaps around? It seems an awful small number to defend this section. Where the hell are the Lewis gun teams?'

Allinson gestured with his thumb to his right. 'Out there. Dead, sir,' he answered bitterly. 'That machine-gun caught them like all the rest. I grabbed who was left and told them to stay here until we received further orders.'

'Good thinking Allinson. Wave to those chaps over there in the open and get them to join us. Do what you can for the wounded. We'll have to make something out of these Boche trenches so have a careful look round and see what you can find. See if you can find one of the Lewis guns and have a look at that German machine-gun back there. It's a bit knocked about but we might be able to use it. Quickly lads.'

Within seconds their numbers swelled as thirty or so men, including some of the wounded who had been the late machine-gunners' targets, hurriedly joined them and began to dig furiously with the discarded entrenching tools they had found. In a short time Charteris was pleased to see they had constructed a sand-bagged mini-redoubt. Not capable of withstanding a prolonged assault, it could be said, but one that afforded them sufficient cover facing the German second line in the meantime. The wounded had their wounds tended as best they could and the rest he moved into position among the revised trenchwork. Allinson had returned with a huge grin on his face, lugging a Lewis gun and several round drum magazines, so he had it sited within the redoubt. The machine-gun he had neutralised earlier was too badly damaged to be of any use so they had flung it away.

Along the walls were several deep, lined dugouts, the ideal shelter from any heavy bombardment. A major drawback was that in an attack they could also be a death trap, damning men to a violent death if a bomb was thrown into such a confined space. The few Charteris looked into had several stiffening corpses strewn in attitudes of having met such an end. There too were also some of his men, gleefully looting the bodies as they searched them for worthwhile souvenirs. Angrily he shouted at these ghouls and reluctantly they gave up their searches and resumed their places in the redoubt.

After checking their immediate ammunition stocks and supply of bombs they lay there, rifles at the ready. Intermittent shellfire swept the ground behind them as the German gunners tried to prevent any reinforcements attempting to make their way across no man's land, but he and his men remained untouched.

He glimpsed a small, inert form lying on the ground over by the ruined enemy machine-gun and wriggled over to see if he could make it out. It was a bird, a dead bird, and as he stared at the bundle of feathers he realised with a start that it was a blackbird. Not the same one from their own trenches, surely? He reached over and touched it. The bloodied, bedraggled body felt warm but all life had left the small creature some time before. Cursing for reasons he couldn't quite fathom he left the battered body where it lay and wriggled back to his original position.

The time passed slowly. It was now well after noon and the shadows were swiftly stretching deeper and deeper onto no man's land as a watery sun finally broke through again. As they watched and waited they could hear heavy artillery firing again breaking out to their front. Smoke clouds from the explosions hid the scene from their view and interspersed with the shellfire they could make out bursts of machine-gun and rifle fire. Who was firing at whom it was impossible to make out so they continued to lie there. By now they had all eaten their emergency rations and the supply of water in their water bottles was starting to run low. Charteris caught several of the men crawling among the earlier casualties, stripping them of their equipment and water bottles. Angrily he gestured for them to return to their positions and with some reluctance they followed his orders.

At some point there was a drone overhead and they all craned their heads back to look up into the sky. Three small dots moving across to their right were the cause of the noise and as they continued to observe another four dots joined them. Lower and lower they sank, pirouetting in a graceful dance. Faintly to their ears came the sound of a rattle and one of the dots began to emit a large cloud of black smoke. The noise of an engine surging and roaring became more audible as the now-stricken craft began to nose over into a dive. It took on a defined shape as it neared them and while still high in the blue sky they could now make it out as a biplane. Another dot disengaged from the others and sped down on it.

The rattling sound reached their ears again. The biplane's wings crumpled and it fell at a faster speed than before. Flames could be clearly seen licking along the length of its body and they watched in horror as the plane's angle of descent steepened until it fell into a vertical dive. Its speed increased enormously until with a massive explosion it slammed into the ground some hundreds of yards from where they watched. The pursuing plane, a lean, silver monoplane, banked over its victim's funeral pyre and Charteris saw the movement of the pilot's head as he jerked around to observe his prey's final moments. He saw also the black Maltese crosses adorning this plane's sides but they were powerless to intervene as it righted itself and climbed to join the others still wheeling high over the battlefield. In seconds they all were lost in a huge bank of dark clouds and the sound of their passing faded in the rain that started to lash the already soaked men on the ground.

It was with some trepidation that he heard one of the other sentries give voice. 'Someone's coming.' One of the men he had posted at the extreme edge of their little redoubt hissed a message in his direction and as he looked up he gestured, pointing emphatically to his right. 'All right chaps, make sure your safety-catches are off and wait until I give the order to fire,' he commanded as he strained to make out the approaching troops. It was hard to identify their uniforms owing to the amount of chalk and dirt covering them but there was no mistaking the imposing figure of Charles Brasher at their head with CSM Frank Mason bringing up the rear. Brasher was carrying a rifle but there was no despondency in his tall, confident manner as he loped along. He spotted them at the same time and exchanging words with the men following he ran to the edge of the redoubt, jumped down into the trench and moved swiftly to Charteris's side. His men quickly followed.

'God, Charteris, you're a sight for sore eyes and no mistake!' exclaimed Brasher heartily. 'We've routed tons of the Boche over there,' he said exultantly, pointing back to the way they'd come. 'Bombed heaps of the swine and now we're to get back to our own trenches. The blighters have retreated to their second line. That's why we went through them so quickly. A runner found me; the message says we're to let the Gordons consolidate this little lot, they should be here shortly, and get back to rejoin the battalion. Just as well too, there's a large party of Boche sneaking back this way. There'll be a great scrap on here shortly. We've lost men, all dead I'm afraid. Young Wordsley's gone; a shell blew him to pieces, poor devil. How'd you chaps do?'

In a few terse sentences Charteris explained their situation, omitting his part in the taking of the machine-gun out of a sense of reticence. There was no sign of any relieving troops and he made a quick decision. 'Take your chaps first, sir, and we'll stay here and cover your withdrawal before making our way back behind you.' The captain hurried away. On Charteris's issued orders his men started making their way back.

One man stood by the trench and looked hard at the men as they exited. He moved forward and grabbed one of them. 'Oi, you, Donald, have you seen me brother? Jimmy Cooke, he was in your platoon wasn't he?' The soldier in question shrugged the restraining hand free and pointed down the enemy trench.

'Jimmy was with some of the others down there,' he said. 'He wasn't with me at all, Harry. Down there, about a hundred yards round the corner. We was too busy bombing a dugout to see how Jimmy got on, but he went off with some other lads. Down there!'

Before anyone could stop him, Harry Cooke took off down the trench shouting loudly. 'Me mam'll kill me if I don't find him. Jimmy, Jimmy, lad? Are you there?' He rounded the corner, shouting loudly, and was lost to view. Private Donald's expression was stricken as he looked in the direction Harry Cooke had run. 'If he'd waited a moment more I could've told him it's no use. His brother's dead. Shot through the brain! They're all dead back there. We was too late reaching them.'

As Charteris frantically motioned for the men to resume moving a sudden burst of gunfire was heard round the corner of the trench. The deep crack of a Lee-Enfield answered the gunfire but was lost in another renewed burst of firing. A group of figures appeared suddenly to their right and Charteris recognised them as German soldiers, advancing quickly in their direction.

He stood up and gestured urgently. 'Rapid fire! Start firing! Over to your right, men, force their heads down!' A crackle of gunfire rang out as his men responded and the grey-clad figures melted into the earth and out of sight. Grabbing the nearest soldier, Charteris pushed him physically forward and ran. 'Come on you men, run! Follow me, now! Quickly, before we get caught in the open! Bring those with light wounds as best you can, leave the rest. Allinson! Expend what ammo you have for the Lewis in the direction Captain Brasher came from and then get yourself away. Don't stop for anyone. You hear me?'

They needed no further bidding. Everyone scrambled to make their way out through the gap in the trench and ran hard back across the open ground towards the safety of their own trenches. Charteris followed, lungs bursting as he tried to keep up with them. In the distance he caught a glimpse of Captain Brasher running hard, his face wreathed in a huge smile. My God, Charteris thought, he really is enjoying this. Behind, the bark of the Lewis was answered by a volley of shots and he heard the hum of bullets pass overhead. One plucked at his left shoulder but he felt no pain and continued running as the man alongside him, a man he recognised as one of his own platoon privates, Tom Sugden, suddenly threw his arms up and collapsed limply without a sound. It seemed to take forever but, his arms pumping up and down, he sprinted fiercely, trying to keep on his feet as he weaved in and around the debris and bodies littering the ground in great swathes.

A strange, unfamiliar shape loomed to his right and he swerved to give it a wide berth. As he drew abreast he was shocked to see the plane that they had all seen fall to earth. The mangled, scorched wreckage lay with what remained of its tailplane pointing forlornly to the sky, an angry accusation to the gods that had deserted it. In the burnt-out confusion of the cockpit he could make out a huddled, blackened figure. The day's events had left their mark and just when he had thought nothing more could shock or disturb him he was horrified to see the grinning, burnt skull of the plane's pilot looking squarely at him, mocking his passage as he ran past. Swallowing hard he turned his head away from the ghastly sight and ran on.

As he neared the trench he had left that morning he was relieved to see hands waving him and the rest of the men on, encouraging them as they drew nearer. Others manning the firestep were firing over their heads at the enemy trenches behind them. He made out the deep, barking sound of a Vickers machine-gun firing rapidly over their heads at the German lines and the sound gave him renewed strength. With a final sprint he leapt up and into the trench, sprawling full length in the mud on the floor. His breath was knocked out of him with a *whoosh!* and he lay still for several, long seconds as he fought to regain his breathing. He sucked in air with great gulps until gradually his aching lungs resumed their normal pattern and he was able to sit up and take stock of his surroundings.

Feeling decidedly winded, he gingerly felt the tear in his tunic high up on the left shoulder. He experienced a tinge of guilt as he thought of the wounded they'd had to leave behind. There was also a deep sorrow as the dead of their company who were lying back there, alone, filled his mind. Poor Wordsley, he had paid a heavy price for his carelessness back there in Folkestone. They had only spoken once or twice since arriving in France but he knew the matter on the quayside had affected the young officer deeply. Well, not any more, he concluded bitterly.

In a short while the grief would overwhelm many of the survivors but for now Charteris could only feel comfort in the relief at his and his men's salvation. A hand on his shoulder made him jump and he turned to see the smiling face of Charles Brasher as he collapsed wordlessly down next to him, proffering a water bottle. Charteris gratefully accepted the offering and leaning back, took a good, long swig. It was full of neat rum and as the fiery spirit reached the back of his throat he coughed convulsively. Grinning, Brasher reached over and retrieved the water bottle from where Charteris had dropped it.

The other men who had made it back with him were also huddled in the well of the trench, uniforms mostly covered in mud stains, some hatless, the lightly wounded among them being attended by the aid parties. Men sat staring vacantly at the trench wall in front of them, lost in their thoughts of the day's events. Others sat weeping silently, their heads in their hands, shoulders heaving as their bodies were racked with huge sobs. Charteris longed to go to them and offer words of comfort but now was not the time. Later they could all grieve together for their lost pals but for now it was better to leave them alone. He supposed someone ought to start making a roll-call to find out the extent of their losses but as quickly as it entered his head he dismissed the idea and took another swig from the bottle that Brasher held out once more.

The men now sat talking and exchanging cigarettes, smoking incessantly. Curiously, they had brought no prisoners back with them and Charteris made a mental note to discover why, later. At the same time he noticed he and the others who had returned safely were being looked at curiously by those men of the battalion who had stayed and taken no part in the action. The day's fighting and those who had participated had already indelibly marked them out. Whatever had happened two hundred yards away was of no consequence now. The 19th Battalion had been blooded.

His hand felt strange and he looked down to see it had started shaking, as if of its own volition. The water bottle almost fell from his grasp, so badly was the spasm, and he reached over with the other hand to steady it. A picture of the dead machine-gun crew came into his mind together with the awful smell of fresh-spilt blood and he gagged, suddenly, violently, doubling up and retching into his fist. From far away he heard a distant, concerned voice and he shook his head vehemently. A hand touched his shoulder but he shook it free and lay in a sprawled attitude, his thoughts on the dead men and the smell. The stomach-churning stench of blood. It was everywhere, and in he wondered if this new feeling of despair would ever leave him.

As they lay or sat around, taking stock of the day's happenings, from over the parapet, somewhere out in no man's land a lone voice shrieked out in pain. Out there, in amongst all the death, surrounded by stiffening corpses, a badly-wounded man lay in his agony and stridently bawled his hurt to the skies. Unable to bear it, one or two brave souls made ready to make their way back over the parapet to see if they could find him but they were roughly bundled back to safety by their NCOs. The harrowing cries carried on for the rest of the day, becoming weaker and weaker as the twilight drew in until at last, as the distant crackle of musketry died away in the gloaming, they too, finally, ceased.

8

Tuesday 28th September 1915

Battalion relieved from front line and returned to billets in and around village of Tress-
bourdes, near Bethune. A burial service was held for those battalion dead recovered and a
prayer service for our wounded in the recent show. New drafts received and absorbed into
companies. 2/Lt. D. Elliot joined. Our very first welcome mail from home arrived. Pay
parade held and men allowed local leave. Three OR's held in custody after a brawl in
Bethune. One OR, Pte Godley, hospitalised.

L. Carey, Captain, D Company

Loos had been a bloody failure. For nearly three days the battalion had waited in
reserve, seeing and hearing the failure of General French and his staff to come to
grips with the situation as it developed. The reserves were sent in, too late, to their
utter decimation, adding bitter recriminations and their corpses to the growing
mounds that littered the battlefield. Loos had been briefly held and then lost again.
Several further assaults on Hill 70 in the vicinity of Loos had been carried out,
resulting in the wiping out of most of the fresh battalions that had been fed in.

The 19th had waited in agonising anxiety, awaiting the fateful orders that
would see them streaming over the parapet to add their futile contribution to the
slaughter unfolding before them. Those orders had never arrived and it was with
some relief they finally received the news that they were to be relieved. This time
the offer of buses never came.

'Hey, Charlie, get a move on or we'll be late!' The speaker, wrestling furiously
with his tunic as he fumbled with his buttons, glared over at the figure lying on a
blanket on the outhouse floor. The object of his attentions languidly turned over
and contemplated his informant before returning to the serious business of picking
his nose. Exasperated now, his companion reached down and picking up an old, tattered boot, flung it in the prone figure's direction. It struck him squarely on the
back and he yelped in pain.

'Worra fuck did you do that for you stupid bugger? Yer could have really hurt
me!'

'That's nothing to what old man Findlay will do to you if you don't get a bloody
move on, you dozy bastard, Horsfall!' his pal retorted. At the sound of the RSM's

name, the body on the floor frowned and sat up, his hand stretched behind him as he vigorously rubbed his aching back. 'Yer 'aven't seen me boots anywhere 'ave yer?' he enquired plaintively.

Shaking his head, his pal pushed past him and walked out into the brightness of the day. In the distance, the rumbling of the guns continued. Death did not give up his daily gathering, even for a church service. At length, the smart upright figure of Sergeant Willox strode round the corner of the building and stopped in front of them.

'All right you lot, listen up now,' he boomed. 'The chaplains are gonna be here in five minutes sharp so let's be ready for them. Got it? Barnet, you and Magilton go and lift a table out of that pigsty you seem to be living in. Don't look at me like that laddie. As I was saying, go and get a table, try and see if there's a cloth somewhere to drape over it and follow me with it. Sharp now!'

The two men he had detailed off obediently did as they were ordered and marched smartly away, reappearing a minute or so later with a rickety, stained table and a greyish, stained cloth. Willox gestured impatiently for them to accompany him. They trailed behind him as he led them around the back of the rough, stone building. An ancient broken gate, hanging loose on its worn hinges, impeded them for seconds only. Willox dragged it back without breaking step and stood aside to let them pass into the field. Walking on the rutted earth they gingerly placed the table down and set the cloth over its surface. Several open, freshly-dug graves beckoned on the far side of the field. Shaking his head and muttering fiercely once more, Willox approached and moved the table slightly.

'That'll do, I suppose,' he said. 'You two, yes you laddie, go and rouse the rest of your company. And if you see the RSM kindly inform him we're all set up and he can bring the CO and the rest of the officers.'

They stood around chatting while they waited for the rest of the battalion. It didn't take long and in dribs and drabs the field started to fill as more and more of the battalion arrived to take their place among them. Charlie Horsfall was there, still trying to tuck his shirt into his uniform trousers as he sought out his pals. All sense of order was lost as old friends greeted each other, mixing the companies up as they broke ranks to exchange news, exasperating their NCOs even further.

A hush came over those nearest the gate and the men behind strained to see what was going on. Without ceremony their CO, Lieutenant-Colonel Cuthbert Snaith appeared, dapper as ever, followed closely by the battalion chaplains, Captain Dundas and Father Keenan. Behind them, a firing party and a slow procession of pallbearers slowly approached, carrying the shrouded, wrapped remains of those fallen comrades they had been able to recover. Captain Dundas reverently laid the large Bible he was carrying down on the table and nodded at the CO.

Snaith waved for the men to come closer and waited for them to close in on him and the chaplains. When all movement had stopped he cleared his throat a trifle self-consciously and began. In a reedy voice showing its emotion he spoke slowly and clearly, enunciating each word as the men leant forward to hear.

'We have come here today to remember our fallen comrades,' he said simply. 'Those men who we left behind on the field of our first battle and those who we bury here today. I am proud of your conduct before the enemy and we can mourn our brave comrades who gave their lives in this struggle. We have rendered them unto God and as we pray for them now, we shall remember them and their grieving families. Men of the nineteenth, lift your heads high. Remember them and your deeds with pride. I now call upon Captain Dundas and Father Keenan to give them and us the Lord's blessing.'

'The Lord giveth and the Lord taketh away.' Roger Dundas spoke simply, his words hanging on the still air. 'Today we are gathered here to remember those of our comrades who gave their lives in our first action together as a battalion. It is right to pay homage and mourn our friends, who will be sorely missed, both here and at home. May the Lord's protection fall on us all while we are so far from our homes. We now bury our honoured dead...' He slowly spoke the words of the burial service while they all listened in grim silence. At length he announced simply, 'Please sing with me now the hymn, Oh God Our Help in Ages Past.' The gathered men burst into song at his raised arm and struggled manfully, if not tunefully, to complete it.

After a few more minutes of prayer Captain Dundas nodded to Father Keenan who read out the names of their fallen comrades. The loss of so many friends had hurt all but the most hardened among them. These were men who had volunteered with them, had laughed and sweated all through their training together with them. And had finally died alongside them.

The service finished with a short rendering of the Lord's Prayer. The firing party stepped smartly forward and at the order, raised their rifles skywards. The *crack!* of the guns and the rattle of the bolts as they were reloaded made some of the watching men flinch. Three volleys were fired before they shouldered their rifles and withdrew. Shortly afterwards the colonel and his fellow officers departed, leaving the men and their NCOs alone again. The thudding of earth behind them told of the burial parties filling in the graves.

Cuthbert Snaith stood by the gate looking on intently as his officers passed him. Recognising Neville Charteris he beckoned him over.

'Neville, I had word today from HQ. I felt it necessary to inform them immediately of the gallant way in which we, as a battalion, conducted ourselves in the field. Congratulations, you're to be awarded an immediate Military Cross, our first and I hope not our last, award. Good man, it'll be in the *London Gazette* at some point I dare say but I couldn't tell you when. See about getting some ribbon for it and while you're at it, take those rank badges off and put up your new ones.'

Seeing Charteris's puzzled look he explained. 'My dear chap, I don't appear to have made myself too clear. Private Pilling gave a report of your exploits concerning that Hun machine-gun at Loos to Captain Brasher and he passed it on to me, together with his report on your stout defence of your position. Saved a lot of lives, Neville. Was only too happy to pass it down the line. Get some recognition for the battalion, heh? Since Sprightly's death, poor chap, we're now short of a major. I'm promoting Benson from HQ company so that leaves a vacancy for a captain, and that promotion is yours. Congratulations yet again. The other bit of good news, God knows we could do with some, is that Corporal Simpson from B Company will get a Distinguished Conduct Medal for bringing in his chap who was wounded in the night working party. Poor chap's still in hospital but he'll find out soon enough. Carry on!' With that he was gone, leaving a bemused Neville Charteris behind to bear the back-slaps and congratulations of his pleased and somewhat jealous fellow officers.

RSM Findlay strode to the front of the ranks and stared at them keenly. 'Parade...on caps! When you are dismissed,' he announced, 'move smartly to your company HQs and you will be paid for the first time in a long while. A word of advice, gentlemen, do not try to spend it all at once. Savvy? Right. Parade...shun! Parade...dismiss!'

They came to attention with a crashing of boots and turning to the right, broke up. They were all caught up in the throng as several hundred men tried to pass through the gate at once. Sweating, bawling NCOs forced them into some semblance of order and eventually the crush thinned out into a steady stream of khaki, flowing from the field to the company headquarters. Here, eager queues built up outside as they waited to be paid for the first time since their arrival in France.

Harassed company clerks rushed in and out, calling out names and dragging men in as they answered. Once inside, a hasty salute to the witnessing officer and a wad of greasy, tattered notes was thrust into the recipient's hand. Swiftly he was ushered outside and the process repeated.

'Well, you're the bloody expert, how much have I got then?' Arwyn Jones rounded on Henry Watson as they stood there, contemplating the banknotes each of them clutched in their fists. Henry looked down pensively and tried to do a quick mental sum in his head. 'C'mon Taff,' he protested, 'it's over two years since I was last in France!'

'Never bloody mind that, you, how much have I got then Watson? What's one of these Froggie notes worth, then?'

'Wait! Wait! Er, if I take roughly what we got two years ago and knock off a bit for the devalued bit because of the war, and then multiply it by a factor of, let me see, um, ah...at eightpence ha'penny to the franc that's, er...'

'Oh, bloody bollocks, Watson, you blethering idiot! Just answer the damn question and none of this professor nonsense or I'll give you such a clout your eyes'll sting!'

'All right, all right…I make it you've got in our money, about ten shillings and eightpence,' Watson explained.

'Jesus! Is that all!' exclaimed Jones. 'I thought I was bloody rich, see, how's a man supposed to live on this? When they going to pay us what we're bloody well due, I ask you?' He shook the fistful of banknotes under Henry's nose and stormed off, disgusted. Henry Watson looked after him with a wry smile. When munitions workers back in Blighty were getting three and four times the salary of a private, and that included the women too, it was no wonder men out at the Front felt betrayed.

'Hey, Wadley, hold up there. Have you heard?'

'Heard what, Murgatroyd?' Private Wadley turned and observed the Irishman suspiciously.

'My chum Fergal Ternan in B Company told me they're going to hand out some leave passes to Bethune at twelve o'clock. D'ye fancy a walk into the town if we can get hold of one and see if we can find a canteen to wet our whistle in?'

At his words, Ernie Wadley's face lit up. It had been a while since he had tasted alcohol and he sorely missed the welcome taste of a good pint of strong beer. He hadn't tasted French beer yet but it must be all right, he supposed. The money in his pocket was beginning to burn a hole and the sooner he relieved himself of the burden of carrying it around the better. His face took on an anxious expression and he hastily grabbed Murgatroyd's sleeve.

'What if they're only giving out a couple of passes?' he hissed. 'We could be too late you know. It's nearly twelve now!'

Sean Murgatroyd shrugged off his pal's hand and backed away. 'Stay here an' I'll go and see me pal now. He works in the company office so I'll get him to filch one for us both. Sure, and you see if I don't.'

The time dragged slowly by and Wadley paced up and down the street, peering around every few seconds to see if he could spot Murgatroyd's figure coming towards him. He was beginning to despair when he caught sight of him and waved frantically. Murgatroyd saw him at the same time and sauntered casually over.

'Well? Did you get them?' Wadley could not contain his impatience. Sean grabbed his arm and led him into a nearby alley. 'Shut up you idiot! Would you be wantin' everyone to know what your business is?' He held up two official-looking scraps of white paper. Wadley grabbed one and examined it closely. It was a leave pass, entitling the bearer to be absent from billets until ten o'clock that evening. He hugged Murgatroyd to his breast in a rare expression of joy.

'What are we waiting for then, chum? Let's be off and the first drink's on me!'

'Sure and that's the most sensible thing you've said all day, yer daft galoot.' Murgatroyd punched Wadley lightly on the arm and linking his through his friend's they proceed at a leisurely pace down the street, laughing at the strange glances they encountered.

Sean nudged his friend and motioned to their left. Along the bumpy, paved road a horse-drawn GS wagon was slowly approaching them. As it drew level it stopped and the driver, a red-faced lanky private with the cap badge of the ASC, looked kindly down on them.

'Where're you two coves going to?' he enquired.

Sean Murgatroyd put on his best smile, turning on all his Irish charm. 'Would you be goin' anywhere near Bethune, sir?'

'Yer in luck, chum,' the driver explained, 'I've just delivered some ammo down the road and I'm back off to Bethune myself. Jump in the back and 'ave a seat and we'll 'ave yer there in no time. Won't we Bessie?' This to one of the horses patiently waiting in her harness. At the sound of her name she neighed loudly and stamped her feet.

'C'mon then girls, let's be 'aving you!' he cried, cracking his whip. At the sound the horses started convulsively and jerked forward, pulling the wagon down the road at a sharp pace until the village receded far behind.

The journey passed in comparative quiet through a neat rural setting of green fields and high hedges, although in the distance the sound of gunfire never abated. The driver seemed content to keep to himself, cracking the whip at odd intervals to maintain the slow, even pace the horses had set. An hour or so later the outlines of Bethune became visible on the skyline and grew larger as the wagon continued its leisurely pace. Before they knew it they were passing through the outskirts of the town. Pulling up, the driver twisted round and gestured with his thumb up a large paved street.

'There you go boys,' he informed them, 'that'll get you to where you want to be. Look for a place called *Les Trois Allees.* Janine's the owner. Keep well clear of her but she'll do you a right good feed and the piss ain't that weak. Enjoy it and watch out for the Provost Corps, they're right bastards.'

Eagerly they dismounted and looked in the direction he was pointing. Ignoring their shouts of thanks the driver hunched down and concentrated on his reins, keeping the horses and wagon in a straight line as he disappeared down the street and around the corner out of sight. Hitching up his trousers Sean Murgatroyd beamed magnanimously at his friend.

'So Wadley, where's this drink you was goin' ter buy?' Laughing once more they moved off in the direction the wagon driver had indicated.

Back in Tressbourdes those men not having been put to work by overzealous NCOs saw a slight, bespectacled figure wearing corporal's stripes walking down the main street followed by two men pulling a large, wheeled cart. He stopped outside the cottage where B Company HQ had situated itself and disappeared inside.

'Mail's up!' announced Corporal Green, the battalion post clerk.

With a cheer they surrounded him, pushing and puling to get to the front and receive their mail, if any, before their friends. 'All right, all right!' he shouted above the din, 'keep back there and you'll get your mail. I've got three other companies to deliver to so for God's sake be patient and we'll get you all sorted.'

Names were shouted out and the lucky recipient pushed forward with a broad grin to receive a letter or a parcel, retreating to the back of the press in triumph. The unlucky few hung around in the vain hope that perhaps a mistake had been made and some of the remaining parcels and letters would miraculously be found to have their names on them after all. It became obvious this was not going to happen and a small stream of disappointed men drifted away and mingled with their lucky counterparts.

'Who's that lot for then?' Billy Lane asked the post clerk as the corporal tidied up the pile still left in the bottom of the cart. The corporal looked at him and followed his gaze. 'I dunno,' he replied, 'But I'd hazard a guess they belong to the company's recent casualties.'

'So what happens to them then?' Billy demanded.

'I suppose they'll be sent back to Blighty for the next of kin to collect. Why, what's it to you?' Corporal Green asked with a touch of acidity.

'Well, its just that me an' some of the boys didn't get a thing. My old woman never was one for writing. Come to think of it, I don't think the stupid cow can write at all. I mean, it'd be a shame for all what's in them parcels to 'ave to go all the way back and be spoiled when they gets there. Or nicked by some thief back in Blighty. D'you get my meaning?'

Corporal Green chewed on Lane's words for a second or so. 'You're right,' he sighed, 'I'll send the letters back and we'll just lose these parcels. All right, Lane, cop hold of them and make sure everyone gets a share.' In seconds the remainder of the parcels were thrown into eager, willing hands. Watching them, the corporal sadly shook his head. 'Let's get a move on, boys,' he motioned to his two assistants, 'We've another three of these to unload yet.'

In the nearest cottage, Billy Lane sat in the ruins of what was once the front room and ripped off the brown paper from the parcel he was holding. 'Hey, this one was for old Maitland. What a turn up. The bastard ain't here to collect his mail 'cos he copped a packet scrounging Picklehaubes.' He opened the parcel and sat back, contemplating the large, moist-looking fruitcake it contained. 'Hey! Alfie, pass us over a knife over will you.' He dug deep into the cake, breaking off a large chunk. Stuffing the piece into his mouth he savoured the taste and texture for long seconds before swallowing noisily.

'Maitland,' he announced at length. 'You might be a shite soldier but your mother sure 'as to be some cook!'

Neville Charteris sat on his cot in the front room of the house they had commandeered as a company officer's mess. Charles Brasher had preferred a move to HQ company, to replace Major Benson, so as a newly-promoted captain, he, Neville, could stay with A Company as their new commander.

That had cheered him up enormously, until he was given his mail. He looked down at the sheaf of letters in his hand. There was one from his father and a nice, newsy letter from his aunt in Devon, but it was the other two he was holding that bothered him. They were both from his wife back in Peckham. The hasty, occasional leaves he had managed to spend with her during the battalion's training had helped but she had begun to resent his being away on active service.

He had received her last letter before they had left for France, in which she had expressed her loneliness without him and pleaded with him to try and obtain a staff job back in England. Neville had replied, telling her how hopeless that would be and had heard no more. Until today, with the arrival of these letters. In the first she coldly informed him that she would be looking for work. The second merely informed him that she had found a position in a solicitor's office, a fortunate occurrence if she should ever need one, she had written tartly. The situation was quite impossible and he continued to sit there feeling slightly depressed. The euphoria he felt from his meeting with the CO had suddenly evaporated and for the first time in a long while he had the urge to get up and go and get very, very drunk.

The door was flung open and he looked up. Framed in the doorway stood a young, fresh-faced subaltern, his uniform painfully free of blemishes or creases.

'Second-Lieutenant David Elliot reporting, sir,' he announced firmly with an elaborate salute.

'Neville Charteris,' Neville answered him easily, proffering a hand 'We don't bother with salutes on active service, old chap. Did you have an easy job to find us?'

David Elliot ignored the greeting and the outstretched hand and looked down at his superior officer with a frown.

'Do you know sir,' he said, 'there are men out there in some disgraceful, slovenly states! Should we not be making them smarten themselves up?' He tugged self-consciously at his obviously-new Sam Browne belt as he spoke.

Sighing, Charteris reluctantly rose. Prig! he thought. 'Oh dear. Come along with me then, young Elliot, I'll take you to meet the CO and I'm sure he'll be delighted to hear your observations.'

Back in Bethune, Murgatroyd and Wadley were in a state of bliss. After several false starts and more than a few drinks, they had finally ended up in *Les Trois Allees*, as recommended by the wagon driver. Entering, they had been greeted by an old crone in a filthy black dress, her hair tied back in a severe bun, who had led them wordlessly to a table at the back of the noisy, smoke-filled room full of soldiers like themselves. Slamming a bottle of sour white wine in front of them and two cracked glasses she had disappeared, reappearing a short while later with two plates of egg and chips which they had devoured ravenously. All this and their previous drinking-holes had severely depleted the roll of banknotes each had left with but after another bottle of wine they were now fully replete and ever so slightly drunk.

'Hey, Ernie, isn't that boy over there young Godders?' Sean prodded his chum and gestured vaguely across the room. Ernie blearily followed his pointing finger and nodded affirmatively. 'Yes,' he agreed, his head bouncing around on his neck, 'Its that little shit, Godley. Hey, Goddersh, over here!' The two soldiers sitting by themselves near the front door looked round in a startled manner and recognising the men waving vigorously, reluctantly got up and moved over to join them.

'What ho, you twos. Would you be having a good time? Me and Wadley here are the star guests today. Are we not, Ernie?' Sean was slurring now. Ernie's head wagged up and down as he tried to agree. The wine was affecting his vision and he tried to focus on the two soldiers sat next to him. He dimly recognised the other man as Titch Magilton. 'Wazza marra, you two? 'Aving the battalion dwarves outing are you?' He giggled hilariously at his own feeble attempt at humour, being joined seconds later by an equally befuddled Sean Murgatroyd.

Angrily, Godley made to rise but he was restrained by a warning glance form his companion. 'It's all right, boy,' he soothed, 'they're just funnin'.' Sean Murgatroyd was not someone to mess with. From the first days of training in Morecambe he had been too ready to settle any arguments he was involved in with his fists. Standing well over six feet and with a well-muscled body he was a bully, a sullen bully with a conduct sheet as long as his arm. Any further attempt at conversation between him and the others was stopped by the dramatic entrance of a stunning dark-haired creature from the back rooms of the establishment.

It was the owner, Janine. A woman in her early thirties, she was in the prime of her life and, looking round at the avid, vacuous faces drooling in her direction, she knew it. She smoothed her hands down over her tight, full bosom and pirou-etted lightly towards the bar, the light from the window falling on her head, making her black hair gleam. Her white blouse enhanced the outline of her hourglass waist, tucked as it was into a thick, dark skirt. She stood by the bar and then turned to face them all.

'*Allons mes pauvres,*' she announced, 'you please drink up now as we must close. We open later in the evening so all are welcome. *Maintenant, allez. Vite!* Go, now.'

Godley began to rise but was restrained by Sean Murgatroyd's meaty hand. 'Stay there, me little fella,' he was told threateningly, 'we're goin' nowhere. I've come to wet me whistle and that's what I'm gonna do. Wid me friends an' all.'

Janine looked over at their table and drew her brows together in a twitch of concern. Looking past them she unleashed a torrent of voluble French at the old woman who had entered from the back. Without a sound the crone retraced her steps and disappeared into the interior of the estaminet. Slowly, Janine walked over to where they sat watching her approach and she was careful to keep on the other side of the table to Sean whilst appealing directly to Godley.

'Please, *mes ami,* you and your friends must now go. *Comprendez?*'

'Shut up woman an' bring us another bottle of plonk. Me an' me fuckin' friends are settin' here a while longer! I'm 'aving another drink or two and then I wants me a woman!' answered Sean darkly, rising from where he sat. She ignored him and appealed to a now-embarrassed Godley again.

'You must leave. *Please.* Now!' Her anger overcame her fear and she pointed assertively at the door.

Before any of them could react to this Sean lumbered round the table and caught her around the waist in a vice-like grip. Bending her sideways so she was looking up at him he pushed his face towards her. 'We'll go when I says so, you hear me you Froggie bitch? An' while I'm at it, you'll give me a smack on the lips for me trouble!'

She screamed, terrified of his drunken, leering eyes. Fruitlessly she struggled but to no avail, he held her easily while pulling her towards him, his lips gaping wide. She caught the stench of his foul, alcohol-laden breath and struggled frantically to free herself from his grasp but only succeeded in tearing open her blouse. The sight of her milk-white breasts spurred on the drunken Irishman's advances and he swapped his attention from her face to bury his slobbering lips in between the valley of her breasts.

'For Chrissakes!' shouted Boy Godley and he launched himself at Murgatroyd. 'Let her go, you drunken Irish bastard!' He flung himself at Sean and punched him on the arm. The blow astonished Murgatroyd more for its insolence than its strength. He rocked back and released the woman, flinging her into the table with his other hand. With a bellow of rage he lashed out and caught Godley square on the cheek. Godley dropped soundlessly to the floor, his cap flying. As they watched, horrified, Murgatroyd advanced to where Godley lay and, drawing back his hob-nailed ammunition boot, kicked him viciously in the head, twice.

'I'll teach you to mess with Sean Murgatroyd, you little shit of an English bastard.' he hissed vehemently, drawing his boot back for another kick.

He never completed the move. A metal-shod pickaxe handle struck him with a resounding crunch on the top of his bare head and with a look of utter surprise he slumped limply to the floor. 'I don't know,' breathed Provost Sergeant Hobson, standing nonchalantly before them surrounded by the rest of his patrol as he twirled the pickaxe handle carelessly in one hand. 'Why is it the dumb-fuck Micks that give you all the trouble?'

Further down the street, Lieutenant-Corporal Jim 'Maddy' Maddison was sat with a pal in an establishment similar to the one his friends were experiencing so much trouble in. Maddy had a pocketful of money in his possession and an urgent desire to spend it all. Fast. One of the soldiers vacating the table they were now sat next to had inclined his head at one of the serving girls in response to Maddy's whispered question and left with his mates, laughing and pulling faces at a coarse remark as they went. Maddy ignored their ribald laughter and stared at the girl with a keen interest. She was unkempt and a bit plump, with greasy dark hair pulled back from her face, but to Maddison in his present unfulfilled state she was one of the most beautiful women he'd ever seen

Slamming his glass down on the table, he wiped his lips across the back of his sleeve and looked round for her. She had served him and his pal, Sid Bates, with two or three beers so he felt confident to approach her on the matter uppermost in his thoughts. Catching her eyes he motioned with his head and wearily she walked over to where the two men sat.

'*Oiu, m'sieu?*' she questioned, her dull eyes peering disinterestedly over their shoulders, tray clasped to her hip as she gazed around the room at her other clientele.

'Er,' Maddy lowered his voice as he frantically searched for the words to convey his needs. 'Um. *Mon amis. Le soldiers departez* just now. They say. Er, *parlez* to *moi*. You, er. *Voulez vous...ah...avec moi...Promenade? Jiggy-jig?*' His face reddened as she stared down at him, her moon face expressionless. Desperately he groped for the right words. '*Combien?* Er, *combien de francs?* You know, how much?'

She stared again at him, a long, searching stare and he felt himself redden again. At length she spoke, coldly. '*Dix franc, m'sieu. Et maintenant!*' Her dirty hand shot out and hovered close to his face.

Ten francs? Ten bloody francs? Christ! Did he have that much on him, he thought, frantically digging into his trouser pockets. He could always borrow what he needed from Sid but that thought left his mind as soon as it slipped in. His questing hand touched paper.

'Aha!' Triumphantly he waved the tattered, creased notes in her face. She took them without speaking, pushed them into an opening in the side of her filthy black skirt and motioned him to follow her with a flick of her head. Excited now, Maddy rose from his seat. 'Watch my seat for me, Sid,' he said with a large grin on his face as he moved off, 'this won't take long, if you get my meaning!' Behind him, Sid Bates scratched his head in a bored manner and finished off his beer. Leaning back in his chair he looked around at the other occupants as he waited for his pal.

Silently she led Maddison out into the back yard and picked a path through broken crates and rotting piles of rubbish. Reaching a space on the far wall she turned round, raising her skirt up to her waist as she leaned back against the wall. Maddy saw she was naked under the skirt, save for her stockings, and his excitement rose further inside him at the sight of her white flesh. Eagerly fumbling with his trousers he undid his braces, loosened the leather belt he wore and allowed his trousers to fall around his knees. He pushed against her and thrust deeply into her, his knees bent to take her weight as he tried to lift her up with the movements of his lower body. She smelled of sweat and alcohol and he tried to kiss her but she moved her head sharply to the side, the breath hissing from between her pursed lips in synch with his thrusts. Her breasts were hard lumps beneath her blouse and he moved his hands upwards to her shoulders as he slammed her backwards into the wall.

Grunting in her ear, he concentrated on moving inside her, his legs rasping against the coarse material of her black stockings, then felt the blood roaring in his head as he exploded deep within her unresponsive body. For a short moment he forgot the war, forgot his surroundings and surrendered totally to the exquisiteness of that one bitter-sweet sensation. He let out a guttural, half-choked cry and held her tightly as the spasms racked his body. Finally, he released her and stepped back to pull his trousers up and rearrange his clothing.

All through his frantic lovemaking she had remained passively silent and now as he moved away from her she allowed her skirt to fall down again and pushed past him. Without a backward glance she walked slowly back into the estaminet, leaving him standing there.

Feeling slightly foolish at the short time it had taken to satisfy his needs and chastened at her total lack of emotion, Maddison tucked his coarse shirt into his trousers and refastened his braces. Looking round furtively, to see if anyone had witnessed their loveless coupling, he shuffled quickly through the back door of the estaminet.

Sid watched him approach, trying to gauge from his pal's demeanour how the tryst had gone. Maddy turned to gaze round the packed room. The girl was at the far side, taking an order from a group of laughing, joking soldiers. She never once glanced in his direction and the satisfaction he had begun to feel suddenly deserted him, leaving him feeling cheapened somewhat at the sordidness of their passionless meeting. He grabbed roughly at Sid's arm. 'Come on, chum,' he growled, 'let's get out of here. The beer's shite! There's better stuff up the road I'm told.'

By the time they'd started to walk up the street though, his good spirits had returned.

'God I needed that!' he exclaimed, twanging his braces under his open tunic with his free hand.

'What was it like, our Maddy?' Sid enquired innocently. 'Was she any good?'

'Good? She was one of the best I've had in a long time!' Maddy punched his friend's arm lightly as he swaggered towards the doorway. 'She won't forget me in a hurry, I can tell you. Now shurrup, it's about time you bought me a beer. Sex always makes me thirsty!'

Four days later, while the rest of his chums were engaged in fatigue duties, carrying supplies up to the front line dumps, Jim Maddison learnt just how 'good' his erstwhile mistress had been when he reported sick to the battalion aid post dugout. The MO, Captain Hughes, straightened up from a close examination of Maddy's flaccid member and looked down at the anxious soldier staring up at him from the makeshift couch.

'Well, old man, it appears to me that you've caught a dose of the clap. And serves you jolly well right, too! What did I tell you chaps about using prophylactics when you go into the town. Half the girls in the establishments you men frequent are rotten with the stuff! You'll have to be evacuated to one of the base hospitals for treatment I'm afraid, but before we get you away I'll give you a shot in the arm to be going on with. Now hold still, I'm afraid this is going to hurt.'

He brought his hand out from behind his back and Maddison found himself staring at the longest hypodermic needle he had ever seen. There was a loud *thump!* and Bevan Hughes inclined his head. 'Private Crockett!' he called, shouting for one of his orderlies, 'Bring me a pail of cold water, would you. This cove appears to have fainted!'

9

Thursday 7th October 1915

Battalion orders having come through in a hurry, we have joined 7th Div on the Somme. Entrained for Albert at 07:00 ack emma. Albert badly knocked about. On arrival at 10:30 ack emma, marched to new billets in village of Grandeville-sur-Somme. We are to enter front line tomorrow opposite Mametz. Battalion HQ to be at Tillemont Farm. Three companies to go into the line straightaway with one in reserve. Our routine once more is to be four days in the line and two days out.

L. Carey, Captain, D Company

Bethune station looked as unwelcoming as it had three weeks earlier and the waiting men shivered in their greatcoats as they waited to board the train. A similar length to the one that had originally delivered them to this part of France waited patiently, the steam hissing forlornly from the ancient locomotive as it contemplated pulling its new load. None of the waiting officers spoke much; the experiences of the last few weeks had sobered them all and left them all feeling flat. The humour had deserted them and they boarded the carriages in silence. Henry Watson had no benefactor this time and he clambered aboard one of the filthy wagons further down the train with the rest of his platoon.

Snaith sat back in his seat and looked over at his fellow officers. They looked glum and he thought vainly of some way to restore their spirits.

'Look here, chaps; it's not all that bad. A bit short notice I'll admit but General Watson told me the Somme's a fine, quiet place to be going. Albert isn't that far so we should make good time. We'll be far better off there than here, what? I'm told they have plenty of hacks down there so a chap's opportunities for riding out are far better than here.'

Walter Ramsbottom turned and looked at his CO reflectively. After a short space of time he spoke. 'The men think, and I tend to agree with them, sir, that we're being sent down to the Somme as a sort of punishment. As if we put up a poor show in the last stunt. Was that why we were left in billets on fatigue duties for the last two weeks?'

Snaith stiffened angrily .'No, no, Walter! Certainly not! We're simply being sent where we're most needed. The general assured me he was most impressed with our showing. Good God, you all should be pleased. There'll be far more leisure time when we arrive, more time to train the men up, you'll see.' With that he sat back and stared fixedly out of the window as with a final, wet blast off her whistle the train jerked forward and they were finally on their way.

Albert was reached over three hours later, a slow, pleasant journey through green, rolling fields similar to those they were familiar with back in England. The town shocked them. The German shelling had reduced it to a shattered ghost town with ruined walls and empty shells of buildings propped up with timber baulks. After disembarking, they formed up in silence and marched glumly in the light rain through the town on their way to their new billets.

Looking up at the Basilica spire as they passed, Titch Magilton pointed to the figure leaning from the top at an impossible angle and remarked to his neighbour, 'Oi, matey, 'ave you seen the way that bint up there is leaning over? She looks as if she could fall off any moment and brain some poor cove.'

'Magilton, shut it!'

Wearily Titch complied. Being told to be quiet was becoming quite a habit.

Friday 8th October 1915

Entered trenches to left of Mansell Copse. Tillemont Farm taken over from Oxford and Bucks Regt as Battalion HQ. Outbuildings to form Officers' Mess. Area quiet, no shelling. A and B Companies in Line, C Company in reserve. D Coy left with HQ. Pte Docking, B Company, killed by sniper whilst working on trench repairs. Late surprise visit from Brigade Commander, Brig-General Grierson.

L. Carey, Captain, D Company

The handover was quickly and quietly effected, with men bagging the best sleeping places as soon as they entered the trenches. Many took out their pipes and puffed away contentedly as they took stock of their new surroundings, being swiftly joined by the cigarette smokers among them. The NCOs gave them a minute or two to adjust, and then it was back to work to make the area fit for the foreseeable future.

Private Arnold Docking from B Company was foolish enough to mount the parapet to impatiently pull some sandbags into position and paid tragically for his impetuousness when a sniper's bullet hit him in the head. He fell unconscious into the bottom of the trench and lay there for four or five long minutes issuing loud snoring noises until he expired. It seemed the lessons of their very first incursion into the trenches had been sadly forgotten. Until now.

Arwyn Jones removed his forage cap and held it to his breast in a quiet act of deference as the blanket-swathed body passed him, borne at a crouch by two sweating stretcher-bearers. As he bent to pull his headgear back on he was sent sprawling by a large hand that clapped him hard on the back.

'What the bloody 'ell...!' he exclaimed as he was helped to his feet by his grinning pal, Willie Bennett.

'Sorry, Taff,' Willie laughed, 'didn't mean to hit you so hard. Tell you what, now that I'm in the general's good books how about you share one of his smokes with me?'

'What the bloody 'ell are you going on about Bennett, have you gone stark raving?'

For an answer Willie Bennett pushed his right hand deep into his trouser pocket and came up with a crumpled packet of cigarettes. 'See!' he exclaimed triumphantly, 'Craven A's! I was standing over there at the traverse, minding me own business, when this toff with a plum in his mouth and general's badges on his shoulders and hat asked me where old Snaithy's HQ was. Called me his "good man" too. So I pointed out where the Old Man's bolthole was and he pushed these here smokes into my hand, told me to take care and waltzed off in the right direction. On his own he was too.'

'Bollocks!'

With that, Arwyn turned and made off down the trench shaking his head disbelievingly.

Saturday 9th October 1915
Working parties out wiring trenches in battalion area under RE supervision. Ration parties involved in bringing up supplies. Six ORs from each company returned to Bethune for instruction on Stokes trench mortar. Enemy movements detected opposite but quiet night. Listening post manned in vicinity of enemy trenches. Light rain overnight. Heavy shelling in pm. 2/Lt Burns killed, 2/Lt Fields severely wounded.

L. Carey, Captain, D Company

'Keep it quiet, you lot!' The order, urgently whispered, carried hoarsely down the crowded trench. Men bent double with the load they were carrying tried to see where the voice was coming from but it was quite dark and they soon gave up and carried on down the trench.

The work parties had been weeded out just before dusk and everyone involved given a task. For many this involved a long, exhausting struggle through unfamiliar trenches to where the rations and stores required by the battalion quartermaster had been dumped. Here they were sorted out into teams and the return journey was begun. Bent over with hay boxes containing the warm food cooked by the battalion cooks, the first teams staggered away. Behind them, bringing up the rear, human donkeys struggled with bundles of wire supports, coils of barbed wire, boxes of rations, sacks containing God knows what and all the paraphernalia a modern battalion required to maintain life in the trenches. Tiring of the struggle, some of the more adventurous climbed onto the parados, pulling their load with them, and walked along on top until angrily recalled back into the trench.

The journey back along the same trenches they had passed through hours earlier was made more difficult by the darkness and the conditions. Stumbling along unfamiliar territory elicited muttered curses from the sleeping soldiers they disturbed in their funkholes in the sides of the trenches. Every now and again a ration sack would be dropped and spill its contents on the floor, holding up progress while frantic attempts were made to retrieve the spillages in the dark. The long snake of men moved infinitesimally slowly down and around the bays and seemingly never-ending traverses. Desultory shelling caused many halts and every now and then an enemy machine-gun, firing on a fixed line, would cause them all to duck involuntarily as the bullets swished wickedly overhead.

The night was never still and it was a tired group that eventually began to recognise their own territory. Spirits rose and aching muscles gained a new lease of life as, like racehorses scenting the finishing line, they picked up speed. Nearer they drew, to be met and directed to the various storage areas where, dropping their loads, they stood with weak, trembling legs and heaving chests. Some knelt down in grateful silence while others drew in huge lungfuls of air.

'Look at those poor bastards.' Howard Arkwright nudged Charlie Horsfall's arm, pointing at the exhausted figures trying to recover their strength two or three yards down the trench in front of them. He grinned savagely. 'Hey, Charlie boy, that could've been us if you hadn't seen the sarge looking for volunteers. What a relief, I can say.'

A quiet voice at his elbow made him jump.

'Horsfall, Arkwright, you horrible little pieces of work, I've been looking for you. You follow me now, I've found something right up your street. Teach you to dodge honest work. Yes, Arkwright, I mean you. And bring your rifles!'

Meekly they reached for their rifles and followed the sombre figure of Sergeant Willox. Twisting and turning he led them wordlessly down the way the work parties had come from until at last he stopped by a white sign, unreadable in the gloom. Turning to face the two bemused men facing him he spoke quietly.

'Hop it over the top here and crawl out about forty yards. You'll come to a shallow trench. Keep yer heads down and go to the end, where you'll come to a listening post. Stay there and keep yer ears open for any sounds of our Boche friends over there. Got that?'

'Er, sarge?' Arkwright spoke with a quaver in his voice. 'How long do we stay there?'

'Until I bloody well tells you to come back!' replied the exasperated sergeant. 'And another thing. Do *not* let me catch you falling asleep. We're on active service here and if any of you thinks that you can 'ave a quiet kip the minute I've gone you're bloody well mistaken. Do that an' yer in serious trouble. Have I made myself clear?'

They both nodded.

'Well, get over there and stay there until someone fetches you. If you hear anything untoward, skedaddle back here, but be warned, it'd better be justified. And take yer greatcoats, it looks like it'll be cold tonight.'

Tentatively they both eased themselves onto the firestep and climbed slowly up onto the parapet. The stars shone brilliantly down from their vantage point overhead and as they crawled away from the safety of the trench a light breeze ruffled the damp hair poking out from underneath their uniform caps. Arkwright jammed his cap on more firmly and concentrated on following his friend, their rifles sliding along the ground, grasped firmly in their right hands.

It seemed to take ages but could only have been minutes when, as the sergeant had promised, they came upon a shallow, muddied scrape in the ground. Entering on their bellies, it soon widened out into a narrow trench that pushed towards the German lines. Holding their breath now as best they could they slid soundlessly onwards until at last the defile opened out into a small, sandbagged enclosure. It reeked of urine and other bodily functions but they wriggled gratefully up to the far end and huddled together under the cover of the layer of earth and bags that made up the protective wall.

'What do you think we should do now then, Charlie?' whispered Arkwright.

His friend snorted mildly. 'What Willox told us to do, you berk, sit 'ere until he sends for us, and listen out for Fritz. Be quiet now, d'ye want them to know we're 'ere? I'm going to go over to the other side so you just stay where you are and keep a sharp ear.' With that Horsfall inched away and shuffled over to the far side of the listening post, pressing himself against the wall and burrowing down into the dirt in an attempt to stave off the gathering cold.

They lay there in contemplative silence for several long minutes, each lost in his own thoughts. From far away they could hear faint sounds, a machine-gun stuttering a short burst, random shots. Now and then a Verey light would illuminate up the sky a mile or so away, throwing the ground around them into sharp relief as it drifted down, etching deep lines on their faces and uniforms, but they were soon extinguished, leaving them alone once more in the darkness.

Horsfall scratched viciously at his breast, writhing as he felt the movement of his own individual collection of vermin moving around the warmth of his body. Like all the others he sat for hours trying to rid himself of the lice that infested each and every one of them, but to no avail. Sitting shirtless he had passed a lighted candle down the seams of his shirt, grunting with pleasure as he had heard the lice popping when the heat had seared them. It had brought only temporary relief; the eggs laid elsewhere in their clothing soon hatched, providing another generation with a readily available source of heat and food in the way of their host's blood.

The night air was cooling now and he gave thanks for the advice about their greatcoats. Snuggling down he took stock of their surroundings. A puttee had become unravelled in their journey down the trench so he absentmindedly wound it back round his leg as he concentrated on listening for any sounds. He had no idea of how far away the enemy trenches were but he guessed they weren't that far and made a mental note to make sure he kept his movements to a minimum. His rifle lay against the wall alongside him and he peered at it in the gloom to ensure that he had remembered to load it and let off the safety-catch.

A sudden sound out there in the darkness made him start. It came from over where he estimated the German lines to be and he grabbed at his rifle. Another sound, shuffling, scratching, louder now, reached his ears and he stiffened.

'Did you 'ear that?' he hissed.

There was no answer and he turned to look at where Arkwright had taken up position. His friend lay slumped against the sandbags opposite him, his rifle on the floor where it had slid down, and as he stared with horror he realised Arkwright was sound asleep. As he watched, aghast, a low noise issued from his companion's lips and he recognised the sound of snoring. The sounds from the other side of the parapet were coming closer and becoming more insistent and his breathing came in short, sharp breaths as he fought off the first stages of panic.

Sweating profusely now, he pulled his rifle into his shoulder, aimed it at the top of the hole they were lying in and crouched down into a ball, looking desperately over to where his friend slept, willing him to open his eyes and join him in deciding what to do. His nerves stretched tight, he listened as the noise grew louder until it sounded as if whoever or whatever it was could only be feet away. As he listened he could feel his sphincter tightening while the fear took hold of him and he had a sudden, irrational urge to urinate.

A rat, a huge brownish-black, evil-looking bloated rat, looked down on him, contemplating his stretched, rigid body as it appeared out of nowhere as if by magic on the parapet. He collapsed weak-kneed with relief, the release of tension flooding out as the dam holding back his fear burst. The rifle sagged nervelessly from his fingers and slid to the floor. The rat watched him intently with shiny, piercing eyes, its lips twitching as its flared nostrils and whiskers tested the air about it. Peering about, it reared up on its hind legs and noisily washed its face and front paws before dropping back down again as Horsfall opened his eyes once more and watched it in terror. At last, satisfied that the two figures below it were still alive, the rat shuffled away, its feet noisily scratching a path in the dirt as it departed in search of easier pickings.

Arkwright slept on but Horsfall didn't notice. Or care. It started to rain, a light, insistent type of drizzle that soaked into his clothing and left him wet through. He didn't acknowledge it. He stayed in his crouching position and was still there two hours later when fresh sounds from down the narrow trench told him of their impending relief. Stiffly scrambling over to where Arkwright slept he pulled his friend into surprised wakefulness. They were both ready when two frightened, soaked soldiers cautiously slid into their listening post, completely filling it as they crushed against its relieved occupants.

'Sergeant Willox says yer to get yerselves back now', one of them explained. 'And we're to take yer place for the time being, chum.'

The dawn was a faint hue on the distant, overhead horizon as the rain eased for the first time in hours. Horsfall pushed quickly past their reliefs and spoke again.

'Come on then, time for some bacon and then bed!'

Arkwright turned to look at the two men and then back at his friend. Horsfall was already halfway down the narrow trench and out of sight. Yawning profusely, he followed his pal.

* * * * *

Lionel Carey frowned as he tried to add up the figures before him. Reports! Always some damn report to fill and send off to someone far behind the line in a warm, cushy billet. Damn them! The wind whistled coldly, noisily, through the cracks in the sandbagged wall, adding to both his discomfort and his bad temper. He glanced up at the two chattering subalterns sat somewhat squashed three feet from him, giggling and pushing each other as they rummaged through a risqué French magazine. God, they were sending them out younger each day.

'Look here you two, clear off and go and inspect your men's rifles could you? Give a man some peace, damn it! Go on, off you jolly well go!'

The two fresh-faced youths looked meaningly at each other at his irritable outburst and disappeared through the dugout entrance. In the distance the sound of shelling reached his ears but he ignored it as he angrily crossed out the total and started again. This time the noise of the shelling was nearer and he ducked involuntarily as a series of loud bangs rocked the oozing sandbags, sending tendrils of wet earth trickling down onto his makeshift desk. He reached for his coffee mug but it had gone cold while he'd been preoccupied. As he bent to take a swig, the scent of petrol from the tins that that the water came up the line in permeated his nostrils and he angrily threw the remainder of the coffee onto the dugout floor.

The dugout flap was abruptly pushed back minutes later and he swivelled round to complain.

'What now, didn't I tell...' The words died on his lips as he saw the burly figure of his company sergeant major, Duncan Green, framed in the doorway and looking decidedly distraught.

'What is it Green, what's happened?'

Green looked down at his boots before replying. 'You'd better come see, sir. It's the two young gentlemen. Mister Field and Mister Burns.' He fought to control himself, then resumed in a more even manner. 'They've just copped a packet. Mister Burns is dead and Mister Field's in a bad way.' He saw the question on his company commander's lips and continued. 'A shell exploded near to them as they come down to see the boys, sir. Blew Mister Burns clean out of the trench and took Mister Field's leg off. I've sent for the doc and he's on his way. A rum do, sir, and no mistake!'

As Carey grabbed for his hat and gloves and made to follow, the sergeant paused, before stepping back to allow Captain Carey out of the dugout. 'No one else was hurt but there's one other thing, sir. Two of the boys went out smartish-like and dragged Mister Burns's body back in. It's not good news I'm afraid, we can't find his head!'

* * * * *

Bevan Hughes breathed in deeply as he finished the dirty mug of whisky he held in a shaky, bloodstained hand. The casualty returns for the day lay beneath his hands, pencil-smudged as he'd been unable to locate a pen. He yawned. Time for bed now, that was him done for the day. He bent to pick up his respirator.

A noise from the other side of the gas curtain made him spin round.

'Who's there?' he called out sharply.

'Me sir, Private Godsman,' a quiet voice answered. 'Could I have a word, like, sir?' There was no mistaking the nervousness in the unseen soldier's voice and Bevan scratched his ear in tired resignation before replying.

'Come in man, and don't let the light show.'

A figure wrapped in a greatcoat squeezed into the dugout cautiously, squinting in the poor light. Bevan Hughes pointed to a rickety chair and the soldier sat down, the mud from his boots dripping onto the duckboard floor in a solid flow of liquid. He twisted the fingers of his hands in a never-ending pattern as he silently contemplated the MO.

'I can't go on, sir, I'm done. I just can't take it any more.'

Hughes sat contemplating the man before him for long, awkward seconds before pushing a chipped, battered box towards him. As Godsman's brow furrowed with bemusement, the MO gestured at the box and spoke kindly.

'Go on, take one, old man. They're cigarettes, State Express. I have a maiden aunt in Birkenhead keeps insisting on sending me them, even though I've told her over and over that I only smoke a pipe, bless her!'

Godsman reached over and took a cigarette from the box. Whilst he lit up and took several deep drags, Bevan Hughes watched him closely, noting the man's shaking, trembling hands as he clung to the burning weed.

'Now then, tell me, what is it you can't face?'

For an answer, Godsman stared into space, squinting as the curling smoke made his eyes water in the confined space of the dugout. He turned his fingers over and over, his right leg moving nervously as he attempted to frame an answer. Eventually he spoke.

'When the Jerry shells come over, I just wants to bury me head in the ground and scream at them to stop. I can sort of feel the pressure and I start to shake. It hurts sir, like my skull's going to come right off, like. The other lads, I know they can see what's happening to me. I'm scared one day I'll just up and run off, leave them to it. And then what'll happen?'

'We're all scared Godsman. But in the end we're all here together, you, me, your chums, and we all have to stick it out until we beat the Boche. Can't you see it's as simple as that?'

'You could write me a note, sir, let me go back to where I don't have to be in the line with the boys. That way I won't ever get to thinking about running off!'

Bevan Hughes looked at the expectant face sitting next to him and slowly shook his head.

'I can't do that, Godsman. That way I'd be just as guilty of letting your chums down as you would be. It's shirking one's duty, can't you see that? I'm afraid I just can't help.'

'I thought you'd say that, sir, which is why I did this with my bayonet before I come in.' Godsman bent and rolled his left puttee down. As he pulled his trouser leg up, Bevan Hughes was shocked to see a crimson gash appear, blood flowing freely down the man's leg into his boot.

'Good God, man, what the hell!' He bent forward and caught Godsman as the soldier collapsed limply in a faint. In seconds he had a tourniquet on the affected leg, high on the thigh, as he selected a needle and a roll of thread. Godsman never moved as his wound was expertly stitched and covered in iodine. On completion, the MO delved deep into his bag and extracted a small, brown bottle. Uncorking it he took a deep swallow before tipping it up onto Godsman's lips. Godsman spluttered and tried to sit up.

'Whassa...?'

The MO spoke soothingly. 'Don't worry, lad, it was just a small tipple of brandy. Seems to have down the trick, too!' He looked down, his face a dark, troubled mask. 'You stupid bastard. Do you know what you've done? Do you know the penalty for self-inflicted wounds?'

Godsman looked up crestfallen. 'Sorry, sir, I couldn't see straight. I just needed to get away. Now what do I do? You won't report me will you, sir?'

Hughes thought for a moment. 'There's no way you can go back on duty with this wound, you'll need a few days' rest in a nice clean bed with white sheets. Right, lad, I'm going to perjure myself and declare that this was caused by a shell splinter. Hear me? For your part, you will jolly well agree with me or we both might end up standing before a firing squad! Let me think...stay here while I go and get the bearers to take you down to the CCS. And remember, keep your mouth shut! Oh, and Godsman, don't think you're getting away with it. When you get back, and you *will* be coming back here, make no mistake, you and I are going to have a talk.

While you're doing some shitty errands for me. Oh yes my lad, I'll see the RSM knows that I want you specifically.'

With that threat hanging in the air he moved through the gas curtain and was gone. Long after the stretcher bearers had moved off, cursing, as they bore a pleased-looking Godsman away, Bevan Hughes sat, his head in his hands. Looking up eventually, his eyes saw the cigarette box. Unconsciously his hand moved across the splintered surface of the makeshift desk and he fumbled a slightly crushed cigarette from the box. Contemplating it he shrugged and delved into his tunic pocket for the box of matches he carried along with his battered briar pipe.

'Oh what the hell!'

Striking a match on the dampish striker he took a tentative drag on the cigarette. His shoulders heaved in a paroxysm of coughing from his startled lungs as he inhaled. The smoke blew out from his mouth in large coughing, retching sounds. When his breathing had returned to something approaching normal he shrugged philosophically and, carefully this time, took another shallower drag.

10

Sunday 10th October 1915

Heavy rain overnight. Light shelling of Battalion area. Four ORs wounded, casualties to shelling. Corporal Benson killed and Pte Shaw, A Company, wounded by sniper during sentry changeover.

L. Carey, Captain, D Company

Monday 11th October 1915

A quiet day. Very little enemy activity in trenches opposite us. Sniper still active. Pte Sherman, C Company, killed at latrine pits soon after companies changed over. C and D Company now in line, A and B in reserve. Shelling of enemy's lines commenced at 17:30 pip emma and lasted for 30 minutes.

L. Carey, Captain, D Company

Crack! He lay still and tried not to let his mind wander as the shot rang out. Hearing the sound meant he had not been the intended target so he relaxed slightly, letting his pent-up breath out very slowly. He ached to move his right foot from underneath him but didn't dare to move for fear of attracting the sniper's attention.

Private Bertram 'Bertie' Ludlow was a man on a mission. In the four days they had been here the battalion had lost three men, two dead and one severely wounded to a very determined and capable sniper. The wounded man had been Bertie's best pal, Jim Shaw, and Bertie was out for revenge. In the quiet hour before the day-break and the men's stand-to he had squirmed over the parapet and slid into the valley separating the enemies, carefully picking his way through the wire and into the deep, long grass of no man's land as he crawled towards the German lines. Although the ground between the lines was pockmarked and churned up with the ravages of the intense shelling that had taken place here over the months, there was still a surprising amount of no man's land covered in dense grass and foliage. Mametz village lay some six hundred yards away, to his right, a veritable hornets' nest of machine-guns and heavily fortified trenches. He had taken with him a white sheet, coloured in several different shades of green and brown paint to match the surrounding geography, and a water bottle to stave off the thirst he knew would catch up with him as he lay out there.

Now he was holed-up, the camouflaged sheet wrapped around him and a piece of netting over his face to break up its outline as he quietly observed the German parapet not a hundred yards away. He had crawled up to a long-forgotten corpse, some poor devil who had lain here for weeks and, being careful not to disturb the dead man's position, had wormed his way in behind him to use his body as a shield and be able to observe and hopefully not be seen. The corpse smelled of raw earth and dry, decomposing flesh but it was no worse that that of the trench he had left earlier so he forgot about its proximity and concentrated hard.

It was a fine morning, sunny with a light breeze, and as the light grew stronger he could feel the warm sun radiating through the sheet. Slowly, infinitesimally slowly, he allowed his face to move until he was staring at the trench opposite him. At first it was hard to focus but as his eyes became accustomed to the light he was able to pick out the details. The German parapet was a jumble of scattered objects, as if thrown there by many careless hands. There was no neatness to it, no orderliness in the multi-coloured sandbags.

He hissed in annoyance and then suddenly froze as his eyes caught a fleeting sign of movement in the trench. His heart was pounding heavily, the sound thumping in his ears until he thought those opposite must surely hear and he tried, vainly, to make his tense body relax. He exhaled slowly and kept his eyes fixed on the trench.

Crack! Another shot rang out, making him almost jump in shock. This one was close, very close, and he lay still as he tried to fathom out from which direction it had come. A sound reached him, a muttered voice in an unfamiliar language. German, it had to be. *'Ja, gut, Wolfgang. Da, nach links.'* An answering affirmative told him the sounds were coming from his right so he inched ever so slowly round to face that way.

There was nothing there, nothing but an old rusted pail ten yards from where he lay and some scattered sandbags another thirty yards beyond. As he watched, one of the sandbags moved slightly. Hardly daring to breathe, he made out the barrel of a rifle, a German Mauser K98. The barrel was wrapped in the same material as the sandbag but he could clearly make out its shape from this range.

As Bertie squinted hard at the barrel he began to make out how the soldier was hidden so well. Another movement betrayed the sniper's shape and Bertie could see his head and shoulders were clad in similar materiel to the sandbags he was hiding amongst. Beyond the man, on the far side of the sandbags, a light-coloured tube draped in netting was slowly traversing and it took a while for him to realise he was staring at a similarly-disguised telescope. Sniper and spotter lay together, working as a team.

The sniper was facing away from him but as he continued to observe he became aware of the man's face sweeping slowly round in his direction. He stopped breathing as, across the small expanse of gently waving grass, they stared at each other. One aware of the other's presence, the other in total ignorance of the nearness of his foe. Then with an inaudible sigh of relief Bertie watched as the enemy sniper's gaze and rifle slid past him.

He was sweating hard now, the liquid running in rivulets down his back, soaking into his shirt. His nose itched intolerably but he forced himself to ignore the maddening urge to scratch it. Such an action could bring instant death so he continued to lie there in agonised silence. An insect meandered aimlessly over his face, beneath the netting, and he forced himself to lie still, gritting his teeth in an effort to stop himself jumping up and swatting the offending creature. Eventually it disappeared into the folds of his outer clothing and he breathed a bit more easily, all the while focusing his gaze on the sniper's lair to discern any movements that might warn him of his having been discovered.

None came. The effects of the sun and his own body heat were causing his eyelids to droop. His water bottle was inaccessible, wedged under his right hip, and he licked his parched lips in an attempt to find some moisture there. The notion of a quick nap took hold and refused to disappear. One minute, he told himself, one minute of warm, relaxed, refreshing sleep. Angry with himself he dismissed the thought and concentrated hard once more on staying awake, alert.

The day passed in a mixture of silence, inactivity and alertness, broken by more desultory shelling from both sides and the noises of life emanating from the enemy trenches. Voices, sounds, the chink of metal on metal, all these invaded the world encompassed by the proximity of the corpse beside him and his own thoughts.

At some point he became aware with a start that he was now alone. The sniper hide was empty, the sandbags a mute witness to the death that had so recently lain in wait there. Darkness came too slowly for him and as the shadows lengthened he became impatient to be away. The pain in his foot had long receded and he began to worry whether or not it was still attached to the rest of his body. He wiggled his toes and was relieved to feel his foot move, although the hot searing pain of the flesh regaining its proper circulation nearly made him gasp out loud.

Judging the time was now right he began carefully backing away from his inert companion. Before leaving he tried to find anything that might bring some recognition of who the poor devil once was, but the dead man's clothing had long rotted and anything not made of metal in his pockets had returned to dust with the cloth. Reluctantly he gave up and shook the corpse's shrivelled shoulder in an act of quiet reverence as he prepared to depart. His last action before leaving was to reach into his trouser pocket and bring out a strip of crimson cloth.

Looking round he spotted a long, dull shard of metal about eight inches long, a shell splinter, and he hurriedly fixed the cloth strip to it. The light was fading fast now so he reached up and stuck the splinter by its sharpest end into the soil, making sure he placed it at the back of the dead man where it would not be seen from the enemy trenches. The cloth caught the breeze at once, jumping and dancing as each puff caught its loose ends. Looking round for one last time, he carefully noted the position of the cloth in relation to the sandbags of the sniper's lair before crawling away towards the welcome sight of his own trenches.

As he approached the trench he heard a rifle bolt being worked and a nervous voice rang out. 'Halt!' it quavered, 'Who the bleedin' hell goes there?'

'Is that you, Smithy?'

'Who's that then?' the sentry asked with an air of suspicion. 'Come out and show yourself. And no monkey tricks or I'll blow yer fuckin' head off!'

'It's me.'

'Oh,' said Private Smith from the gloomy depths of the firestep, easing the safety-catch on and lowering his rifle. 'It's you. Why didn't you say it was you, Ludlow? Where the hell have you been?'

'Never mind.' laughed Bertie as he lowered himself over the parapet and into the comparative safety of the trench. 'You haven't seen Lieutenant Coombs about, have you?'

At the mention of the battalion sniping officer Smith's brow furrowed and he sucked noisily on a tooth. 'Come to think of it he was by here about fifteen minutes ago. Before you came along and scared the shit out of me!' He pointed down the trench to his left. 'You should find him in the company mess dugout.' As Bertie turned to go, Smith continued, 'While you were out there gallivanting, or whatever it was you were doing, Charlie Sherman from C Company copped it. A bullet through his pate as he went to take a dump. An him with three kids too!'

'Oh!' said Bertie, remembering the shot earlier that had so suddenly surprised him. He had known Sherman only briefly so felt no great sadness at the man's passing. Rounding the next corner he could make out the gas curtain over a large dugout's entrance. After waiting a respectful minute or so Bertie stuck his head round the curtain and peered into the gloomy interior.

The fetid air inside the dugout was heavy with the fumes of alcohol and he swallowed noisily to clear his throat. At his entrance the five officers, who were sat on various planks of wood and an old chair, swivelled round to stare at him with a hostile air.

'I say, didn't you knock before entering?' A youthful, dark-set lieutenant with wavy hair glared at him, breathing heavy whisky fumes in his direction.

'Begging your pardon sir, but I did try,' Bertie responded. 'Only I couldn't find anything to knock on.'

'Damn cheek...' Before he could remonstrate further the young lieutenant was thrust aside as a large, hearty-looking officer with red cheeks and a big beam pushed his way in front of Bertie. 'Oh do shut up Bryson, can't you see the lad's in a hurry? Looking for me are you Ludlow?'

'Yes sir, could we speak outside. Please?'

In a few terse sentences Bertie appraised him of what he had seen and heard that day. Coombs's brows knitted together as he tried to picture the scene the earnest young man in front of him was setting. He thought at length, then said. 'So what are you saying Ludlow? Do you think we can shell the sneaky blighters out of there? '

'No sir, I thought I'd lie up and have a crack at him at first light tomorrow sir,' Bertie explained with a touch of exasperation. Coombs was a decent sort of cove but sometimes his thought processes were inclined to be on the slow side. He waited while the officer mulled this proposal over. At last, Coombs spoke.

'I say, I have just the thing. A shot like that would probably be over two hundred yards easily and calls for a different kind of gun. I know you're a bit of a whizz but you need a rifle fitted with a telescopic sight, I'll wager. This calls for something special. Trust me.' He brushed aside Bertie's protests and carried on. 'Leave it with me. Old Bryson back there has just been sent the perfect thing from his mater. Arrived the other day. He fancied a bit of sport himself with the Hun. Give me a mo and I'll go and cadge it off him.' He wheeled round and re-entered the dugout. From where Bertie stood he could hear a short, sharp exchange and seconds later Coombs reappeared, smiling. 'Cheeky blighter wasn't going to give me it but I made him. Rank hath its privileges or so the dear old padre keeps telling me. Right, Ludlow, follow me.' With that he was gone, off down the trench at a fast lick.

Half-running to keep up, Bertie followed. A minute or so later Coombs stopped outside a smaller version of the dugout they had just left and dived inside. Bertie waited as the noises of some serious rummaging inside ensued. At last he heard a triumphal shout and Coombs re-emerged, carrying with him a long, wrapped package.

'Got it!' he exulted. 'Cheeky swine thought he could hide it from me but I've got a damn keen nose for these things.' He proffered the package.

Bertie took it from the officer and almost dropped it. He hadn't reckoned on the weight of it but he caught himself and straightened up with it safely in his hand. Coombs threw back the curtain and motioned for Bertie to enter and sit with him. He squeezed next to the lieutenant and began to remove the wrapping in the light from the oil lamp swinging overhead on a wooden peg. A long, gleaming barrel emerged, but before he could complete the job, Coombs grunted impatiently and, reaching out, grabbed the barrel and proceeded to unwrap the remainder of the rifle. Soon he was soon holding up a beautiful, compact rifle with a long professional-looking telescopic sight mounted along the barrel, its rear eyepiece overhanging the stock.

'Look at that,' Coombs breathed reverently. 'A .280 Ross rifle with a Boche Hensoldt sight. Superb weapon. Will pick a squirrel's eye out at four hundred yards, or so Bryson tells me, but he always did have a good imagination. Not to worry, though, this little beauty will take care of Mr Boche, I'll wager!' A thought struck him and he turned a worried look towards where Bertie sat, his eyes on the rifle. 'I say, Ludlow, you have used a sight before, haven't you?'

Indignantly, Bertie reassured him. 'Yes, sir, before I joined up I took to shooting in the hills above Ullswater with the local gamekeeper. He had a sighted rifle for keeping the deer down for his lordship and he let me have a go now and again. I take it this gun's been sighted in, sir?'

'I do certainly hope so, Ludlow.' Coombs worked the bolt backwards and forwards. 'Lovely Mauser action, do you see here, keeps the thing beautifully balanced.' He squinted down the barrel trying to use the sight but the poor light defeated him and with a disappointed grunt he reluctantly turned the weapon into Bertie's eager hands.

Bertie turned the gun over, hefting it smoothly to his shoulder. He, too, tried to squint through the sights but it was hopeless and he soon gave that up, concentrating on the weight and feel of the gun. It felt comfortable in his hands, the woodwork beautifully marked with a pronounced, lightly oiled, grain. As he sat there, Coombs searched around the dugout once more, and presented him with a tasselled leather pouch.

'Almost forgot, you'll need something to shoot from the bally thing!'

Bertie took the pouch from him and opened it. Inside, gleaming dully, were fifty or sixty brass cartridges complete with copper-tipped bullets. He picked one up and nestled it in the cradle of his palm. Everything worked smoothly, the bolt snicked back and the chamber eagerly swallowed the cartridge he offered up. It disappeared neatly inside, a perfect fit, and he pushed the bolt forward and over, locking it in the loaded position. Coombs's voice broke into his reverie.

'Righto, Ludlow, when our Boche friends start their usual shelling antics tomorrow morning, you and I will go off by the latrines and fire a few sighting rounds to see if this thing shoots bally well straight. Then, if they're stupid enough to hang around, we'll go and bag us a Hun!'

Wednesday 13 October 1915
Enemy shelled battalion trenches from early on, two ORs wounded, one dying of wounds in Battalion Aid Post later. Battalion Sniping Officer, Lt Coombs took offensive to the enemy. After a duel which led to the killing of a sniper that had bothered the battalion for days, Pte Ludlow, A Company, heartily commended by CO. More shelling followed this action. Two ORs wounded, one severely.

L. Carey, Captain, D Company

The dawn rose pink-hued, throwing long shadows across the trenches as it chased the night away. There was a definite change to the air temperature, best acknowledged by the clouds of vapour that rose up as the men from both sides stood-to and then went about their early morning business. Soon the smell of coffee and bacon cooking brought a welcome change to the normal smell of death and decay. Five minutes after eating, enemy shelling in the vicinity of C Company's trenches caused two casualties.

Bertie Ludlow ignored all of this as he lay still, wrapped in his camouflaged sheet in a small hollow ten yards in front of the parapet, just beyond the wire. The rifle faced the German lines in a furrow he had made in the top of the hollow, its telescopic sight rubbed with dirt to try and eliminate any fatal reflection and the gun itself wrapped in sackcloth. He had been there long before the dawn broke and the men were called to stand-to, having wriggled out in the same manner as he had done previously. Prior to leaving he had keenly felt the wind and, gauging in his mind the distance he would be firing over, had carefully adjusted the sights.

His stomach was a small hard knot of anxiety as he eased down into a firing position and slowly pushed the rifle forwards and upwards until it lay snug into his right shoulder. Reaching over he pushed the safety-catch off and nestled down to let his right eye take up its position behind the rearward end of the sight. The crystal-clear image it projected complete with crosshairs jumped into prominence and he waited until his eye adjusted to what it could see in front of him before moving the gun and sights slowly from side to side. His one fear was that the splinter together with it's red flag might be obscured by fresh craters from the previous day's shelling.

It took several seconds but suddenly there it was by the hunched corpse, fluttering as gamely as yesterday and his excitement rose as he moved past it to look for the jumble of sandbags where the German sniper team had hidden.

He saw everything with perfect clarity and tried to control his heavy breathing, readying his body for the response to the shot he would be making in a second or so. His eye looked down through the sight straight at the sandbags, there, there where the remembered angle from the marker said they should be. And then he felt his blood freeze in his veins as he saw the tube of the spotter's telescope pointing squarely at him.

The world stopped in an instant, time compacting into micro-seconds as his brain frantically digested the information his shocked sight sent it. Before he could react something smacked squarely into the grass in front of his face, showering him with dirt. He flinched as the *crack!* of the shot echoed across the valley. His camouflage disguise had done enough to make the marksman opposite him unsure of his exact position and he had fired speculatively on his spotter's urgings. He would not make a similar mistake, so instinctively Bertie pulled the rifle tight into his shoulder, exhaled slowly and, aiming to the left of and slightly above the telescope, gently squeezed the trigger. The rifle kicked hard as it recoiled into his flesh and through the sight he saw the telescope fall over abruptly.

Another shot rang out, mirroring his own, and this time he felt the warm breath of the bullet as it fanned his left cheek before burying itself in the parapet behind him. Good as he was the enemy sniper was firing blind now his spotter had been silenced. Pulling back smoothly on the bolt the expended cartridge case flew backwards and he inserted another round from the pouch lying open beside him, snapping the bolt closed again. A quick mental picture of the man on the other side filled his mind as he imagined him frantically trying to reload. There was no time to consider this, no fleeting thought of pity in his head as he brought the gun up once more into his shoulder and peered once again through the sight.

He immediately saw the sandbag concealing the enemy sniper. He was able to make out the shape and outline of the man as his opponent tried to bring his body back into a firing position. Too late. Bertie made a minute adjustment. A slow breath, exhale, hold, and the rifle jumped into his shoulder again as he squeezed gently on the trigger. Coincident with the sound of the report the camouflaged outline half-rose, slumped over, and was still. Reloading more slowly now, Bertie kept the sight trained on the inert shape. It moved slightly and he fired again automatically, felt the recoil once more and saw a puff of dust spurt up from the centre of the shape. It never moved again.

He lay there for a long time it seemed, the adrenaline draining from his tense body as he contemplated the results of his actions. Strangely enough he felt no exultation, no primeval sense of the kill. Rather, it was as if he had excised a troublesome tooth and he lay there supine as a serene feeling of lassitude washed over him. Above him in the clear blue, above the German lines he could see three observation balloons and wondered how he had not come to observe them earlier.

A shout woke him from his thoughts.

'Ludlow! Get yourself over here, man! Quickly now!' He twisted round and made out the concerned, reddened face of Coombs waving furiously. He scrambled up, the sheet rapidly unwinding as he did so, and ran hard towards the parapet, keeping a fierce grip on the rifle. Gaining the top of the sandbags he dropped lightly into the bottom of the trench. The lieutenant advanced on him and before he could react Bertie felt himself grasped in a crushing bear-grip. A huge hand pounded his back, causing him to splutter as he fought to maintain his breath.

'Well done, Ludlow!' The hand slapped him hard again as Coombs danced with unsuppressed glee in a half-crouch. 'I say, Ludlow, what superb shooting! They never knew what hit them. Bryson will be so pleased. It was a bit hard for me to follow you but this little gadget allowed me to see most of the action.' Coombs's other hand grasped a trench periscope which explained how he had witnessed the outcome of the morning's drama. 'There's talk of sniper schools being set up next year, and I'm going to make damn sure you get posted off to one pretty damn quick as soon as they come into being!'

Bertie pushed the rifle into Coombs's outstretched hands and, without waiting, wordlessly spun on his heels and made his way down the trench, crouching low.

Coombs watched him depart. The title he held had always irked him. There were no rifles or sights specifically put aside in this part of the front for sniping, no tactics, nothing. It was just a position the War Office had deemed every regiment and battalion would have. Being battalion sniping officer just meant getting his arse kicked every time the Boche claimed another victim. But if what he had heard about the High Command wanting to set up schools with the singular intention of taking the fight to the Boche snipers, as Ludlow had today, was true then he was all for it. It could turn out just fine for himself, too. Keep him away from the dangers of serving too close to the Front. Yes, he'd definitely look into the possibility of getting a few chaps away from the Front to these new sniping schools, and have himself a long break from the battalion by accompanying them.

Looking down he keenly examined the rifle nestling in his large hands. He toyed briefly with the thought of cutting two notches in the stock but immediately dismissed the idea. Better not. Bryson's mater was known to be a bit of a battleaxe and if her darling son told her to what use he, Coombs, had put the gun to she'd probably want his scalp. The irony of his thoughts totally escaped him. Whistling tunelessly he followed the hero of the hour.

'I say, Ludlow! Hold on. I'll come with you!' he shouted.

A few minutes after they'd departed a slow rumble of gunfire reached their ears. Behind them the skyline heaved as whizz-bangs and the heavier 'Jack Johnson's' flayed the trenches they had so recently vacated. Swift retribution was soon visited on the hapless occupants. Men crouching down to escape the hail of flying steel and deadly splinters, having seen their breakfast literally go up in smoke, roundly cursed the men whose actions had brought such revenge down upon them. The sun rose as the shells slammed down. Another normal day on the Western Front had begun.

11

Saturday 16th October 1915

Area quiet with very little shelling from both sides. Pte Godley rejoined battalion from hospital. CO away at Brigade HQ to discuss possible trench raid. It has been decided that the Battalion will maintain the offensive and keep the enemy occupied at all times. A small party will go out tonight to cut gaps in the enemy wire unseen, allowing the raiding party to access the German trenches tomorrow night.

L. Carey, Captain, D Company

Sunday 17th October 1915

Planning for trench raid tonight at 23:00 pip emma on German lines opposite went ahead. Salient known as The Ram's Horn, to the right of Mametz, will be attacked and enemy guns destroyed. All Companies detailed to select men. Three officers and eighty men selected. RSM Findlay recommended by CO to take part. Pte Murgatroyd rejoined battalion from cells in Bethune, having served 14 days punishment for brawl in estaminet. CO back at Brigade HQ all day for planning purposes.

L. Carey, Captain, D Company

'Look here, all of you, for goodness sake please pay attention!' Major Roberts sounded exasperated and with good reason. The objects of his entreaties seemed to be more interested in the sharpened cudgel Second-Lieutenant Whiting was brandishing than listening to him. He rapped sharply on the small board he was holding and all three officers reluctantly turned to face him.

Major Roberts gestured at the board. 'This is a map of the area that Brigade want us to attack. You've all seen the model we had made of the ground you'll attack over so please pay careful attention to this map. See that curve in the Boche's trench near High Wood? That small salient is known as The Ram's Horn and we have reason to think it houses a jolly good few machine-gun nests. Lieutenant Derby, you and your men will make your way over there and see what you can find out. Divisional HQ have promised that we're to have good support from the artillery and trench mortar chaps, who'll blow the heck out of the wire in front of the enemy trenches before you make your way over. They'll also provide you with cover for getting back. Lewis guns will protect your flanks as you go in and back.

Tapes were laid by men from 'B' Company last night, as you're well aware, so stick closely to them on the way over and back. The artillery johnnies will make sure the Boche's heads are kept well down for an hour or so before the raid begins, so when you go, rush over and get in there quick before they can react. Take lots of bombs with you and have every third man armed with a rifle and fixed bayonet. Destroy the guns you find.'

Major Ramsbottom cut in. 'If you can take a prisoner or two, good. Don't let that be your guiding thought though, we want to know the set-up of The Ram's Horn, what's over there, how many men manning it, how many guns it supports. That sort of thing. If you can, bring back whatever papers you can find, along with rank badges, regimental epaulettes or anything else to identify the Boche that you can gather.

'Right, gentlemen, report back to your companies, read the reports I've given you, look at the maps carefully and make your final preparations. Make sure that everyone knows his part in tonight's proceedings. One other thing. The RSM will be accompanying you tonight. Mr Findlay is a man of great experience already, gentlemen, so please listen to anything he has to say. My watch says it's three-twenty pip emma so synchronise your watches now. You'll be leaving our trenches tonight at twenty-three pip emma so be sure to be ready. Off you go now and good luck.'

They dutifully filed out and were gone. Sighing, Walter Ramsbottom picked up the latest communications and spread them out in front of him. Indents filled his daily life. Men wounded, sock issues, rum issues, numbers used in ration parties, all these things in minutiae that men miles behind the lines in soft comfortable billets demanded to know on a daily, almost hourly basis. He sat down and stared at the latest. *Daily hay usage for GS wagon-horses.* Sighing deeply again he picked up a pen and began to write.

RSM Findlay stared around him as the unkempt men lying around the floor of the half-ruined barn reluctantly rose to their feet and made their way over to where he awaited them.

'Bates! Get your hands out of your pockets, laddie, stop picking your nose and get over here, now. And pin your ears back!' He turned to pick up the splintered shaft of an ancient farm implement and began scratching in the dirt floor as they watched.

He spoke as he scratched. 'The stunt in the Hun trenches is on for tonight. That's why you're all here, all hand-picked men. The bad news is, I'm coming with you. Highly unorthodox the CO reckons,' he sniffed. 'What does old Snaithy know about it? I managed to persuade him that I need to keep my eyes on you all.' He ignored the gasps of dismay and continued. 'So pay attention to what I'm telling you. I shall quickly go over what you lot were told earlier by the officers, in language you might understand, so do try and keep it in those thick skulls.'

As they watched and listened the men gathered around him felt their dismay growing. This had all the makings of a right shambles.

'Sir?' one brave soul asked, 'are we going over there by ourselves? What's going to happen if the Boche get wind of it and send in reinforcements?'

Findlay drew himself up and looked scornfully at his questioner. 'Were you listening, smartarse? The artillery boys'll begin a barrage to keep any Huns heads well down that wants to interfere. The wire should be well cut with that little lot so getting in amongst the Boche shouldn't be a problem. We'll jump in before they know we're ruddy well coming and pop their square heads up. Didn't I tell you that when we get over there, one of you will fire a white flare? That will tell the artillery battery over here that we're in the Boche's trenches. They'll then fire a box barrage around us to keep us inside and any Boche that might want to join in, well out of it.

'All I want you lot to do is bomb the hell out of whoever is in the area and pick up any information you can. We'll then scarper back to our own lines pretty damn quick, under the protection of the aforesaid barrage, leaving Mr Boche very dead. Listen to what I've said and you'll get back alive, see if you don't. This is not some sort of game, boys. Tonight we want to kill the enemy, not bring him back for tea with us. If you knock a Boche down, leave him for the man behind to finish off. Don't be squeamish either, a wounded Boche is still dangerous. The password is "Wigan's Wives". Remember it.'

He was aware of a silence and looked away, following the men's gaze. In the doorway stood Sean Murgatroyd looking sullenly at the gathering in front of him. RSM Findlay frowned for a second, and then stepped forward.

'Where've you come from, Murgatroyd?' he asked.

The man stood there in silence before answering him in a manner as sullen as his demeanour. 'I was sent back from the cells in Bethune to join yous lot, sir. Mr Whiting sent me down here to report, says I'm to join you for the fight that's going off tonight.'

Findlay looked at him keenly. 'If Mr Whiting says you're to join us then you'd better get yerself over here and listen to what I have to say, Murgatroyd, 'cos if I have any trouble from you, your bloody feet won't touch the ground. The CO wasn't too happy you were only given fourteen days imprisonment for your stunt in Bethune so I'll be watching you carefully, you hear?'

Murgatroyd stared at him intently before looking down at the ground in a gesture of meek submission. 'Ye'll have no trouble from me; I can promise you that sir. I've served me punishment and learnt me lesson.' He walked meekly over and joined the men. The RSM nodded and continued with the briefing. The bombers and riflemen were detailed off and ammunition and bombs passed around until each man's pockets bulged with one or the other. At last the RSM spoke for the final time.

'That's all I have to say for now, lads, so let's all have something to eat and a mug of tea and then try and grab an hour or so's kip before we move up to the trenches ready to jump off. Any questions? No? Good, see Jones over there for any spare bandoliers if you need them.'

They all looked at each other but no one had the nerve or inclination to question what the RSM had taken so long to tell them. At his nod they quickly dispersed and broke up into small groups, each discussing the impending raid. Murgatroyd stood alone, unheeded and unwanted in the centre of the barn. Shrugging his shoulders he slouched over to the far wall and dropped his pack and accoutrements down. He stretched and yawned, then dropped down alongside his kit. Within seconds he was asleep.

The afternoon passed slowly for them all, the day's shadows lengthening as the evening approached and passed. Some men sat and wrote letters, others played cards, ostensibly without money changing hands, while others sat thoughtfully cleaning their weapons over and over again, gazing nervously upwards into the growing darkness. The stars appeared overhead, a mass of silver in a cobalt-blue sky that slowly turned to ink-black.

At length, RSM Findlay reappeared and together with the other two NCOs that would be accompanying them, gathered the men around him. He moved among them, making them aware that he understood and shared in their nervousness. Looking round he observed the demeanour of one of the group. A solitary figure sat hunched by the barn's rear entrance, pulling nervously on a cigarette. Walking over, he squatted down and enquired quietly, 'It's young Simmonds, D Company isn't it? How're you doing?'

The young man gulped, white-faced, and looked around to see if anyone else could see his discomfort. 'I feel a bit queer, sir, sort of nervy...is that normal? I don't want to let my pals down...'

'Look around son,' the RSM reassured him, 'See all yer mates? They're feeling the same as you. Scared shitless only they don't want anyone to know. Anyone who says they're not is a liar, you take it from me. I know, I've been lied to by the best of them. It'll be fine once we get going, you'll see.'

At his quiet command the men shouldered their weapons and prepared to move into the trench system. Those not going solemnly shook hands with the raiding party, slowing their passage down until angrily dismissed by the RSM. As well as the rifles carried by every third man, many of the party carried home-made coshes and truncheons, their pockets bulging as they awkwardly moved on. Further down the trench the three officers joined them.

'Everything all right, RSM?' Whiting asked anxiously.

Findlay nodded tersely and they merged in together with the men. Complying with the CO's orders, none of the officers wore rank badges but each carried a pistol as opposed to the rifles carried by the others. Their soft officer's caps marked them out from the men of their own side and it was hoped this would be enough once they gained the sanctuary of the enemy's trenches, should identification prove difficult in the dark. From far away they heard the sound of their own guns open up and seconds later the shells screamed overhead. The sound of the following explosions comforted them and they moved forward again.

The sentries moved the tapes and stood aside to let them pass and ascend the waiting ladders at the jumping-off point. RSM Findlay stood at the other side of the last ladder and motioned his men on. Richard Whiting climbed up first, giving Findlay a grim, tight smile as he did so, followed by the new subaltern, Elliot, and finally Lieutenant Derby. They spread out in the darkness to await their men. Sergeant Jeffries then followed, together with one of D Company's corporals, a ginger-haired giant called Miller. Dutifully each man mounted the ladder and crawled out into the darkness. As the last man mounted the ladder, Findlay moved forward and grabbed his arm.

'Godley,' he hissed, 'where the bleedin' hell did you come from? Who said you was comin' with us?'

Boy Godley shrugged off his restraining hand. 'Please sir, Mr Whiting said I could come. Bates didn't feel well.'

Findlay snorted. 'Bates, that sloping bugger! I'll "didn't feel well" when I see him next. Well, all right, get a move on then. You boys with the rifles stick close to the bombers.'

* * * * *

Back at HQ there was consternation. Major Ramsbottom was roughly shaken awake from his slumbers to hear some disturbing news. The chaplain, Captain Dundas, met him at the HQ dugout and from his expression Ramsbottom knew the news was not good.

'All right, Roger, let's have it.'

'Its Private Murgatroyd,' the chaplain gasped. 'I've just, mistakenly, been given a signal that's come from HQ. It should have gone to the CO. Its...He's...'

'What is it, man, come on, spit it out. What?'

'God help us. He's...They say...' He shook his head helplessly and held the signal limply in his right hand as he vainly strove to compose himself.

Walter Ramsbottom tore the signal roughly from the outstretched hand and held it up to the flickering oil lamp to make sense of its contents. His eyes widened as he read the message and he looked over at the chaplain to gauge his reaction. The man met his eyes with a dark, troubled expression, tinged with horror. He turned to confront Neville Charteris who had heard the commotion and was coming to see for himself what the matter was.

'It's a signal from HQ about Murgatroyd, Neville, they want him arrested.'

'What an earth for, Walter?'

'It seems the man is wanted in connection with a double murder,' Ramsbottom informed him flatly. 'He was released last evening from cells in Bethune, to rejoin the battalion. Apparently no one saw him board the train they indicated he should. He never left Bethune until today, it would appear.'

'I don't understand, Walter, you said murder?' Charteris asked with a puzzled frown. 'What's that got to do with him not being seen boarding a train yesterday?'

'Everything, apparently,' Walter replied. 'This morning, two women were found murdered in an estaminet in Bethune. The same estaminet Murgatroyd was arrested in for fighting. The women were found beaten to death, and it gets worse, old boy. It looks as if one of them was raped. Someone suspiciously answering to the description of our own Private Murgatroyd was seen running away from there late last night. Brigade want him arrested and returned to Bethune immediately for questioning.'

'Good God!' exclaimed Neville. He thought hard for a second or two then straightened up. 'I'm sorry to be the bearer of even more bad news but it's worse than you think, Walter, I saw Murgatroyd tonight.'

Walter Ramsbottom stared at him uncomprehendingly. 'Where is he then, man? Speak up and we'll go and arrest the swine now!'

'I'm afraid you can't. You see, he's already gone with the raiding party over to the other side.'

* * * * *

Three hundred yards away from where they stood the RSM squinted as his eyes became accustomed to the darkness. The artillery fire had stopped for a moment and all around him he could hear the rustle of clothing and the quick, heavy breathing of nervous men. Looking round for any stragglers or signs of some faint-hearted soul attempting to turn back, he saw no one and crawled on.

A loud shrieking pierced the blackness and with a loud bang a shell slammed into the ground away to their left. Right on time the diversionary barrage restarted, making its presence felt, masking their approach to the enemy trenches. More shells rained down and within seconds the red distress flares of the enemy were making their appearance in the sky overhead. He heard a loud cheer from some-where ahead and the sound of bombs going off intermingled with rifle shots. Hoarse shouts greeted these noises as the Germans awoke too late to the fact that the enemy was amongst them. He rose to his feet, all pretence at concealment aban-doned, and began to run in the direction of the shots. Like the officers, RSM Findlay carried a revolver and he held it in front of him now, pointing it at the trenches ahead. Panting, out of breath, he arrived at last at a huge gap in the enemy barbed wire. The barrage had simply pulverised it and left a massive swathe, flat-tened like summer corn. He leapt forward onto the parapet of the German first line trench and stood on the top, looking down. In the dim light he could see several unidentifiable crumpled bodies, upturned faces gleaming deathly white in the moonlight. To his right he could hear more cheering, followed by bursts of firing and the deep *crump!* of Mills bombs exploding. Making a quick decision he jumped down into the trench and ran towards the sound of the fighting, taking care not to trip over the bodies in his path.

Forty yards down the trench in the other direction, Sean Murgatroyd was enjoying himself immensely. He had reached the enemy trench behind the officers and had been one of the first to jump down into it. A dugout opening had loomed before him and pulling the pin from a bomb extracted from his pocket he had counted three before deftly lobbing it inside. The following explosion and loud screams emanating from the dugout had stirred the savagery in him and he had bellowed his exultation at the sky before running on, searching for more fresh game.

Another dugout entrance appeared suddenly and he pulled the pin from another bomb and threw that down inside the black, gaping maw. More screams followed this explosion and he roared again, his bloodlust well and truly aroused. Rounding a traverse he blundered into a figure pulling at a rifle. A shot whistled past him as the two men collided and he caught the sour unwashed smell of black bread and smoked meat. Panting hard, he brought his large, meaty fist hard down on where he thought the man's face to be.

His opponent went down without a sound and Murgatroyd paused long enough to savagely stamp on the man's head before moving on down the trench. Above the growing noise of battle he heard a sound and whirled as a figure appeared behind him and a voice shouted, 'In there!'

The slight figure was pointing into a dugout he had missed as he had passed by, owing to the heavy curtain across the entrance. Running back he pushed the curtain aside and jumped down into the dugout, fists raised, all coherent thought gone as he looked for another object to vent his wrath and bloodlust on. In the dim light of an overhead lamp he caught sight of bodies strewn on the floor, covered in fresh blood and the sight and smell pulled him up sharply.

The doorway was blocked by the same slight figure that had shouted at him and his brain tried to comprehend this new information. The newcomer continued to look at him and as the raging fire within him began to die down he was aware of the man's face for the first time.

'Hello, Murgatroyd.' said Boy Godley simply.

Murgatroyd frowned. His slow mind tried to recognise the face before him, wreathed in shadow. At last he replied.

'Didn't I batter yous once? Get out of my way, boy, or you'll get hurt again. Now! My fight's not with yous. Not tonight, leastways.' He inched slowly towards the slight figure as he spoke, pulling a large cosh surreptitiously from his pocket as he did so.

Godley smiled at him, a strange, slow smile in the flickering, orange light. 'Sean, Sean. Look at you. All the time I was lying in the bed in hospital being looked after by those beautiful nurses I never really once saw their faces. Just yours, Sean. My head's hurt ever since I left the hospital, thinking about you.'

'Yer feckin' mad. Now get outa my way boy or you'll be sorry. I'm warnin' ye!' His hand tightened its grip on the cosh.

'All right, Sean, I'll move out of the way, only you won't be going anywhere. Here's a present I kept specially for you. Ta-ta Sean!' Godley's hand extended and he lobbed something that landed at Murgatroyd's feet with a dull thud. He ducked back through the dugout opening and was gone.

Murgatroyd looked down and dimly made out the Mills bomb at his feet. His last thoughts before his world exploded in a vivid kaleidoscope of colours and sound were of an estaminet in an alley and a pretty woman framed in the doorway smiling enticingly at him, the bright sun shining on her lustrous, black hair.

Outside, Boy Godley collided with a body that had run full-tilt into him. Both men were knocked off their feet with the violence of the collision but Godley was first to his feet. Swiftly he bent down and straightened up with a German Mauser rifle in his hand. Its barrel was bent but he held it like a club as the other got to his feet.

"I say! Aren't you one of the new chaps? What the bloody hell do you mean by attacking me like that?"

Elliot was in a foul mood. He had become separated from the main body and had wandered around, becoming lost and more and more afraid he would end up in the hands of the enemy. Godley looked at him and not recognising him, moved to pass by. That inflamed Elliot even more.

'I'm talking to you, private, do you hear me? Don't you answer when an officer addresses you? God damn you, I'll have you in front of the CO when we get back.' He made a weak grab at Godley's arm.

All the emotions of the last few moments welled up and exploded in Godley's mind as Elliot continued to rant at him. Without thinking he smartly brought up the weapon in his hand and slammed it into Elliot's face. His nose burst in a crunching spray of blood, black as ink in the darkness, and he dropped without a sound. For a moment Godley stood over him, the rifle raised high. A shout to his left spun him round and he dropped the rifle and ran off in the opposite direction. Seconds later, Corporal Miller ran up and stopped as he saw the inert body at his feet. He bent down in the darkness and started as he recognised the officer's blood-soaked face.

'Christ! Are you all right, sir?' he asked solicitously, as the man beneath him began to retch and moan as he regained his senses. Reaching down, Miller helped Elliot to his feet and supported him as they staggered down the trench together in the direction Godley had run off.

Elsewhere, Richard Whiting had reached the parapet of the German trench with a group of his men. Jumping down in the gloom he caught a glimpse of a dim figure staggering away from him and, breathing hard to steady his aim, he dropped the man with a shot from his revolver. 'Come on! Come on!' He half-turned to shout to his men on when a burning, paralysing pain knocked the breath out of his body. He grimaced and slid weakly down, his legs suddenly unable to support him.

The German reservist tugged hard and finally withdrew the bayonet attached to his rifle from the young officer's body. His greatcoat tails flapping, he ran towards a gas alarm bell hanging down at a corner of the trench, shouting as he ran. '*Alarm! Englanders! Alarm!*' A shot from a Lee-Enfield bowled him over as he reached for the bell's clanger and he slithered nervelessly down the side of the trench to lie in an inert heap. Shouts and screams told of desperate hand-to-hand fighting elsewhere as the defenders woke up to the intruders in their midst. In the close confines of the trench the coshes and truncheons the men had brought with them were put to good use, but the attackers began to suffer casualties as the defence hardened.

A German officer, attempting to rally his troops, was cut down in a blazing volley of fire and his cowering men dispatched with bombs and the bayonet. Many of the attackers, their bloodlust up, shot, stabbed, kicked and punched in a wild-eyed, frenetic flurry of blows. All those in their path were ruthlessly slaughtered as they worked their way along the unfamiliar trenches.

Private Henry Watson was becoming anxious as he scurried along deserted trenches in what had seemed to him to be the right direction. In the dark he had dropped his glasses and this had caused him to lag behind. By the time he had replaced them the others had disappeared. He could hear the noise of the fighting going on all around him but try as he may he could not find a way to rejoin his comrades. A voice shouted hoarsely from his left and his mind filled with relief as he recognised the stentorian roars of the RSM.

'I'm here!' he yelled, breathing hard as he rounded a corner and ran towards the group of men staring at him in the gloom.

Too late he realised his mistake. As his mind frantically scrambled to find the correct words, he began to raise his hands in a gesture of surrender. The two soldiers accompanying the German NCO levelled their rifles and at a barked command both fired simultaneously, the bullets tearing into Watson's body at point-blank range. He fell loosely like a shot rabbit, his spectacles flying off to land beside his body. The bag of bombs he was carrying dropped limply beside him. The NCO barked again and the Germans advanced down the trench nervously. One of them kicked Watson's body as he passed, crunching Watson's spectacles into the duck-board as he did so. The other, holding back, began to go through the dead man's pockets before a curt shout brought him to his feet. Jumping over Watson's body he picked up the bag of bombs and without looking back ran to join his comrades.

Ten minutes later, RSM Findlay was a worried man. By the dial of his luminous watch the box barrage should have already started with the firing of the red flare he had ordered one of the men to fire. So far there had been not one shell fired from their own guns. White enemy distress flares had informed the Germans in the surrounding area of their presence and he was beginning to worry about their ability to extract themselves from a situation that was growing worse with each passing minute.

'To me, get here to me!' he shouted, trying to make himself heard above the noise of battle. 'Come on, let's be having you. Get out! Get out now! Get yerselves back to our own lines, lads. Move sharply now, the Boche will be on us if we don't get a move on. Follow me!'

With that he ran along the top of the trench, waving and gesticulating at the men below. In dribs and drabs they began exiting the enemy trench, some laden with captured equipment. Heavy firing from all round now spurred them on. When he was certain he could see no more of his own men on their feet, Findlay began to make his own way back. The enemy fire chased them across no man's land as they ran and he heard rather than felt the passage of enemy bullets as they cracked past him.

Halfway across he heard a shrill, shrieking sound, growing in volume with every passing second. The realisation had just registered in his mind when the first shells from their own artillery slammed down amongst them, knocking him violently to the ground. White-hot shards of wicked, whining metal scythed through them, flinging men savagely aside to lie in crumpled, broken heaps. A maelstrom of noise battered their ears as the shells poured down, lighting up the night with blinding flashes of deadly colour. Bodies were flung in all directions, some men simply disintegrating as the deadly shells exploded next to or on top of them.

Cowering in a shell hole along with the raiders escorting them back was a small group of German prisoners. Taking advantage of the confusion they rose up and grappled with the soldiers nearest to them. A fierce, deadly game of hand-to-hand fighting broke out amongst the whining, screaming shells as both sides struggled for supremacy. Eventually, four enemy soldiers succeeded in breaking free and began to run back towards the comparative safety of their own lines. They disappeared suddenly in a flash of red, yellow and grey as a shell burst squarely amongst them. Ducking, Findlay squeezed his eyes shut tight to regain his night vision and nodded curtly in satisfaction before turning around to look to his own men once more.

Braving the torrent of fire that threatened to drench them with high explosives they crossed the ground at a mad pace and gained the safety of their own trenches. Some assumed that the deadly rain that had fallen so violently upon them was enemy fire and roundly cursed their own gunners for their lack of response. On the enemy's side the British barrage lifted and moved on, raining shells down on the next area with parade-ground precision as the sweating gunners two miles back followed their flawed fire plan and saturated the next area marked out on their maps.

His uniform torn in numerous places, bleeding profusely from his forehead and shoulder, the result of several minor splinter and shrapnel wounds, Findlay shepherded the shocked men down the trench to where they had started from over two hours previously. Medical orderlies were waiting, along with the battalion MO, Bevan Hughes. Allowing the MO long enough to bind up his wounds the RSM angrily waved him away and went in search of his men.

Back in the barn, as the exhausted survivors gulped down a welcome cup of rum handed to them, a shocked adjutant took the roll-call. Of the three officers who had set out only Elliot had returned, still supported by Corporal Miller. Lieutenant Derby had set off back across no man's land but had never appeared on the other side. Whiting had been seen to fall and of the others Sergeant Miller and RSM Findlay were the two surviving senior NCOs, Sergeant Jeffries having simply disappeared. Of the other ranks, only twenty-seven had made it back and nine of these were injured, two critically. The rest were all missing. One of these was Private Lewis Simmonds, nineteen years of age, of D Company. Some known to be dead had been left, as were those too badly wounded to be moved. Of the others, nothing was known. Morning and daylight might see one or two arrive back safely and this would allow a final count to be made. The price for the night's work was going to be high.

No one had managed to pierce the enemy lines far enough to gain The Ram's Horn. Some captured papers were sent away for analysis along with enemy shoulder epaulettes and weapons taken from the dead. Ramsbottom was relieved to hear that Private Murgatroyd had not returned, as well as being horrified at the cost to the battalion of the night's work. For him the thought of Murgatroyd's possible death was a satisfactory conclusion of the matter back in Bethune as far as the battalion was concerned. For the moment, the fact that Private Ben 'Boy' Godley was missing interested him not one little bit. He would be haunted by his lack of concern in the days to come.

12

Monday 18th October 1915

Casualties for last night's raid amounted to 2 officers, Lt. Derby and 2/Lt Whiting killed,
1 officer, 2/lt Elliot, slightly wounded. 1 Senior NCO, Sergeant Miller, missing, presumed
killed, RSM wounded slightly. 18 ORs returned unharmed, 9 ORs returned wounded, 2
severely. 13 ORs returned during the night leaving 36 missing. Most presumed killed.
Enquiry to be set up into shelling on return journey by our own artillery. Very little intel-
ligence was gained about Ram's Horn situation. Battalion spirits dropped at such heavy
casualty lists. Heavy shelling along the line this morning by Minenwerfers and 5.9
Howitzers left 3 ORs severely wounded when dugout blown in. Rain all afternoon made
conditions very unpleasant. Ration parties sent out later in afternoon. Wiring repairs
carried out in evening under Royal Engineer supervision.

Captain L. Carey, D Company

The rain fell from midday onwards, drenching those unlucky to be caught out
in it and seeping into the clothes of the many trying unsuccessfully to shelter
in the dugouts and funkholes along the line. To those men sharing a shelter the
main topic of conversation was the raid of the previous night. Even the hardened
amongst them realised the loss to the regiment of so many of their companions-
in-arms and the ensuing conversations were subdued in the extreme.

Huddled in a grimy blanket, Billy Lane was an exception as he tried to keep
warm and stared out at the grey sky. The raindrops ran down the wood framing of
his dugout and dripped in a steady stream onto his head, soaking the already-wet
woollen hat he was wearing. Bending forward, oblivious to the rain coursing down
his clothing, he idly pushed fingerfulls of earth and chalk together in a miniature
dam, grunting with pleasure as a small puddle built up rapidly behind the heaped
earth. It crumbled quickly and released the water to run down the trench in a minor
tidal wave. A torrent of water narrowly missed splashing him and he turned
sharply, his eyes narrowing as the stranger glumly squelched past him down the
sodden duckboards. Leaning over he prodded the prone figure lying with its knees
bent alongside him.

'Oi, Jim, are you awake?'

Wearily his companion answered, rubbing his eyes and rising up on his elbows before pushing his own filthy blanket aside. 'No I bloody well wasn't but I reckon as how I am now!'

'Besides giving me a fag you grumpy old sod, you can answer me a question!'
'What?'

'Who's that lanky streak o' piss that's just scuttled down past us then?'

Grumbling, his companion leaned out into the dugout opening and looked in the direction his mate was pointing, cursing as a new stream of raindrops landed neatly on the bare nape of his neck.

'Oh, him. That's Charlie, the shit-wallah. And you're not getting a fag!'

Billy Lane was not going to let the matter end there.

'Keep your gaspers then, you miserable bugger. Shit-wallah eh, Jim? What the 'ell is that fer a name?'

'What I just said. Who the 'ell do you think empties the latrines on a night?'

'Oh, I see, but where did he come from? He wasn't with us on the boat over here, was he?'

Turning back towards him, Jim frowned as he tried to gather his thoughts. 'No, you're right. I think he just appeared one day and attached himself to us. Came from the East Kents I heard. Like Hackett. Quiet sort of a cove. Doesn't say an awful lot, just gets on with it.'

'The point is, where does he put the stuff?'

'What stuff?' Jim answered, puzzled now.

'Christ, do I 'ave to spell it out for you, chum? The shit, man, the shit! Where the bleedin' 'ell does 'e dump all that shit!'

His patience at an end, Jim leant forward and thrust his face next to that of his inquisitive companion. 'You, my little chum, are starting to get on my nerves with all these stupid questions! I haven't a fucking clue where he dumps the crap and neither do I want to know! All I know is that he disappears over the top with a bloody great bucket some nights. Several times a night in fact, if you'd open your cloth ears and eyes! I've seen him. Where and what he does with it from then on is a fucking mystery. I doubt if even the Kaiser knows! Now, I'm going to lie down an' get back to bleedin' sleep an' you will stop asking me any more stupid questions if you know what's good for you. Savvy?'

'Keep your hair on, matey, I was only asking. Christ! Some people...' Billy grumbled indignantly but he refrained from any more questions and after awhile joined his friend in the arms of Morpheus, albeit a trifle uneasily.

The rain continued to fall steadily but they sleepy on. A while later the toe of a boot made Billy Lane start and he woke to see a figure bending down looking at him.

'Oi, sleepy-head, CSM's orders. You and your mate report to him tonight at eight pip emma. Those nice gentlemen from the Royal Engineers are coming up to show us how to sort the barbed wire out and your names came up.'

Later that evening the wiring parties assembled with their props and stakes under the watchful gaze of an RE sergeant and when it was dark, moved out into no man's land to fill in the gaps produced by that morning's shelling. During the course of the night's work a great shout of terror and revulsion rose up, causing men to drop and hug the ground in consternation. Apart from a probing burst of machine-gun fire the other side stayed silent and after waiting a few minutes more, the men slowly resumed their work.

The reason for the disturbance became apparent after the wiring party returned with one of their number wearily bringing up the rear. Billy Lane, wiring diligently with the rest, had over-reached in the dark and fallen full tilt into a shell hole. It was at the precise moment of entering the thick, greasy scum headfirst at the bottom that he had discovered exactly where Charlie the shit-wallah disposed of the battalion's 'soil'.

Tuesday 26th October 1915

'C Coy to billets, being replaced by A Coy. More rain in the morning which stopped by the afternoon. Two platoons of D Coy involved with Royal Engineers in amassing dumps of barbed wire, ammunition and pickets behind Stratford Lane communication trench. ORs hot meal delivered late and cold due to heavy shelling in early afternoon. Two platoons of C Coy marched to bathing station near Havrelles for bathing and clean clothing issue. Heavy shelling on return caused three OR casualties, none severe.

Captain L. Carey, D Company

It was becoming colder and more and more of the men stood-to, clothed in a variety of garments, some official Army issue, and others most definitely not. Company commanders turned a blind eye to the practice of civilian jumpers being worn under the men's greatcoats and coloured scarves being wrapped round faces, as long as it was done only while up in the line. Back in reserve everyone was expected to be smartly turned out.

The thin gaggle of men exited the last of the communication trenches and morosely formed up at the side of the pàve. CSM Miles Hornby strode up and down them, ignoring the thin drizzle that had started under a grey, leaden sky as he looked keenly at each of the fifty men standing around. A career NCO of thirty-five, he had seen service in India and Egypt before the wars. Standing over six feet tall and clean-shaven, his once brown hair now tinged with grey flecks, he hailed from Appleby in Cumbria and had the fierce independent air of a fells man who brooked no arguments from the men in his charge.

'Right, my lucky lads. We're now going for a *promenade*, as they say in Froggy-land, along this here road for a couple of miles and at the end of it you filthy wallahs are going to have a good bath. No! No!' he continued as a chorus of groans rose up behind him, 'Don't thank me. Thank our good General French and his generous staff-wallahs what have all your interests at heart. Now then! Shut the chuntering, collect yourselves and follow me. Squad, shun! Shoulder arms! By the right, quick march!'

With ill-grace they did as they'd been ordered and marched resignedly behind their CSM, following his tall, upright figure as he marched along the cobbled road. Corporal Menzies, a small mousy man who had the air of a perpetual worrier, slunk along at the rear. After a short while CSM Hornby spoke again.

'What, no singing? Come on lads, sing up. Private Parkes, lead the way. '*It's a long way to...*' he croaked lustily, motioning for them to join in. Wearily they obeyed, Alfie Parkes singing the loudest.

The road seemed to stretch for ever and the singing soon petered out as the rain ceased abruptly. For a while some of the more observant took a keen view of the countryside as they doggedly followed Hornby, but after a mile or so their movements became automatic, front foot down followed by back foot, followed by front foot. In this manner they tramped towards the outlines of a ruined village that grew larger as they neared.

'Squad, halt!' Cursing at the sudden stop, the men awaited the next command. Up ahead Hornby was looking inquisitively at a large, blue and white covered tent set up at the edge of the road at the entrance to the village. The tent bore the legend: SALVATION ARMY. ALL WELCOME on a notice hung next to the canvas entrance facing the road.

What had caught Hornby's eye was not the tent or its notice but the shape of a female figure clad in a large, voluminous dark cloak bustling around in its inner room. A large kettle hung there, over a range protected from the elements by a blanket flapping wetly in the wind, and a number of white, earthenware mugs were neatly stacked alongside the range. The figure straightened and moved gracefully through the entrance towards the watching, staring men.

'Good morning, sergeant,' she cried out. 'Will you and your men be resting for a cuppa?'

Pointedly ignoring the titters from the ranks behind him, Hornby advanced towards the tent and its proprietress. She stood there, in her early thirties he guessed, a pleasant, welcoming smile on her face, watching him as he frankly observed her. Miles Hornby saw a cream-complexioned face with green eyes staring inquisitively at him from underneath a thick shock of curling auburn hair. She wore a dark dress with insignia on the collars over a gleaming white blouse under the cloak, and as he looked down he could see she was wearing thick, black leather boots laced up to her ankles. A large dark hat lay behind her on the earth floor where she had carelessly discarded it. She was fully aware of his appraisal of her and his face reddened as his eyes rose up to her face to meet hers.

'I'm sorry ma'am,' he stammered, embarrassed. 'We're on our way to the other side of the village. Should you be here? Has no one told you this is a dangerous area to be setting up shop?'

She laughed quietly, enjoying his discomfiture. 'Don't worry about us sergeant, our Lord looks after his servants well. We have no fear at our being here, tending to the simple wants of those around us.'

Us? 'Hornby asked, 'You said us?'

'Oh, yes, Henry. Captain Henry Blake. Of the Salvation Army like myself. We received permission from your brigade commander to set up a comfort stall in the area so here we are. Have you and your men time for tea?'

He felt like an adolescent schoolboy in her presence. 'No, ma'am, but thank you for your kind thought. We have to get on but if we make up the time during our business in the village beyond perhaps we can stop for a cuppa on the way back.'

She laughed again, gaily this time. 'I'll keep the kettle boiling for you and your men, sergeant. Take care, and God be with you.'

Hornby muttered fiercely at her continued mistaken identification of his rank but she had gone, disappearing around the back of the stall once more. The men tittered again, louder this time and he whirled round to glare at them. 'We're gonna get going now, you spawn of mother's whores! And I don't want to hear a word. Not one fuckin' word. Get me?' They got him.

The houses were the usual hotchpotch of ruins, bare blackened walls clinging to a dirt road, and they soon passed through. Marching down the overgrown track for a mile or so towards a wooded area, a large, intact barn came into view on their right, half-hidden among the trees. Behind it Hornby could make out a number of large canvas structures, supported by sheets of corrugated iron, looking for all the world like outdoor swimming pools. The baths, such as they were, were hidden from prying eyes in the lee of the trees behind the barn, making them hard to spot. As they approached, a bored looking corporal appeared out of the barn, an unlit cigarette dangling loosely from his lower lip.

'Where've you ruddy well been, we've been waiting for ages! Don't you chaps know there's a war on...' He saw CSM Hornby turn his gaze on him and hastily snatched the cigarette from his lips and thrust it deep into his pocket. Straightening up he addressed Hornby directly.

'Er, just my little joke sir. Corporal Diack, sir. We've got the hot water ready in the barn and the boys will flash up the fumigator while you have your bath.'

Hornby continued to glare at him so he continued, more subdued this time. 'We should have plenty of spare shirts and socks so if you'd like to step this way, gents, we'll get you sorted. Just like Fortnum and Mason.'

Hornby snorted as he pushed past him. With large grins his men followed. 'Bit hard to find ain't you?' asked Titch Magilton cheekily as he passed the thoroughly-humbled soldier.

'Yeah? Well you try and pitch this little lot in the open without Jerry blowing you sky-high, chum!' came the laconic reply. The corporal came and stood along-side Hornby as the latter gazed at the baths with a quizzical air. Diack pointed laconically at the structures.

'Bet you're wondering where this little lot came from, ain't you, CSM? They're the reservoirs for the horses and mules, the beggars need lots of water every day so it's stored here before being taken up the line to where it's needed. Simple, see? We give you lot a bath and later on, when the water's settled, we load it into tins and Bob's yer uncle, off it goes for the animals, like!'

He saw Hornby's face and continued, 'So now you know, next time you fancy half-hitching the horses water to make a brew for yourselves, you'll be a bit more careful whose water you pinch!' He ignored Hornby's wintry stare and moved off, hands in pockets, whistling tunelessly.

At Hornby's commands they discarded their rifles and webbing by the barn, stripped off and then dumped their verminous clothes on the floor by the canvas structures. Hopping round, trying to get their breath back, a few naked men tried to evacuate the canvas baths they'd been assigned to but a curt command from their equally naked NCO stopped them in their tracks. Shivering, they stooped under the rim of the baths in an attempt to keep the wind off their bare forms.

Hornby straightened up to shout angrily for the corporal who had somehow disappeared but the words died on his lips as from inside the barn a procession of uniformed men bearing large, steaming buckets appeared. Bending low under the weight they staggered over to the baths and began pouring in the boiling-hot water the buckets contained. Within minutes the baths were full of pink-bodied men soaping themselves vigorously and luxuriating in the first hot bath they'd had in weeks. While they frolicked and joked inside, the supply party men went round gathering up the filthy clothes the bathers had discarded and bore them off back inside the barn.

Watching the horseplay from a quiet corner of the nearest bath where he slowly lathered himself, Hornby let them soak for ten minutes, then ordered everyone out. Grumbling now, they reluctantly followed him back over the sides, to stand once more on the cold, hard ground, shivering. Again, the bathing unit's men appeared, this time bearing armfuls of clean shirts and socks. It was obvious as they handed them out that they were not new, but they were clean, and the men luxuriated once again to the feel of fresh clothing.

They used the long shirt-tails of the grey issue shirts to dry themselves and stood in groups looking like damp, grey herons beside a pond as they waited for their uniforms to be brought out. In minutes they were supplied with the latter, but not before a large amount of swapping went on to reunite each owner with what each thought were his own tunic and trousers. The uniforms were damp from the fumigating they'd undergone inside the barn but to the waiting men they felt like Savile Row suits. No matter that the lice, vanquished for the moment, would return as soon as they were back in the line. For now the smell and feel of clean, fresh clothing banished all such dreary thoughts from their minds.

A private from the bath company strode over to Hornby.

'Now that the sun's coming up sir, be careful. The Hun shell this road fairly regularly and especially if they spot a body of men like yours marching along...' Hornby was grateful for the advice and patted the private on the arm to show his thanks as he moved to the head of his men. The men they left behind waved until they were out of sight and then sauntered back to the baths to make the place ready for their next visitors.

They sang lustily now, full of vigour after their refreshing experience and Hornby joined in, although tactfully refraining repeating the contents of some of the more lurid verses. They passed through the village at a fast pace and as the bright-coloured tent they had encountered on their way to the baths hove into view Hornby waved his right arm in an up and down movement.

She came out of the tent's entrance and watched their approach, the same grave expression on her face as before. She was joined by a dapper and moustached elderly man in the uniform of a Salvation Army captain and together they gazed at the marching men. At the signal from Hornby the men stopped abruptly, level with the stall and he marched forward, saluting smartly.

'Sir. Ma'am. I believe a cuppa was what we agreed on previously.'

Her smile was a dazzling burst of sunlight that lit up the day. She turned without a word and entered the tent, leaving her companion to walk forward and grasp Hornby's hand, shaking it vigorously.

'Welcome, you're all welcome,' he said simply, and stood back to bow and sweep his hand in the direction of the tent. In a short time each man stood armed with a mug of hot, sweet, steaming tea and a large biscuit, chattering animatedly as the two Salvationists passed among them topping up half-empty mugs and thrusting more biscuits into their hands. Eventually she was at Hornby's side, looking up at him with a calm, serene expression on her face.

'My apologies, CSM, for my ignorance earlier at your rank.' She was teasing him and he knew it but this only served to make him more tongue-tied in her presence. As she leant forward to speak he caught the light fragrance of the cologne she was wearing and his thoughts flashed back over the years to a young woman in Aldershot and a hot summer's day.

'Miles, ma'am, my first name is Miles. There's no need here for rank between us.'

'And I am Jennifer, Jennifer Swales,' she answered him, dropping a mock curtsey. 'Now that we've been introduced, Miles, we should be as friends, don't you think?'

He nodded, eager to keep the intimate contact between them for as long as possible. After a long pause she looked at his tunic and noticed for the first time the row of medals stitched on his left breast. 'Goodness, she exclaimed, 'there seem to be rather a lot of ribbons there. You *have* been busy, Miles.'

He laughed at her obvious coquettishness and in return she giggled, the light girlish sound of a woman enjoying herself. 'No, ma'am,' he explained, 'I bought them for a penny down the bazaar in Cairo.'

Another awkward silence grew between them until he said, 'How come you picked this place to stop? Aren't you a bit far from home, wherever that might be?'

She wiped the mug she was holding on her cloak before answering. 'Gloucester is where I'm from originally, Miles, although when the war started it was apparent God wanted his servants to aid those far from their homes. I followed my vocation and applied to serve overseas. Captain Blake and myself came over in March of this year. We were not the first you know, the Salvation Army established a base in France soon after the outbreak of hostilities. We move around, setting the stall up where we feel it's most needed and last week that brought us here. Here we'll stay until we feel Our Lord requires our presence elsewhere.' She gazed at him with an earnest look that moved him to feel slightly uncomfortable at her simple yet steadfast faith.

'It's too dangerous here,' he stated flatly. 'Any moment you could be...'

'Killed?'

'You know what I mean. The Boche won't lose sleep over killing innocent servants of God. They've been doing it for long enough as it is. And this tent sticks out like a sore thumb. Can't you at least move it further back?'

She spoke softly. 'Miles, your concern is greatly appreciated but do you really think that the Germans could be as beastly as to target those whose work is with the Lord? I could quote you the words of one of our hymns: "*Be strong in the grace of the Lord*".'

Hornby finished the line for her. '"*Be armed in the power of his might*".'

* * * * *

She laughed delightedly and clapped her hands in a spontaneous gesture of surprised appreciation. 'Miles, you've read our song book!'

He laughed wryly in return, sharing in her surprise. 'I've had my moments, miss.'

'Jennifer.' She eyed him gravely again.

'Jennifer.'

He continued to look at her and this time it was she who looked away first, her face tinged pink.

After a while she composed herself and addressed him again. 'This is our work, Miles, and I feel God has sent us here for such a purpose. We'll be fine here, I can assure you, tending to the needs of those who need us. Now, I see by your manner that you're eager to be on your way. Would you and your men join Captain Blake and myself in a quiet prayer of thanksgiving and maybe a hymn before you all leave?'

Reluctantly he nodded and allowed himself to be led back towards the main body of his waiting men. Captain Blake joined them and led them in the Lord's Prayer. At a further cue from him the assembly broke into the sweet, heartfelt words of 'Rock of Ages'. When the last words had died on the afternoon air the men stood for several long moments. It fell to Hornby to break the spell. At his command, once again that day they donned their greatcoats and hefted the weapons they had tactfully left on the far side of the road.

Before marching away he looked over to where she stood, gazing at him with an unfathomable expression as she twisted the ends of her cloak in the doorway of the stall. He lifted a hand, half-heartedly, then dropped it again, in a small, futile gesture of helplessness. She saw it and smiled at him, the same dazzling smile that had lit up her face when they had stopped and he felt his heart take a great leap.

'We'll be back, ' he said, looking straight into those green eyes. 'Keep the kettle on the boil now, you hear?'

'May the good Lord take care of you, sergeant,' she replied, emphasising the last word, teasing him again now. 'There'll always be a warm welcome for you here.' With that she turned into the tent and was gone. He stared at the tent's entrance for several, long moments, then finally turned to the soldiers patiently waiting and in a low voice said simply, 'Let's go. Move it.'

They marched away from the village with a firm tread. Hornby looked back but Jennifer didn't appear again. A mirrored flash caught his eye as he turned round but when he looked about him he could see nothing. A song started quietly behind him, as if the men were afraid of his reaction, but he made a pumping motion with his hand to encourage them and the bawdy choruses were soon ringing out across the landscape with renewed vigour as they marched briskly forwards.

It happened again. A flash in his eyes, followed shortly by another. Then another. He looked around wildly, concerned now but again could see nothing. His right arm shot up in a pumping motion once more and the answering clatter told him his men had understood the order and halted. As he turned to speak, his face lifted, the flash struck him squarely again in his questing eyes. As he read-justed to the sudden glare he looked fearfully upwards. There, looming over them, a thousand feet up and a few miles away, floated the sinister, greyish-white sausage shape of a *Drachen*, an enemy observation balloon. When the skies had cleared its crew had operated the steam winch that had sent it soaring swiftly aloft, where it now floated, its wicker basket swaying gently below as the observer it contained shifted about to view the panorama beneath him. As he continued to gaze, the flash struck Hornby's eyes again and he realised, with a wild pounding in his heart, that he was seeing the sun's reflection from the coated lenses of a pair of binoculars.

'Get off the road! Now! For God's sake get off the fucking road!' he shouted hoarsely at the top of his voice, waving his arms at the startled men before running over to throw himself down in the drainage ditch running alongside the cobbles. Swiftly they followed his example, diving for cover without a moment's hesitation.

In the distance a sound like ripping canvas was swiftly followed by the screeching, *whooshing* noise of incoming shells. The shells burst suddenly, frighteningly, with massive bangs around the road, showering all those cowering facedown in the ditch with earth, intermingled with the cobbled stones of the pàve. Whining fragments of white-hot metal zipped overhead as they pressed their faces deep into the muddy water that slowly oozed its way down the ditch. The cleanliness of their earlier bathing was gone in seconds as they pressed down but no one cared, each man trying to make his body as small as possible to escape from the deadly fragments.

Another salvo landed, and another, the noise and colours of each shell exploding driving the shockwaves deep. Dimly, Hornby heard someone scream in pain but he was unable to lift his head to see who or what was making the noise and he stayed in the same position. The shells slammed around them with surgical precision, the whole maelstrom of hate being visited upon them orchestrated by the man sitting in a hydrogen-filled balloon miles away, swaying hundreds of feet over their head.

The rain saved them. It seemed like hours but could only have been minutes before the barrage slowly lifted and the explosions shifted away from where they lay. A large, black cloud had drifted rapidly across their front, the rain slanting down, blanketing them from the enemy observer's view. Slowly, wondering, shocked faces covered in dirt raised a hesitant look over the top of the ditch. Corporal Menzies was first to his feet, staggering dazedly along the now pockmarked road as he tried to make a rudimentary roll-call. Unbelievably, they had suffered no fatalities, just three men wounded by flying splinters, none of them severe.

'A right Blighty one, you lucky old sod,' Alfie Parkes called out enviously as he pulled his wounded pal to his feet and began bandaging the shocked man's bloodied arm, the blood freely mingling with the water that threatened to soak them all.

'Menzies, check the wounded and spread the men out along the road.' The words died on Hornby's lips as he became aware of his corporal's stance.

The man stood gazing back the way they had come, and Hornby followed his gaze with the same foreboding that had come over him just minutes before. The village they had just left was the next object of the German observer's attention. Guessing that the troops he had caught in the open would run back to the village for cover he had directed his battery's fire in that direction. As the two men watched in horror a salvo landed squarely in the middle of the ruins, sending bricks and a huge dust cloud rising malignantly into the air. The shockwave of the explosions reached them a split-second later and as Hornby started forward another salvo followed the first, bursting among the ruins with red and black flashes and loud *crumps!* adding to the smoke hiding the earlier destruction.

Hornby ran, rifle in both hands. He ran, desperately, as he'd never run before. Long before he reached the outskirts of the village the shelling and the rain stopped. In its place was a deathly hush and a swirling cloud of red brick-dust, together with the awful stink of cordite and burning wood, mixed in with the damp, fungal smell of the rain. He stopped, his chest heaving as he dragged in huge lungfuls of air, looking around in a wild, panic-stricken motion as his brain tried to digest the new shape of the ruins and superimpose them on the outlines it had recorded hours previously.

He gave up trying to make sense of the grotesque, scattered shards of splintered wood and shattered brickwork and walked forward, falteringly. He called out frantically, 'Jennifer, Miss Swales! Captain Blake!' but no answering cry came from the wreckage confronting him. Coughing on the acrid taste of the dust he placed his left hand over his mouth and advanced further into the gloom, kicking aside broken beams and pieces of bent and twisted metalwork as he peered into the dust cloud. His heart stopped as, protruding from a pile of misshapen rubble, he recognised scraps of the cloth covering the stall they had taken their ease at twenty minutes or so earlier. Hesitatingly he moved towards it, his mind uncomprehending, willing his brain to be mistaken. Nearing the mangled remains his eyes became accustomed to the light and with a sinking, heavy feeling he realised he was staring down at the broken, pulverized remains of dozens of white, earthenware mugs.

Down on the ground, half-hidden among a mound of shattered bricks, covered in dust, something gleamed. He dropped his rifle and his arms fell helplessly to his sides as he recognised the one thing he was dreading to find. With a groan he sank down, ignoring the pain in his knees as he dropped onto the sharp-edged, misshapen bricks and reached forward to touch the limp, half-buried object.

When Corporal Menzies and a handful of the men reached him minutes later they found him kneeling on the muddied mound, staring white-faced and unseeing into the distance, his hand slowly reddening as he continued to gently caress a shock of bloodstained, auburn hair peeping out from underneath the tattered ruins of a blue and white canvas tent.

13

Thursday 4th November 1915

Sector quiet. D Coy in reserve. In view of heavy casualties suffered by battalion in abortive Ram's Horn trench raid and subsequent actions, CO requested Brigade to allow first leave party to be formed. Brigade agreed. Three officers and ten ORs given three days' leave over the weekend. ORs balloted. Heavy shelling occurred at 09:40 ack emma in the vicinity of A Coy. One OR killed, six wounded, two severely. Wiring parties out in evening. Weather much colder now. Rain for most of the day. Mail arrived. Capt Charteris to Brigade HQ for presentation of his Military Cross and then on leave.

Captain L. Carey, D Company

Neville Charteris laid the paper he was writing on aside and frowned as he looked round for the envelope he had mislaid. Damn it, the blasted thing had been perched on the end of the wooden bench he was sitting on and now it was gone. He looked down and spotted it beneath his feet where it had fallen onto the dirt floor. Picking it up he wiped the mud from the front, picked his pen up once more and began to write carefully by the light of the guttering candle.

He had been asked by the CO to answer a letter. The distraught wife of Henry Watson had written to Colonel Snaith, pleading for more information on the disappearance of her husband. What to say? There had been no information, from either the Red Cross or any other source. It was as if the missing men had marched into a fog bank and never appeared on the other side. He chewed on the end of his pen as he tried to think of some words of comfort, and looked down at his wristwatch. It was three o'clock. Two more hours and he would welcome his relief and stumble off for some well-earned sleep himself.

After a while he laid the pen down on top of the sheet of paper and made his way out of the dugout. It was still dark, the dawn several hours away, and he had difficulty in picking his way down the trench.

'Halt! Who goes there?'

'Friend,' he replied.

'Advance, friend, and be recognised!' came the stern rejoinder. Charteris stepped forward and stood still as a shape in the murk carefully scrutinised him. 'Oh, its you Mr Charteris. Beg your pardon, I never recognised you, sir.'

The sentry atop the firestep grounded his rifle and peered at him.

'That's all right,' he laughed, 'you can't be too careful. Who knows, I might have been a phantom Boche, lost in the dark.'

The sentry joined in the laughter then resumed his watch of the area to his front.

'Look here, its Dawson isn't it?' The man nodded as Charteris approached. 'I say, you haven't seen Mr Elliot have you?'

Private Dawson looked down at him from his perch on the firestep. 'Keep on down the trench, sir,' he replied with a hint of sarcasm, 'You'll find Mr Elliot winning the war on his ownsome in the next bay.' He turned back to his position, leaving Charteris looking at him askance.

Stumbling along, ignoring the occasional curse as he stepped on outstretched arms or legs protruding from shallow scrapes and funkholes in the trench walls he made his way finally round the corner and saw a dim shape in the firing bay. As he moved forwards he recognised the thin figure of the very person he was searching for.

'There you are, old man,' he greeted Elliot. 'I've been looking everywhere for you.'

Elliot scowled before answering. 'I can't think how you've not found me earlier sir, I've been here for the last two hours, checking up on these sentries, making sure none of them doze off. If you don't keep on at them they slacken off and where would that lead to?' Elliot spoke with some difficulty as a result of the large dressing stuck across his broken nose, a legacy of the injury suffered on the night of the abortive trench raid.

'Well, yes, as a matter of fact that's what I want to talk to you about.' Charteris spoke sharply and the young officer in front of him stiffened. 'Look here, Elliot, the Old Man is becoming a bit concerned at the number of men you keep putting on a charge. He's asked me to have a word and see if you can't let up on the men, treat them a bit more gently if you see what I mean. Not that he wants to undermine your authority, you understand, he just feels you might be bearing down on the chaps a bit too hard.'

His voice taut with suppressed rage, Elliot answered. 'Sir,' he hissed, 'I hold the King's Commission and have sworn to uphold his authority over the men under my command. If the CO thinks I shall desist in my duty then I must respectfully ask you to inform him that I cannot, sir. The men in this company are a bunch of shirking slackers and I shall do all it takes to bring them into line. If that means more of them appearing before him for punishment before they get the message then that's how it must be.'

Charteris choked back an angry retort as he contemplated the jumped-up prig standing quivering with rage before him. Elliot would learn soon enough that to lose the respect of the men in his command was to be a lonely person indeed.

'Very well, young Elliot, if that's what you think,' he answered coldly. 'But you'll meet with a better response from your men if you treat them a bit more decently. We're all out here in this damn war together and death is no respecter of rank, mark my words. You have a lot to learn if you want to come through this in one piece and go home to wherever it is you're from.'

'Romford. I'm from Romford, sir,' Elliot muttered in a surly fashion, his voice betraying the anger he still felt at Charteris's well-meant words.

'Are you indeed! I have an old uncle in Romford, my father's brother, Tom. He was always getting on to me to pack up and move down to Romford. Wish I had now, this might have turned out so differently.'

Elliot glanced at him, still annoyed. '*This*, sir? Do you mean the war? I thought someone with your experience would have been glad to be a part of this.'

Charteris laughed, a short bitter laugh. 'Experience my foot! I was a bloody insurance clerk not long ago, not some damned fire-breathing warrior. How could anyone be glad to be a part of *this*? Now, what have you got to report?'

Elliot remained where he stood, stiffly maintaining his aggrieved posture before gesturing into the darkness. 'Dawson thought he heard movement out there half an hour ago sir, but we both listened hard and heard nothing more. Other than that it's been a quiet night. All the sentries are alert, sir. You can count on that.'

Charteris stood for a moment, looking in the direction Elliot had pointed to. It was only a day or so before that he had crouched here in this very same spot as the dawn broke and witnessed the swift retribution dealt to the observer of the German observation balloon that had caused CSM Hornby and the bathing party such grief the previous week. A single aircraft, hugging the contours of the ground, had suddenly risen up and, ignoring the fierce 'Archie' the enemy anti-aircraft gunners had thrown up to protect the balloon, had pressed home his attack. The watching infantrymen had held their breath as the German crews frantically winched down the balloon to no avail. Their ears had taken in the sound of a machine-gun hammering away and a stream of tracer had spewed from the nose of the biplane to rip through the fabric of the balloon. It had caught fire immediately, the hydrogen gas it contained flaring up with an enormous explosion that had lit up the sky for miles around.

To the watchers on the ground the best was yet to come. The observer, swinging helplessly in his basket below the balloon, had decided that now was the time to evacuate his stricken craft. He left it too late, far too late. As his parachute unfurled a tendril of fire had licked down from the collapsing gas bag, setting fire to his silken umbrella. The men looking up from the trenches, crouching far below, had cheered loudly and enthusiastically as he had plunged to earth. Twisting and spinning, legs kicking wildly, he had spiralled down in a long, black-smudged trail of smoke that smeared the sky as the fiery parachute signalled his funeral pyre.

'All right, Elliot, I'm going back to the company dugout to finish a letter. Call by when you've been relieved and we'll make out our report together. Carry on.' With that he spun on his heel and strode back to the dugout. He was still feeling angry and any answer from Elliot might have been enough to tip him over the edge.

He awoke with a start. Leaning over him, tugging at his exposed shoulder with a gloved hand, was the face of Private Evans, the CO's batman. 'Begging your pardon, sir, but Colonel Snaith would like to see you. Now, sir, if you don't mind.' He stepped back as Charteris struggled into a sitting position on the hard plank seat and glanced down at his watch. It was five-thirty. 'What's so bloody important that you had to wake me at this unearthly hour?'

'Dunno, sir,' Evans replied diffidently. 'The Old Man got me out of my scratcher to come and get you, sir. Wouldn't say what it was for.'

'All right, Evans, all right, I get the message. Give Colonel Snaith my respects and inform him I shall join him shortly. Go on then, man, hop it!' Shuffling round he pushed himself stiffly off the plank and stood upright, stamping his feet hard to restore some feeling into them. Running his hand swiftly through his hair he pushed his uniform cap on his head and made his way out of the dugout. The rain had a refreshing feel, helping to blow the cobwebs of his tiredness away, and his mood improved as fifteen minutes later he neared the large, comfortable, deepened dugout that was Snaith's headquarters. He descended the ten or so feet down the wooden steps, carefully avoiding the tangle of wires and telephone cables running haphazardly alongside the steps.

It was a large room, some twenty feet by fifteen, with electric lights and a stove in the corner. Thick planks buttressed the walls, making the dugout impervious to all but the most direct of hits. In the far corner, a battered hotchpotch of wood, thrown up by the battalion carpenter to represent a desk, leant at a dangerous angle next to an opening to a small, dark chamber that he guessed contained the CO's own sleeping quarters. Round the stove were parked a few looted armchairs. Seated in front of the desk was the weary-looking figure of his CO, reading through a sheaf of official-looking forms. To Charteris, it seemed as if Cuthbert Snaith had aged greatly in the last few weeks and he felt a twinge of pity.

Becoming aware of his presence, Snaith turned to face Neville. 'Neville my dear chap!' he cried. 'Come in! Come in! Come on over here, I have some good news for you. A double helping of good news in fact. Evans? Where is the blasted man? Ah there you are. Evans, coffee for the captain if you please. '

Evans appeared from nowhere and trotted over to a large silver pot and placed it on the stove. Snaith carried on speaking excitedly, the words tumbling out as he tried to explain everything in a mad rush. 'Marvellous news, Neville. You're to present yourself to HQ this afternoon. General Hughes will be present to award you your Military Cross and when he's finished you'll be proceeding on three days leave. Is that good news or what?'

Charteris's brain reeled as the colonel jabbered on. Leave. Home. Peckham. Lucille. He tried hard to concentrate on Snaith's words but pictures of his wife kept flitting through his mind. Her hair. The smell of her perfume. Her touch. The images were so strong he could almost reach out and embrace her.

'Are you listening, old chap? I said, how long will it take you to be ready to set off?'

He looked at Snaith's expectant face staring up at him.

'Er, I could, give me an hour, sir, and I think I should be back here packed, ready to go. I don't understand though, why me? How was it decided? Are any more of our chaps going too?'

'Too many bally questions, Neville,' Snaith answered him with a touch of asperity. 'Brigade agreed after the last operation we participated in that it would be in order to grant some limited leave to the battalion as a means of raising morale. Three officers and ten ORs were to be chosen. As you're our first gallantry award winner, I personally decided that you would be first on the list. The rest were chosen by ballot. Now go and get packed. You'll be collected and taken to divisional HQ shortly and after the ceremony you can catch a train from Albert to Boulogne for the leave boat. Go and see the adjutant before you leave, he's got all your travel papers ready. Give my love to Blighty when you arrive and have a good time. Cheerio!'

Behind him, Evans looked down at the mug of steaming coffee in his hand as Charteris departed. He lifted it to his lips and drank deeply. No one said a word.

After a frantic few minutes throwing belongings into a soft leather knapsack Charteris was escorted through the trenches by the RSM and together they walked to where a motor lorry was waiting to take him to Albert.

As they drove away he could hear the sound of shellfire. It was quite close and he shivered. His guilt and fear lasted only a few seconds and he sank back into the seat. The grim-faced driver eventually deposited him in the courtyard of a pretty chateau, where he stood with several ranks in the drizzle to await the arrival of the general.

A posse of flunkeys preceded him, pulling and pushing the recipients into the order in which they were to receive their awards. After a brief citation was read out, Charteris was motioned in front of a gruff-looking, red-tabbed general who mumbled a few inaudible words that included 'Good show! Good show!' He was unable to catch any of it before the medal ribbon of the Military Cross mounted on a clip was pinned on his chest. Before he could look down at the ribbon he was pushed to the side and the next recipient marched forward. On completion of the awards the general and his staff left in a cloud of spray, leaving a bemused group of men in the otherwise empty courtyard. Transport had been arranged for them all back to Albert, the lorry depositing a now-thoroughly soaked Charteris, at his request, outside the train station.

He walked slowly onto the platform and found a hard bench to sit on. He remembered the papers in his breast pocket and he pulled them out. They were a trifle sodden but separated easily and he was able to lean back and open the letter from his wife.

There was little comfort contained within the two short pages, rather a litany of complaints as his wife vented her feelings in bitter words. Her friend's husband, a staff officer, had been home twice so far on leave but he, Neville, had yet to come back once to see his own wife. The money he sent was barely enough to pay the rent on the house and if it wasn't for her mother she would be in severe financial difficulties. Luckily, Arnold, the senior partner of the solicitor's firm, was very kind to her and had raised her weekly money by another three shillings in order, as he put it, 'To do his bit in helping our brave men at the front and their dependants'.

He became impatient and rose to his feet. The platform was fast filling with khaki as more men arrived to await the oncoming train. A loud whistle pierced the air and he turned, only to bump into another waiting figure.

'I'm sorry, I do beg your pardon,' he murmured automatically.

'That's all right sir, it's Mr Charteris isn't it?'

'CSM Mason! How the devil are you, don't tell me you're one of the lucky blighters going on leave too?' he exclaimed.

Frank Mason nodded eagerly. 'I was told only an hour or so ago, sir, seems I was one of the lucky ones what was pulled out of the hat. Not that I'm moaning mind, I reckon as how I still can't believe it. Are you on your way too, sir?'

Charteris was about to answer when a loud clanking noise drowned out any chance of further conversation as the train rolled to a stop in front of them, venting huge quantities of steam as it did so. Frank Mason was lost in the sudden rush so Charteris let himself be borne along the platform. Spotting a sign on one of the forward-most carriages, reading 'Officers Only' he made his way towards it. He swung up into the dank interior and, spotting an empty seat, sank into it with a sigh of relief, ignoring the stares of the other wearied occupants.

The train was on its way in minutes and he sank down in his seat, trying to grab some precious sleep. The day's events had taken their toll on him and he dozed fitfully as the train lurched through the darkening French countryside. As a leave train they had some priority over the local war traffic and he was glad see the coast appear after a few uncomfortable hours on the hard seat. His fellow travellers had kept themselves to themselves, with very little conversation, and he was relieved as they finally slid into Boulogne.

Yawning, he stretched and rose in his seat, grabbing his knapsack and following the other occupants of the carriage as they disembarked onto the side of the quay. Looming over them, afloat on the low tide, was the dark shape of the leave boat, upper decks alight. By her stern he could hear the sounds of an engine throbbing.

It was too dark to make out her name and he gave up trying and allowed himself to be shepherded along with the others into a large series of sheds.

'Here we go!' muttered the man to his right.

'What's all this about?' Charteris asked, to be met with a bitter smile.

'It's the "Ghouls", as we call them sir. We have to be searched before being allowed on the ship, so's nobody can smuggle any souvenirs or contraband into Blighty but what these bastards let you.'

Charteris frowned as he shuffled forward, his gaze settling on the soldiers manning the desks. He became aware of their sleek, well-groomed appearance as he neared the front of the queue and the quick well-practiced way they rifled through the valises and packs hoisted on the desks by the now surly crowd, blithely ignoring their weak protests. At the front of this queue a kilted Highlander wearing the cap badge of the Cameronians and three wound-stripes on his left cuff stood, red-faced, clutching his rifle defensively as a fat, puffing Military Police lieutenant rummaged through his knapsack. The man looked as though he was ready to explode as his belongings were arbitrarily tossed onto the desk.

'Don't get smart with me laddie, or you'll sit this leave out. Now, where did you put it? Answer me, or your feet won't touch the ground. And salute when you speak to an officer, damn you!'

The Scot looked at him contemptuously. 'Ah have nae got it, whatever it was you thought I had, sir.'

'What's going on here?' Charteris enquired sharply, pushing his way to the front.

'Sir,' the officer complained pompously, recognising Charteris's superior rank, 'Please keep out of what doesn't concern you.'

'Lieutenant,' Charteris replied with a hint of steel in his voice, 'I asked you a question. Now, what the hell is going on?'

Sullenly the officer said, 'This man was seen to try and conceal what looked like a pistol in his bag. These sort of things are simply not allowed and if I can be allowed to do my job, without anymore interference, sir, we can find the gun and this...this person here will find he's not going anywhere except to the cells in the town.'

Charteris looked at the Scot, who glowered back as he waited for the blow to fall.

'Do you have a pistol in the bag?'

'No sir, I don't. Just a wee gift for ma bairn.'

'Righto then, pick up all your belongings and get on the ship. I was at Loos with your battalion. Well done there. Now be off and enjoy your leave, you deserve it.' Charteris turned once more to face the lieutenant. The man's face was blazing as he struggled to contain himself. His wild eyes moved from Charteris's feet to his face, taking in both the ribbon of the Military Cross on his chest and his dishevelled and muddied appearance.

'Sir!' he spat out. 'That was against all regulations. I would have your name and regiment so as to report this matter in the most strongest of possible terms.'

Slowly, Charteris looked him up and down. The sounds behind him died away slowly as all those in the hall watched the outcome. The contemptuous intensity of his, Charteris's gaze, brought a red flush to the hapless officer's face. Finally he spoke, low enough for only those waiting near them in the queue to hear.

'You, lieutenant, and all those fat pigs like you, who stand here bullying these men whose boots you are not fit to lace, make me sick to my stomach. While you live the life of luxury here, with your soft beds, cheap drink and tawdry women, men like him are dying in their hundreds, all the while denied of any such luxuries. This man's comrades paid with their blood so you can stand here today. You make me ashamed to share the same uniform as yourself. Now, the rest of the men in this queue are going to march out of here onto the ship waiting to take them home and you, lieutenant, and your men, will stand back and allow them to do so without any hindrance. Do I make myself clear?'

The lieutenant's eyes blazed with hatred at his humiliation but he nodded mutely, his white lips pressed tightly together as he stood back to allow the men to pass. Many of them patted Charteris's back as they went by but he acknowledged no one, his gaze staying focused on the officer in front of him. When the last soldier had gone by, Charteris bent forwards and spoke softly.

'By the way, my name is Charteris, Captain Neville Charteris, and I belong with the 19th Lancashires. Do try and remember it, I would hate for you to get any of the details wrong.'

'Oh don't you worry sir,' the lieutenant replied spitefully, pulling out a grimy notebook and pencil, 'Your name and face are something I shall remember for some time.'

Charteris stared at him for the last time with as much contempt as he could muster and the man blanched white under his scrutiny. He swept past the desk and walked out onto the quay and up the gangway onto the ship. The confined space inside bothered him, so buttoning his coat he made his way to the upper deck and stood there, leaning against the rail as he watched men gleefully run across the quay and up the gangway, oblivious to the sentry's objections.

Feeling weary now, he found an iron bench alongside the ship's funnel. Gratefully he dropped his knapsack from his shoulder and lowered himself down on to the bench and huddled there. The rain had long stopped but it was still cold. Nevertheless, within a few minutes of sitting down, he was asleep.

The ship remained at its berth for several more hours, the spotting of a German submarine in the channel that had eluded the Dover Patrol boats delaying their departure. Neville slept for only a short while before the incessant rain drove him inside where he found a spare seat in the lounge and gratefully sank down. Exhaustion overcame him and he fell into a deep sleep.

A gentle throbbing woke him suddenly and he walked stiffly back outside to see the black water below froth and churn as the ship slowly edged her way out of the harbour and into the open water beyond. The crying of gulls, unseen in the blackness, followed them out into the open sea as the ship turned her prow towards England. Long after she began to plunge with the motion of the heavy seas, Charteris kept his eyes focused on the pinpricks of light, behind them before making his way back inside and regaining his seat in the warmth of the lounge.

They made heavy going in the rough seas and dawn was peeping over the horizon before the ship forced her way into the harbour and docked alongside at Folkestone. Then followed a chaotic dash as the soldiers flew down the gangway once it had been installed, several of them looking green around the gills from the rigours of the crossing. Rifles and packs were shouldered, webbing pulled tight and caps set at a jaunty angle as the tide of khaki wended its slow way up the hill into the town and to the train waiting for them.

Charteris watched all this from his original vantage point alongside the funnel. The more deadly side to their journey became apparent when a few ambulances drove pell-mell alongside the ship. The early morning breeze made his hair flutter and he watched until the ambulances departed, leaning on the rail and rubbing his chin in a pensive manner. Eventually, when the line of disembarking men had slowed to a dribble, he hefted his knapsack and walked down to the gangway. No one examined his papers and he slowly followed the long snake of breathless men up the hill to the train alongside the station platform. The locomotive's whistle hooted impatiently and he crammed himself in with the rest.

They passed through a countryside at peace, utterly devoid of shell holes or craters, no ruined villages, barbed wire or ghostly manors. England ignored them as they passed by, totally unaware of their existence. Somewhere ahead lay warmth and comfort, hope and reunion, but not here, not here in the empty windows of dark, unlit houses that passed quickly out of sight as they rolled sedately onwards. This was England, 'Blighty', the long, lonely hours of yearning now a reality, but they were all too tired to care.

A young fresh-faced lieutenant, his uniform still bearing heavy traces of mud, sat by the door of the compartment smoking incessantly, his shoulders shaking constantly as if with the ague. Staring ahead with an unseeing gaze, his free hand tap-tap-tapped against his Sam Browne belt. In a window seat, a red-tabbed colonel twisted and angrily gestured at the large NO SMOKING sign on the window but the young man pointedly ignored him, staring fixedly ahead as he dragged in huge lungfuls of smoke, exhaling noisily.

At last the rolling fields and forlorn, empty trees began to peter out. A straggle of buildings took shape and began to grow in size and depth, the empty streets stretching out in front of them. As the minutes passed, the streets on either side grew larger and denser. More train tracks appeared, running alongside then dashing off at a tangent, chasing them as they *click-clacked* their way towards the epi-centre of the sprawling metropolis that was London. The smell of burning coal drifted through the carriage and several men coughed as the acrid fumes caressed the back of their throats. Bags were swung down as men stood up to stretch and await the moment the train stopped.

They clanked over The Thames and entered the first of several tunnels. More smoke entered the carriage causing paroxysms of further coughing. Bursting out into the daylight they clattered remorselessly on but all of them felt the moment the train began to decelerate as the long platform that signalled their arrival in Victoria Station hove into view. Slowing down to a crawl the engine let out a plaintive whistle as it came to a juddering stop in a cloud of wet, billowing steam.

Rising stiffly, Charteris waited before grabbing hold of his knapsack and following his fellow passengers. He swung down onto the platform and looked round. The great concourse was tightly packed with people, some surging forward to greet loved ones they had glimpsed in the crowd. On the other side of the track a wall of uniforms stood tightly packed, glowering jealously in their direction and he realised these must be men returning from leave.

He stood watching the scenes before him, awkwardly aware that no one would be here to greet him. Looking to his left he saw a loose collection of young women, elegantly dressed, surveying the new arrivals. As he watched, one of them approached the young lieutenant who had shared his carriage and after a brief conversation the two walked off towards the exit together. Even at this distance Charteris could see the way the boy's body shook and a fleeting twinge of pity passed through him before he pondered what to do next.

Walking in the direction the couple had taken he passed through the exit to stand on the street. A pretty girl wandered towards him, her face alight with expectation but at his shake of the head she smiled gravely at him and retreated into the main part of the station, leaving him alone again. Ten yards or so down the ramp, among the waiting horse-drawn hackney carriages, a single motor car stood, a taxi sign fixed to its roof. The driver, a short, dark-haired individual in a large, grey coat and cap, stood puffing on a battered pipe as Charteris approached.

'How much to go to Peckham?' he enquired.

'Peckham? I reckon that'll be a few bob, mate. It's a way from here an' I've got me lunch to consider.'

'Look, how does five shillings sound?' Charteris asked desperately. It was the only motor taxi and he could see a few more people eyeing the driver up as they contemplated making him an offer. Seeing them, the driver knocked the contents of his pipe out on the wall and turned to Charteris abruptly

'Come on then mate, make a move if you wants to go. Do you think I've got all bleedin' day? Where abouts in Peckham does you want then?'

Relieved, Charteris opened the back door and jumped in before answering him. 'Adys Road. Do you know it?'

The cabbie gave him a look. 'Are you joking mate? Course I knows where Adys Road is. What do you take me for, a bleedin' stevedore?' He slammed Chateris's door shut and walked round to the front of the car to turn the starting handle. A quick twist and the engine burst into life. Climbing into the front seat he took hold of the steering wheel and with a crunch engaged a gear, eased off the parking brake and edged out into the sparse traffic.

Motor cars and buses intermingled with horse-drawn vehicles, all vying for space in the narrow streets. Omnibuses passed them, packed with people on their way to work. Charteris noticed groups of young girls, clad in overalls, with bright yellow faces, walking arm in arm down the streets and realised they must be involved in the munitions industries. The girls were known as 'canaries' because the chemicals and explosives they came into contact with in the shell factories stained their arms and faces. The war had certainly brought about a change in attitude to women working, he mused; they were now doing the skilled jobs that had always been in the male domain. The driver concentrated on threading his way through the crowds, cursing roundly as people suddenly running out in front of him blocked his progress from time to time.

Charteris's excitement grew as the streets began to take on a familiar aspect. He had deliberately forced all thoughts of Lucille from his mind on the journey but now there was so much to discuss and his impatience grew as they turned in to a road of bay-fronted, Victorian houses.

'Stop! Stop!' he cried and the cabbie pulled up abruptly. He opened the door and rose up from the seat. He stood on the corner of the street, next to a newsagent shop he recognised as Miller's, only a short walk from his front door. He fumbled in his pocket to find the change to pay the cabbie but the man had left his cab and put a restraining hand on Neville's shoulder.

'Nah, you keep it mate, ' he said softly, 'this one's on me.' He turned to go but Neville grabbed his arm.

'You must let me pay you, we made a bargain, remember.'

The cabbie looked at him intently before replying simply. 'You have this one on me. Me son Harry, sir, Middlesex regiment, he was killed at Le Cateau last year. He was only a boy, nineteen years old. His mum hasn't got over it yet. Never will.' He moved sadly away and got back into the front of the cab. The gears crunched again and he moved off, waving to Charteris as he drove away.

Charteris stood on the pavement and watched as the cab drove away. It wasn't that cold, wrapped up as he was in his Mackintosh, but he shivered as an empty feeling touched his soul. He looked up and found himself outside the blue door he recognised as theirs and his breathing became shallow and ragged as he fumbled for the house key he had taken from his knapsack in the taxi and placed in his trouser pocket for safety. The lock turned smoothly and at his pressure the door opened silently and he stepped into the cool familiar interior of the hallway.

He opened his mouth to shout a greeting as he took off his coat but the sounds died in his throat as his eyes became accustomed to the change in the light within the hallway and he found them drawn to an object on the bottom of the stairs in front of him. Soundlessly dropping his coat to the floor he walked over quietly and looked down uncomprehendingly. A woman's black silk robe lay on the first stair, carelessly discarded in a crumpled heap. His eyes slowly moved upwards. His heart pounding now in his chest, his breath coming in short gasps, he recognised a black silk stocking draped provocatively halfway up the stairs and as he stared he could see its twin lying further up. Slowly, soundlessly, not wanting to, he ascended the stairs as if in a dream, his arm resting on the polished banister rail for support.

He arrived at the top and stood quietly, hardly daring to breathe as he stared across the corridor to the room on the far side. The main bedroom, *their* room was there, and coming from it were the sort of sounds that in all eternity he had never thought he would hear. The sounds of two people engaged in noisy, uninhibited lovemaking. Lucille, his wife Lucille, and God knows who.

He started forward and nearly overbalanced as his boot caught up in an item on the carpet beneath him. A dark pair of men's suit trousers, cheap trousers, the kind a senior partner in a firm of solicitors would wear, he noted almost absent-mindedly, lay entwined around his left foot, the braces spread over both his feet. He kicked angrily, impatiently, at the braces. They slid off his feet and, pushing the trousers to one side, he advanced to the door of the room. It was partially open and he pushed it gently, enough for it to move a few inches more and allow him to look through the crack provided by the door's hinges and into the room.

His wife lay across the bed, unashamedly naked, her full breasts heaving as she reached up for the half-dressed man towering over her. Her head thrown back, the rich extravagant tresses of her dark hair falling off the side of the bed, she arched her back and drew her bare legs up, drumming them into the back of her lover, his face unseen as he bent down. Reaching for him, pinning him to her belly. He responded by kneading her breasts energetically as he began thrusting rhythmically into her, his white collarless shirt falling open as he moved across her.

'Yes! Yes! Oh God, Arnold darling, yes!' she moved with him as she squealed, her body writhing as she succumbed to his practised lovemaking, eyes wide and unseeing.

Charteris choked, a small sudden noise, but the two people on the other side of the door were too engrossed in each other to notice the alien sound. His limbs were like jelly as he continued to watch, desperately trying to tear his eyes away from the sight. Dry-mouthed he moved to turn away but his legs betrayed him. With an immense effort he fell back against the wall. The lovers were oblivious to him, their coupling becoming more frenetic.

Breathing hard with his mouth wide open, his right hand brushed unconsciously against his service revolver's holster. The idea fled as soon as it had entered his mind and he tore himself from the wall's support to stand upright once more. With faltering steps he retraced his path to the top of the stairs and hesitated momentarily on the top stair. From the bedroom the noises continued unabated, his wife's cries now being answered by the hoarse grunting sounds of her beau. Sickened, Charteris walked, white-faced, slowly down the stairs. His knapsack lay next to his Mackintosh where he'd dropped them and he bent down and lifted them both up.

He turned the doorknob and opened the front door. A gust of icy air greeted him and he shivered as the draught took him unawares. Gently closing the door behind him he paused to don his coat and sling his knapsack over his shoulder. His mind was reeling and he felt the urge to run at the greatest speed he could manage, anywhere, to somewhere he could fathom out the great leap in a different direction his life had just taken. He turned and walked away from the house, reversing the steps he had taken only ten minutes before.

Unseeing, he found himself once more at the corner of the road, opposite the newsagent. The door was now open and a white-aproned, middle-aged man emerged, to begin laying out the day's news on the billboards he was setting out in front of the shop. He nodded at Charteris but received no response. Shrugging, he returned into the shop and left Charteris standing there, head slumped as the scenes he had witnessed behind him played endlessly through his mind. A sharp object in his trouser pocket dug into his thigh and he reached inside and withdrew his house key. He looked down at it a second, frowning, then walked slowly over to the kerb and carefully dropped the key into the drain on the apex of the corner. Pausing for a moment he wrenched the gold band off the finger of his left hand and in a second it had followed the house key into the depths of the drain.

Lips pursed, he made his way back down the road, not caring where his feet took him, the last, windblown leaves from autumn scrunching under his boots. Blindly he marched on, ignoring the curious stares from passers-by. Lucille, the first time they met. Her shy smile, the way she walked, laughed, filled his world totally from the time they first kissed to their wedding day. The first time they had made love, shyly, amateurishly, fumbling frantically with each other once they were alone. Their dreams, hopes, future. Gone, all gone now. Wiped out in a moment, ground to dust in a manner that he could still taste at the back of his throat.

He emerged from his thoughts to find himself sitting on a rough-hewn bench on the Goose Green, streets away, knapsack at his feet. He looked at his wristwatch and was surprised to see the hands read three fifty-five. He must have been sitting there for hours but the time had been a complete blank.

A sound to his right made him turn abruptly. A young woman, her face in shadow, was watching him gravely. As he stared at her she spoke in a low, concerned voice and he had to strain to catch the words.

'I say, are you all right? It's just that you've been sat here for some time. I saw you from my upstairs window hours ago and I was beginning to worry that you were, oh I don't know, not well. You're not ill are you?'

'Thank you,' he replied tiredly. 'No I'm fine. Really I am. I should be getting along now.'

She looked down at him again and noticed for the first time how weary and strained he looked. He made to rise and she stepped forward, lifting her hand in a gesture of restraint.

'Please, hear me out. You look as though you could do with a hot cup of tea, captain. I know this may sound forward of me but would you like to accompany me?' She gestured vaguely, pointing to the row of houses bordering the Green. 'My house is not far, over there, on East Dulwich Street, and you can sit in the warmth for a while before going on your way.'

He glanced up at her as she spoke. He saw an elfin face framed by a set of golden curls. She stood just over five feet he reckoned, slim, in her mid-twenties with a well-defined figure under the black skirt he could see under her coat. Her face was drawn though, her blue eyes shadowed as one who had a great sadness inside, as if a once-bright light had dimmed and gone out. A mirror of his own feelings, somehow..

'You seem to know something about army ranks,' he said, at a loss as to how to answer her request. 'Is your husband a serving man?' He glanced at the thin gold band on the finger of her left hand as he spoke.

'He was. But not any more,' she answered abruptly, her right hand covering the left, hiding the evidence of her status from his questioning gaze. 'It won't take a minute to boil the kettle. Now would you like that cup of tea? I dare say I could throw in a sandwich too and I would point out, captain, that if you stay out here much longer you'll catch your death of cold. If you want to accompany me I'd rather you do it now before more curtains start to twitch.'

Her change of subject threw him momentarily and he scrambled to regain his train of thought. He thought of the conditions in the trenches he had just left and smiled at her innocent mention of the cold, and death. Unconsciously his head nodded at the mention of a hot drink. She had already begun to walk away towards the houses she had pointed to earlier and he realised just how hungry he was, so he picked up his knapsack and followed her obediently.

They walked in silence, her slow, sedate pace being matched by his own. It took only a minute or so before she arrived at a large, brick-faced house with bay windows that almost mirrored the one he had left earlier in the day. Walking down the short path and opening the door she stepped inside. The hallway smelled of roses, a soft aromatic smell that also filled the kitchen at the far end, where he joined her. She turned to face him, a questioning look on her face. When he gazed back, unspeaking, awkward in her presence, she moved past him and placed a large kettle on the gas range against the far wall and, fiddling with the gas knob, lit the ring with a long splinter that she first lit from a match. The gas lit with a small *woomph!* and she moved the kettle over the ring. That done she turned to face him once more and held a small, slender hand out before speaking in an honest, forthright manner.

'I'm sorry, we haven't been properly introduced. I'm Matilda Fairley, Tillie to my friends, and in case you were wondering, I am not in the habit of bringing strange men into my house, captain. Even if they are officers in His Majesty's Forces. You looked so, so forlorn out there that I had to come over and see if you were all right. Besides, you don't look like a criminal. Are you?'

She saw before her a good-looking, exhausted young man who was obviously under great strain. Her observant eyes had already noticed the white mark on his left hand where a wedding ring had been, but she said nothing and waited for him to speak.

Grasping her hand he answered her in a shaky tone. 'Thanks awfully but you mustn't worry, I really am fine you know. I'll have that cup of tea and then be on my way. I'm Neville, Captain Neville Charteris, 19th Lancashires. I came over from France today on the leave boat, just got into London this morning.'

Her hand was cool to the touch and he held it for a brief second before gently letting it go.

'Please, take a seat through there, I know you must be tired.' She pointed to an archway to his right. 'I'll be through when the tea is ready.' He obeyed, and found himself in a small drawing-room with a window looking out to the front of the house. Relaxing into a cold, dark, leather sofa he twisted round to take stock while his hostess busied herself in the other room. There was the usual array of potted plants on a nest of small tables. On the wall above the tiled fireplace, a photograph of a solemn youth, dressed in the uniform of a subaltern, stared down.

'A family member?' he asked of her as she entered bearing a tray filled with a teapot, cups and a plate with some sliced cake on it. She had taken off the dark coat and stood before him clad in a high-collared, white lace blouse and long, flowing black skirt. She looked at him searchingly before glancing at the photograph and then back at him with an expression of quiet pain on her face.

'My late husband,' she replied simply.

'I'm sorry, I shouldn't have asked.' Charteris felt crushed by her words as he tried to make amends.

'No, no, Captain Charteris, it's all right. You weren't to know. Arthur got caught up in the excitement last August when all his old chums joined up after war was declared and he enlisted immediately. We were married in the first week of September and I never saw him again, as he returned to his regiment after our honeymoon. He begged the War Office to allow him to go over to France in October, shortly after being commissioned, and he was killed just a week after he landed there. I was a widow before I knew what being a wife meant. It's strange you know, since Arthur was killed, all I seem to know are dead people. Every week one hears of some other friend or acquaintance being killed in the frightfulness that's going on over there.' She spoke with no trace of rancour but Charteris again saw a expression of pain pass over her face as she explained and, great as his own misery was, he felt the enormous, unspoken sadness within her

An awkward silence descended, broken only by the loud ticking of the clock on the mantelpiece. She broke it by passing him a cup of tea, followed by a slice of cake. They ate in silence and when finished she reached over and poured him another cup, this time pushing the jug of milk and a sugar bowl in his direction. He spooned several large quantities of sugar into the cup and caught her faint smile as he raised it cup to his lips.

'I'll be open with you, Captain Charteris. Something tells me you have no place to stay. Am I wrong?'

He started at her directness. Looking at her, frantically trying to frame an answer, he knew it was fruitless to lie. He thought to make up a story of visiting relatives only to find them out but realised that stood no chance of being believed. Instead, he nodded weakly as he finished the tea. It was the first food or drink he'd had that day and for the first time he was beginning to feel a trifle better. Besides, the young, pretty woman sitting across the room from him did not look like one who could be lied to so easily. What could he say? That he was a cuckold, newly home from the Front to find another man in his bed?

'Look, I don't know what trouble you find yourself in, captain. How long do you have until you have to return?' she asked bluntly.

'Two days. I must be on the night boat back to France on Sunday.'

'In that case, why don't you stay here? No, please don't shake your head! It's not what you think. I shall make a bed up for you on the sofa. You can't wander the streets for the next two days until you have to return to your regiment and it's too late in the evening now to be looking for a hotel room. If indeed they'll take you, looking like that. Stay for tonight and we'll see what tomorrow brings. At least you'll be warm here. What do you say?'

She cocked her head to one side and glanced over to where he sat, waiting for him to answer. He began to remonstrate but all of a sudden he realised how utterly exhausted he was. The events of the morning had also taken their toll so all he could do was nod weakly in her direction.

'Good!' she exclaimed, 'That's decided then. Please stay seated, I won't be a moment.' Leaning forward she lifted the tray and took it back into the kitchen. He heard a door open and the sound of her ascending the stairs. Minutes later she returned, bearing some blankets and a pillow which she deposited at his feet. 'These should help you get a good night's sleep,' she indicated, 'And if you will excuse me for a few moments there is one more thing I need to attend to.' With that she moved back through the open door behind her and shortly he heard her ascend the stairs again. Seconds later he heard another sound, the sound of running water. After a short while she returned again and stood in the doorway, looking at him.

An embarrassed look flitted across her brow as she addressed him. 'I hope you don't feel offended, captain, but I've taken the liberty of drawing you a bath. You *do* need a bath!' There are clean towels in the bathroom and I've also left some of my late husband's clothes for you to change into. You seem about the same size as Arthur. I'm sorry, as Arthur was...' she corrected herself lamely.

It was Charteris's turn to feel embarrassed. 'You're too kind...' he started to say but she interrupted him swiftly.

'Please, don't thank me. You must be feeling tired and a hot bath will do you the power of good. The bathroom is at the top of the stairs so I would go now if I were you, before the water grows cold.' He began to rise from the seat when she spoke again. 'If you could leave your clothes outside the door I'll see that they get cleaned and laundered. I shall be out all day tomorrow, my mother isn't well so I have to visit her. I'll drop your soiled clothes off on my way and pick them up again on my return. There's a water closet out in the back should you require it. Lock the back door before you retire if you go out. And put the lights out when you're finished downstairs if you could. Now, after all those orders I shall leave you in peace. Please forgive me but I have some letters to write so I'll take a tray to my room and retire for the night. I'll leave a sandwich in the kitchen for you should you feel hungry later on. Until tomorrow then, Captain Charteris. Goodnight.' With that, she turned and was gone. A short time later he heard her footsteps on the stairs once more and the house fell silent.

He felt uncomfortable at her sudden departure and the thought crossed his mind that it might have something to do with his being in uniform and her dead husband. Dismissing the dark thought from his mind he bent down and began to untie his boots. Tugging them off he dropped them by the side of the sofa and ascended the stairs. He gained the top of the landing and turned to his right, in time to see the door at the far end of the corridor close firmly as she entered her bedroom. To his left a wet smell of steam leaked out from the open door and he walked into the bathroom and stared down at the wrought-iron, white-enamelled bath it contained. The bath was three-quarters full with steaming, hot water, smelling of lavender and jasmine. He undressed quickly, peeling off his dirty clothes, grimacing as the earthy, sweaty smell of them.

The temperature of the water was slightly on the hot side but he didn't hesitate. Grabbing the sides of the bath he lifted his legs over its rim and slid down, causing a tidal wave of scummy water to lap over the end and splash onto the tiled floor. He gasped as the hot water enveloped him but his guilty feelings at making such a mess lasted only seconds as he luxuriated in the feel of the water encasing him.

The water enveloped him like a second skin and he turned and twisted to feel its effects on his entire body. A soap dish on the wall just above him caught his attention and he reached up and grasped the pink bar of soap it contained. It smelled light and feminine with a delicate perfume and he inhaled deeply before dipping it into the now-filthy water and rubbing it vigorously over his body. It lathered well and soon he felt clean and refreshed.

He could of lain there for a long, long time but the water gradually cooled and he suddenly became aware of how cold he was feeling. On a chair in the corner were two large, white bath towels, neatly folded. Putting a foot over the side he vaulted out, made his way over to them, and towelled himself vigorously as the bath emptied. Hidden under the towels was a small pile of clothing and he examined the clothes reflectively as he dried himself. She had left him a green cotton shirt, some underwear, clean socks and a pair of dark, worsted trousers. The trousers were a bit tight but the length was not too bad. The shirt fitted him loosely, the sleeves not quite reaching the ends of his bony wrists, and he tucked it in before donning the socks and stepping quietly out of the bathroom. Turning, he descended the stairs and re-entered the drawing-room.

He took hold of the blankets she had brought down earlier and lay down on the sofa. The leather was cold and hard to the touch and he moved around in a vain attempt to lie in a comfortable position. Jumping up he switched off the light as she'd commanded and lay down again. Tiredness washed over him and he quickly sank into a troubled sleep.

He spent a long, uncomfortable night, once he had finally managed, restlessly, to fall into a fitful, troubled sleep in which Lucille appeared. She wore an evil, malign expression on her face as she loomed over him, a shadowy male figure lurking threateningly behind her, fuzzily out of focus. He gave a small cry and woke up, bathed in sweat. Disorientated for a while he looked wildly round before realising where he was. Dizzy, his head throbbing painfully, he lay back down and testily rearranged the blankets before dropping off for the second time. He had been asleep for only half an hour when the drawing-room door quietly opened. Tillie Fairley stood there for a moment, clad in a lace night robe, staring down at him with a look of compassion on her concerned face before quietly closing the door and ascending the stairs back to her own room.

He slept deeply and was awakened by the sound of her drawing back the heavy brocade curtains. 'Good morning, captain!' she called gaily, 'there's tea made and a rack of toast in the kitchen for you.' He looked up blearily and saw her, framed in the light from the window, her hair pinned up, dressed in a peach-coloured blouse and long grey dress. It accentuated her loveliness but before he could speak she noticed his look and gestured at her clothing.

'It's been over a year now, since Arthur was killed. Long enough, I feel, to have worn widow's weeds. Perhaps your coming here has made me see that. I have your clothes here so I must dash to make sure Benjamin's clean these today. Take care, I've laid some food out for you so you shouldn't starve. I'll be back tonight.' With that she spun on her heels and took hold of her coat with her free hand before he could respond. He heard the front door open and close and the house was quiet again.

He lay there, cocooned in the blankets she'd given him, and stretched luxuri-ously, his feet hanging over the side of the sofa. Rising stiffly while he pondered on this new direction his life was taking, he scratched his itching ribs, pushed his feet into his boots with an effort and wandered through into the kitchen, his laces flap-ping. The toast rack sat atop the kitchen range with a steaming teapot beside it. She had been kind enough to leave a small jar of marmalade with the butter and he ate ravenously as he drank the tea.

Wiping the crumbs from his face he returned to the drawing-room and delved into his knapsack to find the small wash kit he had packed the day before. Pulling it free he walked back into the kitchen and left it by the sink as he opened the back door to find the water closet she had mentioned. Once back in the kitchen he shaved coarsely, using soap and a sense of touch in lieu of a mirror. He nicked himself a few times but the resultant splash of cologne from the bottle he found buried in the depths of the wash kit made him feel a lot more refreshed and ready for the day ahead.

The thought of returning to Adys Road to confront Lucille entered his mind but he dismissed the idea almost immediately. That part of his life was over, her betrayal had left no way back for them to go and for the moment he pushed all thoughts of her into a recess in the back of his brain as he pondered his next move. He stepped over to the fireplace and stared at the photograph of the young officer above it. The metal badges on his tunic identified Arthur Fairley's regiment as the Coldstream Guards. Always to the front of the action it was no wonder that Tillie Fairley's husband had been killed so early in his service with the Guards. The boy/man's lidded eyes seemed to stare deep into his soul and he became uncom-fortable under the dead man's gaze. A thought of going upstairs suddenly crossed his mind and before he could banish it he found himself ascending.

The doors on either side of the corridor that stretched away in front of him frowned their disapproval but he disregarded their forbidding presence and walked slowly, soundlessly, along the heavy carpet until he arrived at the other end, outside the door he had marked as his hostess's room. Hesitantly, he took hold of the door-knob, turned it and pushed the door open.

It swung easily under his pressure. He took a faltering step inside and stopped. It was a pretty room, a woman's room, with light floral curtains in a pinkish hue that framed the window to his right. A large double bed with a coloured eiderdown filled the room and on the small bedside table he could see a china wash basin in the same colours as the curtains. His hand brushed against something light and soft and he looked down to see it was a white lace night robe hanging on the back of the door. As his hand briefly touched the flimsy material his nostrils caught the sudden, soft smell of her fragrance and he breathed it in deeply.

Turning to his left he gasped in surprise. Hanging in front of him, on a clothes hanger that was hooked in the top lip of a small wardrobe standing against the far wall was a full dress uniform of the Coldstream Guards. The scarlet jacket with its row of shining buttons glared at him accusingly, as if demanding to know what business he had invading the sanctity of the room, and he retreated red-faced in shame.

Once downstairs again, abashed now, he explored the lower part of the house. It was fairly large and well-furnished: another drawing-room lay at the end of the long corridor but when he opened the door it became apparent by its musty smell that it had not been used for some time. A damp smell filled the room and he closed the door quickly. It was also obvious that Matilda Fairley did not employ any servants to help her in the house, but from choice or hardship on her part he could not tell.

A bookcase stood at the far end of the hall and he examined its contents with an enquiring eye. He knew none of the titles, but picking one at random he retired back into the drawing-room and lay down again on the sofa. Pulling the blankets close to him he opened the book and began to read. His choice was a travel book on the ancient city of Petra, in the Middle East, and he grimaced.

The day passed slowly. Once he rose to drink a cup of cold tea he drained from the pot she had made that morning, a trick he had learned assiduously in the trenches. His thirst satisfied, he backtracked and lay down once more. The book fell to the floor and he ignored it as he lay on his back, snoring loudly.

This was how she found him when she returned that evening, as the night was turning colder. 'Goodness me! Could you not light the fire yourself, or do your men do everything for you Captain Charteris?' she exclaimed in mock annoyance, entering the room as she divested herself of her coat. 'I have your uniform here, all cleaned, for you. I'm afraid the socks didn't make it, though. According to Mr Benjamin they simply disintegrated when he put them in the boiler.' She giggled, a light, girlish giggle. 'Never mind, I'll put some of Arthur's out for you and you can put them with your other clothes.' She looked at him appraisingly, dressed as he was in her late husband's clothes, until he began to feel uncomfortable. 'Hmn. Not too bad a fit.' Charteris felt a warm flush cross his face. 'Now then, let me see to this.'

Ignoring his weak protestations she rolled up her sleeves and set about lighting the fire in the cold hearth. Within minutes a warmth spread through the room as the fire caught, orange flames flickering, making shadows dance on the far wall. Disappearing into the kitchen the noise of food being prepared told him of supper being made and shortly afterwards a delicious smell wafted through the open door.

During the evening that followed she changed strangely. She became suddenly distant, as if a switch had been thrown to extinguish any warmth that had sprung up between them. He had thought of trying to explain his situation, how he had found his wife in the arms of another man, which had led to his sitting so forlornly on the bench, but Matilda Fairley's sudden change in attitude confused him and he remained quiet. After clearing away the dishes once they'd both eaten, a meal that was peppered with some desultory small talk, she returned to the drawing-room to quietly bid him goodnight and once again he heard her footsteps as she ascended the stairs.

He switched the light off, moved over to the sofa, and lay down with his hands behind his head as he contemplated the situation he found himself in. He had thought of enquiring after her mother as they ate but the sudden change in her demeanour had unnerved him so he had eaten quietly with the words unspoken. Although she had laughed on seeing him in the ill-fitting clothes, he sensed that beneath all that she seemed lonely, with that delicate air of sadness surrounding her, and he wondered what her response would be were he to ascend the stairs and knock on her bedroom door.

A fierce disgust welled up inside him, and he rolled over onto his side and pulled the blankets more tightly to him. Christ! What was he thinking? The woman was still grieving for her dead husband and here he was, Neville Charteris, late married, cuckolded man himself, proposing to enter her boudoir like some young swain. He tossed and turned again and fell into the same disturbed sleep of the previous night. He never heard the door open nor saw her standing there for the second night running, a troubled expression on her face, framed in the dying embers of the fire as she stared down at him while he muttered inaudibly. Quietly, she closed the door behind her and the sound of her light footfalls ascending the stairs again echoed through the dark, empty house.

The next morning he was up before she rose and dressed quickly into the freshly cleaned uniform she had brought back with her. This time he had the kettle on the boil before she descended the stairs and entered the kitchen. They both looked shyly at one another, then looked away.

'It looks like you have everything in hand, captain,' she teased at length. 'While you get the breakfast ready shall I go and fetch you a newspaper? I believe it's what you army men love to read out there in France.'

'No thank you, Mrs Fairley,' he replied grimly, 'it's most kind of you but I couldn't bring myself to read any newspaper you might care to buy. In truth, the propaganda that the papers contain these days turns my stomach. Even the ordinary man in the trenches hates reporters, did you know that, for the vicious lies they spread!' He spoke with vehemence and her eyes opened wide at his savage response.

'Why? Is it really so bad over there? How can you speak of such things, Captain Charteris, when you wear the ribbon of one who has been honoured for his obvious gallantry? Are the newspaper stories that inaccurate?'

'When next you read a newspaper, Mrs Fairley, please do me the honour of ignoring what passes for the news. Instead, read the casualty lists first. They portray the real horror of what goes on across the water, far, far more eloquently than any oily reporter with a quick pen and poisonous words for those who have never been within a mile of the Front. The empty words of statesmen, armchair warriors and newspaper editors are dwarfed by the silence to be found in the cemeteries of France. As for this,' he pushed his finger forcefully against the ribbon on his chest, 'there is many a brave man who lies in an unmarked grave, unrecognised for his valour and the brave deeds he had carried out. I was one of the lucky ones and I thank God for sparing me so far, but there are far, far braver men over there. Men who face death every day with a smile on their faces and yet are never known or receive recognition for their deeds.'

She stared, white-faced and he cursed himself the cruelty he had inflicted upon her. Her of all people, she who had already paid the supreme price for the arrogance and jealousy of Man.

'What was I thinking of? Good God! What am I saying...please forgive me Mrs Fairley, I meant no disrespect. I...'

'It's all right, Captain Charteris. Neville. Please, don't apologise. It's obvious to me by the strength of your words that the horrors endured by men such as yourself bear no relation to what our politicians would have us believe. Sit here with me if you would, please, and tell me all that you can about conditions over there. It's something I've thought a lot about since being alone. As you can see, I have no one to help with the house. My needs became a lot smaller, what with Arthur gone, so I was able to dispense with the servants. Now, I would be most grateful for you to tell me all that you can.'

He was reluctant at first but she was a patient listener and before long the words tumbled from him in a torrent and she listened both entranced and with mounting horror as he described for her in simple terms the life the fighting men knew as they struggled daily for survival. Her eyes moistened as he told her quietly of the deaths of close friends and the men under him, her small hands kneading the handkerchief she carried. He spoke with little enough emotion but his words painted such a mental picture in her mind of the enormity of the struggle that she found it hard to believe him at times. Her mind reeled as he calmly recounted the happenings the battalion had endured since arriving in France, and it was only the clock striking the hour that broke the spell and brought them back to the present.

'Goodness! I must be going!' Charteris exclaimed. 'I must beg your forgiveness once more, Mrs Fairley, I've talked for far too long. I hope I didn't bore you too much with my talk of the war, you must regard me as something of a fool in that respect, I'm afraid. It's time I was on my way. I have some supplies to shop for in London before making my way back to Victoria Station and then on to Folkestone. The war won't stop for men such as myself. Generals, maybe, Captains most definitely not.'

The awkwardness that had grown between them made him more aware of how he must sound to her. 'Look, I must thank you for all you have done for me over these past few days. You took a complete stranger in and treated him most kindly. I still haven't paid you for the clothes you had cleaned for me.'

She shook her head and he continued. 'Please, you must let me. I can't begin to thank you enough...'

'Then don't, Captain Charteris. I only did what any other person seeing someone in trouble would have done. And besides, as to the cleaning, Mr Benjamin told me in no uncertain terms he would take no payment whatsoever for your uniform.'

She stood back and watched as he gathered his knapsack up, carefully closing the flap before swinging it onto his shoulders. Charteris looked down at her sitting there, gazing at him with the same grave expression on her face as when they had met, and his heart went out to her. Thoughts tumbled around in his brain as he frantically tried to put feelings into words but the emotions of the last forty-eight life-shattering hours welled up inside like a tidal wave and he remained self-consciously as silent as a tongue-tied schoolboy. All that had happened since arriving at his front door had created an enormous barrier that hopelessly prevented him from explaining his situation to the beautiful young woman in front of him. Feeling helpless he turned abruptly and opened the door to the hall.

She followed him in silence to the front door and stood watching as he walked the short path to the pavement beyond.

'God speed, Captain Neville Charteris, take care of yourself,' she cried as he adjusted the pack into a comfortable position. As she watched him walk away the sadness inside her grew as she realised that she had learnt nothing about him, apart from his name and regiment, in the two short days since she had first spotted him sitting forlornly on the bench across from her house.

Charteris looked back to answer her but when he did so she'd gone. He stood for a moment and then slowly moved away, walking towards the intersection at the bottom of the road. She watched from behind the curtain in the drawing-room until he was out of sight, before letting the curtain fall back into place.

* * * * *

CSM Frank Mason had grinned fiercely when he saw Charteris stride away from him. Mr Charteris was a good officer, much respected by his men, and would make an excellent commanding officer of any battalion. If he survived. Frank had missed him in the general mêlée at Folkestone and had just glimpsed him now as they disembarked at Victoria. No matter, he looked like he was in a bloody hurry so Frank wished him well and a good time as he looked around for assistance.

A friendly railwayman put him right and he was soon on his way to Euston Station. There, after surrendering his leave pass he was issued with a ticket for

Burnley, changing at Preston, and was informed he had forty minutes to wait. Eventually, his train was announced and he meandered over to the platform and boarded the train. A small boy sat, staring wide-eyed at Frank's stained uniform and rifle, until his mother crossly pulled him away and moved to sit further up the carriage, wrinkling her nose in disgust. Wearily, Frank sat back as the train wheezed out of Euston, clanking and clanging as the carriages were jerked forward. Some things never change, he thought. Returning heroes? Perish the thought! Where the hell did she think he'd picked up all the mud that was engrained deeply in his tunic and trousers, the parish council tip? Dismissing her from his mind he gazed eagerly out of the window as the train picked up speed and headed north.

He slept part of the way and a clattering of the rails beneath was enough to waken him as they entered Preston. The Burnley train was waiting impatiently on the other side of the platform, wreathed in smoke, so he hurried over the connecting bridge and gained a seat. Minutes later, a mournful whistle let vent its cry and they were on their way.

Frank Mason had retired from the Army as a sergeant in the reserve in May 1914, having served his country for fifteen years. Like RSM Findlay, Frank had seen action overseas and he too carried the ribbons of previous campaigns proudly on his chest. At the age of thirty-three Frank had kept the promise he had made his wife Katherine and returned to the town of their birth to make a home for her and their son, William. He had found work as a shoe salesman and though his pay was small it brought enough into the Mason household, along with Kath's wage as a cleaner, to make life comfortable.

The declaration of war in August 1914 had a shattering effect upon them. Within days the telegram arrived, ordering him to report to the depot at Carlisle. Kath had walked him to the station and watched him depart, her eyes streaming with tears as she hugged their son to her. In a few days, after drawing his kit, he had slipped back into familiar ways, his devastation at being so savagely parted from his family being compensated somewhat by swiftly regaining his old Army rank. His posting as CSM to the foundling battalion of the 19th Lancashires at Morecambe had followed shortly after. He had had one short, sweet leave with Kath and the boy before leaving for France, and since then only her letters had kept him informed as to their well-being.

Hardened soldier as he was, his eyes were wet as Burnley station hove into view and he hurriedly wiped them before anyone could see. The train slowed and came to a halt. A bored guard waved him through the barrier and he marched swiftly outside, turning up the street towards the market and his home in St James Street. It took but minutes and before long he was stood outside a familiar door. He dropped the pack and ignoring the curious stares of passers-by, rapped smartly on the weather-beaten door.

His wife opened the door and looked at him uncomprehendingly, wringing a towel in her hands as she gazed at him with a fearful expression on her face. She opened her mouth to speak and her eyes focused as she took in the stranger on her doorstep. Those crinkled brown eyes opened wide in surprise and then rapidly filled with tears as Frank spoke.

'Hey up, our lass, is the kettle on for a cuppa?'

'Frank? Frank? Oh goodness, oh me...it's really you! I thought, oh God, I thought it was a, a post boy...' Kath tried to speak but her voice faltered and her face dissolved in tears as she buried her head into the welcoming shoulder of his rough serge jacket. He held her there for a long time, murmuring soothing words into her ear as she clung on tight, fiercely refusing to let go of him as if by doing so he would disappear. At length, she disengaged herself from his warm grasp and kissed him long and hard, her tears intermingling with his. Slipping her arm around his waist she twisted to let him enter and they both walked slowly inside. Excusing herself, she swiftly ran back down the hall to close the gaping front door before running back and taking hold of him again, her fresh tears wetting his stubble once more.

The rest of the afternoon passed in a blur. After sleeping awhile on the worn sofa, Frank sat and watched as his wife made their tea. Kath's parents had taken their grandchild out for the day. William was now eight and missed his father sorely. Frank's letters brought a small comfort to close the miles between them and now they rejoiced at being together again.

At last, the door opened and William was ushered in by his grandparents. Their joy at seeing Frank home was nothing to the delight of their grandson. After breaking into floods of tears he sat on his father's lap and resisted all attempts to dislodge him, questioning him endlessly about the war and how many Germans his father had killed. Frank fielded his questions with a smile, making up stories of fierce fighting and promising to show him his rifle and bayonet in the morning.

'Are we going to the bonfire, da?' William asked him anxiously.

'Oh, William, your dad's tired, son, maybe we'll go out tomorrow.' Kath sounded exasperated as she addressed their son. 'He's just this minute stepped in the door and you want to go out.'

Frank looked at his son's expectant face. 'Come on then, you young shaver, get yerself ready and we'll all go and see them burn the Guy!' Katherine looked at her husband as he watched their son run out into the hall. She could see he was tired and appreciated what an effort he was making in walking out with them. She planted a kiss on his head and gave him a big hug as he rose from his seat. William found them like that and he grinned to see his mother smiling again.

Later, after the last ember from the bonfire had gone out and they had walked home, tired from the day's exertions and his excitement at his father being home, young William fell asleep in his father's arms and was taken upstairs to be sleepily undressed and laid in his bed. 'Dad, tell me again about the Germans...' were his last words before falling into a deep sleep.

Kath's parents eventually left them alone and Frank helped her clear the tea cups and plates into the kitchen. She looked deeply into his eyes and letting fall the pinny she had donned to serve the tea, took his hand and led him up the stairs to the bedroom. Unpinning her dark brown hair, she shook it free and kissed him hard on the mouth. They both undressed quickly and climbed into the bed. Holding each other tight they made love tenderly, like newly-found lovers. Passion spent for the moment, they clung to each other and slept entwined until the morning light peeped into the room.

Before breakfast, Kath filled a zinc bath with hot water in the front room for Frank and helped scrub the layers of grime from his body as a wide-eyed William watched. His uniform shirt and underwear were dispatched to the depths of the coal-fired boiler in the shed in the back yard and while it boiled Frank dressed himself in his old civilian clothes. His suit fitted him after a fashion, Army food having put on an inch or so around his waist, making everything tight. The shirt Kath gave him fitted him perfectly though, albeit smelling of camphor from the cupboard where it had hung these past long months.

Having dressed and eaten, the family left the house and wandered down through the town, making their way through the busy market where Kath bought fresh produce from the traders. Old friends approached and engaged Frank in conversation, shaking his hand and asking about the war's progress. Their friends were genuine enough but the questions they asked showed a lamentable ignorance of what was going on in France. He caught his wife's warning glances and answered pleasantly enough, but inside he seethed.

Kath pulled him into a side street. 'Please, Frank, try and keep your temper,' she implored.

'I *am* trying, love, but did you hear Jim there? He actually thinks we live in boarding houses each night and get a bus up to the trenches each morning! I ask you!' He shook his head and brushed past her back into the street. She hurried after him, a worried expression on her face, but he calmed enough to catch her arm and together they meandered happily along with William skipping at their heels.

Father and son sat together and ate a sandwich while Kath watched and afterwards they slept on the cracked, worn sofa together, snoring loudly, limbs entwined. She watched them sleeping together, a sad expression on her face. Her son, her life, looked so much like Frank that her heart felt as if it would burst. She dreaded the morning coming when they would have to say goodbye again. It would break William's heart, she just knew it, and a small tear broke free and rolled unheeded down her troubled face.

A knock on the door in the early evening brought her parents back into the house. Her mother took her to one side and whispered in her ear. Walking over to

Frank she looked down half-fearfully and said, 'Mum and dad have come over to let you take me out for the evening. Would you like to go over the road for a drink?'

Frank stretched and glanced over at his in-laws. He knew the reason behind their offer and was grateful for it. Rising up he reached for his cap. 'Well, don't keep me waiting, woman, go and get yer coat!' She raced away, a broad smile on her face, and he turned to thank her parents.

'No, no, our Frank,' his mother-in-law bobbed her head. 'You go and spend a bit of time together with our Kath. We'll sit here and watch William until you get back. Now go on, go and enjoy yourselves, the pair of you.'

Kath was back with her coat seconds later and together they walked down the hallway and out through the front door. 'Which one then, our lass, you choose,' Frank asked.

'Oh, I don't know, I only go out when you're with me, Frank. How about The Drover's Arms? It's just down the end of the street so we can be back home fairly quickly.'

'Right, love, The Drover's Arms it is!'

The narrow bar and the snug were starting to fill when they entered, the smoky atmosphere of cheap cigarettes and pipe tobacco causing Frank to catch his breath and choke. They found a seat easily enough in the corner of the snug and Frank returned to the bar. As the barman served him he was aware of being stared at. He turned and was confronted by the enquiring gaze of a young thick-set, heavy-jowled man, sat opposite them with two young, foolish-looking women. The women giggled loudly at something their companion said and nudged each other.

Picking the drinks up Frank returned to where Kath sat watching him anxiously. He sat down alongside her and took a deep drink from his glass. 'Frank, please, I know what you're thinking. Let's not have any trouble. Drink your pint, eh, love?'

He patted her hand reassuringly. 'It's all right, sweetheart, don't worry your pretty little head. We'll have this drink and then go elsewhere.'

They drank in silence, oblivious to the looks from the trio opposite. At length, Frank rose and made his way out to the back yard to relieve himself. On his return the two women were giggling openly and as Frank sat down he caught the sight of his wife's flame-red face, staring, looking down at something on their table by his glass. It was a single white feather.

He sat still, contemplating the feather and raised his face until he was staring directly into the sneering visage of the young man.

'Is this yours?' he enquired, gesturing at the feather.

'No, mate, I reckon as it 'appens to be yours.' The man pointed to the nearest of the women smirking next to him. 'She says it should belong to you, which is why she give it you. Asked me to ask you why you're not in uniform.'

Frank's face assumed a puzzled look. 'How's that then?' he asked.

'Seein' as how your sitting 'ere on yer arse while good men are dying over in France, mate,' the young man replied aggressively. 'What's the matter, too scared to enlist?'

'I don't see you with a uniform on either.' Frank spoke quietly, ignoring the question. His adversary bridled at his remark and made as if to rise. Picking the feather up, Frank shrugged off his wife's restraining hand and walked over to the other table. As the young man stood up, Frank dropped the feather onto the table top.

The man's eyes followed the fall of the feather and as he did so, Frank leaned over and struck him once, hard, with all his strength, flush on the chin. The man went down without a sound as if pole-axed and lay inert in a tangled heap at the foot of his chair. The two women jumped up screaming and moved over to him, bending down to tend to him. Frank was aware of Kath shouting at him as he surged forward, a red mist in front of his eyes.

'Frank! Frank! Don't! Please.'

The young man was helped, half-dazed still, to a sitting position where he sat rubbing his aching jaw. Shrugging off Kath's hand once more as she tried to hold him back, Frank stood over the man he had just felled.

'If you have any more of those feathers left, son, I'd like to take them back for my mates in the 19th Lancashires over there in France when I go back off my leave tomorrow,' he said quietly. 'And next week when I'm standing there, knee-deep in shit and water in the trenches, thinking of how I'm there doing my bit just to keep miserable toe-rags like you safe here in Burnley, maybe I could use some of them to stuff a pillow with!'

He turned, disgustedly, and took Kath's arm. Together they walked out in silence, the locals gawking at them as they passed through. Outside, Frank opened his hands in a gesture of helplessness. 'Sorry, love,' he began but Kath covered her hand with his.

'Don't apologise, Frank, I was right proud of you. He deserved everything he got. Biff! Did you see the way he fell?' She laughed out loud.

Neither of them felt like another drink so they retraced their steps back to the house. After sharing a cup of tea, her parents tactfully withdrew, leaving them alone with their son. All three sat together in the front room, William chattering as his parents talked into the darkening evening. At last, he tired, and Frank carried him upstairs to his bed. It was an emotional father who came back down the narrow stairs to sit and hold a worried Kath who had just finished scraping the dirt from his tunic as best she could.

She held him close, clinging to him fiercely, as if by doing so she could shield them both from the evils of the world. Frank sat quietly in her embrace, aware of her fears, and stroked her hair as the dying embers of the fire warmed them. When it finally spluttered into nothingness they retired to bed, holding each other tenderly as they made love.

'Come back to me, Frank,' she whispered tremulously, later, unable to shake her feelings of impending dread as they lay there replete. 'Come back to me and William. Promise? I couldn't bear it if...if...' She sobbed quietly into the crook of his arm.

He held her gently in his arms. 'Kath my sweet, you know I'll be back. Nothing can separate us, you hear me. Nothing.' Long after she had dropped into a troubled, disturbed sleep he lay there, holding her close to him, staring unseeingly into the blackness of the night. Later, easing her from him he moved over and stood up on the bedroom floor. She moaned softly in her sleep and he held his breath, but after while her breathing resumed its even pattern. He padded over to the door and, opening it softly, stood at the top of the stairs. His son's room was next to theirs and he quietly opened the door and stood looking tenderly down at William's tousled head as he slept.

When Kath awoke the next morning with a leaden heart, he was gone. Her hand brushed the wet pillow where his head had lain next to her and she realised with a feeling of wonder and overwhelming sadness that the tears on the pillow were not only her own.

That evening, Victoria Station was crowded with men returning to Folkestone and the night leave boat, together with friends and relatives who had come to see them off. It had a forced gaiety about it, the men trying to remain brave in the presence of so much sadness and tears, ragging and joking with each other and their companions. In among them all Frank Mason moved, swimming against the moving tide of humanity like a fish in a shoal of herring. People bumped and knocked him but he moved on automatically, riding the contact, staying upright as he was swept along. In the distance he recognised a lone figure looking down the line, staring intently into the blackness beyond the platform. He pushed through the crowd and made his way over to the solitary man, clad in the uniform of an officer.

'Mr Charteris! Begging your pardon, sir, did you have a good leave?'

Charteris started and turned around to meet his questioner. 'Oh, hello, CSM. Um...sort of. And yourself?'

His question was drowned out by a stentorian roar. 'Folkestone! All aboard the leave train for Folkestone! The train leaves in three minutes. Step lively there!' The bewhiskered, grizzled railwayman spat on the ground as he delivered his message and squinted down at the fob watch in his beefy right hand. Charteris shrugged wryly and glanced round for a last look

'Come on then, CSM, you heard the man, best not keep them waiting!'

14

Wednesday 10th November 1915

Weather stormy. Rain, followed by sleet in the afternoon. A Coy to billets in reserve. One OR of C Coy killed near latrines in forward trenches by sniper. Five ORs of D Coy wounded, one later dying of wounds by trench mortar fire. Our artillery responded, several good hits observed on enemy lines. One OR, Private Godley, returned to battalion having been missing since trench raid of 17 October. Being held in HQ dugout for questioning. Wiring parties out in late evening, repairing damage in front of D Coy trenches. A very welcome parcel mail arrived and was distributed.

Captain L. Carey, D Company

Walter Ramsbottom groaned softly and eased his shoulders up, vainly trying to encourage the muscles to relax and give him some relief from the tension afflicting him. Tiredly he wiped his hand across his eyes, eyes that were becoming more and more strained in the yellowish light of the oil lamp that illuminated his dugout. Christ! He was tired, a few hours last night to complement the two or three he had gained the night before had done nothing for his physical, never mind mental, state.

The paperwork he had been trying to avoid had left a mountain in front of him. He'd noticed the Old Man frowning at it as he'd made one of his fleeting visits earlier in the day. An hour or so of busy writing had brought the level down slightly but if he could have a good sleep tonight he'd give it a good going over tomorrow and try to sort the rest out. He smiled to himself as he thought of the Germans being kind enough to allow him to catch up on his sleep. Fat chance of that happening! Still, you never knew. Oh God, let him be granted some leave soon. Please. Before he went completely mad.

Besides which, sleet was falling pretty grimly out there now and he preferred to stay in the dry rather than splash his way along the glutinous-bottomed trenches, getting soaked in the process, only to be told by some young indignant subaltern that 'he' was 'handling things, thank you very much, sir'. A rat squealed under his foot and he aimed a bad-tempered kick at it half-blindly. He failed to connect and made a mental note to have a word with Evans about the number of rats in the vicinity of the dugout. Pesky things were everywhere and it would be up to Evans, never mind his ill-grace, to sort things out.

He reached over for the whisky bottle on top of the shelf in front of him. A tot to ease his pain would come in very handy now, just see if it wouldn't. His hand was on the neck of the bottle when a loud cough broke into his reverie from outside the dugout.

'Begging your pardon sir, would you have a moment?'

'Yes! All right. Wait a second and I'll be out.' Reluctantly pushing the bottle firmly back on the shelf he heaved himself out of the battered, wicker chair. Pushing aside the gas curtain that was the only thing affording him any kind of privacy, he climbed up the wooden steps and out into the daylight.

His eyes took a few seconds to adjust and when they did he found himself looking at the slightly embarrassed figure of Menzies, the duty orderly corporal.

'Sorry to bother you sir,' he said, 'but the colonel requests your presence at HQ. Now, if you wouldn't mind, sir. I got the idea it was kind of important.'

Calming down at the air of suppressed urgency in the man's demeanour, Walter Ramsbottom sought to reassure the NCO peering anxiously at him. 'What's it this time? No, don't tell me, I can guess. He's lost his pipe again?'

They both laughed but when they'd finished, the corporal's face took on a sombre expression. 'No, I'm afraid it's a bit more serious than that, sir. They've brought back young Godley, sir. He's not dead after all!'

'Godley? Wasn't he one of the chaps that went missing after the trench raid last month? And "they've" brought him back to us? Who are "they" for God's sake? Where has he been all this time?'

Menzies nodded dumbly to the first question before answering the major. 'That's him sir. Godley never come back with the rest of the lads from the Jerry trenches. I don't know exactly where he's been, sir, but the Provost Marshall's people from Bethune brought him back about an hour ago. Seems he might have been hiding over there all this time. It's best if you come with me now, sir, and the colonel might be able to answer more of your questions.'

'Lead on, let's go and get to the bottom of all this.'

Crouching, they both made their way down the muddy trench, squelching their way with difficulty in the cold, thin, sleet that was falling more persistently. By the time they had reached the HQ dugout both men were freezing, despite the layers of clothing they wore. Stepping carefully down the short flight of steps and squeezing into the dugout they became aware of just how crowded it was. Besides a harassed-looking Colonel Snaith and the battalion adjutant the dugout was filled by the bulk of two large men whose brassards identified them as being part of the Provost Marshall's staff. Huddled next to them against the stove, shivering in a suit of thin civilian clothing, sat the tired figure of Private 'Boy' Godley.

Last seen on the evening of the abortive trench raid on the Ram's Horn, Godley wore a collarless striped shirt under a grubby pinstriped suit. Ramsbottom noticed he still had on his feet his Army issue boots. A dark civilian coat lay crumpled on the floor at Godley's feet as he tried to gain some warmth from the spluttering stove.

'Now look here, Sergeant Horrison...' Snaith was saying as they entered. 'Now, you say you have orders to bring Private Godley back to the battalion for investigations to be made as to his disappearance from the line. And that he was found in civilian clothes in Bethune two days ago? Just what I am supposed to do with the chap?'

'Sir, ' Sergeant Hobson replied smoothly, ignoring the mispronunciation of his name as he answered the colonel. 'I think you will find it all there in the envelope I have brought with me. My orders were to deliver the prisoner to you personally and to let you inform Brigade as to the results of your investigation. And of whatever charges may be brought out of that investigation,' he added darkly.

Snaith ignored him for the moment as he recognised Major Ramsbottom. 'Ah, Walter, thank God you're here. You and Major Roberts here take charge of this matter will you, while I go and speak to Brigade.' Motioning for a pleased-looking Evans to follow, the two men swiftly exited the dugout, leaving Walter Ramsbottom to face the others. Ramsbottom extended his hand towards the patiently waiting sergeant.

'Now then, sergeant, if you would kindly show me where to sign, I'll get you and your corporal here on your way. Many thanks for bringing Private Godley back to us. We'll take it from here.'

Sergeant Hobson laid a brown official-looking envelope on the desk. Ramsbottom carefully and neatly appended his signature on the line indicated. Swiftly pocketing the papers and then unlocking the handcuffs binding Godley and his escort together, Sergeant Hobson stepped back. Murmuring a faint 'Thank you, sir, ' and 'Good luck, chum,' in Godley's direction he and his corporal mounted the steps of the dugout and made their way outside.

As their retreating footsteps echoed dimly, Walter replaced his pen in it's pocket and looked over to where Godley sat quietly waiting, watching him with a calm expression on his face. Walking over and sitting down next to him he said gently, 'Look here, Godley, what's all this about? Where have you been all this time?' Before Godley could answer him, he heard a faint noise and turned to see Major Roberts staring at him, a strained expression on his face.

'Walter,' the adjutant began. 'I think you'd better get one of the NCOs in here right away. If Private Godley is going to tell us anything it had better be written down. In case it's required as evidence, you understand.'

'My apologies, David, you're perfectly correct,' he replied. 'You couldn't get one of the men outside to send for RSM Findlay, could you?'

Before Roberts could react, a noise was heard from outside and a figure pushed aside the curtain and entered.

'Look here sir,' Second-Lieutenant Elliot held out a sheaf of papers in his hand. His face, Walter noticed, was still marked by the fresh scars around his nose and cheeks. 'I've brought the daily ammunition expenditure sheets for the last two weeks as ordered by the CO only to be told he's absent. What am I...' he was cut off by Ramsbottom's upraised hand.

'Thank you, Elliot, just put them on the desk over there and I'll make sure the colonel sees them when he returns.'

'But I...' Elliot rejoined and Ramsbottom raised his voice sharply at the subaltern's insistent tone.

'I said thank you! Now , if you don't mind, there is a more urgent matter needing my attention right now, so If you would be so good as to leave the papers as I asked, the colonel will read them on his return. Good day Mr Elliot!'

Sullenly, the young officer flung down the papers he was holding on top of the desk and prepared to leave. It was then that he saw for the first time the silent figure sitting in the corner by the stove and his countenance changed dramatically.

'You!' he breathed, staring directly at Private Godley. 'Good God, it's you!' He wheeled round to face the major. 'Sir,' he expostulated, 'what is *he* doing here?'

Major Ramsbottom's face mirrored his puzzlement as he looked from one man to the other. Godley continued to sit there serenely, unmoving at the officer's heated intervention, a fact which only served to enrage Elliot further.

'Sir, I must protest in the most strongest of terms at this man sitting here! I wish to have him arrested immediately.'

Ramsbottom looked at him in amazement. 'Mr Elliot, calm down and tell me just what is your point.'

The exasperation in his voice caused Elliot to pause dramatically before pointing a quivering finger in the direction of Godley.

'This is the man who assaulted me in the trenches last month, sir, breaking my nose after he hit me in the face with a rifle during my attempts to regroup the men under my command. He attacked me with no provocation after I had given him a direct order, sir. I wish to bring charges against this man and demand that you arrest him now! Immediately!'

Ramsbottom's mind reeled as he tried to take in the accusations the young officer in front of him had voiced. There had been an investigation into the complaint made by Elliot on his return from the raid. As he had been unable to recognise his assailant from any of the survivors who had made it back from the German trenches, the matter had been quietly filed away. Until today. Godley continued to sit there in silence, having not uttered a word since being brought in.

'David,' Ramsbottom said quietly, 'I really do think it about time you went and fetched the RSM.'

* * * * *

Half a mile away, 'Haddaway' Wadkins of D Company, so called because of his habitual reply to anything he disliked of 'Ah, haddaway an' shite, man!' turned to his left as he lounged, seated on the firestep, and remarked to his neighbour, 'Hey, kid, I see that shirker Godsman slunk back to our lot this morning from his cushy billet in the hospital. By Christ, he didn't half spin that out, the dirty fucker! Must've been gone over a month. An' did ye see Billy's newspaper his mam sent him? The dirty Hun bastards shot one of our nurses! Ah'm telling ye, it was there in black an' white, man. Some nurse called Edith Cavell. Shot her in Belgium for helping our lads trapped behind the lines get away.' He rubbed his nose thought-fully. 'It makes ye think,what the world's coming to. Fancy shootin' a bloody woman!'

15

Thursday 11th November 1915

Early morning barrage in C Coy trenches left three ORs dead and four wounded. Lt Coombs, Battalion Sniping Officer, slightly wounded whilst attempting to spot enemy sniper active in B Coy area. Weather remains grim, sleet and snow falling all day. Colonel Snaith has initiated formal Court Martial proceedings against Private Godley, B Coy, on a variety of charges including desertion. Ration parties shelled all the way up through communication trenches. No casualties.

Captain L. Carey, D Company

The shells were falling thickly as Major Walter Ramsbottom made his way along the communication trench towards the HQ dugout. He paused several times as shells screamed over and impacted in the trenches to his right. Even at this range, large clods of earth and pieces of shell hummed over him and, keeping well down, he shuffled through the mud lining the bottom of the trench. His eyes were streaming with the effects of the sleet hitting him squarely in the face so he kept his head averted and sloshed along through the cloying, sucking embrace of the mud under his feet .

Reaching the dugout steps he stepped down into its entrance and the welcome warmth of the stove. The room was as crowded as yesterday and he winced at the rank, pungent air of sweaty bodies, but this time the attitude of those in the dugout was one of solemn importance. Private Godley sat flanked by the RSM and the adjutant. Godley's civilian clothes had been taken from him and he was now clad in uniform tunic and trousers. Seated at his desk, Colonel Cuthbert Snaith ruffled his hand nervously through his silver hair as he glanced down at the papers before him.

'Ah, Walter,' he exclaimed. 'Glad to see you made it unharmed. Damned Boche want to strafe at the most unearthly hours! Come in! Come in! Have a seat over here.' He waved his hand in the direction of the far corner and Walter gratefully subsided into the chair he had indicated. Snaith continued. 'I've gathered you all here to make a start on the proceedings Brigade have ordered me to initiate in the case of Private Godley's absence from his place of duty and, er, other matters that have since been brought to my attention. The adjutant and I interviewed Second-

Lieutenant Elliot last night and I have his written statement here in front of me. Private Godley has spoken with the RSM and the adjutant and will have to make a written statement today. In short, gentlemen, in view of the seriousness of the charges laid against Private Godley and acting on the advice given to me by Brigade, this battalion will be holding a Field General Court Martial in which Private Godley will be given every opportunity to answer these charges. Do I make myself clear?'

The silence hung around them for several long seconds as each man digested the CO's grave words. No one spoke and at length Snaith turned to the RSM. 'Mr Findlay, if you don't mind, I think now is the time to take Private Godley to where he will be detained until this sorry business is dealt with. March him out now, if you please.'

Godley rose a trifle unsteadily and looked at the colonel. 'Please sir...' he stammered, but was savagely interrupted by the RSM who leaned over him with an angry expression. 'You heard the colonel. Save it for later!' he rasped. Without another word Godley walked over to the doorway and mounted the steps, closely followed by the RSM.

The atmosphere in the dugout as the two men left was one of utter gloom. Snaith sat slumped in his seat examining the papers on his desk while the other two officers waited for him to speak. At length, he pushed the papers away and lifted his head to address them.

'David,' he murmured, 'I would like you to act as the prosecutor at the court martial. As the man's CO I cannot play any part in it. Brigade are sending over another three officers from our adjoining regiments and we should have their names shortly. I have a mind to start proceedings in two days' time, in a suitable building within the small village on the Mametz road about seven miles from here. I think its called Hevemont, is that right Walter?'

'It's Havremont, sir,' Ramsbottom corrected him mechanically.

'Havremont, yes, thank you for that.' Snaith continued wearily, 'Once Godley has made a statement and we find him a suitable person to act in his defence then we'll make a start. This is a damnable business, gentlemen, and I wish to have the matter dealt with as speedily as possible. Is that understood by everyone present?'

'Perfectly, sir,' Ramsbottom replied, rising to his feet, 'I'll follow the RSM and make sure Godley is held securely and then sit down and sort out who he needs to act in his interests.' He pushed his way out through the curtain. The sleet was still whipping across the top of the trench, with an occasional snow flurry, so he buttoned his coat securely and leant forward into the wind as he made his way back the way he had come earlier.

Watching his figure wend its way down the trench, Private Evans turned to his companion and said, 'Cough up me old matey! Didn't I tell you there was something big on. That young shaver, Godley, he's for the bloomin' high jump. You mark my words!' His eyes narrowed as he drew on the cigarette held protectively in his cupped hand. With a snort of disgust the other soldier proffered a tin of cigarettes and Evans grabbed them from him with a wide beam.

* * * * *

Half a mile away, Sydney Coombs lay panting heavily from his exertions as he finished wrapping a scrap of uniform around the shoulders of a home-made mannequin. A cap comforter had been hastily jammed on the doll's head and as a last embellishment the battalion sniping officer fixed an unlit cigarette between its lips. He twisted round to address the three soldiers who had accompanied him, all of them staring unconvinced at the doll as it lay at his feet.

'Look chaps, I know you don't think this bally thing will work but believe me, a chap from the Devonshires was speaking to me and he says they work every time. He said all one has to do is lift the thing up and the Boche sniper will fire at it, thinking it's one of our chaps. You let it drop immediately, as if the chap's been hit, and then we measure the angle the bullet entered the doll and Bob's your uncle! We call in the artillery and that blasted Boche won't bother us again. Simple, eh?'

There was an uncomfortable silence. Slowly, one of his men answered their officer. 'You said, all *you* have to do is lift the thing up, sir. Does that mean you want one of us to try it out?'

Coombs looked at each of the three men in turn and they stared back at him, their faces blank. 'For goodness' sake, you bunch of grannies! It's not that hard to do. Look, give it here. All you have to do is...' Puffing, he bent forward, heaved the mannequin up into position above the parapet and turned to glare at them. *Crack!* The mannequin jumped as it fell into the trench and lay inert in the mud. The three men stared at it intently. Eventually, a note of puzzlement in his voice, one of the soldiers turned to Coombs.

'Sir, I can't see where it was hit. Sir?' Coombs lay slumped against the trench wall, his face creased with pain as he tried to staunch the blood flowing from the neat hole the sniper's bullet had drilled through his exposed wrist.

'Oh fuck!' the soldier exclaimed. 'Are you all right? Hang on there, sir. Stretcher bearers! Stretcher bearers!'

Friday 12th November 1915
In view of the impending FGCM, Brigade issued new orders. Battalion moved to billets in Havremont for rest and training. Battalion was relieved by 8th Leinsters. ORs kit inspection carried out by the RSM prior to moving out. Light shelling on rear roads as battalion moved out. No casualties. 4 officers and 15 ORs departed on leave.

Captain L. Carey, D Company

'Bastard! The utter bastard!' Charlie Horsfall spoke feelingly as he threw his pack and rifle down into the pile of musty, light straw he had selected in the crowded outhouse that was to be their new billet. 'What's up with you, mate?' one of the huddled figures alongside shouted. 'Who's got on your bad side then, Charlie boy?'

'That bastard Hornby's put me on report for losing me water bottle. Christ, as if I'm going to fucking well die of thirst, here of all places!'

There was a short silence then a voice piped up. 'You wanna be careful there, Charlie, they could shoot you for that you know!'

In the longer silence that followed, Charlie Horsfall slowly turned round to face in the direction of the man who had made the comment. He said nothing but stood for a long time, looking at the slowly reddening face in front of him before dropping wordlessly into the straw next to his belongings.

Neville Charteris was making his way past the farmhouse on the outer perimeter of the village, deep in his own thoughts. Poor old Snaith. Brigade had intervened by sending orders which had made for a hasty handover to the Leinsters and in two short days the court martial of young Godley would be taking place here. The Old Man must be feeling pretty low right now. A sound broke through his reverie and he turned to see the adjutant waving him over.

'Good day, David, everything going all right in there?'

'Yes! Fine.' David Roberts gestured impatiently. 'I've got heaps to do to get ready for Monday but I thought I'd let you in on some other news that arrived today. Some blithering idiot from Boulogne has written to us complaining about your conduct while proceeding on leave. Can you shed a light on the matter?'

Charteris gazed at the adjutant resignedly. 'Yes, David, I do remember a pompous ass on the dockside that tried to stop one of the Jocks from Loos going on leave over some triviality. I intervened and the idiot took it badly. Why, what's going to happen about it?'

'Nothing, Neville, old man. Absolutely bloody well nothing, if you'll excuse my French. We have enough to be going on with without dealing with some crybaby MP. I shall write a sucking-up letter back, informing them that you have been severely censured! Now, get along with you. And watch out the next time you feel like rescuing one of our boys from those demons that frequent the docksides of France!'

Charteris resumed his deliberations and plodded on. His mind had been in a turmoil since returning from leave and he had become withdrawn, a fact his brother officers and the men had not been slow to pick up on. Several people had tried to discuss his unusual reticence with him but he had refused to be drawn on the matter. He had received another long, strident letter from Lucille demanding to know why he had not written to her for some weeks. To add to his troubled state of mind he had also received a short note from Matilda Fairley. It had simply read:

Dear Captain Charteris,

Forgive my writing to you in this manner. I remembered the name of your regiment so I hope this letter finds you well, after your short leave in London. I have thought about you since we met and the rather abrupt way in which we parted. If you would wish too communicate with me by letter or by visiting me when next you are in London I would be most pleased. With my best wishes for your safe return.

Yours sincerely,

Matilda Fairley (Mrs)

Confused about the letter's contents and it's effect on him, his mood darkening, he raised his head just in time to avoid bumping into the lonely, troubled form of his CO, Cuthbert Snaith.

'Oh, it's you, Neville. What are you doing, out for a walk?' Snaith sounded hospitable enough although Charteris could see the lines of strain etched on his face. The colonel seemed to have aged in the past few weeks and for the first time Charteris noticed just how grey his hair had become. Before he could answer, Snaith spoke again.

'I was going to ride the surrounding fields but with all that's going on it has somehow lost its appeal. Please, Neville, walk a bit further with me, there's a good chap, if you don't mind.'

Charteris nodded and fell in alongside and they walked on in quiet reflection. At last, Snaith broke the silence. He opened by tapping the ribbons on his breast.

'I won my DSO at Colenso, with Buller's relief column in 1900, you know. We thought then that South Africa had taught us all about killing but this, this senseless slaughter of our youth has changed the world we know forever. The world has become an evil place, Neville, and I'm growing old and tired of my part in it.

'A damnable business don't you think? In two days' time we must try a young man for his life, a boy no older than my youngest son. What an earth have we come to, so much death on both sides and yet if found guilty his own side might well have to execute him.'

Charteris looked at his CO in surprise. 'Do you think it might come to that sir? And, excuse me, you said your son? I'm sorry, you've never mentioned your children before.'

Cuthbert Snaith laughed bitterly. 'Forgive me, Neville, if an old codger like myself may be permitted to have children.' He continued, waving away Charteris's weak protests. 'It doesn't matter, I know what you mean. My children are special to me and as such I've tended to keep their lives private. I have two boys. Alfred is twenty-two and a subaltern in the Royal Field Artillery up in the salient around Ypres, while George is nineteen and a midshipman in the RN. I miss them dreadfully you know, but like you and the rest of the chaps who also have loved ones they miss, I keep in touch by writing.

'And now this, in answer to your first question,' he concluded gloomily. 'Godley was a damn fool but all the same he's only a youngster. Oh well...' He kicked a loose stone out of his way and walked on, his shoulders hunched as if carrying a great burden. Charteris followed and they trudged on together, unseeing, each man's thoughts far away.

Monday 15th November 1915

Light snow fell for most of the day. Men set to work cleaning billets by NCOs. The FGCM took place at Havremont of Private 213652 Benjamin Isaac Godley accused of desertion in the field and striking a superior officer.

Captain L. Carey, D Company

'Good morning, gentlemen.'

The swarthy, clean-shaven, long-nosed officer in a major's uniform greeted the three officers as they solemnly filed into the lower storey of the farmhouse at Havremont. One lone chair for the witnesses sat at the other side of the table with extra chairs further back for the prosecution and defence counsels. In the centre of the room stood a solitary chair, that being reserved for the accused. Some clean sacking covered the empty windows to provide both some respite from the biting wind outside and a degree of privacy. At the side of the table, a clerk in the shape of an older-looking corporal busied himself with a pen and a bottle of ink, fussing with some papers in front of him.

At length, the major spoke again.

'My name is Major James Goldstern. I am a lawyer in civilian life and at present I am attached to the Judge Advocate's Branch at divisional HQ. GHQ has become concerned at the large numbers of our troops facing capital charges for various offences. Many reports have reached us of those accused not being properly represented and defended, so GHQ has seen fit to commission a trial study, whereby advocates will attend such FGCM's with a view to seeing justice properly dispensed. Hence my appearance before you today.

'In view of the seriousness of the charges about to be brought against Private Godley this morning I have been ordered to sit in on this FGCM and advise you gentlemen on the legal points that may be brought up during these proceedings. The charges will be read out in this room and the prosecution and the defence will then have their chance, in turn, to press or deny those charges. Do you have any questions before the proceedings begin, gentlemen?'

No one spoke and in turn each man shook his head. Major Goldstern stared keenly at each of them before looking at the watch on his wrist.

'Roger. It being one minute before eight o'clock, we shall take the time to ensure everything is at hand before we open the proceedings. Gentlemen, you should have in front of you a notepad and some sharp pencils. I must add that nothing is to be removed from this room when these proceedings are over. Is that understood?' They all nodded and he pointed to a large, thick book in the centre of the table. 'That, gentlemen, is the *Manual of Military Law* which contains the format this FGCM will proceed under. Section 49 of the Army Act sets out the duties and responsibilities of a FGCM. If at any time during the proceedings you feel that you are struggling to understand the terms used and information elicited from the various witnesses that may come before you, please indicate your misgivings to myself and I will endeavour to explain the point of law in question. We shall at all times follow the enclosed rules of procedure.

'Make no mistake gentlemen, this is a fully-convened court whose jurisdiction is without question and as such we shall conduct the following proceedings with due respect for the majesty of the law of our Armed forces and our country. Let us now proceed and do our duty. I shall require to swear you to secrecy regarding the proceedings, under oath, on the Bible being placed in front of you. Thank you.'

The tension in the room mounted as each officer rose from his seat and repeated the oath written on a card by the Bible before sitting once more. After all concerned had sworn their oath the major gently inserted the card into the bible.

'Mr Findlay, would you be so kind as to bring in the accused.'

'Sir!'

RSM Findlay drew himself up to his full height and marched smartly out of the room. The men sitting at the table fidgeted and one or two coughed nervously in the seconds before the tramping of feet announced the arrival of the accused and his accompanying escort. RSM Findlay entered first, followed swiftly by a bare-headed and beltless, slightly nervous-looking, Godley between two NCOs. Behind him stood an equally nervous-looking lieutenant. The escort and their charge came to a crashing halt in front of the table and stood there, sweating in spite of the chill in the room.

Major Goldstern broke the silence. 'This is an FGCM convened on active service in Havremont, France, this day of Monday fifteenth November 1915 under the Army Act 1914. We are gathered here today to try Private 213652 Benjamin Isaac Godley, B Company, of the 19th King's Own Lancashire Regiment. Under the existing regulations, Private Godley will be tried by this court consisting of the following officers: the president of the court is Major Charles Dawlish, of the 15th Northumberland Fusiliers. Accompanying him today are Captain Ronald Stanley of the 11th London regiment and Lieutenant Arthur Wilson of the 7th Yorkshire and Lancashire regiment. Do you have any objections to these officers sitting in judgement on you, Private Godley?'

His face a white sheen of sweat, Godley shook his head without speaking. Major Goldstern nodded. 'The battalion adjutant to my left here, Major David Roberts, will act as the prosecutor in these proceedings. Behind the accused is an officer from his battalion, Lieutenant Roger Bradley, who the accused, as is his right, has chosen to be his defender, known as the "prisoner's friend". Now, would you read out the charges, regimental sergeant major.'

'Sir! Private 213652 Benjamin Isaac Godley, you are hereby charged with desertion under Section 12 of the Army Act 1914 in that you did on the night of the seventeenth of October 1915, desert in the face of the enemy whilst engaged in a trench raid on the enemy lines and did remain at large until apprehended in Bethune on the eighth of November 1915. You are further charged under Section 8 of the Army Act 1914, in that you did on or during the night of the seventeenth of October strike a superior officer in the execution of his office, one Second-Lieutenant David William Elliot, a member of the 19th King's Own Lancashire Rifles holding the King's commission. How do you plead?'

Godley moved as if to speak but Major Goldstern moved swiftly forward and addressed the panel of officers at the table.

'Gentlemen,' he began, 'as both the charges laid against Private Godley carry the supreme penalty, the *Manual of Military Law* has been amended to ensure that the only response the accused may make to such charges is to enter a plea of "not guilty". The law will recognise no other plea. Do you understand me?' he asked, turning towards Godley. Dumbly, he nodded. The major motioned to the clerk sitting by the table.

'Corporal Harmiston, please enter a plea of "not guilty" to both charges.' The corporal began to write laboriously. At a gesture from the major, Godley sat on the chair provided for him and his escort stood flanking him. Major Goldstern next moved towards David Roberts.

'Major Roberts, as prosecutor it is now your turn to lay before this court the substance of the charges laid out before the accused. Major Roberts?'

'Thank you, sir.'

David Roberts rose, smoothed down his uniform jacket, moved briskly forward and addressed the waiting officers.

'Gentlemen. The evidence against Private Godley is quite overwhelming and irrefutable. On the night in question, Private Godley along with others in his platoon were told to take part in a trench raid against the enemy position opposite the battalion lines, known as the 'Horn. During that raid, one I might add with many casualties to the battalion, Private Godley went missing. At first he was presumed killed or wounded and captured by the enemy. This assumption existed until his apprehension, in Bethune, three weeks later, in civilian clothes. Nothing is known of his movements during the time he was reported missing. Since his arrest he has consistently refused to answer any questions put to him regarding his disappearance that night. How he managed to clear the trenches and reach Bethune we have not one inkling. Save that, when apprehended, he was found to be wearing civilian clothes, indicating a clear desire to desert and take no further part in the war. What other reason, given his silence, can there be for such actions?

'As to the second charge, that of striking a superior officer, we shall bring witnesses before this court who will identify this man, Private Godley, as the man who struck his superior officer, Second-Lieutenant Elliot of his battalion, deliberately and with malice during the course of the said trench raid.

'I call as my first witness, Sergeant Wifred Hobson, of the provost marshall's department Bethune.'

Calmly Sergeant Hobson strode into the room and took the oath administered to him by the flustered clerk. He sat in the witness chair and stared at Godley as the major advanced on him.

'Now, Sergeant Hobson, would you like to tell the court how you came into contact with the accused?'

'Certainly, sir,' he replied confidently. 'My colleague Corporal Huckerby and I were proceeding on the evening of the eighth of November at approximately six-thirty towards the Trois Allees in Bethune, an estaminet that had been the site of a recent double murder involving one of the 19th battalion when I saw the accused coming out of a side door dressed in civilian clothes. I had a feeling that I recognised him and we caught up with him and asked him where he was going. He did not answer. On his facing us, I recognised the accused as being one of the soldiers from the 19th battalion involved in a fracas some weeks before in the estaminet.

'I demanded to know what the accused was doing dressed in civilian clothes. He refused to answer me. I asked him where his uniform was and why he was not with his regiment. Again, he refused to answer me. Together with Corporal Huckerby I then took hold of the accused and brought him to the provost marshall's office. After making further enquiries which eventually established his identity, myself and Corporal Huckerby were ordered to escort the accused back to his battalion on the morning of the tenth of November.'

'Thank you, sergeant. Now, for the sake of the court, could you say in any way that when you apprehended the accused he was wearing a single piece of clothing that would mark him out as being one of His Majesty's servicemen?'

'No sir, definitely not. When apprehended the accused was wearing a striped civilian shirt and a pair of dark civilian trousers. He was not wearing a single scrap of service clothing.'

'Thank you, sergeant. Lieutenant Bradley, do you or Private Godley wish to cross-examine Sergeant Hobson?' Godley turned to the lieutenant next to him and spoke in a low, insistent voice that the rest of the room struggled to hear. He seemed calm enough but Major Roberts could see that his right knee was trembling violently, a sure sign of the inner turmoil the soldier was feeling. At last, Bradley straightened up and shook his head.

He spoke quietly in a strained voice. 'If it please the court, Private Godley has no questions for the sergeant, sir.'

The president looked up from the table in surprise.

'Private Godley, do you know the significance of your passing over the chance to cross-examine the witness? Will you not reconsider your decision? Lieutenant Bradley, please explain to Private Godley the consequences of his actions. I urge you most strongly to do so!'

Godley stared straight ahead, white-faced, and shook his head in a fierce gesture of dismissal.

'Thank you, sergeant. You may step down.' Sergeant Hobson stood and walked out of the door, giving the young soldier a puzzled look as he passed. The major faced the court and spoke again.

'Gentlemen, if needs be I could call on Corporal Huckerby to back up the evidence of his sergeant but what has been laid before you already this morning is incontrovertible evidence of Private Godley's guilt on the first charge and does not require his presence for the moment. There is no need for further witnesses on this charge. He was last seen in the enemy trenches and was then found and apprehended three weeks later, in civilian clothing, many miles from his place of duty. That must constitute desertion in any language, of that I'm sure you will have no doubt. Bear in mind also, please, that when apprehended he refused to give any information as to how or why he was there in Bethune and not serving with his battalion.

'As to the second charge, that of striking his superior officer, I call on Second-Lieutenant David Elliot.'

An immaculate Elliot was sworn in and lounged back in his seat with an affected air as Major Roberts approached him.

'Second-Lieutenant Elliot, could you please tell the court what happened to you on the night of the seventeenth of October, during the battalion raid on the Ram's Horn?'

Elliot sat bolt upright in the chair, slicked his thinning hair back with a nervous gesture, licked his lips and leaned forward eagerly.

'Certainly, sir. Together with two of my brother officers I went over the top with my chaps and we gained entry to the enemy trenches. It was night but with the light of the various explosions and gun flashes it was quite light, well, enough to recognise someone if you know what I mean.' He saw one or two of the panel nod in absentminded agreement and encouraged by this continued to speak in a thin, reedy voice. 'I had become detached from my chaps and had run out of bombs, due to my having expended them bombing several Hun dugouts. I saw one of our chaps, a person I see before me here today as the accused, and ran up the trench to ask him if he could supply me with some. He began to run away from me. I shouted at him to turn around and accompany me as there were lots of Huns attacking my chaps and I could see he had a bag of bombs slung over his shoulder.

'The accused's response to my order was to bend down and pick up a weapon from the bottom of the trench. As I repeated my order he bore down on me and hit me in the face, breaking my nose. Luckily, one of our NCOs, Corporal Miller, saw what happened and ran to my assistance, otherwise I am sure the accused would have killed me. As I fell I saw him run down the trench in the opposite direction to that which I had ordered him to go.

'I next saw the accused when he was brought back from Bethune and even then I am sure he would have harmed me if he was able.' He finished his evidence and rose from the chair, pointing a dramatic finger in Godley's direction. 'There, gentlemen, there is the swine who tried to kill me! None other than Private Godley!'

'Lieutenant Elliot! Compose yourself!' Dawlish was appalled. 'Remember, sir, you are an officer and should conduct yourself accordingly! Have you finished giving your evidence?'

The other two officers at the table began scribbling in their notebooks, a gesture noted by Major Roberts.

'Lieutenant Bradley, do you or Private Godley have any questions for Second-Lieutenant Elliot?' he asked, glaring at Elliot as he spoke. Bradley cleared his throat but before he could speak, Godley's tremulous voice broke the silence.

'Begging your pardon, sir, how can you say that you saw me? It was dark that night, there were no lights in the trench area that I found myself in and I couldn't have been the person you saw.'

'Oh yes, private? And how do you intend to explain that?' Elliot sneered at Godley sarcastically.

'Well, sir, you say I had a bag of bombs over my shoulder. But that night I was carrying a rifle, sir.'

'What difference does that make, you had the bombs slung over your shoulder. I distinctly saw you! You could have got rid of the rifle earlier!' Elliot blustered, his eyes flashing.

'Please sir, if it please the court, that night only the boys that were told to carry the bombs carried them in a bag. I was one of the men told off as a rifleman. Ask the RSM, sir, he was the one who told me I was to carry a rifle.' Godley's voice had gained in strength the longer he spoke.

The president of the court leaned forward and addressed the RSM. 'Well, RSM Findlay, this is most irregular but is Private Godley telling the truth of the matter? Speak up!'

The RSM's face cleared as he finished searching his memory. He nodded slowly and spoke.

'Yes, sir, there is no doubt of the matter, now that you ask. Private Godley was indeed one of the soldiers in his section detailed off by me personally to carry a rifle.

Private Godley is also correct when he says that only the men detailed off as bombers carried their bombs in a bag, sir. The rest of the men carried the odd one or two on their persons or not at all.'

Before he could speak further Elliot burst out wildly while glaring malevolently at Godley. 'Sir, you must believe me! This is most unfair, the RSM has not been called as a witness. That *is* the man who attacked me! This is just an attempt to have the charge dismissed by calling me a liar!'

' Elliot!' Major Dawlish was furious. 'This is the second time I have had to warn you of your conduct, sir. I shall be making a full report to your commanding officer after these proceedings. The RSM has fully answered the question put to him in respect of Private Godley's role in the night's raid and I see no further need for your presence here as a witness. You may leave. sir.'

'But, sir. I...' Elliot wheeled to face the panel to be met with an icy stare from the president. 'I said you may leave.' The tone of his voice brooked no further argument.

Flushed, Elliot vacated the chair with a sullen expression, saving a vengeful stare for Godley as he passed out of the room. Major Roberts watched his witness leave with an air of consternation. This was not what he had expected.

'My apologies, gentlemen, I am sure Second-Lieutenant Elliot will regret his outburst later, when he has had time to reflect. In the meantime, I would like to call my next witness, Corporal Edward Miller, D Company, 19th battalion.

'Corporal Miller,' David Roberts enquired as he stood next to the trembling NCO, 'Second-Lieutenant Elliot testified earlier that you witnessed the attack on him on the night in question and are able to identify his assailant. Could you please point him out to the court, if he is present here today.'

'No, sir, I'm afraid I couldn't,' Miller replied.

'No? But I thought Second-Lieutenant Elliot said that you were able to identify Private Godley as his assailant?'

'That's for Mr Elliot to explain, sir. It was dark that night. I saw *someone* running away down the trench and found Mr Elliot on his knees in a great deal of pain. I helped him back to where the RSM took over, sir. As to seeing who that someone running away was, I could no easier tell if it was the devil, sir.' Miller stared at him defiantly.

'Er, thank you, Corporal Miller. That will be all. Lieutenant Bradley, would you like to cross-examine Corporal Miller?' David Roberts knew when to shut up but the damage had been done.

'No sir,' Bradley replied with a slight smile hovering on his lips. 'After hearing Corporal Miller's evidence there is no point in my asking him anything!'

Sat behind the table, Captain Stanley leaned forward and spoke. 'Corporal Miller, could you in fact see whether the person who assaulted Elliot that night was one of our own troops or indeed one of the enemy defenders?'

'No sir, I could not tell anything about the person who I saw running away from me. As I explained earlier, sir, it was dark and...'

'Yes, yes. Quite. Thank you, corporal, you may go now.' The captain smiled easily at Miller and bent to write in his notebook.

Another two privates from Godley's company were called but as they were only able to confirm having left their own trenches with him on the night in question and had not seen him since gaining entry to the enemy trenches they were quickly dismissed by the panel without cross-examination.

The last witness to be called was Bevan Hughes, the battalion MO. After being sworn in he sat back in his chair and looked on quizzically as David Roberts approached him.

'Captain Hughes, as the medical officer attached to the 19th you were called to examine the accused after his return to the battalion, while he was being held in custody, were you not?'

'Yes sir, I was.'

'Did you notice anything about the accused's mental or physical condition that could explain the actions taken by him on the night in question, which have led to his appearance before this court martial today?'

'Well sir, I am a medical man, not a psychiatrist, so I find myself unable to comment on Private Godley's mental state of mind. However...'

'Quite. How did he seem during your examination, Captain Hughes? Was he agitated, concerned?' David Roberts seemed eager to press the point.

'Sir, I was called upon to examine Private Godley as a doctor. I made a full *physical* examination of the man. Apart from the recent injuries he seemed to have sustained during some sort of altercation he was unwilling to specify, I found nothing further. During my examination Private Godley made no comment, other than to answer yes or no to minor questions put to him. It can all be found in my written report.'

'Thank you, Captain Hughes. The court notes that you found nothing untoward in the accused's mental state that could have had an influence on his actions on the night so specified in the charges.' With that Roberts spun round and fixed his gaze on each of the officers at the table, looking pointedly at them so they were in no doubt as to his meaning.

'Sir,' Bevan Hughes protested, 'with due respect, that is not what I said. What I did say was...'

'Thank you, Captain Hughes.' Roberts spoke smoothly, his gaze still on the trio sat at the top table. He spoke again, over his shoulder. 'That is all, Captain, you may go now.'

'One moment, please.' Major Goldstern rose and addressed Bradley. 'Do you have any questions you would like to ask the captain?'

Bradley looked at Godley, who shook his head vehemently. Reluctantly he answered, 'No sir.'

An uncomfortable silence followed as the MO vacated the chair and marched smartly from the room.

Major Goldstern rose again and addressed the panel.

'Gentlemen, as there are no further witnesses to appear for the prosecution, we will now hear from Lieutenant Bradley who will speak in Private Godley's defence.'

Bradley was very ill at ease. 'Much against my will and judgement, gentlemen, I have been instructed by Private Godley to offer no statement on the first charge. Private Godley realises the seriousness of the situation he finds himself in and the inference that may be taken from his silence, but insists he will not be questioned on the matters contained within the first charge.

'As to the second charge, Private Godley totally and utterly refutes that charge. Why, those attempting to press this charge against him have themselves, from their very own lips, described the ludicrousness of the situation. There is no point bringing any witnesses forward to refute the charge as the prosecution have done a very good job of that already. You have heard also from the battalion Regimental Sergeant Major RSM Findlay, a man totally above reproach, who testified that it was he who personally who ordered Private Godley to carry a rifle that night.

'This contrasts starkly with the evidence of Second-Lieutenant Elliot who states that the person who attacked him had a bag of bombs slung over his shoulder. Note that, gentlemen, at no point did Second-Lieutenant Elliot intimate that the person who attacked him that night was armed with a Lee-Enfield rifle, something that even on a dark night should be distinctly noticeable. He said his attacker *bent* down and picked a weapon up to assault him with, not used the one he was *already* holding. A small point but a vital one, gentlemen. And one on which our defence now rests. Thank you.' With that, he sat down next to Godley, mopping his forehead with a large, coloured handkerchief he pulled from his trouser pocket.

Dawlish looked up from his notebook and stared directly at Godley with a look of pity, intermingled with exasperation. 'Private Godley, I must ask you once more, and for the final time, will you not stand there and at least try to explain yourself in connection with the first charge brought against you, that of desertion? You must understand, this is a perilous position you find yourself in and it will do you no good to remain silent. Please...'

Godley flushed a deep red and gazed down at his boots before looking up to return the major's inquisitive look. He spoke softly, in a low voice. 'I'm, I'm sorry, sir, there is no help for it. I have nothing to say.'

Major Dawlish sighed deeply, a sigh of utter helplessness. 'Very well. Major Goldstern?'

'It would appear that this is all the evidence we shall have before us this morning gentlemen, from both sides,' he intoned. 'It is now incumbent on the prosecution and the defence to make a closing address before the court retires to consider a verdict. Major Roberts, if you please.'

Roberts sat lips pursed, the fingers of both hands pressed together as if in prayer. At the sound of his name he dropped his hands to his side and stood. Taking a deep breath to compose himself he began to speak, enunciating each word clearly as if frightened his audience would misunderstand him.

'Gentlemen, I take no pleasure in standing here before you this morning, prosecuting the charges laid against this young man in this court today. However, by doing so I am also doing my duty, something Private Godley ignored when he disappeared on the night of October the seventeenth. Wearing the uniform of His Majesty's forces incurs certain obligations, something Private Godley also ignored that night.

'The facts are simple. Private Godley should have returned from the night's raid on the enemy trenches to his place of duty, the 19th battalion, or he should have been left lying dead or injured in the enemy trenches he had been sent to assault. Neither of these things happened. Private Godley simply disappeared, to be found and apprehended twenty-two days later in Bethune. We have heard no explanation as to how he found himself to be there, nor how he managed to travel such a distance. He was apprehended there in civilian clothes wearing, as you have heard from the lips of the person apprehending him, Sergeant Hobson, not a single scrap of the uniform military law dictated he should be wearing while serving his country in this time of war. That action alone clearly displays the intent of the accused to take no further part in his country's defence. A plain act of desertion you will agree.

'Not once, despite having been given ample time and opportunity to explain himself, has one word in his defence been uttered by Private Godley in this matter. A damning silence indeed! On the charge of desertion, I therefore ask you to find Private Godley guilty.

'As to the second charge, that of striking his superior officer, there has been offered a defence that Private Godley was not a bomber and therefore could not have been carrying a satchel of bombs that night. Is it not possible that Private Godley had simply dropped or lost his rifle and had carried on fighting by the use of bombs he had picked up during the raid? Why, if this was not so, did Private Godley disappear that night? Was it because, in striking a person he knew to be an officer, he realised the consequences of that act and so took flight, making his way to where he hoped to hide? Discarding his uniform on the way also, so as not to be recognised.'

He saved his last damning statement until last. 'How is it that Second-Lieutenant Elliot recognised Private Godley as the person who had attacked him, immediately on the day Godley was returned under escort to the battalion? Had he finished his evidence he might have informed you that up to the time he entered the dugout that day he had no inkling whatsoever of Private Godley's presence. And yet, gentlemen, he was able to see in the figure of the accused sitting there, in civilian clothes, mark you, the very man who had assaulted him unlawfully in the execution of his duty, in the dark, three weeks earlier. The facts speak for themselves. I must ask you, gentlemen, to find Private Godley guilty of this second charge also. Thank you. The prosecution has no further statement to make.'

The silence in the court stretched as each person, Godley included, digested the bare facts Major Roberts had outlined. Thoughtfully, Major Goldstern gestured at Bradley. 'Would you or Private Godley like to address the court, lieutenant!'

'If it please the court, Private Godley has indicated his wish that I speak for him.'

Bradley rose hesitantly and moved forward slowly. Facing away from Godley he addressed the panel of expectant officers, all of them staring at him intently. His brow shone with perspiration as he strove to gain their understanding.

'I have no legal experience, gentlemen, and find myself here today in these distressing circumstances only because a young soldier in my company requested I attend these proceedings and speak for him. Nevertheless, I will do my best to outline our defence. I must confess I am almost as astounded as yourselves by the accused's refusal to say anything in his defence on the first charge, that of desertion. Private Godley understands fully the possible interpretation of his silence, and the possible consequences too, but has instructed me to offer his sincere apologies at being unable or unwilling, you might think, to offer any statement to the charge. You must make your own inference from that refusal.

'Private Godley totally denies the second charge, that of striking his superior officer, Second-Lieutenant Elliot. He has already offered his explanation, backed up by the battalion RSM, as to why it could not have been him who struck the second-lieutenant that night. He was a rifleman that night, not a bomber. The differences are quite distinct, even at night. In the heat of battle many confusions arise but in this case there is no confusion. Private Godley did not strike his superior officer for one simple reason. He was not there, gentlemen. He was elsewhere in the enemy trenches. No one has been able to place him at the scene of the assault, not one single person has come into this court and identified him other than Second-Lieutenant Elliot, who quite clearly identified his assailant that night as one carrying a bag of bombs. Not a rifle, as none other a person than the battalion RSM has testified in Private Godley's defence. I therefore ask you to find Private Godley not guilty of this charge. Thank you.'

He finished speaking, touched Godley lightly on the shoulder as he passed, and resumed his seat.

A longer silence than when the previous speaker had finished was broken only by the scratching of a pen as Corporal Harmiston wrote furiously in an untidy scrawl in a desperate effort to keep up with the proceedings. At length Major Goldstern addressed the panel.

'The court will now be cleared while you, gentlemen, debate the evidence from both sides and decide a verdict. Unless any of you have something you wish to say first?' The three officers contemplated him as he finished speaking and after a slow deliberation, each in turn shook his head.

'Roger, gentlemen, that's settled. RSM, would you now kindly clear the court.'

'Sir!' RSM Findlay marched smartly forward and announced. 'Escort, march the accused out!'

Godley jumped up from his seat and took his place between the two NCOs again. The court waited in silence as he was swiftly marched out, followed slowly by the remainder of those present. The door closed behind the last man out, leaving the three officers alone to their deliberations.

Major Dawlish spoke first.

'Well, chaps, this is a strange state of affairs, make no mistake on that. We have a young man here before us, on trial for his life, and he refuses to make any statement on the first charge put to him. How do we approach this? Captain Stanley?'

The captain hesitated and then answered. 'Sir,' he began slowly, 'I must confess to being as concerned as Lieutenant Bradley with the accused's insistence on remaining silent on the charge of desertion. To keep silent is to overlook the fact that he *did* disappear from his place of duty that night, namely the action that was going on in the enemy trenches. Where is the sense in keeping quiet? He must have been informed that the law as it stands demands he make some response to the charge?'

'So what you are saying, sir, is that he's guilty without even opening his mouth?' Lieutenant Wilson spoke for the first time since taking the oath.

'Exactly so!' Major Dawlish interrupted with feeling. 'My God! By not opening his mouth he has admitted, *ipso facto,* his guilt. What other explanation can there be? Even his battalion MO has testified that he could find nothing wrong with the man. All this implied talk of his mental state is just poppycock. Must we sit here discussing the obvious facts?

'The man disappeared during action and was found miles away, weeks later. He had discarded his uniform and was hiding in some, some bloody Froggie café while his fellow soldiers faced the Hun without him! Plainly the actions of a deserter, and a coward to boot!' He snorted derisively.

'Forgive me, gentlemen, but I see no need for us to sit here forever, trying to make our minds up on a verdict when the facts are so plain. Guilty, or not guilty?

Lieutenant Wilson, as the junior member of this court, protocol demands that you give your verdict first. Do you understand?'

'Guilty.' Lieutenant Wilson spoke in a low voice, the single word being echoed by Captain Stanley seconds later.

'Good! Now then, let's get on to the second charge.'

Before he could go on a discreet knock on the door informed them of the arrival of the battalion cook. A tray containing three bowls of thick, hot steaming soup, some fresh bread and mugs of hot tea was passed through and the lieutenant deposited it on the table. All three men ate heartily. After they had finished, Dawlish stretched lazily in his chair before laconically resuming his deliberations.

'In the case of the second charge, mark you, I'm half inclined to believe Godley when he says he didn't strike Elliot.'

Captain Stanley hastily interrupted. 'I think we should take a bit more time over this charge, if you would allow me to say so, sir. Elliot came over as a nincompoop, sir, no manners whatsoever. That's what comes of these service battalions taking anyone as an officer these days. However, and I do have to say this, there is the perturbing matter of his recognising the man straightaway in the dugout a few days ago.'

'Granted, but Private Godley was sat between the two provost's people, sir. That might have given Elliot an inkling that something was up and he could have made the accusation up on the spot. A scapegoat for his injuries if you see what I mean.' Lieutenant Wilson looked half-expectantly at his two superiors.

'I do see what you mean, Wilson, but I still can't see past this recognition thing in the dugout.' Captain Stanley shook his head and twisted his face as he struggled with his thoughts. He looked over to Major Dawlish. 'What about you, sir, how do you consider the matter?'

Dawlish stared a them both with a serious expression before answering. 'No one saw Godley in the trench at the time of the assault, did they? No one saw him at all that night after they left their own trenches. So where was he? What was he doing? The RSM seems to believe that Godley couldn't have struck Elliot because he should have been carrying a rifle and not a bag of bombs. A good point, and the RSM appears to be a truthful witness. However, gentlemen, there is one other aspect that we should do well to consider.

'It is of no consequence whatsoever whether or not Private Godley struck Elliot that night, or any other night for that matter. Private Godley is without a doubt guilty of the first charge, that of desertion. Do we then damn him doubly by finding him guilty of striking such a total incompetent as Elliot? The evidence is patchy to say the least and there is, at least on this charge, substantial doubt as to whether or not he did it.

There is also the fact that we could add '*Shamefully casting away his arms in the face of the enemy...*' under Section 4 of the Act. No one, least of all Godley, has explained where his rifle ended up that night. Did he drop it, or deliberately throw it away as he took flight?

'The man has doomed himself by refusing to answer to the first charge. And besides, gentlemen, officer or not, I do not like Elliot! His evidence was a load of tosh and tommy-rot and his conduct was abominable! Whoever struck him that night deserves our best wishes, if you will forgive my levity... However, I leave it up to you two, but remember, our verdict must be unanimous and I for one do not wish to spend the rest of the day debating the issue.'

The threat was there, subtle in the extreme, and the other two were quick to pick up on the major's remarks. Captain Stanley leant back and looked at Dawlish in agreement.

'I totally agree with you, sir, this business is going to be bad enough for the 19th without us piling on the agony. I move for an immediate verdict. Lieutenant Wilson?'

'Oh, not guilty. Definitely. Not guilty, sir!' Wilson exclaimed eagerly.

'Good man!' Major Dawlish leaned over and clapped him on the shoulder, smiling. 'That's the spirit! Now, what about yourself, Stanley?'

'Not guilty also, sir.'

'Right! Let's get this over with. Wilson, would you be so kind and go inform Major Goldstern that we have reached our verdicts.'

As the court was recalled Godley moved steadily into the room between his two escorts. The RSM's keen eye noted his wan complexion and the way the fingers of both hands flexed and unflexed as the three men came to a halt and stood to attention in the middle of the room.

Goldstern addressed the court. 'Gentlemen, have you reached a verdict on the two charges against Private Godley?'

Major Dawlish took a sip of water from the glass in front of him before replying. 'We have. On the first charge, that of desertion, we find Private Godley guilty. On the second charge, that of striking a superior officer, we find the accused not guilty.'

There was an audible sigh in the room as the verdicts were announced. Watching him, RSM Findlay saw Godley stagger slightly then recover as the word 'guilty' was pronounced. Major Goldstern directed his next question at the RSM.

'RSM Findlay, before the court adjourns to consider the sentence, could you please read out Private Godley's conduct sheet?'

RSM Findlay drew himself up. 'During his time with the battalion, in fact, since his enlistment, Private Godley's conduct has been exemplary. There is not one entry of a bad nature in it and I can inform the court that he has never been on Battalion Orders for any misdemeanour. Sir!'

Major Goldstern digested these facts along with the other members of the court before looking over to where Bradley sat in an obvious state of distress.

'Lieutenant Bradley,' he asked gently, 'before the court adjourns again it is for you to make any plea you may wish to, in mitigation.'

Bradley rose from his chair, rubbing his face, trying to disguise the despair he had felt since hearing the verdicts. 'Thank you, sir, I shall endeavour to make some comments in mitigation. In view of the extreme youth of the accused I would ask the court show some mercy when considering a sentence. We all find ourselves here today, fighting a war that none of us here were ever prepared for fully. Some men take it in their stride, others struggle to come to terms with the daily horrors and the ghastly situations they find themselves in, the young more so.

'Private Godley stands before you convicted of deserting his comrades during battle, a heinous crime. He has not helped himself by being unwilling to explain his actions that night. However, I am sure part of those actions could be traced to a head injury he sustained during a brutal assault on him by one of his own comrades weeks prior to the raid that night. Private Godley refused to allow me to include this in the evidence presented in his defence today but I would be doing him a grave injustice were I not to mention it as I plead with you now. I say part of what happened that night can be attributed to those injuries and I would ask you to look on this young man, just nineteen, far from home, and show him some compassion. I would also ask you to take heed of his exemplary record since joining the battalion. Thank you, gentlemen.' He sat down again and buried his head in his hands.

The simple plea moved them all. Major Goldstern looked down momentarily before announcing simply, 'Very well spoken, thank you Lieutenant Bradley. Private Godley, even though Lieutenant Bradley has spoken, would you like to address the court?'

Godley stood to attention and spoke in a firm, clear voice, showing no trace of his previous nervousness, his hands pressed firmly down the seam of his uniform trousers.

'Thank you, sir. If it please the court, Lieutenant Bradley has spoken up well for me and I thank him for that. I would just like to say I'm sorry I could not answer fully to the charges. I realise what effect this has had on the outcome today but it would have made no difference to my actions. I have been treated most fairly and have no complaints. All I can say is I'm sorry to have brought such disgrace on the battalion and my chums. That's all I want to say.'

'Thank you, private. RSM Findlay, could you please clear the court again while sentence is decided.'

The courtroom was cleared once more and the three men sat at the table were alone again. An uncomfortable silence threatened to stretch further before Major Dawlish pulled his cap firmly onto his head, sat upright in his chair and addressed his companions.

'Gentlemen, there is no point sitting here beating about the bush. We have an unpleasant duty to fulfil and by Christ we shall do it! Let us not prolong the agonies that poor young wretch must be feeling right now. Lieutenant Wilson, am I right when I say the *Manual* recommends death as the sentence if the accused is found guilty of the offence of desertion in the face of the enemy?'

Wilson spoke quietly. 'Yes sir. By shooting.'

'Very well then. Death it is, there's nothing else for it. This is not a pleasant thing to do, but be comforted by the fact that we have the full weight of the law to back us up. In any case, I propose that we allow a plea for mercy, that way the final decision will be taken from us.' Dawlish looked round but neither of the other two men could meet his eyes, save to nod miserably in agreement.

'Right, Lieutenant Wilson, let's not waste any more time. Go and fetch everyone back please.'

The courtroom filled more quickly this time. When everyone was in place and Godley had resumed his position in front of the panel, Major Goldstern walked to the front of the table and looked directly at Major Dawlish.

'Have you all reached agreement on the sentence, major?' he asked.

Major Dawlish kept his eyes averted as he murmured in a low voice. 'Yes sir, we have. The sentence of the court is that the accused suffer death by shooting.'

There was a sharp intake of breath from those listening as he spoke. His face flushed, the major continued, 'However, in view of the extreme youth of the accused we also strongly recommend mercy be shown to Private Godley in this case.'

Major Goldstern turned around to face the court and Godley. Lifting up the clipboard he had been holding, he spoke slowly and clearly.

'Private 213652 Benjamin Isaac Godley, 19th Battalion King's Own Lancashire Rifles, you have been tried and convicted by this court of the charge of desertion in the face of the enemy. The sentence of the court is that you suffer death by shooting, with a recommendation for mercy. The findings of this court shall now be passed to a higher authority for confirmation and promulgation. Take the accused away, RSM.'

As the RSM reached them, the escort and Godley moved smartly to their right and marched steadily out of the room. Godley marched with his head held high, looking neither right nor left as he kept pace with his escort. When their footsteps could no longer be heard, Major Goldstern moved over to where Bradley sat, distraught, and laid a hand on his shoulder as the rest of the assembled court slowly filed out.

'Hard luck, old man,' he said sadly, 'I'm afraid that poor young man never had a chance. Please don't blame yourself for what happened today, you did your best.' He hesitated, as if to continue, then walked away softly, leaving Bradley sitting there, staring at the worn floorboards.

Snaith's mood of depression deepened when his adjutant reported the findings of the court to him. 'What happens now? Can Godley appeal?' he asked David

Roberts plaintively. 'I thought George Bradley was going to have that private appear and speak up for Godley?'

'Magilton, sir,' Major Roberts told him in a placatory manner.

'Yes, Magilton! I thought he was going to appear for the defence and offer an explanation for Godley's behaviour. That beating he took in Bethune. That sort of thing!'

'I'm afraid not, sir,' Major Roberts replied. 'It's my understanding that Private Godley did not want Magilton to speak up for him, Lord knows why. Flatly refused I'm told. As to the sentencing, I believe the findings are passed all the way up the chain of command with various recommendations being attached until they reach GHQ. There's no appeal against the sentence itself. Field Marshall French is the only man in France with the necessary authority to sign the death warrant or commute the sentence to a lesser one. I'm afraid we shall simply have to wait and see what he intends to do with young Godley.'

'I don't know.' Cuthbert Snaith passed his hands wearily over his face. 'Is this all it takes to condemn someone, a single morning's work to sentence a young man to death? How on God's earth did we get to where we are now? I despair, I honestly do. How long will this beastly business take? D'you think there's a chance Sir John will commute the sentence? I shall write a note about Godley endorsing the plea for mercy. Lay it on a bit thick, eh?'

'I can't say sir, it depends on so many things. I'm afraid it's out of our hands now.'

'Right you are David, thank you for that. And Godley, where is he just now?'

'I've put him under the RSM as a messenger, sir. Keep him occupied while we all wait to find out. No need to agitate him unduly.'

'Good! So now we'll just wait until we get orders on what to do next, eh?' Snaith leaned back and closed his eyes. He remained that way for some time and just as the adjutant thought he had fallen asleep his eyes snapped open and he fixed Roberts with a baleful glare.

'David!' he snapped. 'On your way back to billets do me a great favour would you, and send me that little beast Elliot. It's time that young man and I had a talk.'

—

16

Battalion in billets in and around Havremont. Pay parade at 0:800 ack emma. Small arms training carried out in morning prior to church parade, followed by inter-company sports in the afternoon. The football final was abandoned due to irregularities. Work parties employed in building up of reserve shell dumps. RSM Findlay's heroism on night of 17th October during trench raid has been recognised by the award of the MC. Heavy snowfall in the evening.

Captain L. Carey, D Company

After church parade, attended surprisingly by many of the men available, a hasty lunch was prepared and eaten as the men looked forward in anticipation to the highlight of their stay in billets so far. The inter-company sports had been eagerly awaited, with many bets and side-bets being surreptitiously placed among the deadly rivals in each sport. A sports field had been crudely marked out on a field outside the village that had been deemed suitable. A football and a rugby pitch had had their lines sketched out in a mixture of chalk and sawdust and in one corner of the field a makeshift boxing ring had been erected. Urns of tea, strategically placed around the field by the cooks, ensured everyone a warm drink to keep the chill out of their bones while they spectated – volubly in many cases.

'Come on ye daftie, pass the flamin' ball! Shit, Wadley, who the 'ell told you that you could play football, you twerp?' Billy Lane gave full vent to his feelings as he watched Ernie Wadley crudely try to boot the football upfield. His frustration was well-placed as B Company were a goal down (a well-drilled shot past the keeper from Reggie Pilling), and there were only two minutes of normal time remaining. Gamely, Ernie puffed up the far side of the pitch as his watching pals screamed their encouragement. D Company had roundly thrashed C Company three-nil and a place in the final now loomed for the winner of this match.

Ernie went down, knocked by a full shoulder charge from Archie Higgins, and the air was filled with shouts and cries as the watching men from B Company bayed their dismay. Faces contorted, they appealed to the referee. Captain Hughes shook his head and waved play on, oblivious to the howls of disagreement. Billy Lane was beside himself.

'Aw, ref! Ref! Give over, that was a bleedin' foul! Sort the bugger out. That's our fuckin' free kick!'

Bevan Hughes scowled at the private dancing up and down on the line and fiercely waved his arms again. 'Play on!' he called sternly. 'And you there, keep the language down or I'll give a free kick the other way!' That was too much for Billy Lane. He promptly ran onto the pitch and flung himself at Archie Higgins. Both men went down in a welter of limbs, to be followed seconds later as the rest of the onlookers joined in the fray. Whooping and hollering the two companies clashed, several old scores being settled out on the football pitch as the scrum of men surged up and down the pitch in a wild, excited mêlée, fists, boots and caps flying in all directions.

Bevan Hughes scrambled to the touchline where he vainly tried to halt the proceedings as he blew piercing blasts again and again on his whistle. All to no avail. The battle raged on, drawing in more combatants as the sound spread and more men scurried from all points of the sports field onto the pitch. It all became academic when the ball itself was transfixed on the point of a bayonet wielded, some said, but later vehemently denied, by Arwyn Jones, the B Company reserve goalkeeper. A thoroughly disillusioned Bevan Hughes admitted defeat and slunk off, allowing the RSM to gain control and bring the match to a halt. Owing to the difficulties in identifying the culprits, the football tournament was cancelled, to the chagrin of D Company who futilely protested their innocence. The matter of who were the battalion champions would have to wait for another time.

Elsewhere, the team of officers from HQ Company won the rugby sevens, Captain Brasher flattening any opposition with an enormous, wild grin on his face and running in try after try. The cross-country was won by D Company, despite a protest that the tapes had been switched, causing half the field to run off in the wrong direction. Captain Carey, an Oxford Blue in his time, led the field home at an easy pace, hardly breaking into a sweat as he romped over the finishing line.

The best action was saved for the boxing finals. Everyone agreed that the match of the afternoon was that where Bill Thomson slugged it out with Charlie Horsfall in the light-heavyweight final. After being battered round the ring for two rounds, grimly hanging on wherever possible, his face a mask of fresh blood, Thomson had raised a great cheer in the third when he landed a single punch to Horsfall's chin. Horsfall had collapsed as if poleaxed, having to be revived by a bucket of freezing water poured over him by a solicitous referee in the shape of the RSM. As Bill Thomson was carried around the ring shoulder high, no one saw the A Company boxing coach, Sergeant Clark, surreptitiously empty Bill's gloves around the back of the ring before joining in the celebrations.

The battalion cooks had excelled themselves and as the hungry men wolfed down the thick beef stew the cooks had dished up, followed by a rich plum duff pudding, the snow started falling. Thinly at first then thicker and thicker, until every building was soon covered in a mantle of white.

Over in the small labourer's cottage that was their billet, Sergeant Bill Clark sat by a roaring fire in the front room and held out his hand. 'Come on CSM, cough up, there's a good sir.' He grinned at Frank Mason's obvious chagrin. 'It was ten francs wasn't it, Frank? I told you my boy would win.' Grumbling, Frank Mason put his glass of rum down and dipped his hand into his pocket. Something fishy had gone on today and it wasn't the jar of rum that Bill Clark had scrounged from his pal in the stores. Give it time though, he'd find out.

Sunday 28th November 1915
In billets at Havremont. Training on all types of weapons continues. Battalion received new issue of Lewis guns to compensate for loss of Vickers machine-guns. Stokes mortar demonstration to companies. All companies' kit inspections carried out. Battalion has been warned today to expect orders shortly to go back into the line. CO returned from three days' leave.
Captain L. Carey, D Company

'God sarge, its bleedin' freezing!' Percy Hartson blew on his gloved hands as he tried to tuck the butt of the unwieldy Lewis gun into his shoulder. The drum of ammunition had slipped through his fingers twice, falling to the dirt floor with a thud, before he had managed to locate it into its groove and click it firmly into place.

'Look to your front, Hartson, lad, don't look sideways at me whilst you've got your finger on the trigger, for Christ's sake!' Willox snapped in exasperation at the antics of the man lying on the ground in front of him. 'Who the bloody hell gave me an idiot like you as a Lewis gunner? Jesus H. Christ, you'll be more use to the bleeding enemy than to your pals!'

Hartson bore the insults from the sergeant towering above him stoically and sucked in his breath before pushing his forage cap back on his head, settling his body into the firing position and smoothly pulling the trigger back towards him. The gun juddered under his chin as he squinted through the raised sights and a row of holes appeared magically in the centre of the cloth target fifty yards down the range, the frozen dirt kicking up high as the gun barked rhythmically.

'Hmn, not bad, Hartson. Not bad indeed.' Rare praise from Sergeant Willox, who nodded briefly at Hartson's upturned grinning face before moving on to the next waiting soldier.

'Benson! What are you gawping at? Who the bleedin' hell said you could ever be a Lewis gunner? Get that gun butt tucked into your shoulder, lad!'

Further down the range, a small huddled group of figures tried to stop shivering and take an interest in the artillery sergeant facing them as he gestured at the strange piece of piping he had brought with him.

'Right lads, this here piece of equipment is one you'll all become very familiar with over the next few months and I dare say some of you watching today might want to transfer into one of the mortar companies. That is when our blinkin' High Command get their fingers out and make those loafers back in Blighty start producing more of the same. Now, who knows what this is?'

'A piece of sanitary pipe, sarge?' Arwyn Jones asked tentatively.

'Thank you for that, smartarse!' the sergeant replied aggrievedly, 'Was no one paying attention? Some of you have seen these before, I know you have. Did anyone listen to the clue? Come on, speak up!' He was met by silence. His arms dropped to his side in a gesture of disgust. 'You'll thank the boys what operates these when they save your ruddy bacon in the coming months, you see if you don't. Righto, for all you thick-skulled individuals what 'avent got a clue, let me introduce you to the three-inch Stokes trench Mortar Mark 1. This little baby will drop a bomb up to 800 yards right down on Fritz as he's having his sausages for breakfast. You point the tube in the direction you think Fritz is hiding in, drop the bomb down the tube and off she goes to blow him to hell. The bombs weigh in at about eleven pounds each and if you get a rhythm going you can get a fair few in the air at once. I've taken the fuses out of these so they won't explode on landing. Watch what I'm doing.'

He knelt down and fiddled with the base-plate of the mortar, adjusting the angle of the mortar tube by aiming visually. The sergeant smartly plopped the first bomb down the tube. A split second later it emerged with a hollow, metallic *whoomp!* as the cartridge on the base of the bomb fired, throwing it high into the air. The men watched mesmerised as within seconds the sergeant had nine bombs in the air at once, all descending in an elegant pattern down towards the wooded end of the field two hundred yards away.

'Well, what do you think of that, then?' the sergeant exclaimed, straightening up in satisfaction. They observed him in silence before Arwyn Jones piped up.

'Er, I take it that's the end of the demonstration, sarge, is it?'

'Why?' the sergeant asked, puzzled by their obvious lack of admiration of his skill.

'Well, sarge, if I'm not mistaken, those bomb-things are going to land right about where me and the boys dug the officers latrines when we first arrived!' Arwyn shot back. 'So if you don't mind, I think it's time we weren't here, boyo!'

* * * * *

While all this was happening, events were taking place far to the north in St Omer, GHQ of the British Army in France and Flanders.

'Damn!' The dapper figure of Field Marshall Sir John French, commander-in-chief of the British Expeditionary Force, grunted in annoyance as he began reading the letter in front of him. He stopped to take a sip of the lukewarm tea in the delicate porcelain cup he was holding in his other hand before resuming his reading. As he read his annoyance grew, his face reddening.

It was no secret that moves were afoot to try to get rid of him; he had already refused to resign once in the last few days, but the message in the letter he was holding from a close friend in the know informed him that the strident calls for his resignation were reaching fever pitch. What did these people know about waging war, especially a war such as this one?

The failures that year to throw the Germans back and win the war, together with the growing casualty lists, were all taking their toll on his popularity with his masters. The disasters at Aubers Ridge, Festubert and, lately, Loos, were all being laid at his door. It was being whispered, even among his own staff he knew, that it was time for him to move aside and let someone else complete the task he had started all those months before.

A name leapt out from the pages of the letter and he stiffened in rage as he read on. Haig! That upstart! They would replace him with a man like Douglas Haig, a dour, lowbrow Scot with a mind as slow as a tortoise's. He knew Haig had blamed him personally for not committing the reserves at Loos – the leaked correspondence from Haig's treacherous hand to His Majesty had proved his subordinate's disloyal actions without a shadow of a doubt! He tossed the letter aside in his annoyance and sat there with both hands outstretched on the well-polished walnut desk in front of him as he slumped into his seat and struggled to control his temper, breathing heavily into his thick moustache. Damn the man! Damn! Damn! Damn!

A discreet cough broke into his reverie and he snapped round to observe his aide, a red-tabbed full colonel, peering anxiously down at him.

'What? What is it Jenkins!' he barked.

'Er, I'm sorry to bother you sir, I know how busy you are, but I wonder if you have attended to that matter I laid before you earlier?'

'Matter, what damn matter would that be?'

'These papers, sir, the matter of Private Godley.'

'Godley? Godley who?' Sir John was getting more annoyed and testy by the second.

'Um, Private Godley, sir, from the 19th Battalion King's Own Lancashire's. He was convicted of desertion at an FGCM the other week, down on the Somme. The court recommended mercy and I put these papers on your desk earlier to look at them. As the death penalty was handed out the papers concerning the proceedings were handled more quickly, just as you've ordered in these circumstances. The brigade, divisional and corps commanders have accordingly appended their recommendations alongside those of the court so if you could read the papers and, ahem, make a decision on the matter, sir, I can forward the verdict to the proper authorities.'

French straightened up, impatiently grabbed the docket and quickly scanned the contents. Hmm. Cuthbert Snaith, the man's commanding officer, had entered an eloquent plea for sparing the young soldier. It read:

Dear Sir John,

Private Godley has proved to be an excellent, keen and hardworking soldier whilst serving with my battalion. Not *once* had he been before me for punishment for any misdemeanours. I recommend mercy be shown him on these grounds and on the basis of his youth. Good soldiers like him are hard to find and I would beg the sentence of death be commuted to that of a salutary prison sentence, after which he may well be of service to his country.

> Your obedient servant,
> Lt. Colonel. J.C. Snaith, DSO
> Commander, 19th King's Own Lancashire Rifles

A quick glance at the following pages told a similar story, where the brigade, corps and divisional commanders had also added their recommendations for sparing the life of Private Godley. All pointed to his exemplary record and his youth.

The transcript of the trial was included in the file and his mood changed as he read through it swiftly. The man had clearly let his comrades down by his deserting them at the height of an action, so where had the various commanders found any extenuating circumstances? Colonel Jenkins was at his office door, whispering furtively to someone unseen on the other side.

'Jenkins, who is it?' he queried, his anger rising once more at the intrusion.

'Er, it's a message from General Haig, sir. He's here for a meeting this morning and wonders if you could spare him a few moments of your time to discuss a matter of great importance?'

Sir John's blood pressure boiled over. Haig? Here? Without a previous communication? The damn cheek of the man! Come to gloat no doubt. Twist the knife while all the time seemingly concerned for his chief's welfare? He slashed a few words in pencil across the facing page of the file and signed it before slamming it down on the top of his desk. 'Keep him waiting for five minutes and then show the general in!' he hissed and turned away to look broodingly out of the main window..

Jenkins picked up the file and looked down at the words his master had written. In large black letters it read:

I can find no grounds for commutation. Sentence is confirmed. Expedite immediately.

French, CIC, BEF, 28/11/15

Wednesday 1st December 1915
Battalion received orders to return to the front line, departing on foot on Friday 3rd. We are
to relieve 13th Worcesters on the Somme near Auchonvillers as part of 29 Div. Final kit
inspections held and deficiencies made good by quartermaster. Heavy shelling inflicted
severe casualties on ration party sent to assist in build-up of food dumps near front line.
Two officers, five ORs and one NCO of D Coy killed. Confirmation received from GHQ to
expedite sentence of death on Private 213652 Godley, B Coy. Battalion informed by CO.
Captain L. Carey, D Company

'Come in!'

David Roberts stuck his head round the door in response to the shout to find Snaith sat at his makeshift desk in the small cottage he had taken over as battalion HQ. Roberts was shocked to see a half-empty glass and a bottle of whisky, Glenlivet if he wasn't mistaken, on the desk-top and all the indications were that the CO had drank heavily from it. Cuthbert Snaith was seated, staring into the glow of the small fire, his eyes wide and unseeing. At the sound of his adjutant's entrance he gazed blearily at the major.

'I say, sir, are you all right?' Roberts asked anxiously.

Snaith pointed wearily at the two pieces of paper lying on the desk before answering. 'They're from Brigade headquarters, via GHQ, David. Our orders are in, the battalion will march out on Friday to join up with 29 Division up at Auchonvillers. We should be there by Monday. And this,' he pointed at the nearest message, 'this is an order to carry out the sentence of death on Private Godley without delay. Sir John has flatly refused to listen to his commanders in the field and ignored our recommendations for mercy. I can't think, I was sure this beastly business would take weeks to sort itself out one way or another. That GHQ lawyer fellow told me so and now look, a fortnight after the court martial and we have...we have this. God help us, David, we have a ghastly task to carry out in the next few hours. Please gather the officers and men together and let us begin the whole sordid business as laid out according to the regulations.'

An hour later, what could be hastily gathered together of the battalion from the various billets and work places was stood to attention in a hollow square in company order on the remnants of the playing field on the outskirts of Havremont. In the middle of the square, Snaith stood waiting, silently flanked by both the battalion's chaplains.

As they waited the men fidgeted and muttered among themselves, unheeding of the glares from their NCOs. The murmurs grew louder as Godley, hatless and beltless, flanked by the RSM and CSM Mason was marched up the street to the playing field from the house he had been incarcerated in. All three men came to a halt in the middle of the square at the RSM's muted command. As the watching men looked on, Snaith came to attention in front of the small party and began to read from the piece of paper in his hand.

'By order of the commander-in-chief BEF, Private 213652 Benjamin Godley, B Company, 19th King's Own Lancashire Rifles, the sentence of death by shooting awarded you by an FGCM on the fifteenth of November 1915 is hereby confirmed and will be carried out tomorrow morning at first light. That is all. March him away.'

His face white, Godley about-turned and, watched pityingly by all his stunned comrades, marched steadfastly back the way he had came, his escort half a pace behind.

As the men huddled together in small groups after being dismissed the colonel trudged over to the band of waiting officers who had attended and listened stone-faced to the sentence being read out. Cuthbert Snaith looked weary, his head drooped and his shoulders were slumped as he approached them, the message from HQ held in a limp hand. Reaching within a few steps of them he raised his head and addressed the adjutant directly.

'David, could you see that Godley has every comfort we can give him while I find out what the details for tomorrow will be?'

'Certainly, sir.' Major Roberts raised a gloved hand in salute. 'But, er, excuse my asking, sir, am I to collect together a squad of our chaps for...for...you see what I mean?'

Snaith smiled, a wan smile. 'No, David, Brigade have spared us that at least. I am assured that a firing party from one of the Gordons battalions will be on hand tomorrow morning at first light to carry out that little task. You and I, together with the RSM, CSM Mason, Captain Dundas, the chaplain that Godley has requested, and the battalion MO will be the only witnesses from the 19th to attend.

Oh, and David. Let Bradley have access to Godley, would you? I think he would like someone other than the chaplain to speak to and Bradley did request a visit when we spoke yesterday. I refused, of course, but now under the circumstances it might do Godley well to have a last few words with his platoon officer. We'll meet later this evening to go over the details of what will happen tomorrow. Understood?'

Major Roberts nodded and wheeled away, his face set in a grim mask as he walked briskly in the direction the condemned man and his escort had marched minutes previously. After a hesitant pause he was followed by Captain Dundas. Behind them, the remaining officers broke ranks and dispersed to their billets, mutely following the forlorn figure of their commanding officer.

* * * * *

'See! I told you Godley was for the high jump!' Evans later announced with a self-satisfied air, but he was cursed roundly by all those within earshot and slunk off with an aggrieved shrug of his bony shoulders. In the draughty outhouse, Charlie Horsfall threw down his cards in disgust.

'Gaaarrrgh! Who dealt this load of shite? How am I supposed to make me fortune with this crap? What? What're you looking at me like that for, Magilton?'

'C'mon Charlie, you reckon you knows all about what happens at one of these dos. Are they goin' to make us shoot poor old Godley? Can we tell the Old Man to go to blazes if we're detailed off for it? Christ, I'm gonna tell the RSM I've lost me rifle if he gives me the evil eye! I ain't gonna do it, I tell you boys I ain't gonna do it!'

'Shut it, Magilton, you quivering baby, and calm down!' Charlie Horsfall spoke with feeling. 'One, course we won't be putting a few bullets in Godley 'cos he ain't from our company for a start! Two, it's not always the fact that his own mates have to see him into the next world, if you catch my drift. I hears that it'll be some Jocks from down the road who'll be coming to do the dirty tomorrow. That twerp Evans says he heard the Old Man speaking to the adjutant about it. More to the point, am I going to have to spend some spondoolicks on a ham omelette, a sneaky brandy and a glimpse of Mademoiselle Descarte's tits down at 'er mum's caff tonight or do I settle for a tin of Maconochies stew, some bully beef and a brick-hard Army biscuit instead?'

'There's no need to talk like that, Charlie, not with what's going to happen tomorrow!' protested one of his companions.

'Oh, yeah?' snarled Horsfall, throwing his cap at the protester with a savage grin. 'What should I fucking well do then, eh? Start puttin' on me sackcloth and bleedin' ashes? Godley's well out of this fucking little mess if you ask me. Do you really think we're going to live forever, you dozy bunch of clods? We're all going to join him at some point, don't you bleedin' well worry! Now if you don't mind, I'm off to see if I can scrounge some firewood for the caff. That way I might cop a free drink.'

The wind gusted hard with a hint of snow as Lieutenant Bradley made his way through the darkened streets, looking for number 15 Rue des Chats. Godley had been marched back to where he had been quietly and benevolently looked after by the RSM since his court martial. RSM Findlay has used him for doing odd jobs, all the while within earshot and eyesight of one or more of the regimental police. Bradley arrived at the door he was seeking and discreetly knocked. The door opened a crack and a pair of eyes looked him up and down before opening the door wider to admit him. CSM Mason opened the door on his right and murmured, 'He's in there, sir.' Bradley stared hard for a moment at the CSM's retreating figure before stooping to enter the small front room.

It was cold inside, despite the warmth of the fire in the fireplace against the far wall. Godley was sat on a stool, his tunic open, by the only other furniture in the room, a small rickety table, writing on a blank sheet of paper with a pencil stub. He looked up and smiled wanly when he recognised his visitor, his face a trifle pale.

'Hello, sir.'

He stood and welcomed Bradley warmly enough, any fear he might be feeling being well disguised. 'I'll be with you in a mo if that's all right. I just want to finish this off.' He sat down again and resumed his scribbling. Bradley, feeling decidedly ill at ease, stood next to the table and nodded towards the paper.

'Who're you writing to?'

'My sister.' Godley replied simply, screwing up his face as he tried to remember the spelling of the word he was trying to write. He wrote painstakingly slowly. Bradley shuddered involuntarily. Godley caught the movement and stopped writing. Turning back towards the officer he spoke softly. 'It's all right, sir, honest it is. Please don't upset yourself. There's no help for it, there really isn't.'

'Christ, Godley!' Bradley burst out. 'How can you sit there so calmly with all...all this that's going on?'

Godley looked at his platoon officer long and hard before replying. 'I've made my peace with what's happening, sir. I spoke with Captain Dundas about every-thing and he understands. In a way it's right that I pay for what I did that night. No man should be allowed to make excuses for what he done. That's why I didn't plead against the desertion charge. Because of...you know, of the other thing.'

Bradley looked down at him, perplexed. 'What are you saying? What other thing do you mean? The court found you not guilty of striking Second-Lieutenant Elliot.'

'Oh no, sir. I mean Murgatroyd.' Godley looked at him earnestly. Bradley felt his confusion grow. Murgatroyd? What the blazes did that bastard Murgatroyd have to do with this?

Seeing his confusion Godley leaned forward and spoke in a matter-of-fact voice as he explained patiently. 'Private Murgatroyd, sir. I killed him. The night of the raid. Chucked a bomb into the Gerry dugout and killed him. Blew him to pieces.'

'Good God, man! Why?'

'Because he hurt the lady in the café and put me in the hospital, sir. After I got out of the hospital all I could think of was getting my own back. I must have gone crazy the night we went over to the Boche trenches, all I remember is seeing him and remembering how he'd hurt me in the café that night and the next thing was I got him to go into the dugout on a pretext and that's when I killed him.'

'And Mister Elliot, do you remember whether or not you hit him?'

'I don't know about that, sir, maybe it *was* me that night that struck Lieutenant Elliot. I can't say, all I know is that I ran and ran until I found myself back on our side of the lines with a splitting head. I wandered down the support trenches but no one stopped me. Hours later on I was stood by the side of the road. Before I knew where I was in Bethune stood in front of the café where me and Murgatroyd had had our...disagreement, sir. The man serving there saw me and took me inside. Kept calling me his '*pauvre garçon*'. Everyone in there was crying over the two ladies that had been killed. They told me what happened. I reckon Murgatroyd had done it to get his own back.

I slept for nearly a day and when I woke they'd taken my uniform and hidden it. They gave me the clothes I was found in and I helped in the kitchen. They were all so kind to me and it was like I could stay there forever. And all the time, though,

I was thinking of how I'd killed Murgatroyd, murdered him just like he'd murdered those two ladies. I was sort of glad when Sergeant Hobson found me, sir, but I kept quiet so as not to bring the kind people who helped me into trouble. You won't tell on them, will you, sir?'

'No, no, Godley. But why, for God's sake, why didn't you tell me this sooner? I could have explained it all at the court martial. Do you realise what you've done?'

'It doesn't excuse what I've done, sir,' Godley said slowly. 'I still killed Murgatroyd. Murdered him. There was no way the court martial would forget that. They hang murderers don't they? I brought enough shame on my pals and Colonel Snaith as it was, running away like that.'

He turned back to his letter and began to write again.

'Godley, I'm sorry, I don't know what to say. You must let me speak to someone on your behalf...' began , but Godley shrugged his shoulders and spoke sharply.

'No! Don't! Please don't. It's all right, sir, although I would ask one favour of you if I may? This letter, sir, could you make sure it gets sent on to my sister after...' Godley's composure nearly cracked as his voice faltered. He gulped deeply and continued in a steadier tone. 'After tomorrow.'

Bradley nodded. 'Of course I will. Your sister, you say? Is she older than you?'

Nodding, Godley stared into the spluttering fire. 'Elaine's her name, sir, I haven't seen her since I ran away from home over two years ago. I never got on with my stepfather, it was better I was away from him. She'd would've been gone sixteen then.'

Bradley let the words wash over him but then sat bolt upright as the meaning of what Godley was telling him became plain. 'What do you mean, sixteen? If she was older than you and she was sixteen then, that will only make her nineteen at the most now. Great Scott, Godley! What are you saying? How old are you? Speak up!'

Godley broke from his reverie to focus on the officer sat by him. He answered simply. 'I was just over sixteen myself when I volunteered last year, sir. I'll be eighteen next month.'

Bradley stared at him in consternation and damned with all his heart the stupidity of fat, ignorant recruiting sergeants who had allowed patriotism to rule their heads and looked the other way as boys obviously underage volunteered. As the law stood, only youths of nineteen and over could serve in the front line. Looking at Godley sitting so calmly in front of him as he recited his story, so many things became clear. The lack of facial hair, the spindliness of him and how his chums had carried his pack and belongings on so many of the route marches they had undertaken. No wonder.

He started forward. 'Do you realise what this means, Godley? I'll have to inform the colonel at once so he can telephone Brigade and obtain a postponement. This monstrosity cannot be allowed to go on.'

'Sir,' Godley began haltingly, 'as long as I can remember all I ever knew was being hungry and being belted by my mam and stepdad from one room to the next. My sister was the only friend I had and I ran away and left her with them!' he spat out. 'I joined the Army, the battalion, sir, and since then I've known nothing but kindness from the pals I found. I let them down badly which has brought me here, and what's going to happen tomorrow. I'm ready to pay for my sins. For what I did that night, you see? I can't change what happened. Please, sir, don't embarrass me in front of my pals by letting them find out I was just a kid. I couldn't bear them knowing that.'

'Godley, do you realise what is going to happen very soon if you don't let me go to the colonel? They are going to take you from here in the morning and shoot you! And you want to allow it? For what? Do you feel no fear at all? This is madness!' Bradley was beside himself as he tried to make Godley see the sense in what he was saying but he could see from the soldier's demeanour that he had not reached him.

Godley's voice hardened. 'If you interfere, sir, I'll have to deny having ever spoken this way to you!'

Before the astounded lieutenant could answer there was a muffled knock on the door, which then opened slightly. CSM Mason popped his head round and spoke quietly. 'Beg your pardon, sir, but the chaplain, Captain Dundas, has come back to speak with Private Godley. Are you done or shall I have him wait outside a while longer?'

Bradley turned to face Godley, who shook his head slightly, staring at him imperturbably, a white envelope in his hand. Wordlessly, Bradley reached down took the envelope and with his free hand shook Godley's outstretched one.

'Thanks for everything, sir,' Godley said quietly, 'Tell the boys in the company that I died like a man and that I was brave. I'm sorry I let you all down like this'

Seconds later Bradley found himself back in the street.

He stood there pondering for several minutes and then made his way hurriedly down in the direction of HQ. He found a reflective CO drinking a cup of hot coffee laced with whisky as he read through the day's reports. Snaith listened gravely as the lieutenant told him all that had transpired during his visit to the condemned man.

At length he said, 'Just what would you have me do at this late hour? Telephone Brigade to have all this passed on to higher authorities? To do what? Godley attested the day he volunteered, giving his age as nineteen. His enlistment papers will show that. He has just admitted murdering one of his fellow comrades. Do you think the Army will forgive him that, in spite of his age? If we could prove his youth, which I very much doubt. That could take days, weeks. Time we do not have. By the speed with which his papers were returned, our commander-in-chief is determined to make an example of Godley and I for one am in agreement with him on this.

'No, I'm afraid Private Godley's fate is in higher hands than ours now. He disgraced the battalion and if his dying serves any purpose it might make another young man in our charge think twice before trying something similar.'

'But sir, this is murder! He's just a boy!'

Snaith looked at him coldly. 'Bradley, pull yourself together and look around you, man. We're surrounded by "boys", youths of only nineteen and twenty who know nothing of life yet volunteered to serve their country. We commit murder, legal murder, every day we're out here with these "boys". Do you think one more death, tragic as it might seem at this very moment, is going to make the slightest difference? I have in my hands the safety of all the men of this battalion, over a thousand of them, to consider and I will not jeopardise that safety to try and save one young man who let us all down so badly. Discipline, discipline is what will win this war. Godley forgot that and so must pay for his lapse in spite of his youth.

'You did your best for him, but go back to your billet, and try to sleep. In two day's time we go back into the line and the death of this young man will be a soon-forgotten memory. God knows, then there'll be more than enough death for you and all of us to contemplate.'

'But, sir...

'Lieutenant Bradley, for goodness sake! There is no more to be said on the matter, do you hear? Now kindly do as I have asked and go and try to get some sleep.' As Bradley picked up his cap disconsolately, Cuthbert Snaith spoke to him for the last time that evening. 'Keep this discussion to yourself for the time being, would you? I would not want the men unsettled by the news you brought me of Godley's real age slipping out. No need to upset them with us departing back into the line shortly.' With that Snaith poured himself another large splash of whisky into his empty cup and took a stiff slug, grimacing as the spirit burned his throat. When he put the glass down, he was alone.

In the back room where he had sat readying the CO's uniform for the morning, Evans sat with his eyes wide open at the conversation he had overheard so clearly through the shattered walls of the cottage. He let out a low whistle that went unheard in the next room. What news he had to tell the boys, see if he didn't! Shout at him for taking the mickey earlier would they, well wait until the lads heard this little lot. Who would have believed it, that little shrimp Godley being the age he was and the CO not wanting to lift a damn finger to help the poor blighter. This should be worth more than a few fags.

Evans carefully folded the tunic he was holding, draped it over a chair and drained the last dregs from the glass of whisky he'd earlier stolen from the bottle hidden in the colonel's valise. Opening the back door carefully he stepped out into the dark, cold night and stood for a while on the back step, thinking deeply as he buttoned his tunic. Now then, who should he speak to first?

17

Thursday 2nd December 1915

*Last minute preparations carried out as battalion was readied for route march in the
morning to join 29th Div on the Somme near Auchonvillers. Ammunition drawn from
stores and distributed, along with three days' iron rations for the march. Sentence of
death carried out on 213652 Pte Godley, B Company, in the a.m.*

Captain L. Carey, D Company

A hard frost had gathered overnight, covering the ground with a mantle of
white. The waiting group of four men huddled together in the early gloom,
stamping their feet and blowing into their leather-gloved hands in a vain attempt
to bring some feeling back into frozen fingers and feet. The CO stood flanked by
David Roberts, along with the RSM and CSM Mason. They were gathered together
at the far end of the playing field in front of the butts of the makeshift firing ranges.
Here only a few days earlier the men had gathered to watch a demonstration of the
Stokes mortar but today the gathering was to witness something of a more deadly
nature.

Twenty feet from them, placed centrally below the bank of earth that had supported the cloth targets, sat a solitary wooden chair. It's grim purpose was all too
evident by the wall of sandbags strategically placed at it's rear and the loose coils
of rope, one on each arm and another dangling from the back rest. Ten feet or so
from the chair a line of white tape had been stretched along the grass, almost
hidden by the frost. Behind the butts a driver sat patiently waiting on the seat of
his GS wagon, wrapped in blankets. Cap tied on by a dark scarf to ward off the
cold, he and his horse quietly awaited the outcome of the morning's proceedings.
In the back of the wagon was a single open wooden coffin alongside which the lid
lay tilted at an angle. Leaning by one of the rear wheels was a canvas stretcher, the
carrying-handles and canvas stiff and rimed with ice.

Twenty feet from the driver another group of men stood stoically waiting too,
hands grasped around the stocks of the Lee-Enfield rifles they each bore. The dark
Glengarry caps with badge declaring the legend '*Bydand*', each with it's long tassels
trailing down the soldier's neck, together with the flodden-grey cover over their
dark-green kilts, showed them to be Gordon Highlanders.

A young second-lieutenant, resplendent in dark-green tartan trews and khaki tunic, his claymore hanging down his side, stood nervously aloof from his men, staring at his watch in the murk and playing absentmindedly with the flap of his holstered service revolver. Next to him, wearing the stripes of a sergeant and three wound stripes on his left cuff, a tall, fiercely-moustached figure scowled as he walked up and down the ranks, addressing the squad of men before him.

'Now, lads,' he uttered darkly, 'you will no' fuck it up! When we march out of here, quietly, mind, there'll be no speaking, ye hear?' They all nodded mutely. 'Good. We'll march round yon corner to the spot and stop, wheel into line and present arms a'. You'll fire when the officer here drops his hankie. Then when the laddie's pronounced dead you'll shoulder arms an' we're away. Got that?'

Again, all the listening men nodded.

'Right, now then, don't think you'll be doing yon poor laddie any good by not aimin' straight at him. If he's no dead after the volley, Mister Macpherson here will have to finish him off wi' a pistol an' believe you me if that happens, I'll be finishin' off some o' you along wi' yon poor laddie! Understand?'

No one dared open his mouth . The sergeant continued. 'Don't believe all that shite about only one or two of yer rifles bein' loaded with real bullets. They've *all* got real bullets, I loaded the fuckers myself, this morning. OK?'

The day slowly dawned, a blood-red horizon framed by dark clouds as if to blend in with the grim event that was soon to happen. As the daylight grew stronger and the shadows began to retreat a small party marched slowly over the grass. The frost caught the rays of the strengthening sun and glistened and sparkled as the group of four men drew near. Dark figures far to their rear told of the men detailed off to stop any inquisitive, unwanted onlookers from observing what was about to happen.

In the front strode the calm figure of the chaplain, Captain Dundas. Behind him, looking equally serene but with a deathly pallor to his face, walked a bareheaded Godley, his upper arms bound to his sides by a single piece of rope, flanked by two corporals of the regimental police. They marched steadily on, their footsteps showing up darkly on the frost-covered ground until they were only a few paces from the waiting group. As they passed, the RSM wheeled round and marched behind them, heading at an angle that would bring him level with the end of the butts and into sight of the waiting Highlanders.

As they reached the chair Godley's legs almost buckled beneath him but the two corporals gently caught him and eased him into a sitting position. He winced visibly as the coldness of the chair bit through the uniform trousers he was wearing but he continued to sit there unmoving as the two men quickly bent his elbows below the ropes now crossing his breast and tied his lower arms to the armrests. Straightening up they moved back as the colonel approached Godley, accompanied by the chaplain. Standing in front of the bound youth, looking directly at him, in the cold clear air, Snaith intoned in a firm, strong voice, 'Private Benjamin Isaac Godley, the sentence passed will now be carried out. Do you wish to make a last statement?'

Godley closed his eyes and shook his head dumbly, shivering slightly as the cold bit further into his thin frame. CSM Mason stepped forward and taking a folded linen cloth from his pocket, opened it out and began to wrap it around Godley's face. Godley's eyes opened and he started wildly, shaking his head violently as if to rid himself of the blindfold. 'No, sir!' he burst out, 'No! I'm not afraid. Please! Do I have to have that?'

'I'm sorry, son,' Frank Mason spoke quietly, 'I'm afraid you do. It's not for you but for the others.'

At his words Godley relaxed slightly and allowed the cloth to be tied to his face. Frank Mason reached into his pocket once more and brought out a small white disc which he swiftly pinned on top of Godley's khaki tunic, over his heart. Beneath his cold fingers he could feel Godley's heart beating through the thin tunic, racing like a captive sparrow he had once held, terrified, in the palm of his hand. As he turned to straighten up, Godley spoke once more in a calm voice.

'Goodbye, CSM. Thanks.'

Frank Mason reached down and grasped Godley's right hand as best he could. Squeezing the frozen hand tight, he whispered in Godley's ear, 'Good luck, son. It'll be over soon.' He could hear Godley's breathing, fast and shallow as he sucked in air through the linen cloth. Captain Dundas bent over Godley, too, and whispered a few words before patting him on the shoulder and walking sadly back with the CO and Frank Mason. As he did so, the CSM made a sign with his hand to the waiting Bob Findlay.

Seeing the sign, RSM Findlay signalled to the young Scottish officer and his men. Everything now happened at speed. Without a command the Highlanders wheeled out from behind the butts, the white frozen breath exhaled from their mouths streaming around them like smoke from a locomotive's stack. They marched purposefully towards the white tape marked on the ground at a measured pace, rifles held across their chests at the high port with their young white-faced officer leading them six paces in front. Bringing up the rear his sergeant marched with them, watching fiercely for any faltering.

On they came, the tramping of their boots sounding loud in the still, morning air. Macpherson spun round to face the following men ten feet from the chair. As the first rifleman came to the far end of the tape he wheeled into line and came to a halt, followed a split second by his comrades behind him. Eight loaded rifles rose up to the 'present arms' position soundlessly with smooth, practised, professional ease, all the muzzles pointing at Godley from almost ten feet away.

As the rifles wavered in the growing daylight, Macpherson let go the white handkerchief he held nervously aloft in his raised left hand.

The volley of shots burst, shockingly, loudly, from the barrels simultaneously in a flash of orange flame and the rifles slammed fiercely back into their bearer's shoulders, causing those watching to start violently in spite of themselves. In the woods to their right, a black mass of outraged crows leapt into the air, whirling and swirling in their hundreds, filling the air with their loud caws of protest at having their morning sleep so violently disturbed.

Godley's chest erupted in a cloud of rent khaki, the white disc torn to shreds as the metal-jacketed bullets savagely tore through his slight figure and into the sandbags behind. The impact of the volley threw him backwards, legs flying, the chair tipping over in a spray of bright red blood which arced through the air to splash the white ground beneath in a macabre, abstract pattern. Godley lay, sprawled inertly in a twisted, grotesque attitude, and from under the chair a spreading pool of crimson sluggishly oozed, in stark contrast to the whiteness of the frost.

As the echoes and re-echoes of the shots died away the MO, Captain Hughes, ran forward, his stethoscope trailing as he knelt by the side of the limp figure of Boy Godley.2/Lt Macpherson followed, hesitantly tugging at his holster flap as he approached the two figures. A cursory examination told the MO that the deadly bullets had completed their job and he turned to the waiting colonel and nodded with an air of sad finality.

Facing him, their part in the proceedings finished, the Highlanders smartly shouldered their weapons at a sign from their sergeant and wheeled back the way they had come, soon lost out of sight behind the butts. On their departure Captain Dundas walked over and stood by the body in the chair, his eyes shut tight, gripping his Bible until his knuckles gleamed whitely as the two witnessing NCOs approached

The acrid tang of cordite reached the nostrils of all those present as the RSM and CSM Mason righted the chair and reverently untied the ropes binding Godley to it before laying his limp, inert body on the ground. The group of witnesses dispersed and began their slow walk back over the playing field towards the village as the driver of the GS wagon appeared from behind the butts, dragging the canvas stretcher. RSM Findlay reached down as the driver and Frank Mason straightened the dead man's limbs and tore the cloth from Godley's face before they placed him on the stretcher.

The young soldier lay as if asleep, his eyes closed, the smooth unlined face ghastly pale. The RSM carefully laid the cloth over the obscenely bloodied, shattered area of his chest and nodded. Stooping slightly the two men bore the blood-stained stretcher round to the waiting wagon accompanied by the chaplain. At their approach the horse reared up, eyes white in its sockets as its nostrils caught the smell of fresh blood. Cursing, the driver savagely caught it across the back with his whip and its plunging quieted with the feel of the lash. It remained standing, head sunken, trembling, as they quickly manoeuvred the limp body into the waiting coffin. Standing back they watched mutely as the driver carelessly threw the lid on before resuming his seat and driving away to the British military cemetery in the vicinity of Becourt.

RSM Findlay caught hold of his friend's arm and said simply to him, 'A rum do, eh Frank? Poor little blighter. Come on, let's go and get some breakfast.'

In Havremont, many of the men had wakened early, their attention being drawn to the fields far away to their left. As the faint sound of a volley reached them they flinched and looked at each other in disquiet and sorrow. All except one man. Second-Lieutenant David William Elliot smiled broadly as the sound of the shots reached him and took another deep, appreciative slurp of the tea his batman had brought him.

18

Sunday 5th December 1915

Battalion entered trenches in vicinity of Beaumont Hamel late p.m. after a two-day route march. Relieved Lancs Fusiliers. Heavy sleet changing to snow later on. Trenches in poor condition. B Coy in reserve.

Captain L. Carey, D Company

'Would you look at the state of this!'

Reggie Pilling was outraged as he stooped to drop his pack on the mud of the trench floor. 'Who the bleedin' hell were those dirty pigs we took over from? Look how they've left it for us, our kid!' His gaze was held by the condition of the trench he and his pals of A Company were being ordered to occupy. It was not hard to see the reason for his outrage. The trench floor had disappeared in all but a few places, filled with a thick, greasy, churned-up, freezing scum that would make passage down it anything but easy. The parapet was crumbling in several places with large gaps showing, the sandbags and earth that had slid down the walls hidden under the watery, chalky slush. A stench further down the trench gave a hint of the possibility of some unburied bodies, but for now the water hid its secrets.

'Never mind moaning, Pilling,' Sergeant Clark rasped, 'just get down there and find yourself a funkhole. Then you and all yer mates can help to make this pigsty habitable again. Savvy?' He took a quick peep over the parapet and ducked back down.

'Just as I thought. When it gets dark tonight, I want a work party over the top and clean up all those empty bully tins and all the other rubbish those bastards we relieved saw fit to throw over 'cos they couldn't be bothered to collect them. No wonder there's so many rats in the vicinity.' He stormed off down the trench to berate some other miscreants, leaving Reggie and his mates relieved at having got off so lightly.

It had been a long, tiring march up the muddied, rutted tracks that passed for roads connecting the villages bordering the Somme valley to their present position near the Ancre river, with Auchonvillers behind them and Beaumont Hamel opposite. The weather had been foul, rain that turned to freezing sleet and then to snow had dogged them all the way, leaving them all wet through to the bone and feeling deathly tired.

Many men were still somewhere out on the back roads, stragglers from the line of march who were being tended to and then sent on their way to join up with the rest of the battalion. The shirkers hid among the genuine cases and for the most part there was nothing the NCOs could do but swear viciously at the prone figures and get the rest of the men moving.

After marching through the deathly quiet ruins of Albert, the statue of the Gilded Virgin atop the spire still hanging precariously at right angles to the walls of the Basilica, the names of the following villages had been lost to their consciousness. They had struggled their way up through the French countryside, Snaith's head bowed against the weather as his dispirited nag bore him equally despondently at the head of the column. The death of Godley had affected them all deeply, the feelings of the men tempered by the knowledge, amply spread by Snaith's batman, that their own CO had wished to keep his own involvement in the affair a secret from the rest of the battalion. He was reviled for the preconceived notion that he had allowed the execution to take place without lifting a finger to help Godley.

It had made for an air of gloom that pervaded the wretched march northwards through the rolling hills and downs that reminded many of home. The villages they passed through seemed full of whey-faced, unfriendly faces, people who stood apathetically to gaze unfeelingly as they passed. The British Army was renowned for it's renditions of all the popular songs of the day while it marched but this time the battalion could not find the heart to sing and they tramped along in silence. Even the irascible Alfie Parkes stayed silent. Any attempt to rouse the men in a chorus fizzled out lamely, the second editions of *Marching Songs for Soldiers* that most of them carried staying in their packs out of sight.

Whether or not Cuthbert Snaith realised the depths of feeling ranged against him, he continued his lonely vigil without a backward glance at the head of the long snake of men. At night he dined alone in the billets found for them along the way. His fellow officers understood the reason behind his need for solitude and wisely left him alone with his thoughts, save for the few times they needed guidance during the day's march.

Now, at long last, they had arrived at their final destination, late on a wintry afternoon. After stowing their possessions all the companies, save B Company, which was left in reserve, were turfed out to try and clear the stinking mess. As they toiled their NCOs passed among them shouting and bawling, giving out instructions and herding them together into work parties to shore up the gaping holes in their defences.

'Don't forget, lads, when you're finished here and you get back into yer holes, try and dry yer feet and then rub 'em with the whale grease you were issued with.

Any man coming to me with trench foot can expect a right rollicking. Never mind the bloody MO, you'll cop it from me personally. You hear me?' Bill Clark was everywhere, wading up and down the bays and traverses as he tried to get his message across. They bore his exhortations with stoic patience because even if he was a bit loud they knew he was trying to do them some good.

'Like a bleedin' matron at school trying to force cod liver oil down your throat,' Sidney Bates exclaimed later on as he described the day's work to the newcomers who had arrived later from the route march.

After their kit had been stowed, Snaith held a meeting of all his officers who could be spared from their duties.

'Look chaps,' he began, 'I know we're all tired but we're here now and can make plans for a long stay. I'm told that this is a quiet sector and that the Hun is quite prepared to 'live and let live', as it were. After the emotions of the past week I think it best if we allow the men to get used to the surrounding area before we make any strenuous demands of them. I've informed HQ that I would like some time to elapse before we make a start with our training programme, other than with purely battalion matters.

'We shall shortly start on a programme of bringing the chaps together by platoons to train them in the latest methods. That includes everyone knowing how to operate a Lewis gun, in case of casualties, and as many men away on trench mortar courses as can be spared. On the entertainment front, we don't want the men getting stale. All work and no play... There are plenty of cafés and estaminets within easy reach when in reserve and I've asked Brigade to see if we can't hold a concert party soon, have a jolly good laugh, what! Now you chaps go out there and see to your men, and I do *not* want to hear any talk of Private Godley. That subject is now closed. Very well, gentlemen, off you go!'

With several arched eyebrows and a few knowing looks, his officers left. When they had gone, Col Snaith moved over to his valise and took out the bottle buried deep in its confines. He looked at the contents and a frown passed over his face. The level seemed to have dropped quite a bit in the last few days but as quickly as the thought entered his head he dismissed it impatiently and turned back to the valise to find the tumbler he had placed alongside the bottle. Dragging it from the depths he poured a large quantity of whisky into the glass and sat back in his chair, his back digging into the wall. He grimaced as the sharp spirit burnt all the way down his gullet into his stomach.

Godley. No one had mentioned the private's name but he had heard the hisses and murmurings every morning as he mounted his steed and made his way to the head of his men, *his* battalion. He slammed the tumbler hard down onto the sideboard beside his chair in a sudden fit of temper. By God! No one was going to make *him* feel guilty for any of his actions. He reached for the bottle and poured himself another generous measure.

Tuesday 7th December 1915

A surprise attack on the battalion trenches at 08:05 ack emma led to C Coy trenches being severely damaged. Heavy artillery barrage followed the exploding of a mine in C Coy area. Major Benson, C Coy commander and 2/Lt's Whickham and Donaldson killed. Seventeen ORs killed, fifteen wounded, three severely as enemy tried to gain our trenches, being beaten off with great gallantry. Five ORs missing, presumed killed.

Captain L. Carey, D Company

The day dawned slowly. Great dark clouds scudded along in a brisk breeze, the icy blasts finding their way into every chink in the soldiers' clothing, numbing the bare skin unlucky to be caught uncovered. Stand-to came and went with no undue movement from the trenches in front of them and the men relaxed. Several of them lounged on the firestep, ostensibly as sentries, while the others ate whatever they managed to cook or scrounge for their breakfast, cooking salt bacon in home-made cookers and washing it down with a mug of tea. The smoke from the cooking mingled with the acrid smell of pipe tobacco as pipes were lit after their hunger had been assuaged.

'D'ye know, I'm gonna miss you lot when I go on me merry way next week,' announced Howard Arkwright to those in his immediate vicinity as he puffed contentedly on his briar pipe.

'How's that, then, Howard? Where do you think you're going to, like? We've got bayonet drill in an hour's time and you know what Hornby's like if you mess him about,' Percy Hartson asked him innocently as he carefully cleaned the magazine of the Lewis gun propped next to him. The chalk and dirt tended to stick to the gun and its moving parts and Percy was fastidious in keeping it in immaculate firing order.

'Nob off, you dozy bugger!' Howard grinned and pushed him roughly, 'You know bloody well I said *next* week, Hartson! And you want to know where I'll be? I'll be tucked up in clean sheets clinging on to the old woman as we enjoy some "soldier's comforts", that's where I'll bleedin' well be. Mark my words, Percy old man, I'll be thinking of you.'

Hartson opened his mouth to reply in kind but the breath he had just taken was driven out of him as the ground around their trench seemed to ripple and bulge soundlessly then move upwards at a great rate of speed with an earth-shattering roar. The sound lasted for several, long seconds as the ground shook and the air was filled with huge clods of earth and chalk flying in all directions. A billowing pall of dust hung wisp-like in the air, completely blocking the view in front of the trenches that had survived the explosion.

His ears ringing, Hartson struggled to wipe the dirt from his eyes and stand up from the prone position he now found himself in. Dimly he could hear hoarse shouts and the high, thin sound of someone screaming but for the moment he was unable to see or move. His eyes cleared, he glanced round to see how everyone else had fared and was shocked to see the destruction the explosion had wrought upon the trench yards away to his left. Where the line once snaked was a massive hole, the edges of which still steamed gently with the heat of the explosive force that had gouged it from the frozen ground.

He could see no further than a few yards as the haze of dust from the aftermath of the mine's deafening roar hung in the still air, casting a surreal light on the ground beneath. Of the rest of his Lewis gun team he could see nothing. They had been sheltering in a dugout to his left but where it had stood was now part of the gaping hole in their defences.

'B Platoon, to me!' he shouted, but no answer came in the deathly silence.

Equipment and bodies lay everywhere, littering the ground, and he realised with a sick feeling that some of the shapes he could make out were body parts, flung there as the soldiers in the immediate vicinity of the explosion had borne its full force. An arm, its raised fist still clenched, stuck out of the parapet as if in silent condemnation, and further down what remained of the trench he could make out a blood-drenched lower torso, the upper half having been brutally ripped away. Directly in front of him a pair of hobnailed boots stuck out from a mound of earth and as he watched they shook violently as the soldier beneath the mound tried desperately to extricate himself.

Hartson shook his head and felt his aching jaw. Satisfied that he was still in one piece he moved over to the boots and began to dig, slowly at first, then more frantically, using his hands and a metal mug he found upturned by the buried boots. The hands became free and the buried soldier flapped them weakly as he tried to aid his saviour. His lungs bursting, Hartson dug on grimly and was rewarded by the man's head becoming visible.

In a short while he had uncovered the buried man's body and was able to pull him away from the earth that had threatened to become his tomb. He was unrecognisable, covered in dirt and the white chalk, shivering with shock at the horror of what he had experienced. His teeth chattering, the man rolled over next to Percy and began to retch, gasping, taking in great lungfuls of air as his body heaved with the violence of his retching.

'Th...thanks, mate...' he sobbed, wheezing as he inhaled huge gulps of air. 'I thought I were done for, I truly did. God! Me head hurts something rotten.'

'Howard, you dozy clod! It's me. Percy.'

'Percy? Christ, chum. Oh God, Percy, I was, I were, I thought, I...I've broke me fucking pipe!'

'It's all right,' Percy spoke soothingly, 'just sit back and rest a while til you gets yer breath back.'

Before Arkwright could frame an answer a screaming sound filled the air and they both ducked instinctively as the shells landed over the back of the trench and burst with loud explosions, flinging hot, metallic fragments moaning through the air. Within seconds the air was filled with the noise of more shells and they clung together as they tried to make themselves as small as possible. Risking a look up through the concussive effects of the barrage, Hartson was fascinated to see a large, black drum slowly whistling through the air as it curved downwards towards them. He ducked again and a second later a massive explosion was followed by more screams as the *minenwerfer* shell burst in the trench over to their right.

'Christ, Howard, I think the Boche are attacking!' he exclaimed, and looked round desperately to see where his Lewis gun had gone. He spied the butt sticking out of a pile of earth and scuttled over to it to free it. Thanking the God that had given him the foresight to clothe it he stripped the protective sackcloth from the barrel and working parts and clicked home a magazine from the bag at his feet.

The shellfire increased in tempo, the skyline behind them becoming alight with the fire and smoke of the explosions. Dragging the gun over to the parapet, still crouched down, he looked back to where Howard Arkwright sat, looking stunned as he felt his body for wounds.

'Howard, get over here, now! I need someone to feed me ammo. Quickly Howard, for God's sake, or we're done for!'

Slowly, still shivering with the shock of his recent escape, Arkwright numbly moved over to where Hartson lay and caught the webbing straps of the ammunition bag that held the magazines for the Lewis. His rifle lay on its side, the barrel twisted and useless and he kicked it angrily aside as he lifted the canvas ammunition bag. They both whipped round to see a stumbling, terrified figure, bareheaded, scrambling along the trench towards them, his uniform so caked with mud and what looked like blood as to be unrecognisable.

'Run! Run! The Boche are coming. They're right behind me. Run or we're all dead!'

'Howard! Come with me! Keep an eye out to yer left'

Hartson came to his feet and gestured towards the crater lip. Nodding his understanding Arkwright swung the bag of magazines over his shoulder and followed his friend as he ran swiftly towards the crumbled earth. Panting hard, the two men flung themselves on the ground in the comparative shelter of the crater. Percy squirmed onto the front lip of the crater and squinted down the barrel through the sights, ignoring the cold sensation of the freezing ground as he pulled the cocking handle back savagely towards him.

The shells were still falling steadily as around the corner the shocked soldier had fled from earlier a crouching form slowly appeared. Hartson nodded wordlessly in acknowledgement as Arkwright's fist hit him urgently in the small of the back at the sight of the figure in the grey-green uniform of the enemy.

'Come on, come on chum,' he murmured to himself as more crouching figures arrived behind the first, pointing and gesticulating as they appeared from around the corner, weapons held out at the ready in front of them. When the number of them filled his sights he took a deep breath, slowly exhaled and as he did so, and gently squeezed the trigger. The gun bucked beneath him but he held it firmly with his other hand, pulling the butt down as the Lewis barked angrily. The men in front of him, only twenty yards away, melted away as if by magic, falling without a word as the bullets thudded into them.

The gun shuddered and stopped and Hartson banged with his trigger hand on Arkwright's head. Arkwright handed him a fresh magazine from the bag. Stripping the empty magazine from the gun Hartson flung it high over the crater away from him and banged the new one into place. An object appeared over the parapet from around the far corner and he just had time to shout 'Duck!' before the enemy stick grenade burst with an explosion of dirt, showering them with frozen earth.

He waited, and after a minute's pause a head peered quickly round the corner and then just as quickly withdrew. Another long minute passed and then slowly round the corner appeared the body of another German soldier, stick grenade in hand as he stared round keenly at his surroundings. Percy waited until all of him was visible and then coolly fired a long burst into the man's body. The enemy soldier slid to the floor of the trench, the grenade falling harmlessly to the ground. From around the corner came the voices of several men, arguing gutturally, and Hartson grinned fiercely at their consternation.

A sudden burst of firing in the trench where the enemy were hiding made the two men press themselves more firmly into the earth in alarm. Loud screams sounded, intermingled with more gunfire and shouts, and suddenly two Germans appeared, running hard round the corner straight towards Hartson and Arkwright. Hartson fired automatically and they both fell, adding their bodies to the pile in front of the two Englishmen. Cautiously, a hand appeared and waved up and down from where the Germans had bolted.

'Don't fire!' its owner shouted, his voice masked by the trench. 'I'm coming out. We're British.' Around the corner a uniformed figure appeared, caked with dirt, but even at that range Hartson had no difficulty in recognising the austere figure of their company commander, Major William Benson. Percy eased his finger off the trigger and stood up.

'It's us, sir, me and Howard. I mean, Hartson and Arkwright, sir. From B Platoon.'

'Well done, Hartson.' His eyes took in the dishevelled state of both men and he gestured at the still figures at his feet. 'I see you two have had a bit of a scrap here. Good men, I'll make sure the colonel gets to hear about this. Now, are there any other men from your section with you?'

Hartson jabbered away excitedly as he informed the major of their part in the morning's action and when at last he came to the end of his story Benson quickly explained what had happened.

'Fritz blew a mine under our company trenches and then put up an infernal barrage to stop us being reinforced as you two men no doubt heard. We've lost a few men but so has Fritz. Those men you killed were trapped between you and us. We've bombed them all the way back here but we're running short. You don't have any bombs to spare, do you?'

At Hartson's shake of his head Benson continued. 'Mr Whickham was killed by a shell, poor chap, and Mr Donaldson was shot dead by a Boche pretending to be dead as we passed. Well, he's not pretending now! The Boche were a bit too late in making their way into our trenches and we managed to stop them but it was a close thing. CSM Hornby is keeping them back further to our right with more of our chaps so we need to get cracking.'

'Shouldn't we stay here, sir, until help arrives?' Hartson asked, gesturing to where he'd left his Lewis gun. 'This seems to be a good, natural defensive position, sir.'

'Look here, Hartson,' the major rejoined sharply, 'just go and pick up the damn gun and come with me without arguing. Leave the soldiering to me, there's a good chap.'

Feeling annoyed at the major's tone of voice, Hartson turned away and walked slowly back to where he'd left his weapon. Picking it up he bent down and hefted the canvas bag containing the spare magazines. As he straightened, a shrill sound rose to a screaming crescendo and without thinking he dropped the gun and dived back into the crater. Behind him the sound of a deafening explosion and a gout of yellow flame, black smoke and hot air washed over the top of his sheltering place and he crouched beneath the lethal fragments as they whined near to him, flicking at his clothing.

The earth and dust eventually subsided and he crawled back up the crater and peered over the top to where the men from his company had stood with Major Benson. There was no sign of a living thing to be seen, just shattered bodies, some smouldering scraps of cloth and pieces of hot, twisted metal. It took him seconds before he realised that this was all that remained of the men who seconds before had been living entities. All gone, in the blink of an eye and the force of a high-explosive shell.

He began to retch as the coppery smell of violent death reached him. Dropping to his knees he bent over and threw up, his stomach heaving with each involuntary response. A sound reached his ear, amidst all the shelling, and he looked round blearily for its source.

One of the bodies, its blood-soaked uniform rent and torn in many places, moved feebly and he crawled over to it, wiping the mucus from his mouth and nose on his sleeve as he did so. He grasped the man's shoulders to ease him towards him.

'Oh, God. Howard. Are you all right?'

Howard Arkwright looked up, eyes half-closed, as he tried to focus on the man crouching over him. His left arm rose weakly and wavered, hand open, and his lips moved as he tried to frame a word. Only a liquid, gargling, gulping noise emerged and Percy knelt by him and gently lifted him up. 'It's Percy, Howard, I'll get someone. You'll be all right. Don't move.'

Arkwright shook his head and his lips twitched. He tried to speak but a thin dribble of blood slowly oozed out of his mouth. Hartson stared, horrified, and bent over his friend again. He pulled at his tunic to try and free the emergency shell-dressing he carried in his breast pocket but as he did so he could already feel that it was too late. There was no response from his friend, no movement, and he sat back and looked at Howard Arkwright's pale face as his friend's body sagged. The eyes stared blindly past him, glazed, half-open, fixed at a point in space that Hartson was unable to see or fathom.

He was still there when the reinforcements rushed up from B Company reached him minutes later, sat cradling the body of his dead friend as they crowded into the shattered trench. The firing went on for some time but he continued to sit there, cradling Howard Arkwright's stiffening corpse in his aching arms. It was only when a pair of stray stretcher-bearers reached him and gently lifted Arkwright's body out of his protective arms and onto the stretcher that he rose and accompanied them down the trench out of sight of the scene of his friend's demise. The Lewis gun lay behind him, forgotten, half-buried in the dirt where he had dropped it. When at long last they reached the reserve trenches he dropped into a spare dugout whose owners were long gone and flung himself down on the hard-packed earth. And wept.

19

Wednesday 15 December 1915

In billets in Oudrecourt-sur-Ancre. Sleet for most of the day. New drafts reached the battalion, to replace casualties from previous week's action. Battalion relieved by Middlesex Regt after ten days in the line to enable re-quipping and small arms training to be carried out. Leave party consisting of three officers and twenty ORs left in the p.m. Planning for a concert party begun by Capt Charteris.

Captain L. Carey, D Company

Neville Charteris looked down at the sheaf of letters that had newly arrived at their billets that afternoon. His frown deepened as he recognised his wife's handwriting on two of them and he turned them over and over in his hand unconsciously as he contemplated destroying them without reading what was inside. There was no help for it, he had better see what Lucille was wanting him to do now. Finding a quiet corner of the icy-cold room he had sheltered in he slid to the floor and opened the first letter.

It was as he'd feared. An angry Lucille wrote that owing to his silence of the past weeks she had written to his CO demanding to know whether or not she was a widow. The sarcastic tone of her letter continued unabated, bringing a hot flush to his cheeks as he read and re-read her strident demands for him to contact her, *or else.* Nowhere in the letter was there a single question as to how he was keeping and he flung it angrily to the floor. After a moment's hesitation he opened the second letter and read that quickly.

This time she had become more threatening, alluding to her 'dear friend' Arnold' in the office she worked in, and informing Neville that if she did not hear from him shortly she would be forced to begin 'proceedings' against him. The war had emancipated women and she knew 'her rights'. Helped no doubt by her 'dear friend' he thought.

He laughed bitterly as he remembered the last 'help' her 'dear friend' had been giving her when he came upon them in bed, and viciously crumpled the letter in his hand. Reaching down he gathered the other letter up and slowly ripped them both into small pieces, staring into the empty fireplace of the room as he thought of what he must do next.

The third letter was from Matilda Fairley, a few hastily scribbled lines asking how he was keeping now that the weather had turned colder and giving him a brief idea of how people were coping at home, seeing as the war was stretching towards its second Christmas. Her idle chatter made him homesick suddenly and he yearned to be back in normality again, sitting by a warm fire. He shook himself tetchily and stood up, angry with himself for his tired state of mind and letting his thoughts lead him in that direction.

Lucille's betrayal had sunk deeply into his spirit and blocked all his thoughts of a 'normal' life. His thoughts for Tillie bothered him, too. He had replied to her earlier letter, a single rambling affair of conditions and the weather at the Front and how he hoped to receive more leave in the New Year. Nothing personal – his inner thoughts he had kept to himself, hiding away the mixed emotions he was trying so hard to come to terms with. There were nights when he dreamed he was back in the house in Peckham with her and try as he might to dismiss them they kept returning. Feeling decidedly confused and miserable at all of this he pushed the free ends of his scarf down into his jacket and made his way out into the cold.

He bumped into another figure, bent down against the biting wind, and murmured an automatic 'Sorry old chap' as he passed by. The figure grabbed his sleeve and turned him round.

'Aha, Neville, old man!' exclaimed Charles Brasher. 'Just the man I've been looking for. Glad I found you.'

'What is it, Charles?'

'Haven't you heard, Neville, the Old Man's been looking for you. You've been appointed concert party officer, didn't you know? The Old Man wants a Christmas concert for the men. Cheer them up.'

Charteris groaned aloud. 'Tell me you're having a spot of fun with me, Charles? Please! Not me, not now of all times!'

'Look here, old man, buck up and go and see Captain Dundas, won't you. The Old Man has roped him into it too so the two of you should be able to get your heads together and put on a damn good show for the chaps. I'm off, got some ration parties to get together. Nip off down and see Dundas. Last I saw of him he was putting a list together for auditions. See if you can't wangle yourself a spot, eh? Singing or something!'

Charteris stared after him and groaned again. Damn and blast. A bloody concert party of all things! What next? Elocution lessons for the cooks? Shaking his head he followed Brasher. He found Dundas in the house that had been used as the post office, listening with a pained expression on his face as Private Billy Lane gave full vent to his interpretation of 'Come into the Garden, Maud'.

'Yes, yes, Lane, that'll do. Er, we'll see if we can't get you in as a novelty act.' Ignoring Lane's outraged expression as he flounced out of the door the chaplain twisted round to see Charteris in the doorway.

'Neville, my dear chap. Thank goodness you've come, I could do with a hand here.'

'Hello, Roger, nice to see you. I heard you need help. What can I do?'

'That's the spirit! Call in Private Parker, would you? I believe he does something extraordinary with a set of spoons.'

Rolling his eyes upwards, Charteris made for the door again. 'Parker? In here, now. You're on next. And bring your spoons with you!'

* * * * *

Far, far to the north, as the weather changed and the wind swung round to the east, other events were taking place.

On the windswept German coast near the mouth of the Elbe, a tall, slim figure dressed in the uniform of a Kapitanleutnant in His Majesty's Imperial Naval Airship Service stood by the revolving hangar at the Zeppelin base of Nordholtz, casting a keen eye at the weather. Karl Meyer cursed softly as the rain lashed at his leather overcoat, squinting as he tried to gauge whether it would clear in the next hour or so. The forecast had not been too bad and this rain had come as a complete surprise. He cursed again, softly at first then more loudly as his impatience took hold.

Another uniformed figure slipped out of the side door of the hangar and slowly made its way over to where he stood.

'I thought I'd find you here, sir. Chief Holbein said you'd be out berating the gods for not giving us some clear weather.'

Meyer turned to see his observation officer, Oberleutnant Zur Zee Christian Merkus grinning at him.

'What do you want, Merkus?' he growled. 'Come to annoy me? I warn you, I'm in a foul mood just now.'

'Then I shall cheer you up and make you happy, sir. The weather report has come in and it's good news. The meteorological boys say this will clear up within the hour. In fact they say if it doesn't, you can have their tobacco ration for the next fortnight.'

'Cheeky beggars, they know I don't smoke!' In spite of himself, Meyer's face twitched. 'All right, all right, I forgive them. Now, how soon can we get our baby loaded with some presents for the Englanders?'

'I've already started, sir. Chief Holbein is loading the fuel now and the armourers are fitting the bombs to the gondolas as we speak. It shouldn't take more than an hour or two and we could lift off by 21:00 hours.'

Meyer punched him lightly on the shoulder. 'You'll win the *Pour le Merite* yet, Merkus. See if you don't. Come, let's see what's left to do.' He walked away towards the hangar, Merkus following him like a tame lamb.

The airship filled the hangar. Over 500 feet long, containing just under a million cubic feet of highly-explosive hydrogen in eighteen bags within her aluminium frame, the dark-green painted shape of the Zeppelin LZ.29 swayed gently under the hangar roof as men swarming around her and strove to load the fuel and bombs she would need for her deadly mission on the far side of the North Sea. Round her four 210 horsepower Maybach engines Meyer could see the agitated figure of his senior mechanic, Chief Holbein, together with his machinists as they fussed over the oil and greases required to keep the engines performing satisfactorily once they were airborne. From the engine gondolas he could see the barrels of the parabellum machine-guns LZ.29 carried for her protection and already the sweating armourers were hoisting up the ammunition required to service the guns.

Turning back to his operations officer, Meyer spoke again. 'What bomb load are we carrying today, Merkus?'

'I've asked them to load with four 220lb bombs, sir, and the rest we'll carry as incendiaries. Is that all right with you?'

'Exactly. Now then, let's go and fetch some charts and plot our course for...umm.'

Merkus looked at his commanding officer askance. There was something up but he couldn't put a finger on it. He looked into the distance as he answered Meyer.

'Headquarters were most insistent we didn't take any chances in the bad weather we've been experiencing of late, sir. With that in mind I have a course already plotted for Great Yarmouth.'

'Great Yarmouth? Pah!' Meyer snorted as he faced his young friend impatiently. 'I received a telegram from my mother two days ago, Merkus, telling me my uncle Albrecht, her younger brother, had been shot down and killed on the Western Front. Near some shitty town called Ypres. He was an observer, too old they kept telling him, but he insisted it was his duty to continue to fly and serve the Fatherland. Well, Merkus my friend, I am going to pay the Tommies back for Uncle Albrecht. We are going to pay London a surprise visit, so put your charts away and plot me a new course. One that includes the arsenal at Woolwich. I think it's time they had some more explosives delivered to them. Only by us! Go and tell that to operations. And get a move on! I want to catch that good weather before it disappears!'

It was more than four hours later, after a troublesome engine had to be stripped down and rebuilt, with the sixteen crew members aboard and at their posts that Karl Meyer finally gave the command from the control room in the central gondola. The ground crew then took hold of the ropes dangling from the airship and slowly and carefully began the delicate task of moving her out of her lair and into the open ground beyond the hangar. The hangar itself was an innovation, a totally revolving structure that allowed them to dispatch the airships no matter what the weather was doing.

The rain was still lashing down, albeit somewhat weaker now as she emerged and almost at once began to strain at the ropes holding her down. Curbing his growing impatience to be off Meyer signalled again when he deemed her to be clear of the hangar and the great ship began to rise at once, her engines straining. The cheers and waves of her ground crew followed her upwards as she arrowed skywards and was swiftly lost in the thickening gloom.

Once airborne the machinists checked and re-checked the snorting Maybachs as they surged and sang in the rapidly thinning air while the airship gained altitude. In the central gondola Merkus pored over his maps and checked the magnetic compass as he gave orders to the helmsman to bring her round on a course that would bring her over the light at Orfordness, north of Felixstowe. The radio operator was already tapping out a message to HQ on his powerful transmitter, giving course and bearing details to the plotters back on the ground. Well, mused Meyer to himself, they would soon get a shock when they realised where he was heading.

Two and a half hours passed as they struggled against an unwelcome headwind and then Merkus tapped Meyer on the shoulder. He pointed to their left and far below Meyer made out the sweep of the Orfordness light. They were at 3,000 feet and as they swung round onto a new course to the south-west, one that led to their final destination, London, he jerked his hand upwards. The helmsman began to move the great wheel, then shouted suddenly, in alarm. Following his frightened look, Meyer saw that all the metal objects on the outside of the airship seemed to be glowing with a dancing, bluish flame that jumped eerily across the ship's outer frame.

'Don't worry, Hoffenbach!' he shouted to the frightened crew member, 'It's only St Elmo's Fire. A good omen for us tonight. We are under his protection now.' St Elmo was the patron saint of sailors.

Soon after, the airship began to ascend as they dumped some of the tons of water ballast they carried, and she rose quickly to 11,000 feet. Meyer looked over to where the compressed oxygen was situated. No point in passing out through lack of oxygen over the target, he thought, and pulled a tube towards him.

Another twenty minutes passed as they glided along and he began to pick out lights, lots of them, on the horizon. He had bombed London only once before but the sight of the great metropolis as she came into view below took his breath away. Even with the partial blackout the authorities in Britain had demanded, enough light escaped to make the silhouette of the city below shimmer like a string of pearls round a woman's neck. As far as the eye could see the lights sparkled and dazzled, whites and yellows intermingling to make a pulsating sea of colour. In the midst of it all he spotted the silver ribbon that denoted the meandering path of the River Thames and at his command the great ship swung round onto a new heading.

Quickly the engines were throttled back and they slid through the air, deadly silent to those on the ground. A few searchlights wandered in a random manner but Meyer ignored them and concentrated on trying to pick out the bends in the river that would tell him of where his target lay. Comparing the view below to the chart he held in his hand he gave corrections to the helmsman who minutely tried to follow his orders.

At last, satisfied that he had identified his target, he tugged at the bomb release. Nothing happened. He tugged again. Still nothing happened. The cables were prone to freezing at this altitude if not properly greased and he swore angrily, then gave the release cable an almighty tug. A sudden lurch of the airship as she swooped upwards rapidly, relieved of the weight of her bombs, told him he had been successful and the helmsman pulled down hard on the helm to bring her round on a course for home. Those that were able looked keenly down to see if they could spot the explosions below that would tell them where the bombs had fallen.

Far below them, Lucille Charteris yawned and shifted her feet into the centre of the bed. They hit something soft and she looked sleepily over to where the dim shape of the man lying next to her in the darkness snored gently as he slept deeply, unaware of her scrutiny. Poor Arnold! It had been fun but she was beginning to tire of him. He had become so demanding of late and she was sure the rest of the staff in the office were beginning to suspect. Once he had helped her settle the matter of what to do with Neville's persistent refusal to do the right thing by her, she would have to say goodbye to dear old Arnold and find herself someone a bit younger. And with a bit more money.

She shifted her body to the other side of the bed, careful not to wake him. He would only take it as a sign of her arousal and God knows she could do without his attentions at this unearthly hour. She stretched luxuriously and began to imagine her new life opening up in front of her. She would say one thing for this war, it had given women like her the chance to be free from the drudgery that many of their generation had fallen into.

A whistling noise overhead broke into her reverie and she frowned as she tried to make out the strange phenomenon.

The 220lb bomb was approaching the speed of sound when it slammed into the house at the end of the road. As it impacted through the bedroom ceiling there was a slight delay as its shape deformed rapidly on contact with the solid rafters of the house before the fuse operated and the bomb exploded with a deafening roar. Three houses in Adys Road disappeared in the resultant explosion, their brick and wooden structures pulverised into fragments, leaving only a deep crater where they had stood as the soundwave shattered the windows of houses for several streets around. Lucille Charteris had one micro-second of puzzlement, her lips forming a moue of surprised '*Whaa...?*' before her body and that of her sleeping companion were torn apart in the brilliant white-hot heat of the explosion. Before the dust had time to settle a fractured gas main ignited another fireball, throwing the macabre scene into eerie relief. Within minutes, further down the street, a crowd of inquisitive onlookers sleepily gathered at a safe distance to discuss the night's happenings and gawp at the ruins through the dancing flames.

Saturday 18th December 1915

Small arms training and kit inspections in a.m. Battalion Christmas concert party performed in village hall in p.m. Enjoyed by all who attended. Men performed very well, including Pte Parkes who drew great cheers as a concert hall woman's act.

Captain L. Carey, D Company

The concert party was deemed a great success by all those who clapped and cat-called the various acts as they appeared. From poetry to vaudeville, a succession of their fellow soldiers gave their all. The loudest cheers were reserved for Alfie Parkes who tottered onto the makeshift stage dressed in a suggestive outfit he had beguiled out of a young lady in one of the villages further to the rear, without her parents knowledge, complete with a blonde wig and heavy make-up. His pale, rouged face and scarlet lips, together with a large, obviously-stuffed chest had flouted and pouted its way around the stage as he sang his way through a series of bawdy, suggestive songs that at times bordered on the obscene.

Titch Magilton tried hard to keep the atmosphere alive as a badly organised magician whose tricks went from bad to worse. Great gales of laughter rang through the rafters of the hall as he blundered on, dropping cards, knocking his props over and generally making a pig's ear of how not to keep the secrets of the Magic Circle, well, secret. His best trick was saved until last when a bemused magician whipped the flannel hankie off his cardboard top-hat to reveal...nothing. The large, floppy-eared rabbit he had placed in it at the edge of the stage was missing and was never found. It earned him the tears and approbation of the elderly spinster with whom he was billeted and from whom he had borrowed his 'prop', and a hefty fee in compensation for the loss of her beloved pet. Some less public-spirited soldiers coarsely suggested a few doughty members of C Company had spirited it away to make a stew with, a charge they later vehemently refuted. Amidst a cacophony of light-hearted boos and great whoops of laughter, Titch cut his losses and ran from the scene of his glorious failure.

Sweating, Neville Charteris stood by the edge of the stage, nervously watching as his protégés entered and departed. At long last, after Donnie Parker's spoons had finished their chattering, the two battalion chaplains mounted the stage and led the men in prayer, ending with a wistful singing of the latest hit song in London, 'Keep the Home fires Burning'. As the cheers died down and the men filled out into the night Charteris could finally relax.

'Well done you two, where's Roger slid off to?' Walter Ramsbottom exclaimed, patting Neville heartily on the back. 'Good show, old man! Look at the colonel, he loved it, just what he needed to buck his spirits up. Talking of which, how's about a noggin with me, Neville? I have a fine malt arrived in the mail from the wife, come and have a dram with me. What do you say?' Nodding gratefully, Charteris accompanied Ramsbottom out into the darkness before anyone else could accost him.

He woke in the early hours and looked blearily at his watch. Six o'clock. God! His head hurt. Mentally reminding himself never to take up another invitation for a drink from Walter Ramsbottom he rose stiffly from his crumpled sleeping bag, slipped into his boots and staggered groggily outside to the latrine to relieve himself. Lighting the primus stove on his return he quickly boiled a kettle and made himself a cup of tea. While it cooled he donned the remainder of his uniform, shuddering as he caught a whiff of the ripe condition of his sweaty clothing.

Feeling better after the warm, sweet tea, he stepped out into the street and made his way along the pavement to battalion HQ. He stepped inside the old blacksmith's workshop, closed the door and caught the eye of the corporal already sitting at a desk, carefully typing.

'Good morning Corporal Salter, Captain Charteris, I'm duty "bod" today. Is there anything for me?'

'The CO's in there, sir,' he answered. 'Funny, I was just going to send a runner out for you. Could you go in and see him please?' Charteris nodded, knocked perfunctorily on the door and without waiting for a reply, strode inside.

Cuthbert Snaith was sat by a small fire warming his hands. He looked up sharply as Neville entered and his expression changed immediately. 'Ah, Neville, yes. Look here old man, I have some rather bad news for you. It, er, it concerns your wife. I mean to say, I...'

Charteris's spirits slumped. Damn! She'd carried out her threat and written to the colonel. How could he explain all this to someone like Snaith? The colonel began to speak again but Charteris broke in.

'Look, sir, I can explain this. My wife, Lucille, she's been a bit distraught these past few months. Our being apart has affected her greatly. I don't know what she's been writing to you but believe me, I can...'

'Neville, please,' Snaith gently explained, 'I'm sorry but I have to tell you. I have a communication here, forwarded from the police in London. There is no help for it, I must be blunt. I must inform you, Captain Charteris, that your wife is dead.'

Charteris staggered, his mind reeling. His legs suddenly lost their ability to keep him upright and he caught the edge of the windowsill to stop himself sliding to the floor.

'Lucille? Dead? What? How? I mean... Who could?' he stopped, too shocked to comprehend the meaning of the words Snaith had just spoken.

Snaith looked down at his boots.

'It seems as if there was an explosion. A bomb. A Zeppelin raid the other day, Wednesday to be precise. These foul Huns, bombing innocent civilians. Where will it end, I ask you? Your house was one of several hit that night. Mrs Charteris was killed outright when the house collapsed.'

Charteris stared at him uncomprehendingly, thoughts running through his mind at breakneck speed as the colonel continued to speak. He shook his head.

'I'm sorry, sir,' he stammered, 'what did you say? Could you please repeat your last statement?'

Snaith's face slowly reddened and he continued to stare at his feet as he repeated himself. 'Neville. I'm sorry to have to inform you but the communication from the police contained other information. How can I put it delicately? It would appear that Mrs Charteris was not alone in the house that night. I'm afraid another body was recovered, that of a male. Does the name Arnold Walker mean anything to you?'

Charteris slumped against the wall at his CO's words. Arnold. Poor bastard. No doubt he'd been 'helping' Lucille with her problems again. Well, not any more. As he digested the information he began to feel another emotion crowd in on the grief he was experiencing. Anger. How could she? She had always been selfish, oblivious to nothing but her own self-gratification, but he had loved her. Until her betrayal. Now that need had not only resulted in her death but the death of some other poor benighted soul she had fluttered her seductive eyelashes at. His eyes filled with tears as he silently, impotently, raged at Lucille. His dead wife.

The colonel spoke softly. 'Neville, you have my sympathies in all this, I'm sorry to have to be the one to break such bad news. Nothing I say can fully express my commiserations. In view of the situation I've made a decision. I have here your travel orders, Corporal Salter made them up a few minutes earlier. There's also the note from the police. You should take it with you, so you know who to contact when you get back to England. Under the circumstances I've granted you a few days Compassionate Leave. Go home, Neville. Go home and bury your wife and I pray that somewhere in all of this, in the mad world we now find ourselves in, you can find some comfort in the dark days ahead.' His voice rose sharply. 'Corporal Salter, in here if you please!'

Charteris hardly heard his colonel speak. Numbly he accepted the papers pressed into his hand from a sympathetic corporal and automatically retraced his steps until he found himself outside the smithy. He stood facing the street, staring blankly at the houses opposite while he tried to regroup his thoughts. Eventually he was able to make his way back to his billet and pack what few belongings he could think he might need.

It was only when he was sat on the train from Auchonvillers that he looked at the papers. Snaith had given him four days compassionate leave starting from the

Sunday. Four days, he thought bitterly. What price adultery! Lucille's mother lived in Orpington, he recalled, her father having died some years previously. He supposed he ought to make his way there once he had arranged the funeral, unless she had already been informed. It would not be a pleasant reunion, Lucille's mother had never thought him fit to marry her darling girl so contact between them in the intervening years had been few and far between.

The military timetable conspired against him and he found it would take a considerable effort to make his way to Boulogne. After a long, tiring journey in which he had to change twice, he finally reached his destination late that night. Several times on the way their train had passed troop trains slowly clattering in the other direction. He had smiled wryly to himself as he saw in them the cheering, waving troops who sat on the edge of the open freight cars. Oblivious to the cold, a picture of his own battalion as they had made their way to the Front in a similar manner months before, the men he passed sang lustily as they were drawn nearer to the fighting. Poor beggars, they'd soon be singing a different tune.

On arrival he found that he had missed the leave boat. There was another leaving in the early morning so he was directed to an billet in the town. A middle-aged woman who spoke passable English answered the door and warmly welcomed him but he was in no mood to make pleasantries so she quickly gave up and took him upstairs. After being shown to a small, well-furnished room with a single bed, he washed his face in the cold water basin by the bedside and lay down on the rich eiderdown.

Turbulent dreams disturbed what sleep he managed to find. Dreams of his late wife, a dark, fuzzy image too distant to fully make out. Several times he woke with a start, filled with a strange feeling that she was nearby and it was only after having reassured himself that he was alone that he lay down and dropped off again. For some strange reason he kept imagining himself over and over to be back in Matilda Fairley's house at the time that he had discovered Lucille and her lover. On awaking to find a dim glow that preceded the dawn filling the room, he looked round to finally realise that all of this was not some evil dream and that Lucille was really dead.

The leave boat was waiting for him, looming over the dock as he remembered a similar ship weeks before. A khaki-clad, chattering crowd was slowly wending its way up the gangplank, laden with packs and weapons and he took his turn in the queue before being spotted and quickly ushered through the silently waiting men and onto the ship. Of his provost friend from before there was no sign and he soon found a seat in the lounge and slumped into it. A red-faced captain from the Supply Corps tried to engage him in conversation but the man soon gave up, tired no doubt of Charteris's monosyballic replies. A loud blast on the ship's hooter and the resultant shudder from below told him they were on their way, so he sat and gazed out of a lounge window as they headed into open water and across the Channel.

It looked freezing outside and he saw it had begun to snow, the flakes whirling and dancing round in a frenzy of white that soon froze to the window and blotted any further sights from his view. In this way they slowly crossed the open stretch of water and drew into Folkestone. Once again a train sat patiently waiting and they all quickly boarded, eager to be out of the cold. Minutes after disembarking they were on their way to London.

The train drew into Victoria in the late afternoon and as he stepped down out of the carriage he shivered involuntarily and turned his collar up against the biting wind that swept through the building. There weren't that many young ladies expectantly waiting this time so he quickly made his way out of the thoroughfare and stopped once he was outside, to gaze in the direction of the taxi rank. As with everyone else he had met on his previous visit, the taxi driver that had taken him to Peckham was nowhere to be seen, so he hailed the nearest taxi and gave the elderly driver directions.

Sitting back in the cold leather seat as they clattered their way through the dark streets he watched the people with a keen eye. There were more uniforms in evidence this time, from the dark blue of the Navy to the often-muddied khaki of the soldiers. These travelled together in groups, or singly with a female companion on their arms. The people he observed wended their way through the streets for the most part with an air of resigned weariness, glum at the thought of another wartime Christmas.

There also seemed to be more motor vehicles, filling the streets with the noise of sewing-machine like engines and honking horns. The open-topped omnibuses slowly eased their way along their routes, stopping and starting as people on the side of the street waved to be picked up. The tops were mainly empty, a result of the cold weather, he surmised. He closed his eyes at the sight of so many people and pressed back into the seat to let the memories of Lucille and himself come flooding back.

A tap on the glass partition separating him from the driver brought him from his reverie and he opened his eyes to find himself looking at the familiar sight of Adys Road. Opening the door he stepped out onto the pavement. The driver hovered impatiently so he paid him and then turned back to the houses.

A gap in the neat row drew his attention and he walked towards it, slowing as he approached the devastation. Where houses had once stood was a deep, rubble-filled crater, reminiscent of the ruined, shelled villages so familiar to him on the other side of the Channel. Blackened timbers protruded in a haphazard, kaleidoscopic pattern intermingled with bits of furnishings, broken house tiles and twisted, scorched plasterwork. Deep within the wreckage he could discern the gleam of water and in one corner the mangled, rusted remains of a metal oven.

He stood there for some time, breathing deeply as his eyes took in every detail of the destruction in front of him. A discreet cough made him turn and he looked round to be confronted by a large male wearing a white apron under his overcoat. He frowned as he continued to gaze at the stranger and then recognised the figure of the shop worker from the newsagent down the road. The man gestured at the ruins and then pointed inquisitively at Charteris.

'Haven't I seen you somewhere before? Don't you live round 'ere, mate?'

'No. I'm afraid you have me confused with someone else. Good day!'

Without thinking where he was going he walked away from the man, head bent against a biting wind that appeared from nowhere. He walked like an automaton, his feet taking him where they wanted to. When next he looked up he was astonished to find himself stopped outside a gate that looked familiar. He stared back down the street and saw the name written on the street sign. East Dulwich Street, the street in which Matilda Fairley lived. Marvelling at his calmness he walked up to the door and rapped firmly on the gleaming wood.

Any words that he had forming on his lips died when, after a pause of several seconds, the door was thrown back from within and a complete stranger stood there, staring at him from the lighted recess of the hallway. The large middle-aged woman, dressed severely in black with greying hair pulled back to match, glared at him as he fumbled for words.

'Yes? *Pliss*? You want?' she shouted in his face.

'Er, I...'

'No!' she shouted again and slammed the door shut, leaving him nonplussed on the doorstep. From behind the door came the sound of raised voices and after a further wait the door was hesitantly swung open once more to reveal the slender figure of Matilda Fairley. A voice sounded behind her and she turned back before he could speak, speaking sharply to the unseen person on the other side of the door.

'Shh, Mrs Humboldt. I told you, I'll deal with the gentleman.' More sharply now. 'No, don't worry, it's all right Mrs Humboldt, I do assure you!'

She turned back and he marvelled at her loveliness as the light inside caught her in silhouette, bringing out the fresh, pastel colours of her face and hair. He murmured quietly. 'Matilda? Mrs Fairley, it's me. Neville Charteris. I'm sorry, I didn't mean to startle you and your guest.'

He was rewarded by her face turning a deep shade of cherry-red as she stared speechlessly at him. Now it was her turn to flounder. 'My goodness! Captain Charteris! Neville. What are you doing here? What...? Is it...? Have you...?' She looked past him with a surprised air then stopped, unable to continue, gazing at him with a bemused expression on her face. He shivered and lifted a hand.

'Could we speak inside? It's freezing out here.'

'Oh. Yes. Yes, of course.' She stepped back as he walked forward, never taking her eyes off him as he did so. They came face to face, her breath playing over his face as he stepped close, her eyes watching him gravely as he trapped her against the hatstand in the hallway. For long, lingering seconds their eyes met and it was she who broke away first, her face reddening once more as she moved away from him into the house.

To hide her confusion she turned and raised her voice. 'Mrs Humboldt? Please put the kettle on, it looks as if we have a guest for tea.'

A warm fire glowed in the corner of the room that he remembered instantly. The leather sofa he had slept on still stood in its place on the other side of the room and he made his way over to it and sat down, twisting round to face his hostess. She had seated herself in a high-backed chair by the door, where she continued to regard him. She was dressed in a dark-green outfit, her hair gleaming in the fire's reflection.

Looking at her he was reminded of how beautiful he had thought her when they had first met. The weeks since their meeting had only enhanced that beauty and it was with a sad realisation that he recognised the hopelessness of the situation he found himself in. He was here to bury his wife, the woman he had once loved deeply, and the quiet beauty of the woman sat watching him opposite and who caused his mind such mental turmoil only added to the pain of his reason for being there.

She caught his despair and asked quietly, 'Are you all right, Captain Charteris?'

He looked up wanly from his contemplation of her carpet and smiled weakly. 'Yes,' he answered. 'Yes, I'm fine. Honest.'

He twiddled the cap he had placed in between his fingers upon entering the room and wondered what to say next. Tillie Fairley saw his nervousness and her heart went out to him. He looked so tired and there were lines round his eyes that she could not remember from their first meeting. His boyish good looks were strained and she cast round desperately for a way to break the silence growing between them.

'Look, would you like some cake with that tea? I'll go and see where Mrs Humboldt's got to and she can put it on the plate with the rest of the tea things.'

'Mrs Humboldt, is she staying with you?' Charteris enquired awkwardly.

'In a way I suppose she is. Her husband is in the Belgian Army, missing somewhere near Langemarck I believe. The War Committee for Refugees were looking for people to take care of those who had fled the war and made it to these shores so I volunteered. I'm looking after her for a while. Or as you can see, she's looking after me.'

They were still chuckling when the rattle of crockery heralded the arrival of the redoubtable Mrs Humboldt. She bustled in bearing a tea tray laden with pots and cups, together with a plate of cake and biscuits she'd had the forethought to add. As she watched him wolf down the slice of cake he'd been handed, Matilda felt a flash of maternal concern for how thin the serious young man sat opposite her seemed to have grown. That and something else but she quickly dismissed those thoughts and bent forward to pour the tea. While they drank, Mrs Humboldt withdrew diplomatically to the kitchen, but not before she had caught Matilda's gaze with a pout and an arch of her thick eyebrows, causing Matilda to redden again.

He looked over to where she sat, her hands demurely in her lap, the picture of loveliness, and his heart sank as he realised he was going to have to tell her the whole story. Falteringly he began.

'You will think I have such a cheek turning up here like this when you hear my story, Mrs Fairley. No, please!' She made as if to speak but he forestalled her. 'I hardly know where to start myself, my mind is, so, so churned up just now. These are not normal times we live in and my being here in London is not down to chance or generosity. My commanding officer has given me four days' leave to see to a family affair.'

Matilda saw his distress and spoke gently. 'Please, go on, Neville. Take your time.'

He took a deep breath and tried to continue. 'It concerns my wife.'

Matilda's face blanched and when he stopped again it was her who now fought to control her emotions. She felt suddenly faint as the full impact of his words sunk in. Fool! Fool! she raged inside. He's married. Married! God, what a fool she'd been! She half-rose in her chair, her face flaming once more but this time for a different reason. Neville saw the movement and raised an arm in supplication.

'Wait, please. Mrs Fairley, Matilda. Please, let me finish.'

She sat down again, white-faced, her eyes never leaving his and was shocked to see a small drop of liquid well up in his left eye and slowly trickle down his cheek as he vainly fought to regain his composure.

'My wife is dead,' he said at last, simply. 'She was killed in the recent air raid here, last week. I've been granted compassionate leave to come home and bury her. I'm sorry I came here today, my appearance must have come as a great shock to you. I don't know how or why I came here, it's just that I don't know what to do.'

As he finished speaking the lone tear was joined by several more and he hung his head low and buried it in his hands.

The young woman across from him sat in shocked silence as she tried to comprehend the awful news she had just been given. Her mind struggled to make sense of what Neville was saying. The bombings of last week had shocked them all with the realisation of how close the war had come to Peckham. She herself had walked up to the street where the bombs had fallen and gasped to see such wanton destruction. The scene had had a sobering effect on all those who had come to stare at the shattered ruins and Matilda had joined in with the onlookers' sense of condemnation of a savage enemy who could murder innocent civilians in this way.

Now, looking at the distressed man sat across from her, she found those scenes flash vividly through her mind again as she tried to bring her raging emotions under tight control. His wife? Killed there, only a small distance away from her own house. Her mind flew back to when she had first seen him, sitting so forlornly on the bench on the Goose Green and she felt suddenly lost. Had he just visited his wife then? What an earth was he doing here now? What did he want from her? These and a hundred other questions crowded her brain as she sat and watched Neville fight to regain his composure.

'I'm sorry, Mrs Fairley. Matilda. For some strange reason I found myself outside your gate and I had the strongest urge to come in and see you.' He smiled weakly through the wetness of his tears. 'As if you, you with all the pain and heartache you have suffered yourself, could understand my being here.' He shook his head. 'I shouldn't be here, it was quite wrong of me, I see that now. You've been so kind but if you would please excuse me, I shall be on my way.'

He rose to leave but she stood up and positioned herself in front of him, barring his way to the door.

'Please sit down again, Neville. Finish your story. There is more, isn't there? I feel we are friends you and I, Neville Charteris. Friends need not have any formality to bind their confidences.' She looked at him, half-pleadingly, and he sat down. His every urge was to pick up his pack and be away, but the calm, sincere look in the woman's eyes opposite held him fast and he found his resolve to flee crumble as she continued to gaze at him so directly. To break the silence she spoke gently.

'I, too, am sorry, as I know it must pain you to talk about it, Neville. I must say, on first seeing you I could not think what had brought you here tonight but I am gratified that you could look on me as a friend. I am so sorry to hear about your wife, grief is a hard burden to bear in any circumstances but to lose one whom you loved so much in this manner must be doubly distressing. If I can help in any way you have only to ask. But what of your parents, have you contacted them? Do they know of what has happened?' She stopped, unable to continue as her pain and a sense of, somehow, loss, grew.

Charteris looked up slowly to where she sat, so lovely in the firelight and so pale. He rubbed his face wearily and began.

'Thank you for your understanding. Where shall I start, there is so much to tell. Of my parents there is only my father alive. My mother died while I was still young and I'm afraid my father never recovered from her death. He writes often enough but sometimes I think he lives in his own world, a world where he and my mother are still together. I don't bother him much, as you might see from what I've just explained.

'Should I unburden myself like this to you, a woman who I hardly know? And yet... There is so much pain in this life, so much unhappiness and loneliness. I never thought matters would turn out this way. It should all be so simple. One loves and is loved. Or so it once seemed. Therein is the cause of so much of the trouble that eventually forces its way between a man and a woman. You are mistaken in your understanding of my situation, by the way. God would that it was so simple...'

His voice tailed away as he stared deep into the fire and she waited for a second or so for him to continue.

'Go on. Please, go on.'

He gazed up at her briefly before staring back into the fire. In a quiet, emotional voice he told her of his life, his marriage, their separation and, ultimately, his wife's betrayal. As he spoke she felt her eyes fill with tears, tears for the two lives that had been lost. When Charteris painfully spoke of his wife's descent into scorn and then finally, betrayal, she leant back and closed her eyes, overcome by the sadness and finality of it all. Where was the blame, who were the guilty? Who could point a finger at two people that this war had destroyed so completely and say who was right and who was wrong?

He told of how he had discovered Lucille's unfaithfulness at first hand and how he had disposed of the house key and his wedding ring. As if by doing so he could wipe the whole matter from his mind. At last she became aware that he had fallen silent and opened her eyes to see him sitting there, tousled hair shining wetly, a picture of sad despair, and her heart went out to him. As she moved forward in her seat he turned to look at her and she saw his eyes were wet once more.

'I really must be going now. Thank you, Matilda, for listening to me, at least. I'm sorry if I embarrassed you.'

She gazed back at him and her expression changed. 'Neville, I don't know what to say that would comfort you. What you've told me tonight has come as so much of a shock, but please do not feel embarrassed at having spoken so. It's growing late and you cannot go out there in such a state. We seem to have been here before, but this time I hope I can be a better hostess. You must stay tonight. Tomorrow you can make your way to wherever you need but I think it best you rest here tonight. Mrs Humboldt and I will try to make good company for you. '

He shook his head and rose again but she lifted a restraining arm. 'Please stay, it is the only thing to do. Mrs Humboldt can turn down the bed in the guest room.' She laughed quietly, trying to inject some humour into the situation. 'Even I couldn't have you sleep on the sofa again, not in this cold weather. What you must have thought of me the last time you stayed I dread to think.' Without waiting for an answer she raised her voice. 'Mrs Humboldt!'

The door opened quickly, too quickly for Matilda's liking, but she dismissed any angry thoughts she was harbouring as the two women ascended the stairs to the guest room opposite the bathroom. The single bed was quite cold so Mrs Humboldt went to the kitchen to find a hot water bottle, leaving Matilda to arrange the bedding.

As she turned the top sheet down she cast her mind over the words she had just listened to. Neville Charteris seemed to have been telling her the truth, she could recognise genuine despair when she saw it, and she wondered how two people could let their marriage founder in so short a time. Angrily she shook herself as she continued to ruminate. Who was she to condemn, how long had she and Arthur had together?

As the thought of her dead husband entered her head she wondered how he would have faced this, would have coped had she herself been unfaithful. The word jumped out at her and she recoiled from its meaning. Decent women would never entertain the thought and yet... She was only too aware of the new morality the war had brought. It seemed that almost every day one or more of her small circle of friends would come with some other titbit to shock them all, whether it be an item in the papers or something from personal knowledge. It seemed all so frenetic, people taking lovers, changing partners in a wild attempt to find whatever fleeting happiness they could. The ever-growing casualty lists were a prime cause of this sort of behaviour becoming so commonplace and it was this thought that made her realise how quick she had been to condemn Lucille Charteris. She made a mental note to ask forgiveness and finished plumping up the pillows.

'Neville,' she called from the top of the stairs, 'You can come up and see your room now.'

He woke in the early morning, feeling as refreshed as only a good night's sleep in a comfortable bed could make one feel. The bathroom was empty so he quickly closed the door and washed and shaved. The smell of stale sweat still clung to his clothes but he gave himself an extra dab of cologne before dressing and descending the stairs. Both women were up and about and greeted him, Mrs Humboldt a trifle coldly, before she entered the kitchen and was out of sight.

Matilda was dressed in black this morning, whether out of courtesy to Lucille he couldn't tell, but the outfit she wore only served to emphasise her beauty. The pale make-up she wore enhanced her natural loveliness and he felt his spirits lift as he quietly contemplated her before picking up his knife and fork. The breakfast before him was a culinary delight and he tucked in with gusto, watched by an approving cook. At last he finished eating and pushed his plate back.

'Enough! I've not eaten like that for ages.' He was rewarded by a smile from the severe-looking Belgian as she scooped up his empty plate and bore it off triumphantly to the kitchen.

'You've made a convert,' Matilda observed dryly as they both watched Mrs Humboldt march out of the door. She was pleased to see the haunted, strained look she had seen last night was not in evidence so much this morning. As he rose to find his pack she caught herself wondering what he looked like in civilian clothes, how her friends would react if she were to bring him to see them. With a start she looked up to find him looking at her intently and she reddened, wondering if her thoughts had been so plain on her face.

To hide her confusion she asked him brightly, 'So, are you ready then, Captain Charteris?'

'I must go up to the police station,' he replied, 'I need to find out what arrangements have been made for the...' He faltered. His voice picked up, more stronger now. 'I need to find out what funeral arrangements have been made for Lucille. Her family must know by now.'

It was her turn to feel contrite and she lowered her voice in agreement. 'Yes, I understand. Will you be gone long?'

There was an almost unconscious acceptance in her voice of his returning and to his surprise he found himself warming to the idea. She followed him out and stood looking wistfully after him as he marched down the path.

'I'll be back once I've got everything sorted. Take care, Matilda Fairley.' With that he turned and was gone, marching steadily down the road in the direction she had told him to take. Matilda stepped back into the house and found herself gazing into Mrs Humboldt's concerned face.

'Is nice man, Mateelda, but married. No?'

'No, Mrs Humboldt. Neville's wife died. Not married now.'

'Huh!' Mrs Humboldt tossed her head and walked back into the room.

* * * * *

It was bitterly cold and Charteris was glad of his overcoat as he marched through the streets. Within ten minutes he spotted the blue lamp of the station house. A deferential constable, spotting the ribbon on Charteris's tunic breast, hurried over and then scurried away. Minutes later a sympathetic sergeant arrived and sat down next to him with the information he was seeking. A coroner's court had been hastily convened and adjourned. The funeral had been organised to take place on the morrow, Tuesday, at ten in the morning at the parish church, Lucille's mother having made the funeral arrangements.

Mechanically he took the details of the hotel where Lucille's mother was staying but once outside changed his mind about visiting her. There was plenty of time to meet with Mrs Dewar but just now was not one of them. The rest of the morning he spent walking slowly through Peckham. He bought some Christmas decorations and had them parcelled up. It would make the officers' mess that much brighter, wherever they ended up. The colonel had informed him before he left that the battalion would be returning to the trenches over the festive period and he knew from his tone that that meant Christmas Day would be spent crouching low beneath the firestep, observing no man's land.

He wandered on, walking in and out of shops, and it was late afternoon when he retraced his steps to Matilda Fairley's house. The temperature was dropping and a light dusting of snow was falling gently as he made his way up the path to Matilda's door. As he rapped on the door he thought he saw the curtains of the drawing-room twitch but before he could register the thought the front door was pulled fiercely open and he was confronted by the angry figure of Mrs Humboldt.

'Mrs Fairley nice lady! You no hurt her!'

She stepped back, allowing him to pass. Her outburst rang through his head as he entered the drawing-room and found Matilda sat by the fire, a newspaper in her hands. She looked up as he entered and smiled, a warm welcoming smile that filled him with a rich sense of peace. In the far corner of the room a small decorated Christmas tree stood in a cloth-wrapped bucket. She followed his gaze and smiled again.

'You were gone so long Mrs Humboldt and I decided to enter into the Christmas spirit after all. We went out and bought a tree and spent the last hour or so decorating. It makes the room more homely, don't you agree?'

Her smile widened as Neville unwrapped his parcel of decorations meant for France and together they knelt by the tree and hung some of the more suitable items on the branches. When they finally straightened up they found Mrs Humboldt had slipped in quietly and left a tray bearing tea and sandwiches. Matilda sat on the edge of her chair nibbling daintily at a sandwich as she watched Neville eat. Her emotions were troubling her, feelings of guilt intermingled with a strange sense of longing, and to hide them she busied herself with the tray.

'You must look your best tomorrow so Mrs Humboldt asked if you could change now she would do her best to wash and dry your clothes,' she said casually. 'As you can see, I have some more of Arthur's clothes. They fitted you last time, I seem to recall, so if you could change now, Mrs Humboldt will make a start.'

It was Charteris's turn to feel embarrassed but he took the clothes and went to his room to change. They sat and talked into the evening. Charteris made Matilda laugh uproariously as he told her of the concert party. He had embellished the various goings-on that each artiste had produced in order to hear again her deep, rich laughter and they had climbed the stairs together still chuckling at the antics of the men. He had thought of discussing the next morning's arrangements but the idea slipped from his mind as quickly as it had entered. Once in his room he had quickly undressed and fallen into bed where he had slept the dreamless sleep of the mentally exhausted.

He woke with a tight knot in his stomach which he put down to anxiety. He opened the door to walk to the bathroom and was surprised, and touched, to find his uniform, the jacket sponged and neatly pressed, shirt free of grime, lying on the floor outside the door. Picking the clothes up he walked into the bathroom and washed himself from head to toe in the sink. He shaved carefully and then dressed, looking at himself critically in the mirror once he was finished.

A pale, fresh face stared gravely back at him. The dark shadows under the eyes were not as prominent as he remembered them and he noticed with some relief that most of the deep lines that had been etched in his face for the past few days had all but disappeared. With a grim nod of approval he retrieved his cap from his room, fastened his Sam Browne belt around his waist and walked downstairs into the kitchen.

Both women were by the sink and turned together to look at him. Matilda's heart leapt as she took in his clean, youthful features, heightened as they were by the cleanliness of his uniform. The maroon and white ribbon of the Military Cross shone brightly on his breast and she took a deep breath before her words of greeting escaped her lips.

He ate only a light breakfast and after a large cup of tea, hung around the kitchen, impatient to be off. Realising how his emotions were affecting him Matilda wisely said nothing while he ate. Afterwards, as he readied himself to leave she pointed casually to the newspaper lying neatly folded on the table.

'I see you have a new commander-in-chief.'

'I beg your pardon?'

'Sir John French has been replaced. General Haig is now commanding the BEF, with a promotion to field marshall. It says so here.' She picked the paper up and offered it to him. His mind racing furiously he scanned the pages quickly. God! She was right. It was all here... Palace pleased to announce... Full confidence of the War Office... Prime minister assured... Victory will now be ours... War to end soon with new offensive... He laid the paper back down on the table and stood there silent, breathing heavily.

'Does that mean the war will be over soon, Neville? I mean, they wouldn't have promoted him unless they were sure of an early end to hostilities, would they?'

He laughed bitterly. If all the stories about Haig were true the war would still be going on in 1920. The man was a plodder, a slowly-meandering donkey. Far from meaning an early end to the war, this appointment had all the portents of pro-longing it. He shook his head tiredly at Matilda without comment and made ready to go.

She accompanied him to the door and stood as she had done the day before while he straightened his uniform jacket, took a deep breath and began to walk down the path. He turned to give her a smile, a tight, nervous smile, and her heart went out to him.

'Good luck with today, Neville,' she said quietly. 'Come back to us when it's all over. I'll be here, waiting and we can talk once more.'

He smiled again, a smile that reached his eyes and made her feel breathless. She returned the smile and then he was gone from her for the second time that week. Reluctantly, she turned back into the house when he was no longer in sight and closed the door.

The church was easy to find, although he and Lucille had never been parish-ioners. Faith had never played a part of their lives. While believing in the pres-ence of a Superior Being he had never felt an affinity with the need to display that belief through prayer. He was relieved to find no one else had arrived and he slipped into the cold, dark interior to sit in a pew and have a quiet moment to himself to reflect.

Gradually, a few people, well wrapped up against the cold, interrupted those thoughts as they started to appear and fill the adjoining pews. He recognised none of them and ignored the looks they gave him. A commotion at the door of the church told of the entrance of Lucille's mother, Mrs Dewar, being comforted by a man he took to be the parish priest. If she recognised him as she was led past she gave no sign and he felt suddenly depressed. The incongruity of the situation struck him as he looked round at the sparse amount of filled pews. Some of these people were probably at his wedding and now here they sat, soberly dressed, as they came to say goodbye to Lucille. She who had been killed in bed with another man while her husband served his country overseas.

He was aware of a man standing at the end of the pew and as he craned his neck to see him properly the man spoke quietly into his ear.

'I take it you're the departed's husband, sir, would I be right?'

Charteris nodded and the man spoke again. 'Sid Chappell, the, er, undertaker, sir. Your late wife's mother has asked me to inform you that she has no desire for you to take part in today's, er, proceedings, sir. You will not be called upon to speak so I would ask you to sit here and allow the service to continue without interfering. Please.'

Shocked, Charteris nodded his head once and, satisfied, the man moved slowly away.

He bowed his head and allowed the tears to fall as the coffin containing his wife's remains was borne up the central aisle by the funeral director's servants to its resting place by the altar. Whatever had happened between them to cause so much pain, they had been happy once and he felt an overwhelming sense of sadness as the plain, wooden coffin was gently laid on a trellis in front of the altar thirty feet from where he sat.

The service was short and perfunctory. The priest, who obviously did not know the woman of whom he was speaking, managed to look almost bored as he delivered his address, the last spiteful act of a mother grieving for her lost daughter. No mention was made of Arnold Walker also and for that Neville was grateful. The hymns Lucille's mother had chosen further increased his dark feeling of depression and he was grateful when the service drew to a close. After it was over they all stood respectfully as the coffin was taken up again and carried outside for the interment. This time there was no doubting Lucille's mother's recognition of Charteris as she was helped out: the look she flashed him as she passed while being comforted was one of utter hatred.

He waited until the church was clear of mourners before making his way outside and over the short distance to the graveside. The picks the workmen had used to batter a hole in the frozen ground to accommodate the final resting place of the coffin peeped slyly from under a piece of green baize that covered the disturbed earth, and he stood a small distance away and observed the goings-on. The priest murmured a few words after the coffin had been reverently lowered and after waiting a few moments the crowd began to disperse.

Charteris turned to leave and was dismayed to find himself face to face with Mrs Dewar.

'Good day, Mrs Dewar,' he spoke stiffly, uncertain as to what to say. 'As you can see I was able to return for my wife's funeral. I realise this might not seem the time and place, given the circumstances, but I wonder if I might have a word in private. To clear up any misunderstandings, you see.'

'You!' she hissed. 'You unspeakable, loathsome swine! How dare you have the cheek to turn up here! Had it not been for you and your gallivanting, I might still have my daughter with me today.'

Charteris opened his mouth to protest her mistake but before he could speak the woman drew her hand back and slapped him full across the face. The noise sounded like a pistol shot in the confined space of the graveyard, echoing and re-echoing among the tombstones while those nearest gaped in astonishment.

His face burning, Charteris turned and walked slowly away. From behind him came the sound of fresh sobbing as Lucille's mother dissolved into another outburst of frenzied hysterics. A male voice shouted at him but he ignored the sound and continued to walk slowly down the path to the open gate. Without looking back he walked through the gate and turned up the road to the High Street. No one pursued him and he blindly marched away without heeding where he was heading, his mind a contradiction of conflicting thoughts.

He didn't blame Lucille's mother for her outburst. Seeing him must have been like a red rag to a bull. No matter her daughter's guilt in the matter, taking it out on him would have been cathartic, a way of releasing all the hurt. Her refusal to face the facts was understandable and if it brought her some comfort in her loss then who was he to sully the memory of her daughter, his late wife? Retracing his steps as best he could remember, he came to a part of Peckham that he recognised and was soon on his way back to the house off the Goose Green where the two women waited.

Mrs Humboldt let him in and showed him into the drawing-room where Matilda waited anxiously. She looked at his face as he entered and saw the pain and sorrow etched there. With a weary sigh he sank into the chair she proffered. Taking her cue, Mrs Humboldt quietly left to do the one thing in the kitchen she knew would be appreciated. Within seconds the kettle was boiling and a spoonful of strong tea sprinkled into the teapot.

When he was ready, Charteris opened his heart and told Matilda of all the day's happenings, sparing no detail as he unburdened himself to her. She listened without speaking, nodding from time to time as he made a point she agreed with.

When he came to the bit where Mrs Dewar had slapped him in full view of everyone she made as if to speak, then wisely held her counsel and let him talk on.

'Was I wrong to not go to her and take over the arrangements myself?' he asked at one point. 'Would people not think it strange that the dead woman's husband could not take charge of the whole affair? I was there, they saw me, and yet I did nothing, paid for nothing, said nothing. Proof of my guilt, I'll wager. That's how they'll have seen it.'

'Neville, please, calm yourself. What would you have done? Your wife's mother obviously wanted nothing to do with you so it would have been difficult to have approached her. Let the woman get over her grief and then make contact again. Perhaps with the passage of time she may come to see you in a different light.'

He looked so helpless that before she knew what she was doing she had crossed the room and, kneeling by his chair, took him in her arms.

He stiffened as she drew him close, then relaxed. She could feel his thin frame through her clothing, his heart beating near hers as his arms encircled her and she felt a rush of maternal emotion. They were still locked in their embrace when Mrs Humboldt entered the room to announce that the supper she had prepared was ready. Pushing the door open noisily was enough to cause them to spring guiltily apart and when she entered the room they were back in their seats, looking at anything but each other.

The atmosphere between them had changed now, a subtle change. Supper was a subdued affair, the two of them hardly daring to look or speak to the other. If Mrs Humboldt had noticed this change she said nothing and continued to act in her own inimical fashion. It was long after the supper plates had been cleared away before they could act normally again. Between them, too, was the unspoken acknowledgement that on the morrow Charteris would have to return to the battalion and that brought with it its own emotions.

Reluctantly, as the fire's dying embers sputtered into nothingness, they made preparations to retire. Mrs Humboldt had retired to her room an hour or so ago, grumbling about the lateness of the hour in her fractured English, muttering to herself in her native Flemish. Bidding Matilda goodnight, Charteris abruptly left and ascended the stairs to his room. Seconds after his door closed he could hear her follow him. Her footsteps passed slowly by his door and as he waited with bated breath they faltered, momentarily, then picked up, and he heard the door of her room at the end of the corridor open and close.

Matilda Fairley. What was he doing here, what was he thinking of? She was a widow, he recently a widower. What was he to do? Tomorrow he would be on his way, travelling back over the Channel to the hell that was France and try as he might he could see nothing ahead for him, or for them both, nothing that gave him any hope to cling to. With all these thoughts and many more crowding his brain, he slipped into a troubled sleep.

He woke in the early hours of the morning, tossing and turning as he agonised over what he should do, what he must say to her before he left. As he lay there he threw back the bedclothes suddenly and rose. Perhaps if he went to her, talked to her, she might tell him what to do, what the future, if any, could hold. In his agitated state he saw nothing wrong in what he proposed to do, nor in the lateness of the hour. He wrapped the dressing-gown hanging on the door around him, opened the door quietly and stepped out into the corridor. Mrs Humboldt's room lay between his and Matilda's and as he passed a floorboard creaked beneath his bare feet. Holding his breath he waited for a response but the house remained deathly quiet so he moved past and at last stood outside Matilda's door.

His heart thudding wildly in his chest he opened the door slowly and stood inside the darkness of her room. As he gently closed the door behind him and his senses breathed in the sweet, feminine fragrance of the interior his eyes became accustomed to the gloom and he stepped back in surprise. Matilda Fairley sat upright in her bed, her arms wrapped around her knees under the bedclothes as she calmly, gravely contemplated her visitor, transfixing him with those beautiful eyes.

'Neville,' she spoke softly. 'I was hoping you'd come.'

He gave a helpless wave of his hands.

'I had to see you, Matilda. I needed to speak. To say... You see, I...' His voice trailed away into silence, the blood pounding through his head as she pulled aside the bedclothes, stepped lightly from the bed and approached him. She was wearing a white lace robe pulled tight, tied in bows under her bosom and his words died as she stepped close. Their eyes met and even in the darkness of the room he could see hers were wide open with a warm, sensual glow. As he tried to speak, desire suddenly thickening in his throat, she put a finger to her lips in a *shh-ing* gesture and stepping closer, placing her lips over his and kissing him.

Her perfume filled his nostrils, he drank in the heady, aromatic smell of her and her touch was like an electric shock. As their lips met, he felt her push herself against him and with a sense of wonder felt himself harden in excitement. She, too, felt his arousal and strained her body harder against his, rocking him backwards on the balls of his feet as she pushed hungrily, tantalisingly, moulding her body to his. Unconsciously, as they embraced, his hand reached up to cup her right breast through the thin material of her robe and he felt the nipple harden as he brushed it with his thumb.

She moaned deep in her throat, a sound that was both yearning and pent-up longing and pulled him closer still, her teeth biting down hard on his lip, her right leg entwining with his left as she ground her pelvis into his groin. He felt her left hand frantically reach for the tassel that held his dressing gown together and as she finally undid it she put both hands on his shoulders to his lapels. Pulling the dressing gown fully open, pushing it backward, she let it slide to the floor. He responded by undoing with his free hand the lace ties that held her robe closed and it too slid to the floor, leaving them both naked.

In what light there was from the final dying embers of the fire he saw the milk-whiteness of her skin and then felt the softness of her breasts as he reached up and caressed them, softly at first, then harder as she writhed gently under his questing hands. Her small hands found him and held him fast. Her mouth opened wide as her head fell back and she moaned, softly, pleadingly. 'Please, Neville. Please...'

His excitement mounting, he took her shoulders and pushed her backwards towards the bed. As she fell onto the mattress he lifted her thighs and slid quickly forwards into the slick, warm wetness of her, her eager, urgent hands guiding him as she arched her back to accept him. Her legs wrapped round the small of his back as he thrust into her, his hands stroking her breasts, their breaths coming in short gasps as each fought to control the raging fire building inside. A roaring noise filled his ears as the tidal wave of emotion that had built to a crescendo burst around him with a shattering crash and beneath him he felt her stiffen and her teeth bite hard into his shoulder as her body moved wildly in response to his release. Her hot breath hissed in dying gasps around his head as the same tidal wave swept over her and she clung tightly to him until the moment had passed, before limply collapsing, passion spent.

They stayed entwined like that for several, long minutes, saying nothing as he caressed her body gently in small soothing motions. Becoming aware of the growing chill in the room he rolled away from her and pulled at the bedclothes around them, joining her in the bed and continuing to hold her as she lay against him, her eyes closed. Eventually her eyes opened and she contemplated his face as she softly stroked his hair.

'Is this what blasphemy feels like, Neville Charteris?' she asked. 'Here you are, having just buried your wife today and now you're in bed making love to another woman, me, a virtual stranger, the same night. God forgive me, I've behaved like a wanton, an adulteress, a woman with no shame or morals. What must you think of me now?'

'What a strange thought,' Neville replied gently. 'If you remember, it was me who came to your room, not the other way round, Matilda. I came to say I think I'm falling in love with you. I'm lost, can this be happening so soon? Feelings I thought had been lost forever have been awakened again.'

He felt her body tremble, then suddenly shake beneath his shoulders and realised with apprehension that she was crying. Lifting her head he quietly kissed her lips, then her wet eyes. 'Don't cry, please, Matilda, if there is any blame then it must fall on me. These are not normal times we live in. Lucille and I belonged to the old world which has gone. She loved me once, and I loved her in return, but that love disappeared some time ago and we became strangers. In the end I couldn't live as she wanted me to and that drove her away. I mourn her, for all we had together once. With all that means, a different part of my life that has now changed since meeting you. Does that make me a monster, or you an adulteress?

Who can say what is right and what is wrong? All I know is that I met you and life has never been the same for me since. My life has changed. I love you, Matilda. Is that an unspeakable thing to say when we have both been so sorely treated by what we call life?'

She sobbed bitterly into his shoulder, crying freely with a sense of guilt for her dead husband and the new, strange feelings the man alongside her had aroused. While he continued to hold her tenderly she clung to him like a child.

'I'm scared, Neville, scared of losing you if I love you. After Arthur's death I thought I would never want another man and then you came into my life. I couldn't bear to lose you, not now. I've been lonely for so long and now, just when I've found you, you must go back to...to...' She started to sob again, quietly, and he felt his heart fill with the enormity of his love for her.

Gently he soothed her, rocking her in his arms while she clung to him fiercely until she fell asleep. She lay against him, sleeping like a baby. Before the dawn broke she stirred and reached for him. They made love again, tenderly this time. At the height of their passion she cried out loudly in wild abandonment, before he bent forward and covered her mouth with his lips, stifling her cries with his kisses. They slept, entwined deep within the bed, their limbs wrapped together loosely at the end of their journey of exploration. Before she awoke he slid out of the bed and wrapped the dressing gown around him. She moved softly in the bed, a small moan of satisfaction escaping her, purring like a cat as he stepped quietly from the room. He crept down the corridor back to his own bedroom and as the door closed behind him he never saw the figure of Mrs Humboldt standing briefly in her doorway before her door shut also.

The day dawned and with it the realisation. With a grimace he rose from the warmth of the bed and stood there, thinking deeply. What had happened between them hours before had changed things forever and he felt lost. Too much had happened in the few, short days he had been here for him to take in. He knew he would feel the silky, warm feel of her on his skin for days to come and the feeling that he must soon be on his way had brought with it a sense akin to loss. Sighing, he found his clothes and began put his trousers on before making his way to the bathroom to wash.

Both women were in the drawing-room and as he entered he could see the figure of Matilda Fairley stood by the window, dressed in a sober black outfit. Her face was turned away from his but as she spun round to face him he could see her eyes were wet with tears once more. He gave her a wry smile and she burst into tears, sobbing loudly as she lurched blindly forward to collapse in his arms. Helplessly he held her tight and looked over her shoulder to where Mrs Humboldt stood, a sombre expression on her face as she watched them both, wringing her hands in the white apron she wore over a grey dress.

'Matilda. Darling, please. Calm yourself. There's nothing for it, I must go.' Looking to Mrs Humboldt he gestured helplessly. 'Please, help Mrs Fairley.'

The Belgian walked over, her eyes brimming with tears too, and pulled Matilda silently from Chateris's grasp. Oh Lord! he thought, they're both at it now. The two women hugged each other and wept.

'Please,' Charteris pleaded for the third time, 'Mrs Humboldt. Help Matilda sit down and make a cup of tea for us all, could you?'

Wiping her eyes Mrs Humboldt helped Matilda to sit and disappeared through the door to the kitchen. Charteris knelt by Matilda and took hold of her shaking, heaving shoulders.

'Look, you must buck up or I shall lose all my courage to go back. Would you want to come and see me in prison when they jail me for desertion?' he said half in jest. She raised her head and contemplated him with a serious manner through her blotched eyes and the wetness of her tears.

'If that's what it takes to keep you safe, then, yes I would.'

He spoke soothingly. 'My little bird, you mustn't fret. I must go. I simply must. Dry your tears, Matilda, and let us enjoy what time we have left together before I have to take the train.'

Reluctantly she nodded, then roused herself to brush her hair back into place and repair the damage her tears had done to her make-up. Even with the ravages her crying had left she looked gorgeous and he felt a wave of tenderness sweep over him. Leaving her was going to be a great wrench but it would have to be faced. But not now. He rose up from his kneeling position and shouted desperately.

'Mrs Humboldt, where's that tea?'

Afterwards, they wrapped up warmly, Matilda in a black overcoat and fetching hat. Unconsciously, Charteris took her gloved hand in his and drew her in protectively. Looking anxiously at the darkening skies overhead they walked down the path and over in the direction of the Goose Green. The rose-tinged clouds gave a hint of snow to come but for now it was dry but bitterly cold. In spite of the weather there were other people out walking, couples like themselves chattering animatedly as they passed. In a corner of the Green, by a large mound, Charteris spied some strange markings on the ground. They turned out to be small wooden crosses and seeing his puzzlement Matilda explained.

'Those are memorial crosses left here by the families of soldiers who've been killed in France or Belgium. I see it as a small way of expressing their grief. It's so poignant, don't you think? If you look closely you can see the name of the person etched on each cross.' Charteris shuddered as he looked down. For some reason the sight of the miniature crosses had aroused a feeling of deep depression and he was quick to take Matilda's arm and guide her away from the area.

Walking away, Matilda noticed the admiring glances they received as people passed by and she looked out of the corner of her eye at her walking companion as they strode along. Neville Charteris looked extremely handsome in his uniform she had to admit, his striking blue eyes complementing his pale skin and boyish looks perfectly, and she recognised how they made for a handsome couple together.

Their lovemaking of the night before had overwhelmed her, awakening feelings that she thought would never see the light of day again, and she fought to compose herself in the knowledge that in a few short hours she would lose him again. It had been so different when Arthur was killed. They were almost children, so young, and had married quickly in the excitement of the moment, a romantic gesture in the coming of the war. He had left her in such high spirits and when he was killed it was as if her heart had shrivelled and died also. Now, a new man had come into her life and thrown all her emotions into turmoil once again.

It frightened her that of late she had woken in the small hours smitten with feelings of overwhelming guilt, unable, as much as she desperately tried to, to recall what Arthur's face had looked like. As time had passed his memory was becoming dimmer with every day, his face only a blurred outline. How could this be? Was it possible to fall in love so quickly? She didn't know the answer to the questions crowding her mind, she only knew that in Neville Charteris she had found someone who aroused deep feelings in her and that she would only ever be happy again if she was with him. She clung to his arm, never wanting to let go and together they walked around the Green, making small talk and laughing gaily at the various things each one of them said. Both were determined to remain cheerful for the sake of the other but conscious all the while of the clock ticking remorselessly on.

All too soon it was time for Charteris to pack his things and make his way to Victoria. Matilda overrode his protestations and accompanied him. As they left the house, Mrs Humboldt ran down the path after them and hugged and kissed him, her eyes wet.

'Don't worry, Mrs Humboldt,' he reassured her, 'I'll be back soon. You see if I'm not.'

'Bert-ha! Pliss. My name ees Bertha! *Zalig Kerstfeest*, Meester Neville!' She kissed him one last time, thrust a brown-paper wrapped parcel into his hands and ran back indoors leaving him astounded, looking after her in puzzlement.

He spoke thoughtfully, 'I think Bertha just wished me Merry Christmas in Flemish.' He looked down at the parcel. 'What on earth do you think she's put in here?'

'Oh, I think you'll find a few creature comforts. We've put a small Christmas Day feast together for you. Make you think of us here at home. It's not Fortnums I'm afraid, but we think you'll like it.'

They walked slowly through the streets, not wanting their time together to end, and Matilda excelled herself by finding them a taxi at Peckham Station.

They rode in silence, each one's heart heavy with the knowledge of the impending parting. At last they reached Victoria Station and alighted, Charteris paid the driver and they walked slowly into the hall hand in hand, each reluctant to let go.

The place was full of troops waiting patiently, laden down with packs, weapons and festive paraphernalia, many with weeping womenfolk and young children hanging onto their arms. In a small corner a Salvation Army band struck up Christmas carols, their sweet voices breaking through the air of gloom. The tension mounted until at last the guard announced the imminent departure of the train to Folkestone.

She clung to him fiercely and he had to gently prise her from him. He could see she was fighting to control her emotions and he held her close, to whisper teasingly, softly into her ear in an attempt to make light of their parting. 'You must be strong for us both, Matilda, otherwise I fear I shall embarrass myself in front of all these men.'

She laughed, weakly, and replied, 'That male thing again. A stiff upper lip in front of "the chaps", what?'

He laughed at her attempt to humour him and she reached across and drew him fiercely into her shoulder. 'You never asked, Neville, but you shouldn't worry about me. I have the house and the money Arthur left me. I shall cope because you would want me to. I've been thinking for some time of joining my friends in the VAD, it will give me something to focus on until your next leave. Come back to me, Neville Charteris, don't let me be lonely ever again. Please. You've given me the best Christmas present I shall ever want. Don't let them take you from me. Give me your word?'

He nodded, too upset himself to speak now. Eventually, pulling away from her embrace, he spoke quietly, gazing into the distance.

'It's funny, but in a way I do miss being "there".' He gestured with a finger, pointing high over her head. 'In France everything seems so clear-cut. There is the dread of death and injury of course, but one feels a completeness, as if being there together with one's friends and one's men gives a purpose to life. It's not *that* bad you know, life in the trenches feels like one tenth fear and danger and nine tenths total boredom. Sometimes it can even feel like we're engaged in some, I don't know, a Christian crusade against the powers of evil. Amid all the horrors it gives one a feeling of being borne up by the souls of all the dead. And now there's you to consider. How strange it's all become. I shall be fine, you know, so there's no need for you to worry either. Promise?'

She nodded, too upset now to brave speaking again for fear of breaking down completely.

'I love you and I *will* be back. Count on it. Take care, Tillie Fairley. Merry Christmas.' As she stared, astonished at his first use of her nickname, he bent forward and kissed her hard on the lips, then marched away, head erect. Her last sight of him was as he turned and waved briefly before entering a carriage.

She stayed, a forlorn figure left with only the fading scent of his cologne in her nostrils. She watched with all the other relatives, some openly weeping, as the train passed out of sight and was finally gone, its whistle a forlorn reminder of its passing. Feeling lonely, desolate and somehow empty now, she joined the throng making its way silently outside. Behind her the band played out its last carol to an empty station.

Charteris sat quietly all the way to the boat, his parcel on the seat next to him and his mind filled with the experiences and emotions of the last few days. It had all been too much and he had let matters slip by that he really should have attended to. With a guilty feeling he realised that he should have made more of an effort to contact Lucille's mother and try to come to some amicable agreement over the property and legal expenses. No matter, he resolved to write once he rejoined the battalion in France.

France. His thoughts turned back to reality and the coming days ahead in the front line. It loomed just over the horizon, luring all of them on the train towards it, drawing them ever closer. Trapping them under its all-encompassing spell with a promise of only death or disfigurement as the reward. Sitting on the train he fancied he could hear the angry thudding resonance of the guns already, feel the icy cold, cloying embrace of the mud. What *was* waiting for them over 'there'? He shivered, and turned to gaze unseeingly out the window until they finally clattered into Folkestone.

20

Thursday 23 December 1915

Battalion endured forced march throughout the evening to our next duty stint in front line. We are to remain in the Somme area. We were forced to stay in communication trenches for the night, owing to lack of guides and shelling of front line areas on arrival. Kit musters and issue of cold weather clothing took place prior to leaving. CO held defaulters' parade prior to battalion marching off.

Captain L. Carey, D Company

In the billets, a large number of bundles were being closely examined.

'Phew! What a stink! What the 'ell are these?' Archie Parkes held up a white and black-stained jerkin in front of him as he looked round for enlightenment.

'Dunno, Archie, but they don't 'alf bloody pong!'

Corporal Menzies snorted derisively. 'You ponces, doncha know nothing? They're goat skins, to keep your little undernourished bodies all snug and warm when we go back up the line this evening! Look at the hair on them. They'll keep you warm all right.'

'Well, I don't know about that, corp, they smell too much for me to wear one. Cor, just like the army to send crap like that!'

When Archie looked round again, the bundles had been untied and all the jerkins were gone, adorning the backs of the men in his section as they paraded up and down in them like mannequins in Harrods.

'Aw, c'mon lads,' he whined, 'I was only funning. Be a sport. Who's nicked my one? It's bloody freezing out there.'

Friday 24 December 1915

Battalion entered trenches to left of Authuille, opposite Leipzig salient. We are now attached to 32 Div as part of X Corps. Carried out relief of Hampshire Regt. A Coy in reserve. Bitterly cold weather turned to sleet in p.m. Rations brought up early in anticipation of the morrow. Coy's stood-to in p.m. A false alarm and Bttn stood down after 10 mins.

Captain L. Carey, D Company

'Christmas Eve! Christmas ruddy Eve! For Christ's sake, why us? Why now?' Billy Lane griped as he trudged through the deep slush lining the bottom of the trench he'd been ordered to. 'Paradise Street? You must be bloody joking! It's bloody well Shitstreet if you ask me! Who had the sense of humour failure, then?'

He turned to survey the area around the dugout he'd commandeered and read the faded sign leaning askew at the entrance to the traverse of his particular length of trench. Shaking his head in disgust, he slung his pack and rifle into the dugout, noticing that it seemed to be swimming in water and swore loudly as he leant forward, the rain pouring off his cap as he did so.

A more cheerful-looking Arwyn Jones poked him in the back as he tried to pass. Wearing his new lance-corporal stripes, Jones was not going to let Lane's bad humour spoil his Christmas. 'Shut up boyo, and let me through! All you've done on the march up here is bloody gripe, man. Give it a rest, can't you?'

Lane glowered at the new lance-jack as he slid past him but Jones was too busy looking out a nice shelter for himself to notice.

The march up from the communication trenches they'd spent the previous night in had left them all soaked through in the sleet as they approached the front line. Luckily the weather had been too severe for the German artillery observers to spot them and the relief had gone smoothly with no shelling. The troops they had relieved, a battalion of the Hampshire regiment, had been cock-a-hoop at their departure from the trenches so near to Christmas. In the near distance the guns muttered incessantly. Elsewhere in the world it might be Christmas, but out here in France the serious business of killing carried on unabated.

Now the weapons were made ready. Lewis guns were sited and loaded in position, trench mortars placed into their firing pits and each company's personal arms kept at close hand as they filed into their new positions and made themselves as comfortable as they could, given the conditions. One or two braver souls took their lives in their hands and risked a quick peep over the top. There was nothing to be seen. Through the grey murk of the freezing sleet lashing down, the ground between the two sets of trenches resembled the lunar landscape familiar to them all from their previous tours in the line. Shell holes had gouged out huge overlapping, water-filled holes, covering the ground thickly in profusion as far as the eye could see. There were no trees, no vegetation, nothing to tell of the two armies watching and waiting astride the line. Only a dark smudge on the horizon, several hundred yards away, told of the presence of the enemy trenches.

Barbed wire was everywhere, great thick belts of it, designed to keep the enemy out and the defenders secure behind its sharp enclosures. The beaten zones had been carefully worked out and Vickers machine-guns sited to sweep these with a lethal dose of lead should any attacker be careless or stupid enough to come within range. Further back, the artillery batteries had the ranges marked on all their maps, ready to respond to any call for help with an immediate barrage of shells.

The battalion settled into its new positions quickly, the foul weather helping to get everything squared away as the men not required for sentry duties eagerly sought some respite from the driving rain. Later in the evening, ration parties toiled up the communication and support trenches, bringing with them an early supper as they lugged the heavy containers in sandbags through the crowded lines. If the enemy spotted this they made no sign and no shells whistled over to speed the ration parties on their way. Cold bully beef stew and hunks of wet, stale bread were not what the waiting troops had in mind, though.

It was as he was contemplating reluctantly trying to force some of the mush in his mess tin down his throat that Bill Cox of D Company first heard a noise coming from his front. Hurriedly dropping the tin onto the firestep he crouched down and concentrated hard as he tried to determine its source. There it was again! Rising and falling on the air, somewhere from the direction of the German front line. He reached up and began banging hard with his rifle butt on the metal triangle sunk into the parapet by his right hand.

'Stand-to! Stand-to! The Gerries are coming! Quick, stand-to!'

The response to his banging was instantaneous. Men tumbled from all directions out of holes and dugouts, their meals spilling uneaten. The air was filled with the rattle of bolts as rifles were hastily loaded and the soldiers leapt on to the firestep and crouched there, breathing heavily in shock and sudden panic. Within seconds the line was fully manned, the men waiting for orders as they exchanged worried glances.

'Who raised the alarm? Who was it? Speak up!'

Second-Lieutenant Rodney Patterson, pistol drawn, waded manfully along the bottom of the trench towards where Bill Cox crouched at his post. A figure further down the trench pointed a laconic finger up at Bill and the young officer scuttled along until he was looking up at the crouching, anxious soldier peering down at him.

'Cox! What was it? What did you hear?'

'Sir! I thought I heard a... There it is again, sir! Can you hear it? It's coming from over there!' He made as if to rise but his officer waved him down urgently. 'Stay there, I'm coming up.' He pulled himself up next to Cox and listened hard in the direction the trembling soldier was pointing, his breath coming in short, excited gasps. Yes, there it was, there was no mistaking it. He could hear it too. He took a deep breath, spun round and shouted down the trench at the white faces gaping alongside him..

'All right, men, panic over! Stand down, I repeat, stand down!'

He recognised the concerned figure of their company commander, Captain Carey, making his way along the trench towards him and shouted at him. 'It's all right, sir, false alarm. No harm done!' Lionel Carey made a disgusted grimace and turned back for the warmth and safety of his dugout, adding his bad-tempered comments to those of the men as he did so.

With relief the men relaxed and clambered down, some muttering choice phrases in view of their now-ruined meal at a visibly abashed Bill Cox who stood there, feeling more embarrassed as the seconds ticked by. Patterson holstered his pistol and leapt down to join his men. He looked back at the soldier staring transfixed at him and tried, unsuccessfully, to hide a grin.

'Good show, Cox!' he called, his grin widening. 'Keep a sharp lookout, that was good work on your part just now.'

'But what was it, sir? I heard something, I know I did,' a puzzled Cox rejoined.

'Listen again,' Patterson answered him as he walked away, 'You certainly did hear something, Cox. The Huns. They're singing! It is Christmas after all!'

Faintly on the air from the German trenches, for anyone who strained long enough to hear, came the fading chorus of '*Stille nacht... Heilige nacht...*'

Christmas Day, Saturday 25 December 1915
Battalion's first Christmas in front line. In accordance with brigade orders, men expended small arms fire at enemy trenches at 07:30 ack emma. Heavy shelling of enemy positions carried out by RFA battery in rear. Cooks served Christmas dinner to men in the trenches. CO visited all companies with other officers in attendance.

Captain L. Carey, D Company

Walter Ramsbottom acknowledged the wave of the sentry further down the trench as he stood at the top of the steps leading down to his dugout. The sleet had fallen all night and rivulets of cold water were pouring down his neck in spite of the scarf he had wrapped around it. God! What a way to spend Christmas Day! His thoughts turned to the precious days he'd spent back in Sussex with his wife Gwendoline and their daughters. Was it really three weeks ago? How time had flown, especially here. Gwen would still be fast asleep in their bed, missing the warmth of his body alongside her. Damn this weather but more especially, damn this bloody war!

He looked down at the message sheet Cuthbert Snaith had handed him last night as they'd shared a nightcap and re-read its contents.

Confidential Memo, Div HQ
23-12-1915

To all Commanding Officers. You are reminded of the unauthorised truce and fraternisations which occurred at this time last year and are further directed to ensure that *nothing* of this nature takes place on Christmas Day of this year.

Accordingly, a slow artillery barrage will commence at dawn on all fronts and *every* effort made to inflict the maximum casualties on those of the enemy who expose themselves.

Signed

Col. Maximillian C. Stannard

There had been rumours of the goings-on of last Christmas and tales had abounded of the fraternisation that had occurred between the two sets of protagonists far from the all-seeing eyes of the General Staff. Truces in no man's land, football matches, exchanges of gifts of food and alcohol in some places. Well not today, not this Christmas. Dawn was not far off, he surmised, a faint smudge on the horizon, and as he gazed down the trench at the crouching men lining the firestep he looked briefly at his watch. Any second now.

A rumbling noise far to their rear reached their ears as the sky behind them lit up in a sullen red glow. This was swiftly followed by another flash, and then another. Seconds later came the screaming noise of the shells tearing their way overhead, to be followed by the dull *crump!* of explosions as they impacted on the German lines. There was a noticeable pause after the first explosions, followed by another bout of firing as the artillery batteries slowly reloaded and fired again in accordance with their orders.

'All right, CSM,' Major Ramsbottom ordered, 'let's do what the staff wallahs want. Get the men up and let's show the Boche some Christmas spirit.'

'You heard the officer!!' Miles Hornby shouted, 'stand up and give 'em twenty rounds rapid fire! Now! Come on, move it!'

C Company had been patiently waiting since six o'clock for this moment, stood-to on the firestep, taking the brunt of the weather. An early tot of rum, their Christmas present from the 'stores-bashers' as Hornby had sarcastically put it, had failed for once to warm them up. Stiff limbs groaning under their exertions the men rose up, swinging their rifles onto their shoulders. The rattle of musketry was added to that of the shells now, the hot expended cartridges flying through the air into the bottom of the trench as the bolts were worked backwards and slammed forwards again.

'That's it, lads! Keep up a good rate of fire. Let those Huns over there know who they're facing!' CSM Hornby made his way down the trench, dodging the flying brass cases. Suddenly he stopped and reached up, knocking a soldier's arm skywards.

'Oi, Wadley, what the bleedin' 'ell do you think you're doing?'

Indignantly Wadley looked down at the irate NCO's angry, twisted face.

'Waddya mean CSM? I'm only doing what we was ordered to do. Shoot at the enemy!'

'For God's sake, Wadley, you stupid fucker! Point that rifle up to the sky! Do you want to kill someone, you dozy clod? Don't you know it's Christmas?' Miles Hornby swept down the trench shaking his head disgustedly, leaving a thoroughly bewildered Ernie Wadley staring after him.

Later, 'Dod' Benson of C Company eagerly tore at the brown wrappings of the parcel he'd been hoarding for over a week.

'Come on, man, open the bloody thing then!'

His fellow Lewis gunner, Percy Hartson, was beside himself with excitement as he watched Benson struggle with the paper. The visitors buried deeply in his clothing had begun their incessant irritation of his armpits and groin in spite of the cold, and as he scratched futilely at the affected areas he urged his pal on with a will.

'Keep yer bleeding hair on, Percy, will you! I'm going as quick as I can!' Benson pulled at the last bits of string holding the parcel together, then hissed triumphantly, 'Gotcha!'

'Socks? Bloody socks! For Christ's sakes! Doesn't your old lady know what time of the year it is?' Hartson turned away in utter disgust, leaving Dod to carefully examine and shake each of the four pairs of socks that the parcel held. Nothing fell out of them and he tossed them angrily into the corner. Wait til his next letter home, he'd give her what for! Fancy not hiding some booze in the damn things. He fished a packet of cigarettes out of his pocket and prodded Percy in the ribs, offering him a chance of a smoke.

'Not even a fuckin' card in there! Oi, Perce. Merry Christmas!'

Mollified, Hartson pulled a cigarette out of the packet Dod was holding and stuck it between his lips. As his mate bent forward to give him a light from the match he'd struck Hartson recognised the humour in the situation and began to chortle. Dod Benson stared at him amazed and then he, too, joined in. Within seconds they were both laughing and coughing helplessly, the tears rolling down their cheeks as they sucked in huge lungfuls of tobacco smoke.

Popping his head out his funkhole Donnie Parker witnessed the novel sight of 'Rasher' Parkinson, one of the battalion chefs, puffing hard as he dragged a large, metal container through the wet, freezing slush lying in the bottom of the trench.

'Jesus, Rasher,' he ejaculated, 'what the 'ell are you doing up here slumming it so far from the warmth of the cookhouse?'

'Shut yer face, Parker!' snarled the overwrought cook. 'The RSM told me to bring you bastards some Christmas dinner up here. Now get out here and take some o' this grub I've brought or I'm out o' 'ere as quick as Christ can let me. Unless you've neglected to notice, I doesn't 'appen to enjoy freezing my bollocks off!'

The panting, anxious cook leant down and whipped the cover off the container and Donnie Parker caught a whiff of the unmistakeable smell of plum duff.

'Fuck me! Is that what I thinks it is?'

'Course it is yer berk. Now get here bloody quick or I'm off. And give yer mates a yell, too!'

Within seconds a mass of men were thronging round the hapless cook in the confined area of the trench as he tried to fill the numerous mess tins that were thrust at him. Cursing and lashing out at those who tried to take too much he managed to eke out the contents of the container until all those in the immediate vicinity had had their tins filled. A hush fell over the trench as its occupants eagerly gobbled their meal.

'Where's our main course then?' shouted Haddaway Wadkins as the cook prepared to depart.

'Oh, I forgot to tell you,' replied Parkinson diffidently, 'The boys in C Company are having turkey for their Christmas dinner. Yous lot are having their puddin'. Ta-ta! lads. Merry fucking Christmas!' A howl of indignant curses sent him on his way.

In the C Company area the men were tucking into a dish of warmish turkey and boiled potatoes when Titch Magilton became aware of Snaith struggling down the trench towards him, waving his bamboo cane in the air. He made to rise but was waved down again by Major Roberts, following behind.

'Carry on as you were!' Roberts sang out as they picked their way through the water-filled trench and Titch warily shovelled another piece of warm, leathery turkey into his mouth as he watched the officers approach.

'Merry, um, Christmas!' the colonel stuttered as he came abreast of Magilton, thrusting out a gloved hand. Shaking it, Titch thought: my God, he's smashed! The colonel stood swaying over him, a bright beam on his purplish-tinged face, and as he bent closer Titch detected a pungent whiff of stale alcohol.

Snaith burped before delving into his pocket and bringing out a crumpled, foul-smelling cheroot which he pressed into the bemused Titch's hand.

'Merry Christmas, Private Thingey!' he beamed again, before lurching down the trench to the next waiting group, followed by a now mightily-concerned adjutant. Behind him, Titch gave the cheroot a cursory sniff before screwing his nose up and launching it high over the parapet into no man's land.

'Cheapskate bastard!' he muttered darkly before turning his attention back to his rapidly-cooling meal.

Neville Charteris sat in the relative quiet of his dugout and eased the belt off his aching stomach. The fare in the company officer's mess had filled him to the brim. He had dined well on consommé soup, followed by choice Norfolk turkey with lashings of potatoes and vegetables, the turkey having been brought from England by one of the younger second-lieutenants. Pudding had consisted of plum duff, as enjoyed by the men, with the addition of brandy custard, followed by a selection of cheeses and water biscuits. All of which had been copiously washed down by liberal pourings of Bordeaux wine and large glasses of malt whisky. A Christmas hamper from Fortnum & Mason rested against the wall and they had all picked at its contents from time to time as the fancy took them

He had tried to make sure that his men were well catered for, donating some of the extras that had found their way into the officer's mess, but he was well aware of the paucity of the rations the ordinary rank and file were served for their Christmas dinner. Any guilty feelings, however, had disappeared with his third glass of red wine.

Now, as he sat against the dugout wall in the best of the reserve trenches, trying to ease his groaning stomach, he looked inquisitively at the parcel he held in his hand. It was the same parcel Bertha Humboldt had pressed into his hand on leaving Matilda's and he glanced at it ruminatively before ripping off the wrapping. Inside was a hand-knitted pair of black woollen gloves, a small box of dark chocolate and a brown leather wallet.

He opened the wallet. Staring at him from under a clear cover in the flap was a miniature photograph of Matilda, her curls hanging loosely around her elfin face as she smiled for the photographer. In the lower right corner she had written in her neat handwriting,

Merry Christmas, darling Neville.
Love, Tillie. xxxxx

* * * * *

Gazing at the photograph he felt a wave of longing overcome him and he pressed it to his cheek and held it there for a long, long time. Whatever thoughts he had of Lucille now stayed trapped within the recesses of his mind, deliberately pushed out of awareness. She belonged to a different period of his life, in the past, one he wished to forget, and with Matilda Fairley he had a chance for a new beginning again.

Back in the trenches, Roger Dundas squelched along the bays and traverses, doling out tins of cigarettes and small packets of chocolates to the dispirited men hanging off the firestep or lounging in their holes in the side of the parapet. At one of the larger dugouts he gathered several of its inhabitants and together they prayed and sang a few carols, the men's faces lighting up as they belted out the words. The men responded well to the banter he brought with him and later on, as he made his way back, the chaplain could feel justly pleased with his attempts to bring some comfort to the men so far away from home at a time like this.

The rest of the day passed quietly. The Germans responded in a desultory manner to the shelling from the British lines, which carried on all day, by hurling a few shells back by way of retaliation. No casualties were suffered by the battalion, except for those officers who over-indulged themselves in the various messes up and down the lines, plus the odd OR who managed to scrounge more than his fair share of rum. From the German trenches came the faint sound of singing once again but it soon petered out, as if they too recognised the futility of trying observe the birth of the Saviour of Mankind in such ludicrous conditions.

For the men huddled in their holes trying to keep warm and dry, a sometime impossibility, for the most part it was just another day in the front line with the promise of another one tomorrow. And another one after that. Ad infinitum. Save for one man, Private Bill Evans, the colonel's batman. His feet sticking out of the hole he'd made in the trench wall, Evans snored blissfully as he slept off the effects of the whisky he'd pilfered from the colonel's valise. Well, it was Christmas, after all.

Boxing Day, Sunday 26th December 1915

Work parties involved in trench repair work. Enemy shelling in a.m. caused six casualties in B Coy area. Four ORs killed, two wounded, one severely. More sleet and snow in the p.m.

Captain L. Carey, D Company

The shells screamed out of the sleet, exploding around the trenches before men had a chance to react. Harry Sheldon ducked as shrapnel whined over his head. One of his puttees trailed behind him as he frantically sought shelter, but he ignored it as he dived into the hole next to the Lewis gun position.

'Oi, watch it, you stupid berk.' An indignant voice gave full vent to its feelings as he landed on a soft body already jammed inside the comparative safety of the hole.

'Oh, sorry, corp, didn't see it was you.'

Harry grinned and rubbed the aggrieved soldier's tousled head.

'S'all right, Wadley, if I'd known it was you I'd've landed a bit harder. Knocked some ruddy sense into you. Now, hold still while I tries to extricate myself! Who the bleedin' 'ell woke the Boche up, then?' He pushed himself away from the soldier beneath him with a gloved hand, ignoring Wadley's smothered cries.

A blinding flash and massive explosion tore the breath from his body, turning the world black in an instant as the earth wall of their funkhole caved in. Harry Sheldon came to, his mouth full of foul-tasting dirt and his head and ears ringing, his body held fast in a vice-like grip. Dimly he was aware of someone struggling beside him but for the moment he was too weak to respond. After a second or two he managed to free an arm and after clearing his mouth and taking in huge gasps of breath he frantically began attempting to dig the rest of his body free from the all-encompassing embrace of the wet, frozen earth.

It must have only been minutes but to the entombed NCO it seemed like hours before he heard the sound of digging. Seconds later the metal shape of an entrenching tool smashed through the dirt, nearly striking him in the face and he called out in terror and alarm. The noise of digging slowed as the metal implement was slowly withdrawn before being cautiously pushed back into the earth and used in a backward-digging motion. Within a short space of time a large hole had been excavated and he could see the anxiously-peering faces of men from his platoon. A hand reached into the hole and he grabbed it, interlocking his fingers with the man outside. An almighty heave and he was pulled through the hole to land shivering with nerves and exhaustion, covered from head to foot in dirt, on the frozen floor of the trench.

Ernie Wadley soon followed him and together they stared up at their saviours. 'Thanks, mate, thanks. God, I thought we was done for!' Sheldon exclaimed, still trembling from their near escape as he held his hand out. 'Anyone else near us cop it?'

Billy Lane took the proffered hand and shook it solemnly before pointing a thumb over his shoulder, down the trench.

'The new boys, corp. Four of them. Only joined us a week ago. They're all dead. The dugout they were in took a direct hit. We tried to dig them out but there's only bits o' bodies in there. Mister Bradley says to leave them there so we just filled the lot back in. An' Wilson caught a packet, a nice Blighty one. A shell splinter got him right in the arse!'

His chest heaving, Sheldon listened to Lane's tale and tried to picture the faces of the new men who had joined them only a short period before. He failed, and leant, his legs suddenly weak, against the side of the trench as he took in the damaged state the shelling had left it in.

'Merry bloody Christmas and no mistake, eh! That's the last time I listen to a recruiting sergeant! You wouldn't have a spare fag, would you?'

* * * * *

'Walter? A moment if you please!'

At the sound of the voice behind him, Walter Ramsbottom turned to face the figure approaching him in a crouched manner up the trench. The telephone lines to B Company were down, probably cut by the shelling, so against the advice of his orderly corporal he had stuck his head out of the dugout. Hearing no sound of guns, other than firing in the distance, he had judged it safe enough to take a stroll and see for himself what the damage was.

'Oh, it's you, David. What can I do for you?'

Major Roberts looked round to see if anyone was in earshot before drawing nearer. Reassured that they were alone, he nevertheless kept his voice low as he explained the reason for seeking Walter out.

'Look, I don't know how to begin but it's like this...you see...'

'Oh for goodness sake, David, spell it out, man!' Ramsbottom was exasperated as his fellow officer stumbled over his words. 'What's the matter? That blighter Evans been caught with his hands on one of the CO's bottles again?'

Roberts caught himself and started in surprise. 'I say, how did you know about that? I thought I was the only one who knew Evans was helping himself. No, sorry to take so long to come to the point, Walter, but it's the CO himself.'

'The CO? What has Snaith done now?'

'Look, Walter, swear you won't speak a word to anyone else? He's hitting the bottle. Please, hear me out. I mean really hitting the bottle. He's tight most days now, or hadn't you noticed?'

Ramsbottom frowned. 'Now that you come to mention it, I did think he'd had a bit too much yesterday but as it was Christmas Day I forgot about it. Do you really mean every day?'

'Yes. It's to do with Godley. Since that business he's taken to the bottle even harder. I think it's his conscience, you know. Bradley told me about the evening he tried to stop the execution, when he told the CO about Godley's true age. That information seems to be all round the battalion, by the way. Ever since then the colonel's lost his grip. I'm worried he'll do something stupid when he's drunk. And now that Brigade are involved...'

'What do you mean, Brigade are involved?' Ramsbottom asked sharply.

Roberts looked at him with a miserable expression on his face. 'Somehow, the news of the manner of Godley's death has reached Britain. I think one of the men must have written and told Godley's sister what happened. Don't ask me who or how they got it past the censoring officer, please, I'm as much in the dark over it as you. Whatever the facts, a telegram was sent from her to the War Office asking them to confirm the details. Brigade's now in an uproar. Some blighter in Parliament has already been asking sensitive questions on the matter of under-age youths serving at the front and now this has come up.

'I've been ordered by Brigade to look into it and get back to them immediately. They want to know Godley's true age, if we can verify it, and the exact circumstances of his trial and subsequent execution. Walter, this could blow up in all our faces. What shall I do?'

Ramsbottom thought quickly. 'Stall them for a few days to give us time to come up with something. I'll let you know shortly. And for God's sake keep that thieving blighter Evans's hands off the bottle! Christ knows, it's probably him that's been shooting his mouth off. Thanks, David, for coming to see me. We'll sort this out, you see if we don't.' Roberts gave him a tight smile and hurried off the way he'd come, leaving Ramsbottom rubbing his chin in a pensive manner before he, too, carried on his way.

New Year's Eve, Friday 31st December 1915
A quiet day on all fronts. A Coy had an unusual visitor in the late evening. 2/Lt Elliot of
A Coy personally shot a German officer who strayed too close to our lines.
Captain L. Carey, D Company

The evening was chilly. The temperature had long dipped towards freezing and Bill Thomson was looking forward to being relieved. Overhead the stars gleamed silvery-white and a cold wind moaned over the top of the trench he was guarding. No matter how many layers of clothing he dressed himself in before going on sentry duty, the cold always permeated through every item to leave him feeling chilled to the bone. To compound his misery, in the two days they'd spent in the front line since relieving C Company there had only been cold bully beef and hard biscuits for sustenance, apart from some rare rashers of bacon in the early morning. The rum ration that Sergeant Clark had come round and liberally dispensed each day had helped, but only for a short while, before the numbing cold seeped in again.

He blew fruitlessly into the palms of his thick woollen gloves in a vain attempt to restore the feeling to his fingers and shuffled his feet inside his boots. His toes had long appeared to have parted from his body and he was beginning to wish he'd covered them in whale grease, when from out to his front he heard a sudden movement. He crouched down and tried to work the bolt of his rifle in order to chamber a round into the breech. The metal parts were frozen stiff and he cursed soundlessly as he heaved and pulled at the jammed bolt. The sound grew louder and he abandoned any attempt at loading and stuck his head slowly over the parapet.

'Halt! Who goes there?'

A voice answered him and he had to strain to catch the words.

'Don't shoot! I am unarmed. Please let me approach.'

'Stay where you are!' he yelled back at the unknown and as yet unseen voice out there beyond the wire. He leant back over the trench. 'Quick, get the captain up here! There's someone outside wants to come in!'

Within seconds Frank Mason was on the scene. He took the information from a scared Bill Thomson and half-ran down the trench to the company officers' dugout. Bursting through the flap he peered into the cramped, fetid interior. Spotting Neville Charteris wedged into a cramped cot and reading a letter, he cried, 'Captain Charteris, sir, you're needed out here!'

Glancing over Charteris saw immediately from Mason's concerned expression that something serious was afoot. Folding Tillie Fairley's latest letter into his pocket to be read later, he pushed himself off the cot and stood up, buckling on his holster. Together the two men moved up the trench towards the disturbance, Mason filling Charteris in with the information as he had gleaned from the sentry. They arrived at the place where Bill Thomson was anxiously waiting on the firestep, surrounded by curious men below him.

'Right you lot,' CSM Mason exclaimed, 'Clear a space and let's see just what we've got. Thomson, tell Mister Charteris what you told me. Smartly now!'

Thomson leant down and spoke in a rush. Leaping onto the firestep alongside him, Charteris cautiously took a look over the top of the parapet. He could see nothing but darkness, a black stygian darkness whipped up with snow that covered everything, leaving just ghostly shapes that shimmered on the other side of the barbed wire entanglement to his front. As he was about to duck back down a voice called from the darkness.

'Hello! Is there someone there? Can you hear me?'

'Who are you?' Charteris called out in puzzlement. Whoever it was spoke perfect English and yet nothing made sense. Who could be out there in such weather?

'Kapitan Werner Grundheim von Rechlen, 14th Brandenburger Regiment at your service. May I come in?'

Charteris shook his head. What the devil was going on here? He took his pistol from his holster and kept it pointing in front of him.

'I don't know what your game is but if this is a trick then you will not live to see it out. Approach the wire slowly so we can observe you!' he shouted. Out in the blackness something moved and he made out the shape of a man, moving slowly and carefully as he approached the wire. He was carrying a sort of rucksack on his back and had both his hands held up high in a gesture of surrender.

'Cover me, Thomson, I'm going out to see what on earth this is all about.'

Charteris was over the top of the parapet and moving into the empty space between the trench and the wire before a startled Bill Thomson could answer him. He stopped abruptly, so that both men were staring at each other from either side of the great coils of wire. Dropping his gloved hands to his side the German officer snapped into an immaculate salute and smiled broadly.

'Ah, I see you wear the insignia of a captain. A fellow officer. To whom do I have the pleasure of addressing myself, sir?'

'Captain Neville Charteris. You'll forgive me if I don't give my regiment. And you, sir, what is a German officer doing out on this side of the line by himself? Do you wish to surrender, kapitan?'

The German laughed heartily. 'No, no, my dear chap, I'm not here to surrender. My brother officers and I thought we would bring you a few luxuries. To help celebrate the New Year, you understand. To let you know we are not all barbarians. We may be on opposite sides, Captain Charteris, but that does not mean we must hate each other. Hate is for politicians. As soldiers we must do their bidding but in any war there is also respect. *Nicht wahr?*'

Still feeling decidedly perplexed, Charteris nodded. 'I see what you say, Kapitan Grundheim, but that still doesn't explain your presence here tonight.'

He took a good look at the man opposite him. He saw an intelligent, handsome-looking face, with a firm jaw and a gleam in the dark eyes examining him. The German was dressed in an immaculate uniform, dark, shining leather boots and a thick, greyish greatcoat with an enormous fur collar. A uniform cap sat jauntily over one side of his forehead.

'You speak impeccable English, kapitan. Did you learn it at school maybe?'

'No, captain. Thank you for your compliment. I had an English nanny and it was she who taught me how to speak the language.' He took a step forward and Charteris tensed. 'May I hand this over?' Kapitan Grundheim shrugged the rucksack off his shoulder and let it fall to his feet. 'We are all God's creatures, captain, and after tonight, as enemies, we will no doubt try to kill each other in the morning. But for tonight let there be a sort of peace between we fellow human beings as we celebrate the start of a new year. I bring you some small comforts as a mark of respect from the men on the other side of the lines. It is getting colder so I will not detain you long. Here, let me show you.'

He reached down to the rucksack.

Bang! The report sounded explosively close to Charteris's ear and he leapt back at the deafening sound of the shot. Across the wire from him the German looked disbelievingly down at the hole in his greatcoat. He staggered and made as if to speak. A rattle, and another shot rang out. He spun round and dropped onto the hard ground without a sound, his hat flying off in the wind as he fell.

An incredulous and shocked Charteris wheeled round at the sound of the shots. David Elliot dropped the muzzle of the rifle he'd taken from Bill Thomson before climbing up and staring evenly at his superior's astounded expression from where he stood, five feet away.

'I think I just saved you, sir. That damn Hun was going to shoot you!'

'He was unarmed, you bastard! He was bloody well unarmed!' Charteris exploded in fury at the smug expression on Elliot's face.

'How was I to know that, Captain Charteris?' Elliot ignored Charteris's rage and stared back with a sanguine expression on his face. 'For all I know he was reaching into that bag for a pistol. You know how treacherous these Huns can be, sir. Just like women... Now if you don't mind, I shall go and check on the other sentries.'

He turned away, threw the rifle casually at an astonished Bill Thomson and jumped back down into the trench.

Charteris stood for a long time looking at the corpse lying close to his feet, a white-hot rage coursing through him as he digested Elliot's words. They were meant as a personal insult, of that he had no doubt. He walked slowly through a gap in the wire until he stood next to the body and reached down for the rucksack the dead man had been carrying. The top was open and he peered inside before flinging the rucksack angrily in the direction of the watching men of his company.

'Chocolates!' he called out brokenly as the wind moaned keenly around his shoulders, 'He was bringing us some bloody chocolates!'

An hour or so later a great profusion of flares erupted from the German lines and lit up the sky in a red and white glow, casting eerie shadows on the ground beneath as they slowly drifted back to earth. Quickly the battalion moved to man the parapets, watching the other side with their trench periscopes for any sign of movement. When none came, Charteris stood-down the great majority of his men and stood, crouching, as he tried to fathom out the bizarre goings-on.

It was as he stood, deep in thought, that he heard Frank Mason begin chuckling next to him. Before he could frame a question, a hand dug into his ribs and he turned to see Frank's grinning face in the dying light of the flares, the CSM's other hand stuck out in front of him.

'Happy New Year, sir, Happy New Year! That's what those blighters over there are signalling!' He pumped Charteris's hand vigorously and the two men turned back to face the parapet and look up at the sky, each man's thoughts taking them far away: 1916 had arrived.

A new year indeed. After all that had passed since the war's beginning, each man wondered what was still to come, what more would they all have to endure. Charteris thought of his father, Peckham, and Tillie Fairley. What would she be doing right now? Was she standing in the garden at this very moment looking up at the stars and thinking of him? He looked around and saw the same yearning on the faces of the men surrounding him.

Frank Mason's thoughts were of a bonfire and a young boy, his eyes wide with excitement as he ran down the street towards his laughing mother.

New Year's Day, Saturday 1st January 1916
A new year in our service here in France. Weather very cold. A small unofficial patrol sent out to reconnoitre in the early a.m. observed enemy activity. Gas attack on A Company lines followed. Eleven ORs killed, one in no man's land. Seven ORs and one NCO wounded, four severely. Attack gallantly repulsed by Capt. Charteris and men, with heavy enemy casualties.

Captain L. Carey, D Company

His feet crunched noisily, too noisily for him, on the frozen ground and he paused, watchful and waiting to hear if his movements had been detected. Nothing stirred and he slowly eased his foot down. Bertie Ludlow was sweating under the white sheets wrapped around his body, in spite of the ice-cold temperature. The broken-walled ruin of the shelled cottage that had been his objective loomed up out of the dark and he held his left arm up warningly. He listened keenly but heard nothing save the moaning of the wind. Satisfied they were alone, he waved impatiently and his companion scuttled forward out of the darkness to take his place alongside him.

'It looks quiet, Archie, but you never can tell. Keep an eye on the right, can you, while I go and have a dekko over to the left?' Archie Higgins nodded vigorously and watched as his friend slid away and was swiftly swallowed up in the gloom. He pushed his sleeve back and looked at the watch on his wrist. Dawn was not far away and he hoped Ludlow would be back soon so they could get back to their own side as quickly as Christ would let them.

Above him the stars spangled, twinkling coldly as they shone down on the battlefield. If he listened carefully enough he could hear the muted sounds of the night. Over there came the strangled cough of a nervous sentry and in the far-away distance the mutter and grumble of artillery made syncopated beats on his eardrums as some battery carried out a rehearsed plan of harassing fire. Nearby, a rat squeaked and he shuddered. Loathsome creatures, the rats he had seen scuttled everywhere in multitudes, disturbing men's sleep in their voracious search for sustenance. Sid Bates had insisted he'd seen one as big as a domestic cat and when the rest of the men in his dugout had roared with laughter at his tale he had stormed outside in a temper. For himself, Higgins treated them with equanimity, but not tonight, not here. He breathed deeply and watched his breath stream out into the frozen air, wreathing his head in a white, hoary mist.

What a way to be celebrating the New Year! After the fireworks of flares and artillery fire it had all gone quiet again. He felt terribly homesick, alone and afraid. He glanced at his wrist again. Three minutes only had passed since he had last looked and he was beginning to feel a blue funk coming on, regretting the mad impulse that had seen him accompany Ludlow out into no man's land. To take his mind off things he examined his watch more closely.

He could make out the time quite clearly, owing to the luminous dial on the watch's face. It read five-thirty-three, still a few hours until daylight came. The strap was a bit loose for his liking but it fitted well on his arm otherwise. The name on the face was in a sort of italic script and even if he had been able to decipher it, it would have meant nothing to him. He had taken the watch from the body of the dead German officer that Mr Elliot had shot earlier in the evening, as he and Bertie had passed the body on their way into no man's land.

Ludlow had hissed his disapproval but he had ignored him and continued to search the dead man's pockets before rejoining him. He had stuffed a nice silver cigarette case in his greatcoat pocket and the officer's leather wallet now reposed in Archie's tunic, to be picked over when they returned.

A sudden noise to his front made him crouch down in alarm but to his relief it turned out to be the returning figure of his friend. Bertie spoke quietly.

'I don't like it, Archie, there's something queer going on out there. Lots of movement and weird noises coming from the Hun trenches to our left. Best we get back.' Higgins nodded eagerly and made ready to retreat the way they'd come.

His sleeve was grabbed suddenly.

'What was that? Can you hear it?'

'Hear what?'

'That noise. There it is again! Can you hear it now?'

He strained his ears in the direction Ludlow was pointing but could hear nothing save the noise of the wind. His friend grabbed his arm again, savagely this time.

'Listen, Archie!'

He turned his head again and listened intently. After a short while his brain cancelled out the noise of the wind and his ears picked out a new sound.

'That's strange,' he commented, 'it's a sound of...I dunno, Bertie, like...'

'Hissing?'

'Yeah, that's it. A hissing sound, like a kitchen tap, like as if it was...

'Gas?'

'Oh God, Bertie!'

They both squinted uncertainly and looked to their front as the noise grew louder, slowly, with a menacing edge to the quiet hissing noise Bertie had heard. Archie was the first to spot it, a low evil-looking cloud that looked just like the early ground mists they had been accustomed to seeing as the day broke. This mist, though, had a deadly greenish tinge to it as it sinuously snaked, rolled and billowed its way along the ground, falling into and filling the shell holes in front of them as it edged its way nearer to their position. Chlorine gas – deadly if inhaled, and coming their way. Fast.

'Christ, Archie, we'd better get back and let the lads know about this or it'll overrun them.'

'Look, Bertie, look over there!' Following his friend's trembling finger Bertie glanced in the direction Archie was pointing. Dimly, behind the cloud of green he could see unearthly figures stumbling, demons, weapons held ready as they followed the cloud of deadly gas towards the British lines. It took him a second or two before he recognised these monster-like figures as German soldiers, clad in their gas-masks.

'Get going, now! Get back to the lines and warn everyone. I'll hold them here for as long as I can before joining you. Go. Quick!'

Higgins contemplated the other man, a look of consternation on his face.

'But Bertie, you haven't got your gas mask with you! You can't stay here, mate. Come on, come back with me.'

Ludlow was already working the bolt on his rifle as he chambered a round into the breech and released the safety catch. He looked up and his brow furrowed. 'Don't argue with me, Archie. Get going now before we both get stuck here. Go! I'll be with you in a sec, I'll just stop a few of these buggers getting through so's you can warn the boys. Now, Archie! Don't let me 'ave to say it again.'

Higgins took off, keeping low as he scuttled away from the shelter of the wall and into the darkness. Shell holes loomed up before him and he scrabbled desperately to avoid sliding into them as he ran, lungs bursting. Behind him, Bertie smiled grimly as he brought the rifle up to his shoulder and tried to sight on one of the ghostly figures drawing nearer with every second. The Lee-Enfield was a superb weapon in the arms of a top-class shot and Bertie was such a man.

A noise burst out of the darkness and his eyes opened wide in alarm. Before he could react a boiling mass flowed around him, threatening to overwhelm him. Rats, thousands of them, all sizes and colours, squeaking their fear and anxiety as they frantically sought to escape the poisonous wall of death that silently stalked them. Biting and scratching their nearest neighbours they ran, squealing, surging over and around him like a tidal wave. In a trice they were gone, leaving him alone once more.

A movement to his left made him jerk round and he fired automatically as the rifle sights were filled. *Bang!* The shot broke the restored silence of the night and he heard a groan from out in the darkness as he quickly reloaded. Good! One less Hun to worry about. A sound to his right caused him to swivel frantically round and he caught sight of another shape. The gun exploded before he could think and a body flopped inertly down as the bullet tore into it and he quickly searched for a new target.

A whorl of green mist slowly engulfed his legs and he frowned as he watched the tendrils climb higher up his body. Another noise to his front alerted him and as he wheeled round a soldier tore out of the gathering mists and bore down on him. Ludlow shot him at point-blank range and the body collapsed soundlessly, just feet from where he crouched.

He coughed violently as he inhaled a small portion of the mist that was gathering around him. It had risen to the level of his shoulders and he took an involuntary gulp as he worked another round into the breech of his rifle. The acrid taste hitting his unprotected lungs caused a paroxysm of retching and his eyes began to water profusely. He half-stood to gain some relief and caught sight of a shape creeping slowly towards him, rifle at the ready. He raised his rifle and shot the soldier high in the chest. The enemy soldier fell, making strange noises through the material of his gas mask and Bertie shot him again as he lay squirming on the ground.

The taste of the gas was now overpowering, suffocating him, making each breath an effort. His eyes and nose were streaming badly and it was becoming harder to see. His lungs were filled with the sensation of drowning, and coughing furiously, painfully trying to draw a breath to ease the pain in his chest, he began to retreat away from the cottage wall. Several shots rang out but nothing came his way. Rifle held high he floundered like a man underwater, back towards the direction of A Company's trenches. His breath was coming in great gasps now, panting, his chest heaving as he tried to draw a clean breath. A sound behind him made him stop and whip round, the heavy rifle coming smoothly up to his shoulder again. He was too late, far, far too late.

The German soldier's bayonet slid brutally into his midriff and he gagged in agony as the tempered steel tore into his body. His rifle dropped from his nerveless fingers and he made a weak, futile attempt to disengage from the metal that pinioned him, clawing with both hands at the sharp blade to pull the bayonet from him. The soldier holding the rifle pushed further, stronger, and Bertie screamed, a thin high scream of mortal agony as the bayonet ground deeper into his stomach. His knees gave way and he collapsed, his cut and bloodied hands fluttering from the blade. He fell backwards, the soldier attached to him, grunting as he was pulled forward, vainly trying to free his Mauser rifle from his enemy's embrace. Stooping, he put a nailed boot on Bertie's chest and tugged hard.

The bayonet make a sucking sound as it slid out and Bertie screamed again in agony at the burning sensation in his stomach as it withdrew. Leaving the fallen man where he lay the German loped off to catch up with his comrades. On the ground behind him, Ludlow weakly clasped both hands, soaked with his blood, to his abdomen in an attempt to keep his innards from spilling out as mounting waves of pain washed over him. The gas now enveloped him fully, wrapping him intimately in its deadly embrace as he struggled and fought to stay conscious. Another bout of coughing drew more gas into his lungs and he dropped his hands from his stomach to tear futilely at his throat. It was proving impossible to breathe now and he began a long, choking slide down into blackness. His last conscious thought before the dark overtook him was a twinge of regret that Mr Bryson wouldn't take as good care of the Ross rifle as he had. It was a pity, he could have…

Higgins ran as he'd never run before, sliding and stumbling in the dark as he desperately sought the shelter of his own trenches. His white sheet flapped around him as he ran but he ignored it, wrenching himself off the wire entanglements and ripping it to shreds. Behind him he heard the crack of Bertie's rifle and the answering reports of a Mauser. That spurred him on to greater efforts and he gulped in great mouthfuls of cold clean air as he ran. After what seemed like ten minutes or so he heard a welcoming voice from the darkness and he nearly fainted with relief.

'Halt! 'Who goes there?'

'It's me, Archie Higgins, I'm coming in!'

'Advance and be recognised!' came the stentorian answer.

'Christ! Forget all that, you berk! The whole fuckin' Fritz army's behind me! Can't you hear them? I'm coming in. Quick, there's gas coming, sound the alarm!' He slithered the last few yards or so and faintly made out the top of a questioning head peering over the parapet at him.

'Get the CSM up here, quickly, or we're done for! There's gas coming! Hurry…!'

The head disappeared and he made for the gap he could see in the wire. He passed through it at speed and fell awkwardly into the trench, landing below on a soft body.

'Jesus H Christ! What the fuck's going on? I think you've busted my arm, you idiot!'

Ignoring the man's protests and scrambling to his feet Higgins looked desperately round for a friendly face in the gloom as he tried to catch his breath.

'Jim! Jim! Quick, get Mr Charteris or the CSM or we're done for. Fritz is heading this way, behind a bloody great cloud of gas. They'll be here any minute and if we don't look sharp we're all going to cop it!'

Maddison listened in grim silence as Archie poured out his story then turned quickly.

'Right lads, you heard Archie here. Sound the alarm. Gas! Gas! Gas! Get those masks on, now, and get out of the trench onto the parados. Smartly now! You, Thomson, go and get the captain. And spread the word as you go.'

They needed no second bidding. Along the trench the sound of iron being struck rang out as the gas alarm was sounded. Frantically the men heaved their masks from their pouches, In seconds they had scrambled up onto the parados where they lay, panting from their exertions through the heavy cloth masks with their mica eyepieces. Seconds later, Charteris, followed swiftly by Frank Mason, joined them, both men tugging on their equipment. Charteris heard Archie Higgins's story and looked round at his men spread out along the top of the trench.

'Right, men!' he shouted. 'Keep calm and watch for my order. When the Boche appear, I'll fire a red flare. Open fire and keep firing. Got that? Have your rifles ready and stay on the top, that way the gas won't cover you.' He knelt down, loaded the Verey pistol and laid it down next to him. Trying to stop his hands from trembling he broke open his service revolver and shakily filled the empty chambers with cartridges. Joining his men he lay down and waited.

A stick grenade bursting on the parapet to their right heralded the approach of the Germans, the flash from the grenade glowing eerily as the tidal wave of chlorine gas lapped over the parapet at the same time. The gas flowed down into the trench with a lifelike eagerness, voraciously seeking out its prey, filling each dugout, nook and cranny as its choking tentacles sought to squeeze the last breath of life from all it encountered.

To the men lying waiting the world took on a greenish hue as the gas engulfed them, each man's consciousness being filled with the sound of his own tortured breathing in the suffocating confines of his mask as he tried to see through the rapidly fogging eyepieces. A sudden movement and one of their brethren reared up, tearing at his throat and pulling off his mask in agony as the gas found an entry. Before their horrified eyes he retched and gargled, twisting and turning in a paroxysm of bloated, purple-faced coughing before falling out of sight into a sea of green, back into the trench they had lately evacuated. Hearts thudding painfully quickly in their chests they waited with terrified, tortured breathing for the signal.

Exhaling slowly to calm his nerves, Charteris spotted a group of figures stumbling blindly along the parapet opposite, rifles with fixed bayonets at the ready. Their outlines looked wrong and he recognised them as the enemy. Snatching up the flare pistol he pointed it skywards, jerking the trigger. The pistol bucked savagely and a bright red light shot towards the heavens. Instantly, a volley of shots rang out and the group of men he had spotted melted away. A heavier burst of fire to his right made him drop the flare pistol and grab his revolver.

The swirling gas clouds brought a surreal hue to the desperate exchange as the two sides fought with savage strength, bombing and firing at extremely close range. No quarter was asked for or given. Out of the darkness a burst of machine-gun fire swished along the trench, catching both attackers and defenders unaware as the German gunner fired blindly. Bodies dropped in silent agonised heaps while those still standing fought on. The firing grew heavier, gunfire, flashes, the sounds of combat coming from all directions as Charteris tried to contain and direct his men's fire in the confused struggle. Men shouted, screamed, fired and died as the deadly bullets struck home.

Charteris paused, panting with the exertion of breathing within the claustrophobic confines of his flannel mask as he reloaded his revolver. Fumbling with the brass-jacketed rounds he managed to load three of the chambers, spilling the rest on the ground through trembling fingers that shook with both the cold and apprehension. Looking up he noticed a group of Germans gathering to jump across the trench to the side where his men lay.

'Urrghhh!' was all that came out of his mask as he tried to warn those nearest to him. Realising the futility, he jumped forward and emptied his revolver into the midst of the cowering group. Two men fell and the others retreated in confusion, leaving Charteris standing alone on his side of the trench.

A bullet plucked at his sleeve but he ignored it as he strode quickly to where a group of his men were firing blindly into the green mists swirling around friend and foe. Unseen by him, a German, spotting him standing alone, made as if to fire but before he could pull the trigger a watchful Sergeant Clark had seen the danger and fired first. The German dropped limply into the trench from the parapet where he stood.

It was the Germans who broke first. Turning away suddenly as if from some unheard command, they melted back into the swirling clouds, leaving behind only the scattered groups of their dead. Passing down the line, Charteris pulled and pushed his exultant men, pointing vigorously as they were unable to comprehend the grunts emanating from his mask. A German moved weakly on the ground in front of him, gas mask wrenched off alongside him. As he approached, a British soldier walked over to where the enemy soldier lay and casually shot him from close range. The muzzle flash burned the German's face as the bullet smashed the life out of him.

A whistling, screaming noise grew to a crescendo and a torrent of shells crashed down as the Germans covered their men's withdrawal. Frantically waving to the men around him, Charteris dropped down and hugged the earth as the whizz-bangs burst, the air filling with dirt and flying splinters. The ground shook and heaved for only a few minutes before the shelling stopped as abruptly as it had started. It had the effect of rapidly dispersing the gas and it wasn't too long before the braver among them tentatively began to remove their masks.

Sergeant Clark moved among his men, warning them of the dangers of taking too big a gulp of air. Slowly, as if waking from a drugged, dreamlike state, they began staggering around, inspecting and tugging at the scattered, inert bodies before dragging them from the scene of the fighting. Their wounded were carried away to the aid post, the dead being reverently passed down to a collection point for registration before burial.

Finished, they all crowded together in the communication trenches, waiting for the deadly gas to finally disperse. It was long after daybreak before it was pronounced safe to return to their own trenches and then only after being forbidden to enter the dugouts until they had been pronounced clear of the gas that still lurked dangerously in the low-lying hollows.

Weakly, Charteris leaned against a corner of the firebay and gave his orders. The strain of trying to keep in touch with all his men during the savage fighting had taken its toll and his head felt as if it would burst. Frank Mason busied himself making out the casualty report. They had got off lightly, considering. Ten ORs were dead, excluding Bertie Ludlow, whose fate was unknown for the moment. Seven ORs had been wounded, along with Corporal Charlton from 3 Platoon and he wasn't expected to see out the day. Around them, though, they had counted thirty-odd German bodies and bits of bodies. No wounded Germans were found on either side of the trench, the lightly wounded having been evacuated by their own side under the cover of the gas cloud.

Later in the morning the CO made an unusual appearance. He slapped a weary, dishelleved Charteris heartily on the back and congratulated him as he took in the scene from the lens of a trench periscope.

'Well done, Neville, old man. Splendid, simply splendid! I'll see you get a good mention in my report for this, make no mistake. That'll teach them to try it on with us!' He rambled on excitedly and Charteris wearily listened, hardly taking anything in until a name pierced his shattered senses.

'I'm sorry, sir, what was that you said?'

'Elliot, Second-Lieutenant Elliot, Captain Charteris,' Snaith patiently explained, speaking slowly as if to a child. 'What luck, eh? If he hadn't shot that treacherous Boche blighter earlier, we'd never have been placed in such a heightened state of alert. Could've lost this whole area, eh? I'll see he gets a mention too. Good to know, thought he was turning into a bit of an encumbrance but you see, you never can tell. Good man!' He patted Charteris's arm and was gone, leaving Charteris looking after him in utter disbelief.

Sitting down later that evening, swilling from a welcome mug of whisky in the deep dugout that passed for the officers' mess, Charteris became aware of an animated conversation between Bevan Hughes and David Roberts.

'Look here, old man,' Hughes was remonstrating. 'How on earth can you say these men are cowards? I've already had to send two men back to the casualty clearing station today after the attack we suffered, both of them with neurasthenia. Some men can't take the shelling. You know that, David.'

'Balderdash!' Roberts leaned over and tapped his pipe angrily on the rough-hewn table to make his point. 'Those men *are* damned cowards! You treat them far too leniently, Bevan! Neurasthenia indeed! All it takes are a few shells and they go to pieces, let themselves and their comrades down. I know what I'd do with such fellows, if it were up to me. Every last cowardly swine. I'd...'

'Shoot them?' Charteris stood up and headed for the steps. His question hung in the air between the two officers a long time after he had disappeared.

The night wore on, a white frost springing up along with a freezing, biting breeze. The stars shone silvery overhead, looking icily down on the shivering masses. Frozen vapour rose unchecked above the parapets as the sentries stamped their feet together to ease the numbing ache, and blew chattering lips lustily into their hands in an attempt to warm fingers that had long since lost any sensation.

Eighty yards away from the snaking line of the trenches, David Elliot rolled over onto his back and looked up at the star-filled sky. The cold threatened to bite deep into his aching limbs as he lay there, shivering as if with the ague. He had sneaked over the parapet half an hour earlier with a stern warning to the sentry, Private Allison, not to say a word. Allison knew to keep his mouth shut. Well, he'd better, Elliot thought grimly. One word from the man would bring trouble in a big way down on his head.

Gazing at the panoply overhead he cocked his head first one way then the other, listening intently for any sounds. The colonel had been fulsome in his praise, unwarranted if only he'd known. At the first sign of trouble, Elliot had dived into a deep hole fairly smartly and stayed there until the all-clear. Still, the CO thought he had played a major part in the fighting and it would be foolish to let him know otherwise. Let them think him a hero for a while yet.

Out here, in amongst the shellholes and the debris, he reigned over his own little fiefdom and so long as he was quiet he could scuttle about for hours before making his way back. Whether it was sneaking further down parallel to the trenches to observe and listen to the muted, idle chatter of the sentries without being observed, or making little discoveries of discarded items of kit, there was always something to amuse him.

He knew the men in his platoon despised him, as did his superior, Captain bloody Charteris. At the thought of the man his face darkened. He'd get that swine Charteris, just see if he didn't. Fancy acting so outraged over him shooting the German officer like that. He was the bloody enemy after all!

He suppressed an giggle at the memory and rose onto his knees. A faint rustle came from his right and he dropped instantly back into the frozen earth, heart beating wildly. The noise came out of the darkness again, a faint scratching of something being dragged slowly over the ground. As he listened, his straining senses picked up the sound of a faint groan.

Carefully, Elliot began to crawl towards the sound, eyes searching the blackness ahead of him for any sign of the origin of the noise. This time he heard a cough, an agonised wheeze, suddenly stilled as if a hand had been drawn across a mouth and he bore off to the left now in the direction from whence it had come. Even with thick mittens on, his hands began to lose all sensation of feeling but he ignored the cold and crept on. A large hump impeded him and as he made to go around it, the hump spoke, making him start suddenly in surprise and fear.

'Hilfe!'

He reared up, fumbling madly with his holster, cursing wildly under his breath as he tugged frantically on the revolver's lanyard.

'Aaach! Hilfe mich!' The breath hissed out sibilantly as the man lying huddled before him groaned in pain, the frosted greatcoat he was wearing making audible cracking noises as he tried to ease his body into a comfortable position.

Heart thudding madly in his chest, Elliot looked round, but they were alone. He peered closely at the soldier. A large tear in the side of the greatcoat, liberally splashed with encrusted black patches that must be blood, told of a severe wound. This must be one of the men wounded in that day's fighting, left behind by his comrades in their indecent haste to regain their own trenches. By some miracle he had managed to painfully drag himself away from the scene of the fighting and only his thick winter clothing and iron will had stopped him succumbing thus far to the bitter, penetrating cold.

A cruel, cold smile hovered on Elliot's lips and he edged closer. The soldier, sensing his approach, raised an arm weakly and made to speak.

'Wasser? Hast du wasser? Ich habe durst... Ach Gott, meine...'

'What? What are you saying, old man? No speaka der lingo.' Elliot could see the man was wearing a dark muffler around his neck. Brushing aside the soldier's arm he reached over, pulled the free ends of the muffler from the confines of the greatcoat and began to twist them together, staring deeply into the man's eyes as he did so. Sensing blindly what was about to happen, the soldier tried to fight back, but his strength was gone. His body writhed agonisingly as he tried to rise up but to no avail, and with a weak sigh he fell back. A gargling noise dribbled from his clenched lips while Elliot calmly, pitilessly, throttled him. The man's legs drummed feebly, helplessly, on the icy, hard-packed ground.

The unequal struggle did not last long. With a final rattle deep in his throat the enemy soldier's body went limp under Elliot's sustained pressure. He continued to twist the ends of the muffler together until he was satisfied the man was dead. Whistling tunelessly, he rolled the body onto its back and began to rifle the dead man's pockets.

'Aha!' he breathed as a fat, bloodstained wallet came into view. 'Happy New Year, Fritz.'

A bloodstained photograph was the first item to be withdrawn and he scowled as he tried to make out the images it contained. In the dim light could see what looked to be a woman surrounded by three young children. He tossed the photograph carelessly to one side and delved back inside the wallet. A succession of folded papers and some paper money was all it contained and he snorted with disgust before throwing the wallet to one side and rifling through the corpse's other pockets.

Long after Elliot had disappeared into the waning night, the German soldier's eyes stared blank and unseeing at the photograph of his family which had fallen where it had been so carelessly tossed, to lie on the ground by his cold and stiffening face.

21

Wednesday 5th January 1916

Working parties engaged in trench repairs. Kit inspection carried out on B Coy in reserve after fighting of New Year's Day. Burials took place yesterday of our dead. CO to Brigade HQ for most of the day. Snow in the p.m.

Captain L. Carey, D Company

Snaith squirmed in his seat as he glanced down at the floor before looking up at his questioner.

'Come now, Colonel Snaith, the question wasn't that difficult was it?' the dapper man asked him suavely with a high, arched eyebrow. 'Look, I'll ask you again, just in case you didn't hear properly. When did you become aware of Private Godley's true age? Was it before or after his execution?'

Cuthbert Snaith's mind raced into overtime as he saw the trap opening in front of him. Frantically he tried to regroup his thoughts. Grimacing, he finally spluttered, 'Do you mean his real or his alleged age? I was in no position prior to, or indeed after, the court martial, to ascertain the full facts, given the difficult conditions under which the battalion was serving.'

'Do you deny that one of your own officers came to you prior to the execution and laid facts before you, Colonel Snaith, facts that had come into his possession that could prove the youthfulness of one of your soldiers? Indeed, the very same soldier sitting under sentence of death?'

His questioner waited some long seconds before carrying on in the same vein.

'Look, Colonel Snaith, this is not some kangaroo court trying to trick you into condemning yourself out of your own mouth. Serious allegations have been made that an underage soldier serving in your battalion was executed and that no attempt to halt or delay the execution was made by you or any of your officers, despite this knowledge coming to your attention some time before the man, or rather, boy, was shot. Do you see my point?'

Snaith spoke slowly and forcefully. 'I can only reiterate that we were serving under very difficult conditions. Private Godley had been found guilty in a legally-constituted court of military law and sentenced in accordance with the findings of that court. He was found guilty of deserting his comrades during a trench raid. Why he...'

'Yes, yes! I know that, Colonel Snaith. My point is, that having been found guilty and sentenced, his real age was apparently intimated to you prior to the date of his execution. It is alleged that you ignored this information and allowed the shooting of Private Godley to take place without once attempting to contact your superiors. We are not discussing the shooting of a man here, colonel, we are talking about a mere boy! Good God, man! The press would have a field day if they but knew. And if we allowed them to publish the truth, if it ever came out. Do you realise the damage this could do to the men's morale, not to mention the British public's reaction. What were you thinking of?'

Snaith coldly stared at the clean-shaven colonel sat opposite him.

'Please do not take offence at my words, colonel, but when did you last serve under the conditions that my men do, in knee-high, freezing, glutinous mud, taking hours to gain a few yards? Or bury a comrade that an enemy sniper killed in front of you, his brains spilling over your hands as you tried to save him? Without the comforts of a warm bed and a good night's sleep! You have no idea what it's like to serve in the front line, yet you sit there in judgement of me, taking notes in condemnation, totally unaware of what conditions are like not that far from where we now sit in comfort and safety.

'Private Godley was rightly and justly convicted of an offence committed against his comrades and the laws of the uniform in which he served. The legal sentence that was passed was that he suffer death by shooting. That sentence was carried out in a legal and proscribed manner. Private Godley was treated with the utmost kindness during his trial and subsequent incarceration up to and including his execution. I carried out my orders to the letter of the law, unpleasant as they were, and by God! I will not have you sit there and impugn me in this manner!

'Private Godley let down his comrades and his battalion and he paid for that with his life as military law demanded! The man had attested to being nineteen and he was dealt with on that basis, in a formally constituted court martial that, I might say, conformed more with military law than that to be found in regular battalions. Under the difficult circumstances we found ourselves serving in I was not in any way able to confirm the truth of the matter until after his execution. An execution sanctioned, no, *demanded*, with some indecent haste I might add, by the highest-ranking officer in the BEF. Tell me, colonel, if you will, just where did *we* transgress? Hmn? What did *we* forget, out there in the mud and the cold!'

Across the room from him, his accuser sat back red-faced as Snaith's words hit home.

'I'm sorry Colonel Snaith, but this non-cooperation on your part is unacceptable. I will note your comments for the present but I'm afraid that when Brigadier Blackley returns from London you will be sent for again. I had hoped you would see sense and talk to me in a frank and sensible manner but it is obvious this is not to be. You are free to go and next time I hope you find yourself able to furnish us with the information we require.'

Stiffly, with as much dignity as he could muster, Snaith heaved himself to his feet and looked down at his fellow officer, who had the grace to look away in embarrassment. Spinning on his heels he reached out and jerked open the door of the office. Ignoring the salute of the sentry positioned outside he walked briskly away. After a few minutes he passed a small, clean-looking café with a sign, 'Officers Only' stuck in a prominent position in the front window. He pushed open the door and marched quickly into the dark yet welcoming interior.

'A brandy *s'il vous plait*. And make it a large one!'

Saturday 8th January 1916
Snow for most of the day. Planning begun for fighting patrol to ambush enemy patrol in no man's land in two days' time. Light shelling on D Coy area in p.m. No casualties. One OR of C Coy wounded by sniper, not severely. Rations brought up late p.m. by C Coy ration party.

Captain L. Carey, D Company

The snow petered out late in the afternoon, decorating the trenches with a mantle of white where it settled. The sentries suffered the most. No matter how many layers of clothing each man put on before venturing out, the snow still found its wet, cold way under the lapels of overcoats. After a welcome hot mug of tea the frozen sentries gave up their places to their reliefs and retired gratefully to the warmth of the coal braziers that had begun to make their appearance in the company support trench areas.

At HQ, situated behind the second support trench line, a small meeting chaired by Walter Ramsbottom was taking place. Captain Lionel Carey and two other junior officers from other companies examined a map laid out on the rough table-top in front of them. Aerial photos lay scattered around the edges of the map as they concentrated hard on the acetate overlay defining the trench system they presently occupied.

'Gentlemen,' Ramsbottom began, 'we have information gained from a number of sources that Fritz regularly sends a large patrol out on this line here.' He pointed with a cane to the map. 'Leaving their lines here, and regaining them, there. Brigade want us to intercept this patrol and bring back a few prisoners for interrogation. Under the command of Captain Carey here, you will lie in wait for the buggers in no man's land and nab a few of them after you've dealt with the others in the patrol. Seems a piece of cake but I've brought you here so's we ensure we have no foul-ups.'

'Just small arms will be carried, you officers taking only your pistols, although encourage the men to take what they want, just in case Fritz decides to make a fight of it at close quarters. Bombs as usual, four each, will be carried by all ranks. Riflemen will be positioned here to cover your retreat and once you're safely on the move back, our artillery will put up a jolly good strafe on the Boche lines to keep their heads down while you make good your escape. Now, anyone have any questions they'd like to ask?'

A keen young officer from D Company by the name of Parsons bent over the map for a closer look and then straightened up.

'If you ask me, sir, I think we could have a damn good shot at them about here. You'll see it has...'

Monday 10th January 1916

Fighting patrol successfully intercepted German patrol and captured prisoners. 2/Lt Parsons killed and two ORs missing. One NCO wounded. Much valuable information gained from prisoners who were forwarded to Divisional HQ. Battalion to billets tomorrow for welcome relief.

Captain L. Carey, D Company

Thursday 13th January 1916

Small arms training in a.m. New draft joined us in billets. CO to Brigade in p.m. Quiet day, local leave granted in Authuille.

Captain L. Carey, D Company

Snaith pulled his tunic straight and flicked some imaginary dust off his uniform before nodding to the harassed clerk holding the door open for him. Walking into the room he surprised the two occupants speaking quietly, heads together. Springing apart as they became aware of him, the senior, a tall, austere officer wearing the insignia of a brigadier-general, gestured for Snaith to sit in the single chair on the opposite side of the table. Snaith sat, removed his hat and laid it on his knees.

All three men regarded each other. The brigadier broke the silence.

'Look here, Cuthbert, I have here your recommendations for bravery awards for the action on New Year's day. Is this all you want considering?' He looked down at the single sheet of paper in his hand. 'Captain Neville Charteris MC, recommended for the Distinguished Service Order. Second-Lieutenant Elliot, the Military Cross. Sergeant Clark and Private Higgins, the Distinguished Conduct Medal. You have the requisite witnesses and recommendations on paper, I trust? Good. Well, there should be no trouble passing those through, your fellows acquitted themselves well. Charteris, Charteris? Wasn't he the fellow that did well at Loos? Hmn, thought so. He seems to be just the sort of chap we need if we're to go on and win this damned war. See my clerk, Corporal Westmacott, on the way out and he'll sort it for you.

'As to Private Ludlow, all we have is an unconfirmed statement from your chap, what was his name? Oh yes, Higgins. I see you have indicated your intention to press for the highest award possible and I do understand your motives. If what you say is true, Private Ludlow sacrificed his life to save those of his comrades. This was indeed bravery of the highest order and should not go unrecognised. However, with no witnesses to his actions my hands are tied. See if you can come up with something more substantial and we'll see what can be done. Now, there *is* another matter I need to discuss.'

Snaith continued to regard him in silence and the brigadier fidgeted uneasily. Turning the cover of a second folder he opened it and, reluctantly it seemed, began to read the opening page.

'Trouble is, Cuthbert, this situation with Private Godley. GHQ is becoming uncomfortably difficult over this. Want to know all there is to know about the matter. Bending my ear with almost daily with demands for information. You see, it isn't—'

'Sir, I spoke to Colonel Shannon here a few days ago about this matter. Am I to understand a formal inquiry is to take place?'

Brigadier Blackley squirmed under Snaith's gaze. 'Look here my dear chap, no one is saying anything just now. Not until we know the facts. The—'

Cuthbert Snaith answered him coldly, breaking into his sentence for the second time. 'We have been over this matter, sir, here in this very room only days ago. I informed Colonel Shannon of the facts of the matter and had hoped that would be the end of it.'

This time the Colonel Shannon broke in.

'Colonel Snaith, you were asked questions by me a few days ago, as you rightly point out. You refused to answer most of them. A boy died...'

'Do not begin to lecture me Colonel Shannon on the facts. I know who died! He was a *soldier,* do I have to remind you of that fact again, colonel? Men are dying in this madness every day! I received orders to carry out a most unpleasant duty and carried out those orders! Now I find my obedience to those orders being questioned in a most sinister manner. A manner to which I object most strongly!'

'Gentlemen, gentlemen, please. Let us calm down and look at this matter dispassionately. Colonel Snaith, I must inform you that based on the evidence laid before me so far I *will* be instigating an inquiry into the execution of Private Godley. If it is found that you concealed his true age before the sentence passed upon him by the court martial was carried out, without first informing Brigade, then it is more than likely this will lead to your being removed from the command of your battalion. It is also likely you will find yourself answering charges in a military court. Do I make myself clear?'

Snaith nodded dumbly, taken aback by the sudden personal attack upon him.

'Good!' The brigadier spoke more gently. 'I want a full and accurate report on my desk within the week, Cuthbert, detailing all the facts as you knew them. All of them, mind. Everything you know about the matter. Now please leave us and return to your battalion, I know you have plenty to ponder. Colonel Shannon, please remain here, I wish to have words with you, sir.'

Feeling deflated and suddenly depressed, Snaith rose from his chair and left the room. Wordlessly he dropped the piece of paper from his tunic pocket onto the clerk's desk at the end of the hall and stood there, waiting. The corporal picked it up and glanced at it. 'Oh yes, sir, these are the names the brigadier said you'd be dropping off. Shall I order transport for you now sir?' The words died in his throat as he saw the expression on Snaith's face.

'Look, sir, take a seat over there. I'll get someone to bring you a nice cup of tea and then we'll get you back, all right?'

* * * * *

Back in the village of Combleville, dubbed 'Crumble Vile' by the men, the arrival of the mail had sent everyone scampering to see if they were one of the lucky ones that day. Reclining on a broken sofa in the cottage allocated him, Ernie Wadley puffed contentedly on a cigarette as he scanned the crumpled letter in his free hand. 'Eh, you two, listen to this. Our Harry has only gone and—' The door opened and he looked annoyed as a blast of cold air entered the small room.

'*Non, non, Madame Sophie. Nous tired. Ne distubez us pas. Regardes les cold.*'

It wasn't their landlady who entered but two soldiers bearing their packs and rifles which they dropped unannounced, together with their greatcoats, in the centre of the room as Lane's fractured Franglais spilled out.

'Oi, you two, what the fuck do you think you're doin'?' Billy Lane yelped as one of the packs narrowly missed his foot.

'Sorry, mate, the corporal up the road told us we was to kip down here with you lot, until we can find more comfortable lodgings. I objected but he said we was lucky to get in here. Apparently no one wants to billet with you lot. Something on account of the smell, like!'

Billy straightened up but the angry retort died in his throat as he recognised the dark, saturnine face of Fred Maitland. 'Well I'll be damned! Fred Maitland! We all thought you was dead. Where've you come from then?'

'Well, it ain't fuckin' Heaven I can tell you, matey,' Fred Maitland answered, beaming broadly. 'Although from all those lovely nurses, who weren't averse to a proper man now and again, it certainly felt like it. Nah, me and Bob here,' he gestured at his companion standing alongside him, 'we're part of the new draft sent down to reinforce you shower of shite! Ain't we, Bob? Show you lot what real soldiers look like.'

'Christ! Bob Simpson too!' Billy Lane's widened in astonishment. 'How did the pair of you manage to swing it so's you landed back here with us? I thought we'd seen the last of you after that stunt round Loos back in September.'

Bob Simpson looked over at his travelling companion. 'Tell them the truth, Fred,' he smiled. 'We're only here because of Fred and some missing money from the hospital matron's office. Stupid sod, he swore blind it wasn't him but he was seen going into her office while she were on the wards. I told him to keep out but the bugger wouldn't listen. I got lumped in with him, they thought me 'an him were pals so we were both got shot of. Lucky we weren't sent to the salient, it's bloody murder up there at the moment we were told. Nah, Fred worked his magic and we managed to end up back with the battalion, didn't we Fred? I could've done with another few weeks rest but we were lucky not to get thrown in the clink!'

Maitland straightened up with an aggrieved air. 'It bloody well wasn't me. Well, not all of it, anyways.' He sniggered. 'I was, er, seeing to a young lady in the records department of the hospital me 'n the corp landed up in. Near Southampton, a place called Netley. Was as easy as pie once we was told we was 'aving to come back 'ere to get her to change our orders. No one gives a fuck really, as long as you go back. Some poor sods have ended up in Flanders instead of us. Up to their necks in shit and bullets but that's their lookout. Now then, who's going to offer us a drink? A real drink, not a cup of char or any of that piss they call wine over 'ere. My mouth's gagging for a stiff chota peg.'

Billy laughed. 'Aye, lad, that'll be right! Where the 'ell do you think we can get hold of alcohol, then? We only started getting local leave today!'

'Shit! I thought you'd say that!' Maitland bent down, undid the straps of his pack and pushed a hand inside. There was a brief tinkling sound and his hand reappeared, holding a bottle of Black & White whisky.

'Bloody 'ell, Fred, where did you get that?'

Maitland laughed again. 'Let's just say, some ponce of an officer on the boat over here was too careless leaving his valise unattended. Call it a sort of donation to the real fighting men. Now, go find us a clean cup while Bobby here and me tell you all about our adventures since we last saw your ugly mugs! It was great being looked after like we was heroes back in Blighty, and then you come out 'ere again and find its still the same old crap!' He glanced back to where Bob Simpson, the ribbon of the DCM prominent above his tunic breast-pocket, stood uncertainly near the doorway.

'Come on, corp, get yerself in here and close that bloody door. Don't want these little dears catching their death of cold now, do we!'

Monday 17th January 1916

Re-equipment took place of items of kit recently lost. Bayonet practice by platoons in a.m. CO, Major Ramsbottom and Adjutant to Brigade HQ in p.m. for briefing. Leave party returned from four days' leave, 3 officers and 12 ORs.

Captain L. Carey, D Company

Wearily, Snaith alighted from the motor car and kept the door open while his two fellow passengers alighted. The other two men looked round inquisitively at their surroundings but for Snaith HQ was becoming all too familiar. 'This way, you two,' he called despondently, and obediently they swung round to follow him, being taken swiftly along the corridor by the same corporal clerk who had administered to Snaith only a few days previously.

Brigadier-General Blackley sat with two other officers wearing staff insignia, examining a series of maps as the three men entered. He grunted briefly to acknowledge them, then went back to pointing out several features on one of the large-scale maps in front of him. Eventually he straightened up and nodded.

'Good day, gentlemen, thank you for coming. Please allow me to introduce my two colleagues, Major Briar and Colonel Stanley. We've asked you to come here today to discuss a matter which is to be treated as top secret. Do I make myself clear on this? You've been invited here as it was your battalion, Cuthbert, who provided us with a pretty damn good intelligence coup.'

Seeing their puzzled looks he gestured at the large map lying on top of the others. 'Last week, gentlemen, the 19th sent out a fighting patrol which brought in two prisoners. One of those Boche prisoners was so grateful he spilled his heart out to us. Probably still talking now, I'll warrant. Seems this chap was sort of batman to one of his regiment's officers. Anyhow, apparently this officer decided to take some presents over to our front line on New Year's Eve. Fellow simply vanished. Was never seen again. Our little Boche was then sent to a penal squad, got all the dirty work, for not looking after his officer properly. They sent him out on all the dangerous jobs as a way of punishing him. On the patrol your men intercepted, in fact.

'Fellow was quite cut up at being treated this way by his own side. Anyway, gentlemen, he has given us some pretty startling news. It seems our Boche friends are planning a massive offensive against the French. To take place next month, we think. Now, we know, and the French know, that they're up to something down there. Our intelligence chaps have been noting for some time the movement of heavy guns and troops down to the south of us. Just didn't know exactly where or when.

'This chappie doesn't know either, just says that his officer told him their regiment would be moving to have a crack at the Froggies shortly, in a big way, in the south of the country.'

Snaith leant forward, his face a puzzled frown. 'Excuse me sir, but what has it got to do with the 19th?'

'My dear chap,' Blackley replied patiently, 'GHQ are terrified that if our Froggie allies cave in just because of a major attack by the Boche it will allow the Boche the perfect chance to wheel around the back of us and cut us off from the Channel ports. Paris would then be wide open and the winning of the war would just be a matter of time. For the Kaiser, not us! D'ye get my drift?'

'Yes, sir, I see that. But what have we do with all this?'

'Cuthbert, Cuthbert, please allow me to explain. We are formulating a plan at the moment. At pretty short notice we're going to transfer four or five battalions down near to the French sector on the Somme, maybe more if they can be spared, before the Boche are ready to attack, and start a small offensive of our own with the aid of the French. It all adds up to a large diversionary attack to pull the Boche reserves back up from wherever it is they're heading for. We're not going to hide our movements, nor our preparations for the attack. This will make the Boche think we're going to support the French in a big way and we hope will stop them transferring troops south and instead switch them back up to the north to meet the new threat.

'I know your battalion has been moved from pillar to post these last few months, Cuthbert, but GHQ simply had no choice. Your chaps have been placed where gaps have occurred. However, I can now tell you that you and your battalion have been chosen as one of the participating battalions, along with the West Kents and a battalion from the Cheshire regiment for now, in this operation we've just begun the planning for. We'll sort out the rest of the attackers later, once we've got the whole thing properly considered.'

Having dropped his bombshell, Blackley leaned back, folded his hands expansively behind his head and gazed at the shocked faces opposite.

Finding his voice, Ramsbottom spoke for the first time.

'Do the French know about these developments, sir? And when do we think the Germans plan to open their offensive?'

Blackley laughed, a horsey braying laugh. 'Goodness me, of course not! At least, I hope not. What I mean is, the French intelligence sources must be telling them *something* is in the air, the Boche can't move that many men and equipment without someone smelling a rat. Besides, do you think we want to give our esteemed allies any excuse to start withdrawing a single *poilu* from our sectors, gentlemen? General Joffre would take our telling them what we do know as a godsend and we'd be on our own in no time flat.

No, good question though it is, major, I'm afraid the French will not be told the whys and wherefores. Or at least, not until it suits us to tell them. All they will know is we're prepared to hold a minor show of arms down near them, with their assistance of course, and for that they'll be pathetically grateful. As to your second question, we think the Germans plan to attack around the beginning of February. Our plan must be to cause them to either delay or postpone their attack.'

Ramsbottom looked from one man to another searchingly, but those sat opposite remained impassive.

'But we'll need artillery support, sir. Am I to understand this will be provided by the French? And equipment, ammunition, lots of it. How long do we have? And what happens when we get into the enemy trenches, are we to consolidate our hold on them or are we to—?'

'Questions, questions, major!' Blackley began to sound tetchy. 'Look, we've brought you here to discuss the planned attack. I know it's all a bit sudden but we can do this, with the proper integration of all our thoughts. I can tell you that GHQ are very interested in what we're planning to achieve here. General Haig is looking very keenly in our direction, he has some ideas of his own, I understand.

'Right, must go, have another staff meeting to attend. Please remember what I said when you first came in. No one is to know about this stunt until it's all ready.' He stopped by the door and looked back archly at Snaith. 'Cuthbert, that report I asked you for. Be a good chap and get it to me shortly.'

* * * * *

On the way back late that afternoon they were all silent, each man lost in his own thoughts. Eventually, Roberts looked at his two fellow travelling companions and shook his head emphatically.

'This is utter madness, you know that don't you? Four or five battalions? What on earth can we hope to achieve with such small numbers?'

Ramsbottom agreed. 'Yes, my thoughts entirely. It seems to me as if we are to be sacrificed just to keep the *Entente Cordiale* alive. What our battalions, with God knows what support we can garner from the French, can do to a well dug-in enemy I shudder to think. What are we expected to achieve? How are we to plan if we don't know what the objectives are? This is sheer stupidity of the highest order. Mark my words, the butcher's bill for this is going to be paid for in blood. Our blood. We're expected to agree to a plan which involves us attacking over ground we've never seen before, let alone reconnoitred, using troops whose qualities or quantities are dubious, to say the least. Why, it defies all —'

'That's enough, Walter!' Snaith interjected stiffly. 'May I remind you, we've been given an order to prepare for an assault on the enemy lines shortly. The hows and whys will be imparted soon. In the time we have left I would like as much training as possible to be carried out so our men are fully aware of their objectives. This is an honour that GHQ has bestowed on the 19th and I trust you will do your utmost to uphold that. Let me make it quite clear, I expect us to be ready on time. Do you understand?'

The remainder of the journey was spent in a gloomy silence.

Thursday 20th January 1916

Battalion to remain in billets for intensive training. All rifles inspected by company commanders. Extra small arms ammunition ordered, along with bigger supply of bombs. All Lewis guns returned to armoury for overhaul. Major Ramsbottom and Adjutant to Brigade HQ all day for planning meeting.

Captain L. Carey, D Company

'Come on! Come on! Move it, move it! You're too bloody slow! Get a move on there! Follow the white tapes for Chrissakes, will you!' CSM Mason's voice rose to a roar as he urged the panting, heavily-laden men of A Company on. Stumbling over the frozen ground under the weight of packs, extra ammunition, entrenching tools, coils of barbed wire, wooden stakes and a plethora of other digging-in equipment, each man attempted to keep pace with his neighbour, made all the more difficult by the undulating nature of the ground they were struggling over. Slipping and sliding they meandered, trying to keep their lines straight as they followed the white tape laid on the ground before them.

A hundred paces in front, a line of men with arms stiffly outstretched walked swiftly onwards. This was meant to represent a new innovation, the 'creeping barrage', under whose safety the men would advance up to the enemy trenches. This was all right in practice but as they walked forwards some of the soldiers comprising the imagined barrage walked quicker than others, while some just treated it as a lark and gambolled about like young calves, shouting and whooping as their overburdened mates attempted to catch them up. In no time at all they had gained the sanctuary of the far side of the field where they stopped to look back in expectation.

'Right, you smartarses, let's be having you!' CSM Mason roared his disapproval. 'Get back here now and let's see if we can't get it right this time. Double, you shower! There's no hot meal til you get it perfect so the quicker you start...' Grumbling and casting angry expressions at the imaginary barrage imitators, the soldiers about-turned and made their way back to the other side of the field.

In the next field, in a series of hastily-constructed trenches, the men from C Company were being instructed in the art of bombing and then consolidating the enemy trenches once they were gained. Dummy bombs were thrown in profusion, following a well-practised drill as the bombers swept down the trenches, chucking their deadly bombs into dugouts, round firebays and traverses. The riflemen, following closely, mopped up the supposedly-dazed opposition. Eventually they regained their lodgings in the village where a welcome meal of hot stew warmed their bellies and they looked forward to a rest, wherever they could, before it all started again on the morrow.

In one of the cottages, Bob Simpson ripped open his mail after smelling it appreciatively.

'Ah, that's proper perfume that is, you lot.'

'Garn!' a voice snapped from the depths of the bed its owner was burrowed in. 'Stuff to clean the ablutions with, more like!' Bob grinned, then his smile widened even further as he eagerly scanned the lines written on the cheap, blue writing-paper.

'Oh my gosh! Oh, God, oh golly!!'

'What, you berk? Come on, spill it out.'

'I'm going to be a father. It's my wife, she's pregnant. Lizzie's pregnant. What...? I mean how...?'

Hoots of laughter erupted. 'Two months married and you don't know how she's preggers? The poor girl! What do you want, corp, shall I draw you a bloody picture?'

Billy Lane opened his letter with a beam and then turned white as a sheet.

'Wassup, our Billy?' one of the other occupants shouted as he saw Billy's expression. 'You've not got a bill from your tailor 'ave you?' The laughs died away as they saw Billy's stricken face.

'It's from our lass.' he said lamely. 'She's gone an'...'

'Hang on, hang on! Didn't you say your old woman couldn't write, Billy?'

'Aye, I did. It's her damn sister what's wrote. That bitch never did like me! She says our lass has taken up with some bastard from the glass factory! Some conchie shirker from West Derby! She doesn't want to hear from me again on account of he can take better care of her! She could never manage on the allotment I sent her but he's earning a decent wage. The bloody cow!' He crumpled the letter and threw it viciously into the empty grate then sat there, his head bowed. Ernie Wadley slowly approached and laid his arm around his chum's shoulder.

'Don't you worry, old mate. Me and a few of the boys will sort that home-breaker out when we go on leave next week. You see if we don't. Even his own mum will have trouble recognising him when we finish. Now, I happen to 'ave a nice bottle of *vingt blonk* in me haversack here, so I thinks you and me are going to sit here and 'ave a good swallow or two.'

'Thanks Ernie, you're a real pal. But what about me kids? Who's going to look after the kids?'

Ernie couldn't answer him. Instead, he reached for the bottle of wine in his pack, wrenched the cork out with his teeth and began pouring. 'Get some of this down yer. She don't know what she's missing.' Billy looked round him, gave a stran-gled, derisive laugh and grabbed the bottle from Ernie's hand.

As the wine flowed freely down his mate's throat, Ernie Wadley looked round at the silent figures watching.

'Right you lot, turn and look at summat else, can't you? The bloody show's over. Eh, 'ang on, 'ang on, our Billy, leave some for me, like!'

Saturday 22nd January 1916

Battalion training continued. Fresh draft of men arrived, bringing battalion numbers up to full strength. Bayonet sharpening carried out by companies. Small arms training on ranges for D Company. Last leave party rejoined. CO, Major Ramsbottom and Adjutant at Brigade HQ again all day. Capt's N. Charteris and C. Brasher left for London.

Captain L. Carey, D Company

Walter Ramsbottom frowned. This was the fourth time he'd scanned the map's contours in under half an hour and try as he might he could not see the same picture of success that the staff at HQ were forecasting. There were too many imponderables. *If* this happened and *if* these French guns were moved in the time left and *supposing* this were to take place... He sighed. Too much left to chance, far too much.

No good going to see the colonel. He'd made his position clear right from the first meeting of those dunderheads at Brigade. Since then he'd washed his hands of it, becoming more and more morose as he saw the gaping pit of the burgeoning Godley affair yawning widely beneath him. This plan was just plain suicide and Walter could see no way out of it, other than disobedience, and that was just not going to happen.

In the far distance he could discern the muted sound of the guns and he felt a passing twinge of pity, swiftly suppressed. At least today it was someone else catching a pasting. He shuddered, and the noise was lost in a discreet cough outside his door

'Come in, come in. Thank you for coming over, gentlemen, I needed to talk to you both.'

Charteris and Brasher entered and waited patiently for him to continue.

'Look, this is how it is. Brigade have asked us to forward the names of two officers we consider suitable for training for the General Staff. GHQ are being stretched on all sides by the lack of suitable officers so wartime needs being a priority, it has been decided to hold an immediate staff course in London at the War Office. To fill the gap, so to speak. You two chaps come highly recommended and I've brought you here for the express purpose of enquiring as to how you'd feel if we were to recommend you. Any questions?'

Brasher sat bolt upright. 'Does this mean a trip back to dear old Blighty, then?'

'Don't get excited but I'm afraid it does,' Walter Ramsbottom answered dryly, a wry smile on his face. 'Of course it means you get to wear red tabs on your uniform and all the pretty girls will throw themselves at you in all the best restaurants. D'you think you could handle all that attention?'

'I say, sir, lead on! Put me down, please. Where do I sign up?'

Charteris looked from one man to the other, slightly puzzled. 'Excuse me sir, but if we were to assent to our names being forwarded, when would we be expected to leave?'

'You'd need to be on your way today. The Army being what it is we have only just received these requirements a minute or so ago. And of course they should have arrived yesterday. Now GHQ are simply screaming for us to nominate men and get them over to the War Office as quick as we can so they can get down to some proper training. You can see where the difficulties lie. I sometimes wonder whose side they're on! Any problems with that so far, Captain Charteris?'

'No, sir. It's just that it seems to be, well, so, um, so quick, sir. At such short notice.'

Brasher leant over and thumped Neville soundly on his upper arm.

'Neville, my dear chap! Don't be such a cad! Do you want to miss all the fun back home? Stop these stupid questions, shut up, say you agree and let's jolly well go now!'

'Hang on, Charles. There is another reason for my misgivings.' Charteris looked squarely at the major, who watched him carefully. 'All this training we're doing, sir. Are you telling me it's just part of our being out of the line or is there another stunt coming up in the near future? I would hate to think of my men going into action without me, we've been through so much already and it would feel as if I was deserting them at the last minute.'

Keeping his face deliberately blank, Ramsbottom met Charteris's gaze. 'Captain Charteris, we are in the process of training up the new drafts to work with their fellow soldiers. Training is of paramount importance as and when we can give the chaps the instruction they need. Now, I have heard nothing to the contrary, other then we will probably be going back into the line for a week or so. Which brings me back to my point, do you wish to be considered or not?'

Reluctantly, Charteris backed down from the major's gaze and answered him in a stiff, formal manner. 'Thank you, sir, if that is indeed the reason, I would be delighted to accept.'

'Good man!' Brasher thumped him on the arm again.

Walter Ramsbottom exhaled in relief.

'Fine. Now then, the pair of you, run away smartly and go and get packed. I'll sort out your travel papers with Major Roberts while you're away so be back here in approximately an hour.' He rose up and extended his hand. 'All I can say on behalf of the CO and myself is that you will be sorely missed. The battalion is proud of having had you serve with us, gentlemen. Now go. One last thing, Neville. Congratulations are in order, I'm reliably informed that you've been awarded the DSO for your actions in our last fight. The message from Brigade also confirmed the CO's other recommendations for our last action. They were all approved. Off you go and well done. We'll speak later.'

The two men solemnly shook hands and departed in haste. Five minutes later David Roberts entered the room, his arms full of papers.

'Did you see them, Walter?' he asked.

'Yes, they both accepted,' Ramsbottom told him flatly. 'Charteris was a bit suspicious but I think I managed to allay his concerns. He's no fool, that one.'

'Exactly why we formulated the plan to get them away, Walter,' Roberts responded. 'This monstrosity we're in the middle of planning could spell the end of the battalion. I've looked over the topographical map Brigade sent us again. It seems to be all open ground. They want us to advance with all of our battalions, with what minimal infantry and artillery support we get from the French, over open ground. No word yet on what support in the way of infantry, if we get *any*, the damned French are going to provide. For the love of God, even a madman would call it murder!'

'Quite so, David, which is why I want to see Charteris and Brasher leave us as quickly as possible. The Army is going to need officers of the calibre of those two to make some sense of this futility. Both men have bags of pluck, especially Charteris, and I for one am not going to see them expended wastefully on some foolish stunt some red-tabbed ass has dreamt up after a particularly good bottle of red wine! David, your job is to intercept the CO and take him on a tour of the cookhouse to keep him out of the way. How you do it is your affair. I shall see these two young men get away without his knowledge and without any interference. Go on, scoot!'

'You know he's going to be mad when he finds out.'

'Yes, but what can he do? He's got enough to worry about, what with this forthcoming attack and the Godley affair. He won't find out until Monday. Besides which, I've already asked Brigade to send two replacements. They should be here on Tuesday.'

David Roberts smiled. 'You sly old dog, Walter. You've thought of everything, haven't you?'

Imitating his drill sergeant from all those years ago when he was a young subaltern, Walter Ramsbottom looked up and tapped his forehead then pointed at his feet.

'Up 'ere for finking, son, dahn there for dancing!'

* * * * *

Standing on the open deck of the leave boat watching the darkened coastline of France rapidly receding in the distance, Charteris tried to collect his jumbled thoughts together. It had all happened too soon, too quickly. A hurried goodbye, a final shake of the hand and they were on their way to the railway station. A northbound train had eventually arrived, after a long, impatient, fretful wait, but their luck had changed and another connection further down the line had sped them north just in time to take their turn in the queue to board the waiting ship in the early hours of the morning.

There had been little time to say proper goodbyes and Charteris had been disappointed not to have paid his final respects to the CO. Walter Ramsbottom had told him about the colonel's sudden desire to go on a tour of inspection and he had accepted that with a little sadness. It would have been fine to have said goodbye personally but Ramsbottom had assured him he would pass on his respects. He had left some of his kit behind in the haste to pack everything, but the adjutant had promised it would be sent on as quickly as possible.

Now, as he gazed blankly rearwards, he was beginning to appreciate the good fortune that had come his way. Tillie would be overjoyed to see him. He must send her a telegram as soon as they docked. No, his mind corrected himself, a telegram would not do. Britain had come to dread the sight of a post boy bearing those small brown envelopes. No, he decided, no telegram.

She would just have to wait. His heart leapt at the thought of seeing her, holding her, kissing her. Breathing in her perfume, the warmth of her body against his. He thumped the guardrail in a rush of sudden relief, grinning as his good fortune sank in. It was over, the strain of holding himself in, of ducking, trembling as a shell flew overhead, the cringe at each whiplash *crack!* of a bullet. Gone. All gone. If he kept his nose clean he could see the rest of this madness out in safety. Let someone else face the dangers, let someone else take the risks. He had left it all behind, back there in the mud with the 19th.

It had come too quickly, leaving him unprepared for this moment, and he felt giddy, reaching a hand out to the guardrail to steady himself. A twinge of conscience struck him for the men he had left behind, but the moment passed and he concentrated on thinking about what lay ahead.

The sudden realisation that he was going to survive made him breathe in deeply, taking deep lungfuls of salt-laden air in his appreciation that from now on his future, and that of Tillie's, seemed to be secure. He suppressed the desire to shout his feelings at the stars overhead and walked off across the swaying deck to find his travelling companion.

The rest of the journey passed in a blur. Too soon they were on dry land on the dockside at Folkestone and pushed and pressed into the carriages of a train. In what seemed like minutes they were clanking along, swaying with the motion of the train as it sped towards London. Victoria Station came and was gone and when next he had collected himself together, Charles Brasher was gone and he found himself in the back of a taxi making its way to Peckham.

Tillie met him on the doorstep and was in his arms, crying and laughing, her face tear-streaked as she clung desperately to him. Mrs Humboldt swept outside to see what all the fuss was and soon the three of them were all clinging together with Charteris trying to calm down two weeping women. Once in the safety of the warm house Mrs Humboldt's character reasserted itself and she bustled off while Tillie sat beaming at Charteris from across the room.

'How? I mean, what? Neville, where on earth have you come from, darling? And at this late hour. Oh, it's just too much to take in.' She promptly burst into tears again. Charteris rushed over and, dropping to his knees, embraced her while she sobbed helplessly into his shoulder. After a while he drew gently back and gazed at her as she blew her nose loudly into her handkerchief and struggled to regain her composure.

'It seems like a dream,' he said. 'One minute I was thinking about inspecting my chaps' rifles and the next I'm being told by the battalion second in command to pack my stuff up as I'm leaving for London. It's so unbelievable, I keep having to pinch myself to tell myself I'm really here. Some of my chaps have never been home once, yet here I am again, sitting here, safe, holding you. It doesn't seem right.'

'But how? I don't understand, you're not home on leave again, are you?' She looked at him through her tears in a puzzled way. Pulling her to him again, he proceeded to tell her about the stroke of good fortune that had sent him and Brasher on their way that previous afternoon. As he was coming to the end to his story Mrs Humboldt entered, bearing a large tray loaded with food. He grabbed a sandwich eagerly.

'Sorry,' he spoke sheepishly. 'I haven't eaten since yesterday. It seems all I do when I come here is eat.'

'I wouldn't worry about that, Neville,' Tillie informed him. 'Now that you're here Mrs Humboldt will keep you fed. She's been looking for someone to try her excellent cooking on and I think you fit the bill. We have special news too. Bertha's husband, Gilbert, is safe! He's not dead, Neville. After all these months of the poor dear crying herself to sleep, he's alive. The Belgian Red Cross finally got in touch to advise her that he's a prisoner of war in Germany. Isn't that wonderful?'

'I'll say! To have gone so long without knowing, it must have come as a blessed relief.'

'It is. So, how long will you be staying? Will they send you back once your training is complete? Will it mean promotion?'

'Oh, yes,' Neville interrupted airily. 'I'm told the course lasts about six weeks. Then I shall have to go back, you understand. But I shall be stationed far from the Front, sleeping in white sheets on a proper bed, hobnobbing with generals and the suchlike. And of course, being pursued by all the loveliest, good-looking French women around, I dare say.'

'Beastly swine!' she said, sticking her tongue out at him and bursting out laughing. Growing more serious she looked him up and down. He looked thinner again and the lines of deep strain were back on his face, making him look years older. She knew from what her friends told her how deep was the men's suffering at the Front and looking at Neville she could appreciate the horrors he must have seen on a daily basis to make him look so tired.

They talked animatedly for the rest of the afternoon and long into the evening. Bertha Humboldt had retired by then, discreetly withdrawing to her room to allow the lovers time to relax in each other's company. At length, with a thousand and one subjects animatedly discussed, an awkward silence grew between them. Neville made as if to speak but shyly, almost self-consciously, Tillie came over and wordlessly took his hand. Without speaking she led him to the stairs and began to ascend. When they reached her door she turned back to him and kissed him passionately on the mouth. Responding to her lips he pushed her gently inside and closed the door.

It was still dark when he awoke and looked at his watch. Ten to six. Time to get ready for the new day and the new job. He pushed back the covers, stood on the cold carpet and looked tenderly down at her sleeping figure, curled in a ball as she tried to retain the warmth of the bed. She protested quietly in her sleep, her nose wrinkling and a small frown appearing as she unconsciously pulled the covers back over her body and snuggled down once more. Leaning over, he gently kissed her forehead. She moaned softly, a pleased, satisfied sound, and slept.

Their lovemaking the previous night had been tender, made the more intimate by the warmth of her embrace. Long after he had laid back, replete, she had curled herself around him, pressed languidly into him. She had kissed his back before falling asleep and he had lain there, wondering at the completeness of his feelings for this beautiful, sweet woman before joining her in a deep and peaceful sleep.

At the bottom of the stairs he stepped back in fright as Mrs Humboldt, clad in a formidable dressing gown, swept by him bearing a plate groaning under the weight of a fried breakfast.

* * * * *

Full now, Charteris stood by the mirror to ensure his hat was set at the right, rakish angle. Most of the officers in the front line took the stiffener out of their hats to make them look softer, a sign to those who knew of one's service in the trenches. Satisfied that his looked suitably authentic he opened the door to leave. A large pair of arms encircled him and before he could spin round Bertha Humboldt grabbed him in a bear hug.

'Meester Neville, you take care. Mateelda love you much.' She released him and watched as, touched, he walked down the drive and turned towards the Goose Green.

He managed to catch an omnibus into Central London, followed by a brisk walk to the War Office. A bored sentry saluted him and having inspected his papers directed him as to where to go. He walked down long corridors filled with the babble of self-important bustle to the office he was to report to. A sergeant, a wounded, disabled veteran of the retreat to Mons, sat at a small desk just inside the door.

'Good Morning, sir, you must be Mr Charteris,' he said as he held his one good hand, the right, out for Neville's travel papers.

'Yes, I am, sergeant. How on earth did you know?'

'The names Mackinnon, sir. Two things. The Military Cross ribbon, sir. Not many staff wallahs here are wearing that, and if you'll excuse me saying so, sir, the smell of your uniform. Good old eau de French earth if I'm not mistaken! Ah, and I see you've been awarded the DSO too, sir.' He looked up from his inspection of Charteris's papers with a new light of respect in his eyes. 'Begging your pardon, sir, but could you see about having the ribbon stitched onto your tunic? General Bigelow is a bit of a stickler for things like that.'

'Um, yes, of course, sergeant. Look, you don't know if Captain Brasher has arrived yet, do you?'

'No, sir, you're the first. And I wouldn't be in too much of a hurry to get down to work either, sir. You're over a week early, what must they have been thinking about? Seems to me like your regiment was trying to get rid of you in a hurry.'

'What? Is that so?' Charteris thought about the way Ramsbottom had been so keen for them to leave immediately. 'You may be right, sergeant, er, Mackinnon isn't it? What will happen now? You say the course doesn't start for another week?'

Sergeant Mackinnon laughed. 'Oh don't you worry, sir, the general will make sure you're kept busy before the next staff course starts. He can be a right bugger, pardon my language, sir, so he'll find you plenty to do. Now, do you have a billet yet?'

Charteris thought quickly and the lie tripped easily from his tongue. 'Would it be all right if I stayed with my fiancée and her parents out at Peckham? I could catch a tram or something in to make sure I was here on time each day. You see...'

'I'm sure that would be most agreeable, sir. We're struggling to find places for everyone and I'm sure there would be no problems put in your way. As long as you realise that you may have to stay late some nights to finish off some of the work set for the day?'

'Quite. Sergeant Mackinnon, that will be fine.' Inside he hugged himself, trying to keep the look of sheer delight from spreading over his face. Tillie would be overjoyed as they would see each other every day. Mackinnon looked up at him and caught some of his happiness.

'Look, sir, some ladies from the Red Cross have set up a canteen down the corridor, on the right-hand side. You can't miss it. You'll be able to catch a cuppa in there and read the morning's papers. When Mr Brasher arrives, I'll send him down to you and you can have a chinwag until the general gets in. Which won't be early, knowing 'His Highness'. He had a cocktail party to attend last night, so it'll be a while before he surfaces. You just get yourself off, sir, and have a nice relax.'

Charteris took him at his word and beat a hasty retreat. Sitting in the comfortable canteen ten minutes later with a hot, steaming cup of tea served by a bevy of pleasant ladies eager to please, his smile turned to a frown. The contents of the paper he held before him painted a different picture to that which he knew really existed. So much optimism he had never read before. It was pure tosh. The man in the trenches, grimly trying to stop himself from slipping deeper into the liquid goo he was standing in, would laugh long and hard to read about how the public perceived his conditions to be. It was almost criminal and his anger rose at the thought of politicians and the like. Those men who made flowery speeches exhorting their fellow man to volunteer, while ensuring their own, permanent safety ought to be shot. He flung the paper down in disgust and finished his tea.

After dinner that evening he recounted his adventures of the day for Tillie who sat by the fire across from him. She had noticed the new ribbon on his tunic and listened gravely as he told her the reasons why he had been awarded his DSO. He told her of meeting General Bigelow, together with Charles Brasher who had turned up late looking decidedly the worse for wear. Too much champagne the night before, no doubt. The general had been as puzzled as themselves to find they had arrived almost a week too early but after remonstrating with the remarkable Sergeant Mackinnon he had promised to find them gainful employment on the morrow.

Before lunch, Sergeant Mackinnon had appeared and spoke quietly to Charteris. 'Look, sir, the general has gone off on an inspection. He'll be away for the remainder of the day. Why don't you and Mr Brasher leg it quietly, like. I'll cover for you.'

The rest of the day had been spent in finding a suitable tailor who could run them up a decent spare uniform and, in Charteris's case, stitch the required ribbon onto his existing tunic breast. They had found one at long last, off Piccadilly, and the small Jewish tailor had taken the length of ribbon the sergeant had procured for Neville and stitched it onto his jacket while they waited, but not before first wrinkling his nose at the smell. Neville and Charles had laughed all the way down the street before turning into a small bar and enjoying a whisky before leaving.

All in all it had been a good day and Charteris felt at ease and relaxed as he and Tillie talked long into the night again. Several times he had tried to bring up the one thing that was beginning to trouble him but each time he had shied away from opening his heart to her. Tomorrow, he'd do it tomorrow. There was plenty of time now.

* * * * *

As Charteris laid his head on his pillow and looked into Tillie Fairley's eyes, the 19th Battalion was preparing for its biggest day.

Tuesday 25th January 1916
All company commanders reported to plan impending attack on German trenches in the French Sector near Maricourt Wood. We are to take part in a major attack on the enemy lines, and push towards Hardecourt-aux-Bois. Five British battalions will take part in the assault, assisted by an as yet unknown number of French regiments. The objective is to

disrupt enemy troop movements to the south and prevent enemy reinforcements leaving for the new offensive planned against the French. A copy of the planned attack is to be found at the rear of the Diary.

Captain L. Carey, D Company

'Attenshun!' the RSM barked out as Colonel Snaith swept into the room. Lifting his hand diffidently, Snaith made his way over to the table that had been prepared previously in the centre of the room and pulled back the sheet covering it. The eyes of the men focused on the map taped to the top.

'Thank you for coming here this morning. Today is a day that will go down in the history of the 19th. We have been chosen especially by our new commander-in-chief, General Douglas Haig, to spearhead an offensive against the German lines in the south, assisted by our French allies.'

The officers pressed forward, murmuring in astonishment, as he continued. 'Accordingly, in two days' time we shall entrain for Albert, to rest the men prior to our march to the forward areas. We shall then march through Carnoy to our jumping-off positions on the other side of Maricourt Wood where at 08:45 precisely, on Friday morning, we shall assault the German trenches. As you will see, our area of operations takes us into the French Sixth Army positions but we will be operating independently, albeit with some French support. '

A hubbub of questions were hurled at him from all directions but he held his hand up. When the room had quieted, he spoke again. 'Major Roberts and Major Ramsbottom here have all the information you require, from French artillery timetables to the amount of equipment each man shall be carrying. I will now turn you over to them. Listen well, gentlemen and I'll speak to you all again before we leave for the south. Walter, David. If you please.' He turned and swept out of the room as quickly as he had entered, leaving his two subordinates to face an increasing barrage of excited questions.

An exasperated adjutant waved a sheaf of papers at the men now crowding around the map atop the table. 'We've tried hard to put a feasible plan together, notwithstanding those blithering idiots up at Brigade and GHQ, so please listen carefully to what we're about to say. Feel free to take notes and ask questions. One at a time, though. Sorry, chaps, but this is still pretty hush-hush.'

Walter Ramsbottom stood waiting patiently. 'Walter here will start the show off and I'll come in when and if required. Walter, could you give the chaps the background to all of this?' He nodded. Speaking slowly but clearly he outlined the reasons behind the forthcoming attack, using the map as a guide. He drew out the various dispositions of the troops facing them, as well as the positions of the French troops who would also be involved in the assault.

'As you can see, the German lines protrude into ours in a kind of salient, not dissimilar to that up at Ypres, only this time the Boche hold the bulge. Our aim,

289

gentlemen, is to nip that salient out, capture the ground and, if we can, push deep into Boche territory causing him to bring troops back to meet us. This is to be a diversionary stunt, but one big enough to make the Boche sit up and take notice. When we advance towards Hardecourt-aux-Bois, hopefully, the enemy should be concerned enough to divert considerable numbers of troops to meet our advance and that, gentlemen, is the whole reason for the assault.

'We shall attack here, opposite the key point known as the "Osnabrucker Stellung", at the head of the salient, supported by three or four regiments of our French allies. Total numbers to be committed by both sides are still as yet undecided but we should know the final numbers shortly. The West Kents, we do know, will go in to our left and the Cheshires to our right, both being supported by French troops. The rest of our chaps will follow soon after, supported by more French troops. The artillery barrage will start at seven-thirty ack emma, in order to overwhelm the defenders before they can respond and will stop ten minutes before we go in. A creeping barrage will then follow us all the way up to the Boche lines.

Take a good look at the map, gentlemen, I want you chaps to be under no illusions as to how difficult this is going to be. The Osnabrucker Stellung, according to Froggie reconnaissance, is bristling with machine-guns and heavily defended by artillery. This strongpoint holds the key to unlocking the whole advance so let's make sure we get in there and take it out of the way early. The Boche is not going to give it up easily, so I want you to give him a bloody nose and hit hard.'

After speaking for nearly an hour and answering many questions he concluded, 'You now know as much as we do. GHQ are desperate for this stunt to succeed and pull the Boche reinforcements that would have gone south back up to the north. We shall be striking a blow that could alter the course of the war, I'm told. The Old Man is also pretty keen that we get it right, so look at your notes, make sure you tell your chaps exactly what's required of them and we'll get the job done. And especially the runners and signallers. I want it impressed on each company's runners just how important their role in this attack will be. Got it?' Everyone nodded hurriedly.

'We march to the railhead at 05:00 ack emma on Thursday so ensure everything in your company is tickety-boo. I want every man accounted for, everyone to know what they're doing and all of them carrying the correct equipment. There will be an issue of extra SAA when we reach Carnoy, to save weighing the chaps down, 200 rounds more per man, and we'll issue extra bombs just before reaching our jumping-off positions. Dismiss now and go sort your chaps out!'

When the men were informed of their impending departure to the south and the reasons behind it there were mixed reactions. Arwyn Jones snorted derisively.

'Bloody French, is it? Christ, we can do without those buggers backing us up. From what I've heard all they need to hear is one shot and they won't stop running til they reach Paris!'

Harry Sheldon frowned. 'Oi, Jonesy, spare them a thought would you. That old biddy in the last place we were at, what's 'er name, Missus Fresnay? She were telling me about how she's lost two sons already, and how most of the village was mourning someone or other. You tell me these Frogs don't fight? Go back and ask her how fast her sons could run, I'm sure she'll tell you different!'

The officers were in no less a pensive mood later that night.

George Bradley sipped his whisky slowly, his face a florid colour. It was his third and the drink was beginning to tell. 'I tell you,' he slurred, 'we're in for a hiding, make no mistake. God, what has GHQ foisted on us, eh? What a foul-up!'

One of the youngsters, a fresh-faced second-lieutenant called Greenhaulgh, looked over at him.

'Do you really think so, sir? The colonel seemed pretty keen on this show, if you ask me.'

'Well, I'm not, so wait until your opinion is called for!'

'All right, George, for heaven's sake, the boy was only commenting on your remarks.' Lionel Carey looked over with a concerned frown. It wasn't like George to be so rude. 'Come on, admit it, we'll stroll over to the other side, stick a few Boche and then retire to bore the pants off our grandchildren in later years with our tales of heroics.'

George Bradley stared back savagely and after throwing his head back and tossing the remainder of his drink into his mouth he tottered to his feet.

'Grandchildren? You bloody fools! We'll still be here, killing each other in ten years' time. If any of us here are still alive. What makes you think you're going to bloody well live for ever, Lionel? God has gone, gone west with all the other chaps that once inhabited this hell! Just pray that yours is quick, that you're not left lying with a bullet through the guts, slowly sinking into this...this...shit!'

'Oh, I say!'

The choked response fell on deaf ears. Lurching through the doorway, Bradley fell against the door, drew himself up and disappeared outside, leaving just the sound of the wind whistling into the now silent room.

22

Neville Charteris slid out of the bed, hopping from one foot to another on the ice-cold carpet as he tried to locate his uniform. Pulling on his trousers and socks he moved soundlessly over to the door and made his way to the bathroom to shave and make himself ready. Twenty minutes later, after some toast and a cup of hot tea he quietly closed the door and looked down the drive. It was cold, a deep frost lay everywhere, its icy talons decorating the houses and foliage, painting everything white as far as the eye could see. He patted his overcoat pocket automatically. It was still there, the package he had picked up from the jewellers yesterday, making a hard lump through the lining of the pocket.

He had meant to surprise Tillie with its contents the day before but he had arrived home from the second day at his new job to find her gone for the evening. At her VAD training, as Bertha Humboldt had informed him with an expressive shrug. When finally she had returned, full of excitement at all she had been shown, the moment had passed and it was far too late to surprise her.

The journey into London went quickly enough and as he had thought, it started to snow lightly as he alighted from the tram. He was not surprised to find his office empty as he turned the knob – punctuality was not Charles Brasher's strong suite. Charteris chuckled as he rifled through the papers already stacking up on the desk.

Nothing of note, heavy shell requests along with casualty returns for the First Army. He had a week of this to bear, which was nearly over, and he went home every night to Tillie. What else could a man need? He picked up more papers, dropped them on the desk and took off in search of a cup of tea.

The door of Sergeant Mackinnon's office was open and he waved to him as he passed. Mackinnon responded by gesturing urgently.

'Problems, Mackinnon?'

'Not really, sir. Just a memo here you might be interested in.' Charteris bent down and picked the docket up. The room faded as he read the first lines, thunderstruck.

'Dear Christ!' he murmured.

From a distance he heard the concerned voice of the sergeant. 'I say, sir, are you all right? I only asked you to take a dekko because I knew you were with the 19th weren't you, sir? Looks like some rum do they're about to go into!'

'Where did you get this from?' he asked.

'It was lying there this morning when I came in, sir. Must have been put there last night. Looks like a big show. Another of GHQ's ideas for winning the war. Huh! Does it give all the details, sir. Who else is involved?'

Charteris read on, his mind racing. All the subterfuge, all the lies! Here was the reason Walter Ramsbottom had been so desperate to get them away and no wonder. Even his untrained mind could see the futility in the plan formulated in these few, dry, dusty papers.

'Christ!' he swore again. 'This doesn't stand a chance. Not the way it's been thrown together! What date is it today?'

'I beg your pardon, sir?'

'The date, quick, tell me what the date is!'

Mackinnon looked down at the large diary on the desk. 'Sorry, sir, it's Wednesday. Wednesday the twenty-sixth.'

Charteris looked again at the paper he was holding. Wednesday. That meant the attack would go in the day after tomorrow. Without him. His men would meet their enemy without him next to them. He looked at his watch. Eight-ten. His mind a whirling sea of emotions he glanced at the sergeant as he spoke savagely.

'How long to get to Victoria from here? Come on, Mackinnon, think!'

'Er, about fifteen minutes if you can get a cab, sir.'

'Right. That ought to do it. Sergeant Mackinnon, find me a cab could you while I write a short note. I'll need...'

'Pardon me, sir, but just what is it you intend doing?'

He looked up and his eyes narrowed. 'Sergeant Mackinnon, I went over to France with one of the finest bunch of men it has been my privilege to lead. In two days' time they are going to assault the German lines in what looks to be an utterly hopeless attack. What would those men think if I were not there to lead them? To be with them in the culmination of all we have been through together, all we have trained for?'

As the sergeant looked at him, dumbfounded, Charteris continued in a softer tone, almost pleading. 'Sergeant Mackinnon, you've seen action with your men. Do you see what I mean, what I'm trying to say? Now, are you going to help me? Can it be done, do I have time to reach them?'

After a lengthy stare Mackinnon turned to look broodingly out of the office window. 'I think a lot of what happened to the chums I left out there in France, sir. I only left an arm but they left widows and orphans. You've done your bit, sir, you've nothing to prove to anyone. Look at the ribbons on your chest, no one could accuse you of anything, let alone cowardice. I think you must be mad to want to return to what's waiting over there.' He brooded for several more seconds, the silence stretching until he turned abruptly.

'Right, sir, let me make a call to the switchboard. I've a chum who owes me a favour or two. If you make the afternoon boat and if the trains are running smoothly on the other side, it could work. It's a long shot, sorry, no pun intended, but let's see if we can't do it.'

Charteris and raced down the corridor to his office. His service revolver sat in its holster in his drawer and he pulled it on in a frenzy. He was reaching to pull the door open again when the thought of Tillie hit him like a blow to the stomach.

Sitting down at his desk he pulled a sheet of paper towards him and began to write furiously. He hastily folded the sheet and pushed in into a buff envelope, wrote Tillie's name and address in a firm, steady hand, sealed the envelope and left.

He bumped squarely into a young man, even at that time of the morning smelling strongly of alcohol.

'Whatho, Neville!' Charles Brasher greeted him blearily, 'what the dickens are you up to, old man, so early?'

'Look, Charles, I haven't got time to explain. Must dash. Be seeing you!' He pushed past and strode rapidly down the corridor, ignoring his friend's protestations behind him. When he reached Mackinnon's office the sergeant was absent. He bustled in ten minutes later, folding some papers into a canvas map case.

'Ah, there you are, sir. Here it all is. My chum in the... Oh, never you mind where he hides, sir. My chum has managed to make travel papers out for you. These should get you to Amiens. After that I'm afraid you're on your own, sir. These should pass muster unless some cove gets really suspicious but it ain't as if you're running away. Anyway, you'll find a cab outside to get you to Victoria and from then on its up to you. I've put the times of the boats and the train timetables over there, as far as I could make out, in the case here sir. I've also stuffed two of the general's clean shirts in there. He'll never miss them. Good luck, sir, I think you're going to need it. I still reckons as how you're mad to be doing this. The general's going to have a blue fit when he finds out.' He held out his hand.

Shaking the proffered hand vigorously, Charteris replied, 'Thanks awfully, Sergeant Mackinnon, for all you've done. Could I ask a special favour of you? Could you see that my fiancée receives this after I've gone? I was going to give her it myself tonight but under the circumstances I...'

Mackinnon leant forward and took the package from Neville's outstretched hand. 'Don't you worry, sir. I'll deliver it myself. Mrs Mackinnon will just have to have her supper on her own tonight. And I'll have mine when I get back, if she hasn't given it to the dog. Now quick, sir, you'll have to go if you want to catch that boat.'

He grasped the sergeant's hand again and pumped it furiously. Rushing from the room he collided again with a totally bemused Charles Brasher in the corridor. Knocking him down for the second time he raced on, making for the front entrance. He espied a cab about to pull away but by running hard he caught it up and hammered on the driver's window. Seconds later he was on his way, leaning back into the leather cushion breathing heavily as in front of him the cabbie grumbled continuously all the way.

It was only when he was on the train, rattling on its way to Folkestone, that he was able to contemplate the enormity of what he was about to undertake. A picture of Matilda's face hovered before him, crowding out the faces of the men he had served with. He shook his head wearily, hoping that she would understand his reasons, the apparent madness that had overcome him. She had to understand, she just had to.

Folkestone was strangely deserted, a lone steamer standing patiently alongside the dock. He was early, far too early and so he sat onboard in an agitated state for hours, his mind racing as he weighed up the options before him, before he was able to watch a receding shoreline as the ship headed out of the harbour and set her head for France. It seemed strange to be desperate to reach the other side, the wrong side, and he took a long, hard look as England slid away behind them. Who knew when, and under what circumstances, he would see it again?

The afternoon was fresh and he walked round and round the swaying deck as he gathered his thoughts. Tillie. She would find out soon what he had done and he feared for her reaction. It was done now though, no amount of words in an envelope could convey his feelings they way he wanted to but for her would come the agony of not knowing where he was or how he was faring. He prayed she would forgive him for that. He hoped so.

France. He would need to be extraordinarily lucky to rejoin his men and the battalion but with God's help and a spot of luck he could do so. He looked down at the wake threshing behind the ship and willed it onwards.

When the ship finally docked in Boulogne he raced down the gangway, shoving his papers quickly into the face of an astonished RTO before racing away for the station. He burst into the station-master's office and looked round wildly. In the corner, an elderly, careworn lieutenant in his fifties with several rows of ribbons on his stained tunic chest looked up from pouring a cup of tea, pipe in the other hand, as the dishevelled officer entered.

'Quick!' Charteris panted, 'I'm trying to rejoin my regiment. I need to know if there are any trains that can get me there tonight. It's of the utmost importance. They're headed for Carnoy, in the south. Can you help?'

'All right, old chap, take a seat and calm down. Carnoy you say? Hmnn, now then...'

Charteris remained standing, his blood pressure rising. God! 'Come on! Come on!' he breathed impatiently. Could the old fogey not see how much of a hurry he was in? He quelled the sharp retort rising in his throat as he watched the man carefully lay his pipe down. The lieutenant sat down stiffly, placed his cup carefully in the centre of his large, wooden desk out of harm's way and rummaged around, shuffling various papers.

'Give me a mo', I know I put it somewhere. Now where is it?' Charteris's anger began to rise and he looked over at the man contemptuously. It was obvious he had never even smelled the Front. What a cushy way to let someone else do the fighting. Damn the man! He leaned forward to speak.

'Ah, here it is. Thought I had it!' The elderly officer held up a creased, worn booklet. 'My timetable. Now, let me see…' He thumbed through it agonisingly slowly as Charteris looked on with mounting impatience. 'Yes, I thought so. Arras is a no-no. Priority traffic there just now, big attack going on, no room for anyone. No. Ah, right.' He snapped the booklet shut. 'That's settled then. I can get you to Amiens right now. There's an ammunition supply train leaving from track twelve in ten minutes, if they've loaded all the shells. You know how utterly lazy these Chinese labourers can be. No? Well, no matter. It's an express service too, no stops, should be pretty damn quick. Perhaps you might be able to hitch a ride on a local service for Albert once you get there. Now that's settled, I'll take you over there myself.'

'No. Please. Don't get up. I'm sure I wouldn't want to keep you from your tea, lieutenant. Just point me in the general direction and I'm sure I'll find it. You stay here and catch up with all this, this paperwork. I'm sure you've lots to get on with. Track twelve did you say? Do I have to ride on the flatbed with the shells?' The sarcasm was lost on his opposite number.

'Of course not my dear chap. They normally put a spare carriage on the back for strays just like yourself. Look here, I'll take you over there now. I can catch up on my tea later.' Leaning over he bent down beneath his desk and re-emerged with a heavy black cane. 'Right, that's me! Let's be off, then.'

Charteris caught him up as he limped down the road into the mass of railway tracks and steaming locomotives. He noticed how heavily the man leant on his cane for support. Seeing this, the lieutenant reached down and tapped his left leg. It sounded hollow. Seeing Charteris's surprise, he smiled bleakly.

'Marvellous what they can do these days, eh? Left the bally thing at Pilckem Ridge last year. Surprise attack, you see. Surprised me all right! Hadn't even finished eating my damned breakfast when a shell from a Fritz howitzer burst into my comfy dugout and blew my leg off. Damned inconsiderate don't you think, disturbing a chap's tea and toast like that? No real pain, though.'

He carried on walking. 'Lost my boy, Roland, a month later, at Hooge. Now that really hurt. Still, no point in thinking about it too much. Just got to get on with things. Ah, here we are.' He pointed with his cane at a long collection of flatbed carriages, topped by a white-wreathed locomotive, every one of them filled with long-nosed, heavy artillery shells.

Feeling thoroughly ashamed of himself and his earlier thoughts Charteris followed his pointing hand. He hardly dare look at the man as he hurriedly shook his hand and climbed aboard. The door slammed shut behind him with a grim air of finality. A jerk from the front told him they were on their way.

They reached Amiens as the daylight was slowly fading. The journey had not been as quick as he had been promised. The train was slowly shunted into a siding for unloading of the shells to commence and Charteris quickly alighted as soon as it came to a hissing stop. A light shone at the end of a long, dark, low building and he ran over the tracks towards it.

Gangs of coloured labourers, already sweating in spite of the cold, moved forward and manhandled the heavy shells from the flatbeds, to be placed on the light railways that had sprung up and transported to the various artillery dumps in the area. The notice on the door read: 'Railway Transport Office. Amiens.' Turning the knob he stepped inside.

A bright fire burned in a hearth on the other side of the room where a uniformed officer sat at an oblique angle to the door scribbling furiously in a large ledger. He waited a moment or so for the man to respond to his entrance but the officer scribbled on, oblivious.

'Ahem!' he coughed. 'Good evening. I wonder if you could help me, you see I'm trying to...' The words died in his throat as the officer straightened and looked at him for the first time.

'You!' the stranger hissed, his eyes narrowing in distaste as recognition hit him. With a feeling of disquiet Charteris saw the thoroughly unpleasant RTO he had encountered in Boulogne the year before.

'Captain Charteris, I believe,' he sneered, looking down at Neville's dishevelled appearance. 'And to what do I owe the pleasure of our acquaintance this time. Sir!' The last word was drawn out, an obvious insult and Charteris flushed hotly.

'I'm trying to rejoin my battalion tonight, lieutenant,' he answered as evenly as he could in an attempt not to provoke the man. 'They're on their way to Carnoy, I believe, and I would be obliged if you could assist me in rejoining them as quickly as possible. It is fairly urgent.'

'Tut! Tut! Lost our regiment have we, sir? How careless. Let me see.' The lieutenant looked down at his fingers and pretended to inspect his fingernails. 'Of course, I'd love to help you, sir, but I'm afraid my hands are tied. You know, rules and regulations, old man. I'm not supposed to, well, just help any old so-and-so who turns up at odd hours, wanting assistance. There are proper channels to go through. I know, why don't you come back in the morning and speak to the major? He might be able to help. Now, if you'll excuse me...'

'Lieutenant, ' Charteris asked desperately, 'you and I may have had our differences in the past but it is vital I rejoin my men tonight. Is there no way you can help?'

'Listen to me, sir,' snarled the lieutenant, his nostrils flaring, 'it was all very well for you to humiliate me last year but now you want a favour from me, everything has changed. Your "intervention" might have looked good to the chaps on the dockside but I ended up with a posting to this god-forsaken back of beyond! Well, let me tell you, sir, nothing has changed. Now, if you'll kindly step back and allow me to continue.' The look he gave Charteris as he swept past him was one of utter malevolence.

'In fact, if you don't mind, sir, I think I shall have to inform my superior officer right now. It'll mean dragging him away from his supper but I'm sure he won't mind. Your travel papers *are* in order, I take it?'

'Turn around, lieutenant. Now!' Charteris commanded, an edge to his voice. Slowly, the RTO did as he was told, and found himself staring into the barrel of Neville's cocked service revolver. Waving the revolver at him, Charteris gestured for him to step back into the room. Trembling, the badly frightened officer did as he was ordered.

'Now then, you bullying, cowardly bastard, I never normally swear at a fellow officer but today I am more than happy to make an exception in your case! I need to know where my battalion is. Right now.' The man nodded frantically, his terrified eyes staring at the barrel of the gun waving under his nose. 'Good! Now that we have that out of the way, why don't you see if you can accommodate me? Sit down here, lieutenant, and see if you can't dig up some reports concerning recent troop movements. Now! And please, don't make any sudden movements, I must confess to feeling a trifle jumpy and if you were to move this pistol I'm holding might go off. You do understand, don't you?'

The RTO nodded before slumping down at his desk and leafing hurriedly through the folders scattered before him. After a few seconds he grunted and waved a thick sheaf of papers triumphantly. He skimmed through them rapidly, looking up fearfully with a handful of forms clutched in his fist.

'Who was it you're looking for?' he stammered. Charteris told him tersely, the anger showing in his voice and the man bent back down over his desk and rapidly flicked through the papers. He straightened up again.

'The 19th were to have passed through Albert and detrained there early tomorrow morning. We have no spare trains at present so they'll have to make their own way forward. They were to march to Carnoy, according to this, and there are no further reports as to where they're headed to from there. Is that all you were looking for?' He sat back and cowered under Charteris's gaze.

'Good. See? That wasn't so hard after all!' Charteris's voice hardened as he contemplated the wretched man in front of him. 'Now, how can I get to Carnoy tonight. lieutenant?'

The lieutenant sat and thought for a moment, a sly smile hovering around his lips. As the barrel wavered in his direction once more he gulped and spoke. 'You can't. There are no more trains south, today at least. All supply traffic is going to Arras to try to stop the Boche there. So you see, its all been to no avail.' His voice grew stronger, more cunning. 'And I'm sure my superior will want to take the strongest action against you when I inform him as to the manner of the threats you made against me. If you'll just hand over that revolver, captain...'

'Go to blazes, I'm not finished with you yet!' As his eyes wandered around the office he espied a set of goggles on the cabinet next to the desk and he gestured at them with his free hand.

'Motorcycle goggles, whose are those?'

'Er, my sergeant's, sir, and he's gone to get our supper.'

Charteris raised his hand as if to strike him and he flinched. 'And left his goggles behind? I think not! On your feet, lieutenant. You and I are going for a walk. Move it, man, I've not time to dawdle!' He pointed at the door with his revolver and the RTO obediently moved in that direction. Charteris leant over and swept the goggles into his other hand. Outside, when his eyes had adjusted to the darkness, he pushed the man down into the alleyway. At the far end he spotted a shape leaning against the wall and manoeuvred his captive in that direction.

It was a motorcycle, a BSA 550cc single, caked with mud but looking well-cared for nevertheless. Charteris's heart leapt as he remembered the days before the war spent tinkering with his friend's motorcycle. Now was the time to remember all that he had spent hours learning.

'Quick! Your boots, man, take them off. Now!'

Startled, the RTO bent down and began unlacing his well-polished officer's riding boots. When he had finished Charteris took them from him and threw them high into the night. He slipped the goggles over his cap and fastened them around his eyes. He bent down and turned the fuel lever to 'on'. A quick dabble with the decompressor and the bike was ready to start. Pushing down smoothly with his right foot he engaged the kick-start lever. The machine's engine coughed and then died and he caught a savage, triumphant look appear on the watching man's face. Gripping the throttle again, he kicked harder this time and was rewarded by the sound of the engine coughing heartily into life.

Engaging the lever on the tank he found first gear and gingerly let out the clutch. The bike lurched forward viciously and he hurriedly pulled in on the clutch lever. Motioning to the hapless officer watching glumly, he ordered, 'Give me your maps and then walk this way. Move!'

Obediently the RTO handed over the crumpled maps and began to stagger down the cinder track, gingerly picking his way along the icy route. Slipping the clutch once again, Charteris rammed his pistol into its holster and let the bike slowly move forward. As he came level with the dawdling figure he put out his left leg ang pushed the man violently in the small of the back. The RTO was catapulted head first into a large pool of half-frozen liquid slush and as he floundered about in a vain attempt to claw his way out, Charteris opened the throttle and roared off into the night.

* * * * *

Back in Peckham, Tillie heard the doorbell ring. 'I'll get it, Mrs Humboldt!' she cried. The welcome in her voice died away as she pulled open the front door.

'Mrs Fairley?' Tillie responded automatically, looking past the stranger on her doorstep, down the path, squinting to see Neville hiding in the gloom behind the uniformed NCO.

'Ah, yes, then it is you I've come to see, ma'am. It's about Captain Charteris. I'm Sergeant Mackinnon, from the War Office.'

'Neville? What's happened? Oh God, there's not been an accident, has there?' She swayed suddenly and he reached forward to catch her.

'No, ma'am, it's not like that. You see, the captain, well, he gave me something for you. Made me promise to deliver it tonight.'

'But I don't understand. Where is Neville? What has stopped him delivering whatever it is in person?'

The sergeant looked pityingly at her before continuing. 'Look ma'am, please take this inside and see for yourself. I must be off, the missus is expecting me. Goodbye, ma'am.'

He lifted his hand to his cap in a salute and strode away, leaving her stood there in consternation looking down at the package. Slowly she turned back into the house and closed the door. The door to the drawing-room was open and she moved into the warmth mechanically, still unclear as to what was happening.

Bertha Humboldt found her there, minutes later, staring down stricken at the letter she held in her dainty hand, a small velvet-covered box on the chair beside her. 'Mateelda, what happens?' she asked falteringly, her concern rising at the look of sheer misery on the white, tear-streaked face of the young woman sat looking so distraught in the chair.

'I've lost him. He's gone, Bertha. He's gone.'

Bertha Humboldt rushed over and clasped Tillie to her bosom. Soothing her in her native Flemish, she hugged and rocked her as Tillie sobbed into her shoulder as if her heart would break. The two women stayed that way for long minutes until Bertha felt the flood subside and she pulled back to contemplate her mistress and friend.

'I no unnerstan, Mateelda. Meester Neville? What happens?'

Tillie began to sob again, quietly this time. Eventually she pulled herself together with a fierce movement and gestured at the letter Sergeant Mackinnon had delivered.

'It's Neville, he's...' She gulped. 'He's returned to France.'

'But why?' Bertha spread her shoulders wide in a gesture of total puzzlement.

Wiping her eyes, Tillie raised the single piece of paper and began to read in a flat monotone:

My Darling Tillie,

When you read this letter I shall already be well on my way to rejoin my battalion in France. Please do not hate me for this unexpected departure, but I could not stand idly by, safe and well, whilst the men whom I love as dearly as yourself faced mortal danger without me. It is hard to try to explain the comradeship that develops between a group of men in times like these. Suffice to say that today I discovered that my being sent home was, in part, a ruse to save me and another officer from the dangers facing the men I went over to France with, so many months before. Knowing this, I could never face myself again were I not there with them, sharing whatever is to come in their hour of danger.

I love you, Matilda Fairley, with every sinew of my body. I thank God for every day that I have spent with you and hope that same God watches over us both and allows me to come home, safe and sound, to pursue my goal of your utter happiness. As a token of my love I have enclosed a small box which I ask you to open. Please wear the contents you find within, until that happy day when I can hold you in my arms and never part from you again. Do not think badly of me.

Yours now and always,

Neville, xxxxxxxx. I love you.

She picked up the box and opened it. Nestling within, on a bed of black velvet, sat a gold ring, topped with a small, perfectly-formed diamond. Lifting it from the box, she held it aloft so the diamond sparkled as it caught the firelight. The tears flowed again as she slipped the ring onto the finger of her left hand and pressed it tightly into her bodice. It was slightly too big and she twisted it round her finger as she sat there.

'He's gone and I never told him. Now he'll never know...' A translucent tear edged its way down her face to her chin. The ticking of the mantelpiece clock sounded louder in the silence between the two women.

'Meester Neville come back, you see, Mateelda.'

'I didn't mean about that, Bertha. I meant. Oh...' She burst into fresh tears again.

'About baby?' Bertha asked soothingly as she leaned over and hugged her again.

'How did you know?' Tillie asked, wonderingly, a catch in her voice. 'I don't know for certain myself. I'm not sure yet, it's just that I feel different. I'm over three weeks late and that should have told me something. I was going to speak to Neville but... Oh God, why now, why today of all days! I can't explain, it's just a feeling. I should have said something. I should have told him.'

Bertha's tears intermingled with Tillie's now and the two women sat there clutching each other as the fire flickered and slowly died.

23

Thursday 27th January 1916

Battalion marched to Albert, no transport being made available. Light rain all day. Marched on to Carnoy. Short rest and then on to positions alongside 67th Infantry Regiment of French 6th Army near Maricourt. Hope to arrive in early hours of Friday morning. French trenches said to be in great state of disrepair. Men badly tired although spirits high. Left Carnoy in late evening. Captain Charteris rejoined us. Attack will go in early tomorrow morning. Colonel has high hopes of success.

Captain L. Carey, D Company

Stretching themselves, they rose from where they had fallen out to rest in a small square not far from the centre of Albert and shuffling about in the light drizzle that had begun to fall they donned their arms and equipment over the top of their greatcoats.

The journey down the rutted tracks and muddied roads had taken too long and all of them were soaked and feeling the effects of the march. Confirming what the RTO in Amiens had informed Neville Charteris, the promised train had never materialised, having been cancelled at the last minute. At least their packs and heavy equipment had gone ahead, to be collected at Carnoy. After ranting for several minutes at this latest twist of fate and cursing *all* transport officers, Cuthbert Snaith had cooled down and swung swiftly in action. The company commanders had been given revised orders and had set off in the early hours of the morning on the five or so miles to Albert. Watching them, Snaith felt a warm glow of pride. These were *his* men and by God, tomorrow with him alongside them they would give Fritz such a bloody nose. His features twisted into a frown as he recalled the only bit of unpleasantness that had occurred before they had set off.

Talking over the dispositions for the next morning with Walter Ramsbottom, he had been accosted by a rather rude corporal from headquarters who had peremptorily thrust into his hand an embossed official-looking envelope and then scurried quickly away. He had quickly scanned the contents and looked up to see Walter's anxious eyes on his crestfallen face.

'Is everything all right, sir?'

For an answer he had offered the limp page he was holding in Walter's direction. 'I'm afraid it's bad news, Walter, from Brigadier Blackley. It seems I'm to hand over to you and present myself at HQ immediately, to answer those infernal charges against me concerning the Godley affair. What a humiliation! Relieving a chap the day before his men go into action together as a battalion for the very first time.'

Walter had looked at him closely before simply taking the message, reading it quickly and then ripping it to pieces. His hand had opened and the torn pieces of paper had drifted down in the breeze like confetti into the mud at his feet.

'Come along now, sir,' he had replied, 'we have work to do and a long way to go. We don't want to arrive too late tonight, do we? Isn't it amazing how so many messages go missing? I really must remonstrate with HQ when we get back. Those damned clerks, they can be so bally careless.'

Having spoken, he had walked off without a backward glance. After gazing down at the soiled, mud-clogged pieces of paper Snaith had followed his second in command with a broad, relieved smile on his face.

Now, surrounded by the reassuring mass of his men, his spirits rose. Within half an hour the long column began its onward, snakelike progress out of the battered town in the direction of Carnoy, the proud, mounted figure of Lieutenant-Colonel Snaith DSO at its head. No one sang, fatigue was etched on too many faces for them to feel like singing.

Carnoy was reached later that evening, as night began to fall, with no fallouts or hindrances of any sort along the way. Here they were introduced to their French liaison officer, a youthful sous-lieutenant, and after collecting their packs, equipment and an issue of spare ammunition which, miraculously, had arrived on time, they were very quickly despatched. Along with some pack mules for the heavier equipment they departed, staggering under the heavy weight down the muddy track that led to their final destination. After an hour of marching, the order to halt was given and they relaxed gratefully by the side of the track for a much-needed rest. Fred Maitland craftily took the opportunity to divest himself of several bottles of wine from his pack to some eager buyers at a good profit, keeping a sharp lookout for the company NCOs as he did so.

A loud cheer rose up from the last files of men and the word spread. 'Mr Charteris is back!' The message carried from the back of the column to the front in no time and the cheers increased as a familiar figure, his uniform stiff with ingrained mud, walked its length, a smile spread from ear to ear on his face as he acknowledged the salutes.

It had been a near thing. The lack of transport which had forced the battalion to proceed on foot had saved Charteris from missing them altogether. He had become lost on leaving Amiens and had wasted precious time trying to find his bearings and regain the right direction through the unfamiliar tracks and rutted roads. A much-needed nap on the side of the road, crouching shivering against the motorcycle engine for warmth, had hindered him further. On reaching Carnoy eventually, after an adventurous journey via Albert through the countryside, during which the motorcycle had stalled several times and slowed him up, he had been distraught to find the battalion had already left. Using the map the lieutenant in Amiens had grudgingly provided, and gunning the bike's throttle to its full extent, he had set out after them. Luckily, a sympathetic sergeant had pointed out the direction the battalion had taken and with the engine coughing ominously he had frantically slewed the machine round and taken off after them.

He'd only travelled a few hundred yards when the bike, its petrol tank totally empty, finally quit on him. Hastily abandoning it on the side of the track he half-walked, half-ran, after the column. The decision to call a rest stop had allowed him to join them and now he moved quickly to the front. Marching tiredly, stiffly, up to Colonel Snaith, he saluted and asked, 'Permission to rejoin the battalion, sir?'

The CO touched his cane to his forehead. 'Captain Charteris, no doubt you will have an explanation for your sudden reappearance, sir! For now, please take your place with your old company. I'm sure they will be pleased to see you. We'll speak later about your adventures.'

Charteris walked back to where the eager faces of A Company awaited him. Joining them, he surreptitiously shook hands with a delighted CSM Frank Mason while behind him, Second-Lieutenant David Elliot MC scowled deeply at the sudden appearance of the one man he feared and hated most. Minutes later, all talk ceased as the column swung back onto the track and they resumed the slow march eastwards through the night towards Maricourt.

The darkened sky was lit with the sudden bright-red flashes of shellfire and the slow, dazzling descent of flares. The young French officer marched confidently alongside the CO, one hand tucked through the leather of Cuthbert Snaith's steed's bridle while he made frequent references to the folded map in his other one. The sounds of battle were becoming louder and louder as they finally reached a junction in the road. Large white signposts read 'Napier's Redoubt' and 'Brewery Redoubt' and over to their left the flashes lit up a jumbled collection of ruins which was once Maricourt. The track continued on into the night off to the right, in a quagmire of mud and shell holes, and it was down this track the Frenchman vigorously waved them. Slipping and sliding, with stifled curses the 19th Battalion followed him. The curses grew more frequent as men floundered, slipped and fell, sliding into foul-smelling water-filled holes as their feet left the narrowing track in the unfamiliar landscape.

The column halted several times while rescues were effected, all of which added to the growing mood of frustration and surliness as any humour the men had been feeling evaporated in the face of their journey through the morass before them. The slow moaning of shells passing overhead did nothing to improve their spirits and it was with a feeling of fatigued relief that the leading files at long last saw the Frenchman raise his arm in an arresting motion.

They arrived at their destination utterly exhausted in the early hours of the morning. The French trench line loomed before them and as they cautiously approached, the sound of mules braying somewhere in the dark made them start. Their fears were dispelled as out of the gloom more officers in the *Horizon-bleu* uniforms of the French Army appeared and after some quaint exchanges the men were broken up and led down the narrow, thin, crumbling walls to find shelter and rest where they could.

'Bloody 'ell, I'm fuckin' shattered!' Charlie Horsfall exclaimed, wrinkling his nose, 'Oi, can you smell that? What the fuckin' 'ell is it?'

Archie Parkes looked round and then answered him. 'Charlie, me old, these Froggies aren't like us, I reckon. What you're sniffing smells to me like what I reckon we're stood in. Shite an' dead bodies. I heard they don't bury their dead, they just make them part of the furniture, so to speak. So for Chrissakes don't go hanging yer rifle on that peg what's sticking out of the parapet over there. It looks like some poor cove's arm! Thank Christ we're only here for a few hours.'

Horsfall carefully swung his pack onto what was left of the parapet and clutched his rifle tightly to his chest. 'Dirty buggers, what a way to fight a bleedin' war, I ask you!' he grumbled.

Further along the line of crumbling earthen works, Fred Maitland stooped to lay his rifle and pack against the dirt wall. As he straightened up he collided with another figure making its solitary way along the trench.

''Ere, watch it, you stupid berk!'

'Hello, Fred, I've been looking for you,' the figure calmly replied.

Maitland squinted in the gloom as he tried to make out the identity of the man facing him.

'Christ! What the bleedin' 'ell are you doin' 'ere?'

Sergeant James Hobson, late of the Bethune Provost Marshall's office, smiled grimly as he stared back at Maitland.

'The oi-polloi what makes up our High Command these days decreed that someone from the Provost Marshall's office should get themselves down 'ere to make sure you buggers go over the top tomorrow when you're told, Fred. Look who they sent? Me an' Corporal Thompson.'

'Oh, aye, you'll be right behind us, then,' Maitland answered him sarcastically, 'shouting at us ter get out from behind the safety of the trenches, like. Fuckin' typical!'

'D'ye know, Fred, I asked to come down 'ere,' Hobson mused thoughtfully. 'That business with the young lad, Godley wasn't it, made me see things different. How could a young cove like him do what he did? He showed no fear, about to face what he was. Oh, I know what you think of me, an' others like me, but the way that poor lad took his medicine without grumbling made me stop and think. Take the piss if you like, but tomorrow I'll not be stayin' 'ere while you lot go over. I've got me a spare rifle and some ammo and I'll be right alongside you. I'll see you in the morning then, Fred.'

Hobson stood there awkwardly as Maitland stooped over his pack without answering. 'Look Fred, the other reason I came over to see you was...I just wanted to say I'm sorry for all that went on before, between us. You know. Anyway, good luck tomorrow.'

Maitland continued to ignore him and rearrange his pack, pulling it this way and that. When he looked up again, Hobson was wending his way down the trench.

'Watcha gonna do to the Boche when we get in amongst them, then, sarge? Arrest the whole fuckin' lot of them?' Maitland shouted at Hobson's retreating back.

The dugout the colonel and the officers were taken to was a ruin. Snorting his disgust at the poorly-lit, foul-smelling, rubbish-strewn, waterlogged interior, Cuthbert Snaith waved his staff into its tight confines and gestured impatiently as Walter Ramsbottom unpacked his map case, emptying its contents on the rickety table in the centre.

'Right, gentlemen, gather round if you please.' he pulled a large map towards him as he spoke, 'I want to make quite certain you all know your place in the attack. We're all tired but we'll simply have to make do. I don't want any foul-ups because someone has forgotten his part. We've only a few hours until the attack and a strict timetable we *must* adhere to, so please pay attention.

'I've already spoken to the RSM. Mr Findlay and Major Roberts will form the nucleus of the left out of battle party, along with a section from each company. A Company, Captain Charteris, you will assist your old company and your men will assault the Stellung from this direction, being supported on the same front by D Company and Captain Carey. You must get your men in amongst the Huns quickly. Bomb them out of the trenches, leaving B Company to follow on and mop up the blighters your chaps don't kill in the initial assault. Got that, Redford? Myself and C Company will cut in from the other side and split their defensive fire.

'A French battery of their 75mm's will assist us. They should have arrived last night and will start firing at almost point-blank range shortly by my watch, keeping the Huns' heads down long enough for us to get in amongst the enemy's front line trenches. When we're clear of the Hun second line, marked in red on your maps, gentlemen, we should be able to pass through their third defence line fairly quickly and meet up with the Kents and Cheshires about here.' He pointed at a spot on the map.

'Here is where the French assault will go in, supported by the other British troops and by merging around this point we can all advance on a broad front in the direction of Hardecourt-aux-Bois.'

'Excuse me, sir, do you really think we shall reach that far?' A voice broke into his instructions and Snaith straightened up with annoyance.

'Captain Charteris, what is it you would like to say?' he said, with a note of exasperation, looking at the strained, boyish face opposite.

'It's just that, sir, if the Boche have the sort of defences we seem to think they do then we're going to find it a hard nut to crack. Where is our artillery? Where are the other British troops and how many French regiments are going to back us up? This looks more like a large trench raid than a serious attempt to take and hold the enemy trenches, sir. It seems to me that we should—'

'Captain Charteris, I am well aware of your bravery, sir, and your efforts in rejoining the battalion at the hour of its attack on the German lines are something to be applauded, but you do not have the full facts, coming back to us at this late hour. This attack has been planned and approved, I may add, by GHQ and General Haig himself. I have it on good authority that our attack tomorrow will be keenly watched. The other regiments *will* be forthcoming, you mark my words. The guns will start firing before dawn, for maximum surprise. A new attack is being planned on the Western Front this year and this assault will be the proof of the new tactics GHQ intend to utilise later. They are quite happy for us to attack in this manner and so, sir, should you!'

Squarely meeting his CO's gaze Charteris looked again at the map. 'Nevertheless, sir, I think it would be most prudent if we—'

'Prudent? Prudent? That's enough, Captain!' Colonel Snaith's eyes flashed dangerously, and turning back to the other officers he pointedly ignored Neville Charteris. 'Amongst other things we shall have the benefit of this new innovation, the creeping barrage, to keep the defenders' heads down until we're amongst them. This attack will go in shortly, *exactly* as I have described. Are we quite clear on this?'

Major Ramsbottom coughed discreetly as the colonel spoke and Snaith wheeled round on him. 'Yes, Walter, what is it now?'

'I'm sorry, sir, but the RSM had a word before we came in. The noise we heard as we arrived. Some of the supply party and their mules have gone astray. It looks like we'll be missing quite a bit of the other equipment that was to join us here for the morning. That means some chaps won't be as loaded down as the others but we'll miss the stuff when we need to dig in on the other side. There appear to be no scaling ladders. We were promised they would be available but they simply aren't here. The men will have to go over via the firesteps. Luckily our French allies have left these trenches in such a filthy state that it won't be too much of a hop over.'

* * * * *

As he waded through the mud-filled trench CSM Green of D Company spotted a solitary figure hunched by himself on the ill-kept firestep. The CSM spoke quietly. 'How do, lad, are you all right, got all you need?'

Bill Godsman looked at the NCO, a miserable expression on his face. 'Do you think you really do pay for your sins, CSM? I mean, if you die is there somewhere you pay for what you did?'

Duncan Green stared at the youngster's anguished expression. 'I don't rightly know, son. Why, who's talking of dying?'

Godsman stared down at his feet. 'It's just that, tomorrow...if something happens...I don't know. It's been on my mind for months now!'

Green reached forward. 'Go on, son,' he said softly, 'Speaking out is sometimes better than keeping it in.'

Godsman shot him a grateful look. 'It were at Loos, CSM, when we took part in our first attack. I were detailed off to take some Gerry prisoners back, two of them. I were dead scared. Anyway, on the way back, a shell knocked us over and one of the Gerries, a young lad he were, he just started screaming. My head were ringing, real funny like, and before I knew it I'd shoved my bayonet in him, took him in the throat. Of course he shut up but the other lad, he took to his heels so I pulled my bayonet back out of his pal and shot him in the back as he ran. Mr Charteris's lot found me later on, I reckon I'd lost my head and wandered off.'

Green gazed at the young soldier with a pitying expression and shook his shoulder. 'You ain't to blame for that, son. Terrible things happen in a war like this. You tried to do what was right but it didn't turn out that way. Don't worry about God making it a personal thing with you, either, he's far bigger fish to fry than the little ones like you and me and the rest of the lads. Those bastards at GHQ for example! I hope he makes it *real* personal when they come up before him! Try and get some rest and put what you just told me out of your mind. Go and check your equipment and make sure you're carrying all the extras you was given. We'll need every bit of it when we get over there.'

He patted the young man's arm again and moved off, leaving Godsman looking up at the black sky behind him.

'They're waiting for us, the bastards. I can almost smell them!' Percy Hartson kicked morosely at the chalk wall he was leaning against before flicking his cigarette end onto the dirt floor. He shifted his weight and straightened up, standing head and shoulders above the crumbling parapet as he peered out across the darkness in front of him.

'Come on, our Percy, get yer head down lad, you'll catch a packet if one of them spots you. Come on now, get down and don't be so daft! The colonel says tomorrow's going to be a huge surprise to Fritz, you wait and see. If we ain't all dead of the cold first!'

'Aye, maybe yer right, Archie. But if yer not, we're all in for it. You mark my bloody words.' Hartson slid back down again and for the umpteenth time checked the cocking mechanism of the Lewis gun at his side.

* * * * *

Eight miles away, a French train driver leaned out of his cab and spat his cigarette from his lips as he contemplated the track ahead. A lucky German shell had hit the embankment in front, creating a minor landslide that had ripped away the earth, undermining the tracks. A gang of workmen were working frantically with picks and shovels to effect a repair but from where the train driver was standing, as soon as they shovelled the earth beneath the tracks the driving rain was washing it away.

He glanced back along the carriages making up the load he was pulling and shrugged his shoulders philosophically. *Merde!* Someone, somewhere, would soon be cursing the non-arrival of their supply of shells, but how could they blame him, Henri Reynaud? It was not his fault. *C'est la guerre!*

* * * * *

Time passed slowly. 'Waddya reckon, Harry, boyo, do we stand a chance, then?' Arwyn Jones nervously licked his lips as he knelt down in the muddy bottom of the trench. It stank, a different, foreign smell to the other trenches he'd crouched in since their arrival in France, and the strangeness of it was making him feel decidedly anxious. Corporal Harry Sheldon smiled a trifle uneasily back at his pal as he pulled a cleaning cloth through the barrel of his rifle and blew on his freezing hands.

'To tell you the truth, Taffy, me old, I'm not feeling too chipper meself about this stunt. If Fritz is waiting for us then God help us! I don't know about you but I wish I was back in Blighty tucked up in bed with the missus.' He digested what he'd said then laughed. 'Gawd, there's a thought! On second thoughts I'll take my chance with Fritz!'

'Careful, boys,' muttered Jones, 'here comes Mr Findlay.'

The men looked along the crowded trench to see the figure of the RSM pushing his way through purposely. If he was disappointed not to be accompanying them this morning, Bob Findlay hid it well. The three men following dutifully behind him were bent double under the wicker panniers they were carrying and on the morning breeze came the strong, pungent smell of neat rum.

'Right lads, CO's orders, have a good stiff one on him before you go over. Not you, laddie, you look far too young to be supping this!'

The soldier in question looked aggrieved as a light, nervous ripple of laughter rose up around him but his expression changed as the RSM grinned and thrust a tin mug containing a generous tot into his hand.

'Give 'em hell lads, give them one for me and the boys left back here who'll be waiting to join you over there when you're safely dug in. Dig deep now, I don't want to 'ave to shout at any of you when we meet up again.'

* * * * *

Cuthbert Snaith looked up from the letter he was writing in the gloom of the dugout and met his second-in-command's gaze as Walter Ramsbottom squeezed inside without a word. He moved past the CO and sat down gingerly on the rickety seat opposite the colonel. The candle sitting on top of the plank of wood that served as a table guttered smokily as he moved, almost blowing out before the pale orange flame reasserted itself. In the dim light the two men stared at each other. At length, Snaith cleared his throat and spoke.

'Well, Walter, what is it? Speak up, I know that look. What's on your mind?'

Ramsbottom spoke slowly, hesitantly. 'We're all a bit knocked up over this show, sir. It seems that we're being asked to pull off a great deal with no real chance of success. Too many ifs and buts. It's no wonder the men are so restless. They're worn out after today's efforts of just getting here.'

'You're quite right, Walter,' the colonel sighed. 'I do share your concerns totally but what would you have me say? As it is, it's only thanks to you that I'm here at all. Were I to list all the doubts I have over our attack it would run to several pages and still not be finished. All we can hope for is that we can get in among the enemy trenches before they are fully awake and who knows? We might yet pull it off.'

He pushed his unfinished letter aside. 'It's a strange set of circumstances that have brought us here. From the first day we landed in France I've seen the hopelessness of what we've asked human flesh to endure. The waste, the sheer bloody waste of it all is sometimes beyond comprehension. I have tried to do my best and bring you all through this with as little loss as I could. Some of my actions have earned me the hatred of the men, the Godley thing, I know, but I will tell you this, Walter. God help me, but could I go back I would not change a thing. Discipline *must* be maintained and if that young man had to die so that his comrades learnt what that discipline means, our survival in battle as a unit, then so be it. As you know I was at Colenso with Buller in Natal, back in December 1899. We lay all day in the baking heat being fired at if we so much as blinked an eyelid. I was a major then and that day my company lost twenty men, shot by a farmer enemy we despised as non-soldiers. The Boers taught us a lesson then and the tragedy of it all is that sixteen years on our generals have forgotten everything they learned in South Africa.

'Tomorrow we're going to ask our men to make a supreme effort, to give their all, in a cause that some think has already been lost. How can I go amongst them and say, "Boys, I'm sorry, but we're going to fail today because your commanders have no faith and didn't send enough men or artillery to assist you". Do I say, "You're dispensable and so will be frittered away like chaff on the wind because someone in a cushy billet far back behind the lines had a good idea?"

'I'm writing to my wife, God bless her, in a similar vein. What she'll make of it heaven only knows, she'll probably think I've lost my marbles. Well maybe I have. But, Walter, we will go in and give Fritz a bloody good scare, whatever happens!'

Major Ramsbottom looked pityingly at his CO. 'I'm sorry, sir, I never realised you felt like this. There is another matter. Do you really think you need to accompany us? You could easily stay here with the others and no one would say a word.'

'Come, come, Walter,' the colonel chided him. 'To answer your first statement, do you really think I've swallowed all that guff GHQ sends us? Someone has had to keep up appearances and as the CO of this battalion it has fallen on my shoulders, but please, spare me the thought of being a total believer. As to the attack, this time my place is at the head of my men in their hour of danger and I want everyone to see that the "Old Man" is going with them into whatever is waiting out there for us. No matter that he may be a duffer and an old codger to boot! Now bugger off, old chap, and let me finish this.'

As Ramsbottom rose to leave, Snaith spoke again. 'The only good thing in all of this for my wife is that our boys are safe. Alfred's battery is being withdrawn from the Ypres sector for re-equipping and George, our youngest, has just been posted to a new ship. It's a cruiser, HMS *Hampshire*. I thank God that as our fleet is idle for the most part these days, his most arduous task will be to count the shackles on the anchor chain. Off you go, Walter, get some rest and we'll meet before we go over. Which isn't that far away.'

They shook hands solemnly and as Ramsbottom made his way out, Cuthbert Snaith's voice echoed gently in the stillness of the dugout.

'It isn't the dying that's hard, you know, Walter. God knows, we must all die at some time. It's just the thought of it being for absolutely nothing!'

Ramsbottom made to answer but words failed him. After he'd gone Snaith slowly finished his writing and leant back. 'Evans!' he shouted, and in seconds Bill Evans's ferret-like face appeared in the entrance.

'Sir?' he enquired.

'Private Evans, try and get a little fire going and see if you can't rustle me up a nice cuppa, could you? And while you're at it, go into my valise and take my whisky out. You know, the one you've been taking sly nips from. Don't stare at me like that man, do you think I hadn't noticed? Take the bally thing out and you and your chums polish it off. I'll not be needing it again!' He chortled at the look of utter surprise on Evans face.

* * * * *

Further down the trench, Neville Charteris straightened up from cleaning his revolver and placed it back into its holster. He looked around him at the two snoring bodies that shared the hole they had found in the side of the trench and smiled humourlessly. It was amazing how men could adapt to almost anything and fall asleep in the tightest of spots. And why not? In a few hours a lot of them would be sleeping forever. He shivered, and for once not due to the cold wind that was blowing strongly, straight down the crumbling, snaking line.

Somewhere, out there, Tillie was lying asleep, and his spirits sank. It had seemed such a noble thing to do, to dash out to France and rejoin his men, but for the first time he felt a twinge of regret at his hasty, impetuous actions. How much easier to have stayed at home with her, safe and secure. Angrily he shook himself. It was done now, whatever the rights or wrongs he was here and he had a job to do. Tillie was the future, one he desperately yearned for, but for now there was only the present and what they must all face together in the coming hours.

In the dim distance to their right, before the sun's rays told of the approaching morning, the heavens opened. A low rumble grew in intensity as the skyline filled with an incessant winking of bright flashes. The gunfire went on and on, red flashes filling the air as the NCOs woke those that had managed to sleep with cries of 'Stand-to! Stand-to!' Stomachs churning, dry mouthed, the 19th took up weapons, shrugged shoulders into packs and ascended onto what was left of the firestep, each man loading onto his neighbour's back the bundles of extra equipment each had to carry.

Rolls of wire, wiring pegs, spare ammunition for the Lewis guns, extra rations, all were affixed to the mildewed webbing the men wore. Last of all, spare bombs were thrust into pockets as they readied themselves, trembling, waiting for the moment. The battalion officers, accompanied by their NCOs, waded through the crumbling trenches and took up their allotted positions by their men, each anxiously checking their watches.

'Check your equipment, lads," their NCO's bawled, "and make sure your rifles are loaded before we go over. Keep your distance and dressing. Remember, don't stop for anyone. If your chum goes down, leave him. Your job is to get in amongst the enemy and secure our position.' There was a clatter as the NCOs shouted 'Fix bayonets!' and the long steel bayonets were affixed to each rifle. The 19th was ready for its hour of glory.

Frank Mason's preparations were disturbed by a shove in the back. The angry words on his lips died as he wheeled round to see Bill Clark staring at him.

'What is it Bill?' he demanded. 'You've picked a rum time to come and bum some fags off me, haven't you?'

Clark thrust the dirty notes he was holding in the CSM's direction. 'It's yer ten francs, CSM, the money I took off you at the boxing. I can't go over with it on me conscience, you see. Not after cheating and whatever...' Mason listened in silence as Clark confessed to the trick he had played on the sports day, detailing the metal he had put in his own man's gloves before Thomson had poleaxed Charlie Horsfall. When he finished his sorry tale, Mason shook his head in half-sorrow and amusement.

'You cheeky beggar, Bill. Doing me over like that, and you a vicar's son!' He shook his head again. 'Right, well, get back to your own boys and maybe when this is all over you and me might just have to meet up and don some boxing gloves ourselves. And don't you worry, matey, I'll check yours bloody carefully before we go in the ring!' Go on, off you go. And good luck, Bill, we'll all need it. I only hope you kept a lucky horseshoe for yourself!'

Fred Maitland looked round anxiously as he checked and re-checked his equipment. Along the trench, to his left, a waving arm caught his eye and he recognised the pale, grim face of Hobson looking wanly at him. Nodding his head in reply, Maitland re-busied himself with his pack, tense now, waiting for the whistles to blow.

Back in the dugout the CO and his party readied themselves. Snaith pushed among them, shaking hands with each individual. When he reached Walter Ramsbottom he stopped and both men looked into each other's eyes.

'Well Walter, it's nearly time. All these months of sticking it out have come down to this. I want to thank you for all you've done and for listening to me last night. I know just how loyal you've been these past few weeks. I must confess the Godley affair nearly did for me. Well, it's all behind us now. I haven't touched a drop since we got our orders for this attack. Mustn't let the men see their CO tottering around for the wrong reasons! One of the men spoke to me on my way up here. Said he was sorry for writing about Godley to Brigade. I told him it didn't matter, nothing matters anymore. Only today, only this moment. No, don't ask me who the chap was, it's his secret and mine. Good luck. old man. I'll see you on the other side.'

'Which "other side" would that be, sir?' Walter asked, tongue in cheek, and after a moment's hesitation, Snaith threw back his head and laughed heartily. The dugout flap was suddenly thrown back and an agitated soldier in the person of Sous-Lieutenant Dassaux entered. Spotting Snaith, he threw up his hands and announced volubly.

'*Mon colonel, c'est une catastrophe! Une catastrophe!*'

'What is it, man? Speak English, can't you? What's happened?'

Taking a deep breath the young officer gathered himself before continuing. 'Please forgive me, Colonel Snaith. *Les Boche, les salle Boche!* The Germans, they have attacked not far from here, in the direction of Frise. We are overwhelmed. *Une grande* assault you must understand. My general, he says, I must tell you this. For today it is not possible we can support the British attack this morning. We must send all available troops to halt this sudden attack on ourselves. We can permit the firing of the French battery, it is in position and would take too long to move but for troops, *mais non, c'est impossible*, there is none to give. I must also tell you, no more British troops have arrived to assist you. My general reports, alas, I am sorry.' He whirled on his heels and disappeared.

Colonel Snaith stared at him thunderstruck. The noise they had heard for the last hour had been *German* artillery, not the French support fire they had been promised. He tried to digest what the Frenchman had said. Ramsbottom made to speak but Snaith cut him off with a chopping motion of his hand. He rubbed his forehead in a gesture of despair and finally looked up at the dumbstruck officer staring at him.

'This changes nothing. The attack will go in as planned.'

Ramsbottom stared at him aghast. 'But, sir, we can't...'

'Walter, how on earth are we going to get word to the Cheshires and the West Kents in time to stop them going over?' As he spoke a fusillade of fire erupted from close by as the French battery that had arrived overnight unleashed a torrent of 75mm shells in the direction of the German lines. Snaith gestured in the direction of the firing.

'You see? It's already started. There's no hope for it, we'll have to go. Gentlemen, join your companies and make ready to advance on the signal. When we take the position we'll sit tight and hope for whatever support the French can give us before we decide whether or not to continue our advance. Make no mistake, we can succeed if we keep our nerve. Now go, and good luck! And not a word of this to the men.'

Stunned, Ramsbottom joined his CO and without a word they made their way down the crowded trenches to where the men from C Company waited for them. The rain was falling steadily, the promise of a watery sun had disappeared and the low grey clouds adding a sombre, atmospheric touch to the day. To their left the French guns fired in a continuous stream, the shells screaming over at a flat trajectory as they slammed into the enemy trenches 300 yards away.

As they stared a mass of explosions erupted to their left and they all spun round. The skies had opened in a veritable torrent of red fire and flame and as they watched aghast the British lines behind them to their left were obscured by a rising cloud of dirt and dust as hundreds of shells landed squarely in amongst them. The noise was indescribable, tearing at their eardrums as the enemy shells screamed over, non-stop.

'What's happening?' Ramsbottom screamed into the colonel's ears, trying to make himself heard above the din.

'I don't know!' Snaith yelled back. 'The Boche must be preparing an attack but those shells are landing miles away. They're not firing at us. Quickly, go take your place with the others, Walter, and we'll push on before they switch to firing in our direction!' White-faced, Ramsbottom nodded and hurried away.

Crouching down at the bottom of the trench, Snaith checked his watch for the last time and then nodded to the signaller crouching alongside him. Raising his arm high, the man made a circling motion with a large red flag he was holding. Squinting through the gloom, Captain Carey spotted the movement and blew a series of piercing blasts on the whistle hanging round his neck. The sound was taken up by the adjoining companies and within seconds the air was filled with whistle blasts and the shouts of officers and NCOs screaming at their men to pull themselves up over the parapet and form up in no man's land.

''Ere we go then, boys!' Archie Higgins exclaimed, 'last one in's a sissy! See you over there an' make mine a Blighty one. Please!' He stood and clambered up awkwardly onto the parapet, weighed down by his pack and the spare rolls of wire he was also carrying. He was followed seconds later by the rest of his section.

One of them pointed at the mud-filled, pockmarked landscape. 'Which way do we go from here?'

Higgins grinned, pointing into the murky, rain-lashed ground stretching before them. 'You berk, Donald! Follow the orficers, why do you think they're coming with us today?'

To their left the gunfire stopped abruptly. The French battery had run out of shells, having expended its entire supply in those opening minutes. The train driver had been proved correct. The repair crew had deserted them, leaving him and his ammunition train stranded all night. No further supplies would reach anyone that day. The 19th were on their own.

Unaware of the reason for the stoppage the men continued to pour out of their trenches into the gloom of the dawning day, rifles as ordered in the high-port position. The whistles blew again and ponderously the battalion began to move off across the shell-filled ground before them. Their confidence grew as they advanced in the direction of the German trenches with no response from the enemy. Some did notice the absence of the creeping barrage they'd all been told to expect but thrusting the question from their minds they plodded steadily on, heads bent against the driving, freezing rain.

D Company were the first to die. On the other side of the pockmarked, water-filled ground that separated them, a sweating German machine-gunner frantically urged his loader on as he lifted the gun onto its mount. The shells that had exploded shockingly close to their concrete blockhouse had been the first inkling of an attack, catching them unawares. Running to their position he had broken open the ammunition boxes and now they worked smoothly as a team, readying the gun for action.

His young charge slapped him on the back to signify all was correct and that the canvas ammunition belt was securely in place. He pulled back the cocking handle, squinted through the sights and gently, almost caressingly, depressed the firing handle. The gun bucked but he held onto it securely and watched anxiously for the patters of earth in the distance that would tell him if he was firing at the right elevation. In the dim light he was unable to see properly but from where he crouched he could just make out a thin line of khaki-clad men appearing from out of the dark in front of him and he aimed hurriedly in their direction. The bullets spat out at a cyclic rate of 450 rounds per minute and at first he failed to observe the results of his firing. It was only when the men in front of him began to topple over that he knew he was firing at the correct elevation, so making a small adjustment, he watched carefully as the strikes lengthened. The gun barked rhythmically now and he walked the rounds into the groups of men as they began to advance. At the other end of the trench, a fellow machine-gunner also opened up and together their bullets arced towards the distant men in unison.

Captain Carey looked over his shoulder as he waved his men on, his pistol making small circles in the air above his head as he moved his arm. A swishing noise caught his attention and as he turned back to face his front the machine-gun bullets struck him first, punching through his body before ripping into the men behind him. Carey was dead before he hit the ground. In a moment, the air was full of screams and groans as the line of men took the full force of the incoming bullets, the impact of the rounds throwing men sideways into loosely crumpled heaps.

Bill Godsman heard the staccato bursts of firing as he plodded alongside Haddaway Wadkins. A dull thudding noise came from his right. He bent forward to look along the row and watched horrified as the men to his right toppled limply without a sound as the machine-gunner traversed his gun along their toiling figures. Haddaway threw up his arms as his head exploded in a shower of blood and he fell. Godsman felt a hammer-blow strike him high on the shoulder, his rifle dropped out of nerveless fingers and he collapsed onto the ground. Squirming painfully round, the breath knocked out of him by the impact, he watched wonderingly as the ground all around him seemed to be alive with dancing earth. The machine-gunner continued traversing his gun up and down the rows of men who plodded steadfastly on, heads bowed down in a vain attempt to deflect the storm of fire lacing into them.

The machine-gun was joined by another, and then another and soon the air was filled with the humming of thousands of bees as the bullets arced towards their intended targets. From behind the German trenches a deep cough sounded and seconds later the first shell exploded among the men of the 19th, to be followed closely by another, and another.

'Keep moving! Keep moving!' the officers screamed at the men as they hesitated momentarily, shocked by the avalanche of fire and shrapnel being aimed in their direction.

Bodies began to pile up in greater heaps, men being flung aside by the shells that slammed in among them or knocked down like nine-pins as the deadly machine-guns stuttered continuously. Racing along with the men of C Company, Snaith watched in anguish as his men fell around him. He shouted at Ramsbottom alongside him but his words were blown away by the impact of a shell which threw him high into the air in a shower of mud, stones and huge splashes of bright, red blood.

As the dirt and mud cleared, Ramsbottom stood up shakily from where he had been deposited by the explosion. By some miracle, none of the shrapnel had so much as touched him, although his tunic was drenched in what looked and tasted like blood. Shaking his head to clear the ringing noise in his ears, he looked around for the CO.

Snaith lay limply on his side, his arms outstretched, unmoving. Tottering over, Walter looked down at where his CO lay. Cuthbert Snaith's face was untouched save for a thin stream of blood that dribbled slowly from the side of his mouth. His spine had been torn out, his pallor assuming the ghastly, bluish-white hue that Ramsbottom had seen in many of the dead and dying, and he turned away, overcome.

On the ground next to Snaith's body was the bamboo cane that he had carried everywhere with him and, bending down, Walter Ramsbottom picked it up. Lifting the cane high over his head, he shouted 'Colonel Snaith!' and ran on. A figure appeared at his side, the slight figure of Evans, the CO's batman, his face a contorted mask, tears streaming down his cheeks. With a bellow of rage the men followed them, shouting loud imprecations as they broke ranks and raced fearlessly into the barrage, towards the German trenches.

Fred Maitland lay crumpled full-length, a sardonic sneer still evident on his face. A neat row of holes across his chest bore witness to the burst of machine-gun fire that had killed him. He had thrown away the wooden stakes he had been ordered to carry and filled his pack with extra bottles of wine in readiness for the eager market he expected once they'd consolidated their position. Now, blood slowly filled a small indentation in the ground next to him, flowing in a steady scarlet stream together with the red wine from his shattered pack.

Alongside him, Provost Sergeant James Hobson, late of Bethune, coughed spasmodically as his wheezing lungs tried to drag in the oxygen they sorely craved. A bright red froth tinged his lips as his body shivered violently with the onset of shock. The blood oozing from his shattered chest flowed quicker as he struggled to rise. Another bullet slammed into him, high on the forehead, and he collapsed soundlessly, his outflung hand pointing in an empty, futile gesture at Fred Maitland's stiffening corpse.

Lying nearby, Bob Simpson pressed himself hard against the cover Maitland's inert form provided, his own useless right arm beneath him, the uniform sleeve in tatters. Maitland's body jerked again and again as bullets thudded into it and Bob concentrated hard on making his own body as small a target as possible. Darkness was a long way off but to try and make one's way back now was to invite a death sentence. He bit his lip hard and clung on with the bitter-sweet taste of blood, rain water and wine on his lips, the blood his own and that of his late friend.

The rest of B Company were scattered across the lunar landscape, hugging the ground for whatever cover they could find. In shell holes and hollows they lay and it was here that the enemy fire sought them out and killed them. Ernie Wadley was hit trying to pull Billy Lane to safety and both men fell, lying sprawled together in death in a grotesque parody of a lover's embrace. George Bradley, weeping at the futile loss of his men, was bowled over by a savage burst of fire that cut him in two as he raged, his clenched fists raised to the dark, brooding sky. Battered and bewildered, the survivors, many of them hit repeatedly, kept their heads down and prayed as they frantically sought cover.

Charteris was pushing his men on as they emerged from the trench, urging them forward, when he saw a figure pressed into the firestep, unmoving as the rest of the men clambered up. 'Get up here!' he shouted, but the mud-caked man ignored him, pressing his trembling body closer into the dirt. Jumping down into the trench, Charteris shook the figure by the shoulder and recoiled as Elliot glared at him.

Charteris placed his mouth next to Elliot's ear and bawled loudly above the sounds of battle that were erupting all around them. 'What are you doing here? Get up, man, and join your men!'

Elliot's response was to lash out wildly with his pistol, catching Charteris on the side of the head, knocking his cap off. Elliot's eyes were wide open with fright and as Charteris watched he cocked his pistol and waved it in his direction.

'You can't make me go out there, it's bloody murder! We'll all be killed! Damn you, Charteris, I'm not going!'

Swallowing his own fear, Charteris tried to appear calm. 'Second-Lieutenant Elliot, don't be a fool, where do you think you can go? We have to join our men. Put up your pistol and come over with me, it'll be all right.' He reached out.

Elliot shook off his hand and gestured wildly. 'Don't come any closer, Charteris! You've always had it in for me. Come any closer and I'll fire, I swear I will.'

Charteris looked down at him contemptuously. 'You utter coward, Elliot. Get to your feet, man, and show me that you earned the medal whose ribbon you wear. Show your men what you're made of.'

'No!' Elliot screamed again and fired. The impact of the bullet knocked Charteris over and he fell backwards into the thick, glutinous mud at the bottom of the trench. Curiously, he felt no pain, only a warm lassitude as he lay in the freezing mud looking up at Elliot. The second-lieutenant pointed the pistol at him and as he prepared to fire again there was a loud *bang!* in Charteris's ears and the expression on Elliot's face changed. His mouth dropped open and his eyes glazed over, losing their look of madness. The pistol fell from his fingers and he collapsed soundlessly into the mud.

Astonished, Charteris looked up to see the anxious face of Reggie Pilling looking down at him. 'Are you all right, sir?' he called. 'What's going on? Mr Elliot was trying to kill you! I couldn't shout so I had to shoot. Will I be in trouble?' Reggie jumped back down into the trench and dropping his still-smoking rifle, discarded his pack and helped Charteris up into a sitting position on the firestep. Charteris cautiously felt his right hip. The bullet had entered the fatty part, exiting through the back of his tunic just above his belt. Touching the area around the wound made him feel sick so he sat there awhile, supported by a trembling Pilling until he felt he was able to breathe a bit better.

'We'd best get you to the aid post, sir, wherever that is,' Reggie suggested.

'No!' Charteris spoke sharply. 'Look Pilling, I'll be all right in a moment. Do me a favour could you? Pack my side with a wound dressing and help me up. We'll need to crack on otherwise the other chaps will be long gone. And no, you won't be in trouble, you saved my life. Mr Elliot had gone temporarily insane.'

Reggie did as he was told. It was a struggle pulling Charteris over the parapet but eventually both men made it and stood there, panting. The ground in front of them was strewn with bodies, some still moving, and to their front came the sound of renewed firing as shells burst amongst the figures running in the distance. Grabbing Pilling's arm for support Charteris gestured painfully in the direction he wanted to take and both men staggered off together.

Some men reached the enemy wire, drawn like moths to a candle to the gaps the French guns had opened. It was here that the machine-guns concentrated their deadly fire, cutting huge swathes in the lines of men that attempted to force their way through. CSM Miles Hornby and what was left of his platoon desperately crawled up to one such gap, weaving their way through the bodies in their path. He recognised the twisted bodies of Percy Hartson and the rest of his Lewis gun team and his anger rose.

'Quick, lads, throw your bombs and we'll run through!' he shouted. Obediently, a string of Mills bombs was hurled through the air. Screams from the other side told them they had had some effect and Hornby ran forward into the smoke of the explosions. 'Come on, come on!' he screamed as he raced through and gained the far side of the wire. A roaring noise filled his ears above the din of the battlefield and he was savagely flung sideways as a shell exploded with an ear-splitting shriek alongside him.

He came to, his uniform smouldering in spite of the rain, and peppered with holes where the shrapnel from the shell had tore into him. Dazed, caught securely by the twisted barbed wire of the German entanglements, each breath an agonised intake, he fought to stay conscious. Hoarse shouts told him his men had reached the immediate safety of the enemy trench and he smiled, a brief, tired smile as he felt the life drain out of him. The sounds faded around him, all feeling gone now from his limbs. It was getting harder to stay awake now, the temptation to close his eyes and drift away into sleep was overwhelming and as his eyelids began to droop, a figure bent over him. Slowly he opened his eyes with an effort, weakly brushing the fresh blood from his face as he squinted painfully up at the shape before him.

'Hello Miles,' she said, smiling sweetly down on him.

He smiled back.

'Jennifer.'

Her presence seemed perfectly natural and his hand moved feebly as he tried to raise it in greeting. Her auburn hair swirled around the dark of her cloak and she reached down.

'Come along, dear Miles. Come, walk with me.'

A feeling of strength surged through him and he reached up and took her hand. It felt warm and he felt himself rise up until he stood next to her, breathing once again the rich, deep smell of her perfume. He looked into the green eyes that had so bewitched him when they had first met and held onto her hand, wrapping his callused, bloodstained fingers round hers in a tight embrace. Together they turned and walked away into the light mist that had sprung up around them.

* * * * *

Walter Ramsbottom and the rest of C Company ran on. At the edge of a shell hole Bill Evans stood screaming his defiance, working his rifle bolt furiously as he blazed away at the distant enemy trenches. Donnie Parker grabbed his shoulder but the man shrugged him off angrily and recommenced firing.

'What the fuck are you firing at?' Donnie yelled at him.

'Anything!' Evans yelled back. 'They killed old Snaithy!' He tore the empty magazine from his rifle, discarding it as he drew another from his pouches. Donnie nodded and fumbled in his pouch for another Mills bomb. Ramsbottom made to go round him but a burst of machine-gun fire scythed into them and all three men dropped limply to the ground as they were hit. The grenade fell from a dead hand alongside them.

Ramsbottom lay there for a moment or so before being thrown sideways, winded, as the grenade exploded violently, shockingly, only feet away. Painfully raising his head above the two blood-soaked corpses lying next to him he was hit again as he tried to ascertain the direction from where the enemy fire was being directed. The bullet hit him in the throat, spinning him round in a welter of blood and limbs and he was knocked back savagely to the ground. He crawled away, one hand feebly pressed against his neck wound in an effort to halt the bleeding, but his weakened limbs betrayed him and he found himself sliding inexorably down the steep side of a nearby shell hole.

Landing with a splash in the cold, scummy water at the bottom his head slid under the surface and he struggled helplessly to extricate himself. His fingers sinking deeply into the sucking, cloying embrace of the mud, he tried frantically to drag himself backwards. It was an unequal struggle and his strength quickly drained away. His legs thrashed convulsively, then slowly relaxed as his inert body floated head-down. Fragments of shrapnel continued to pepper the filthy surface of the pool, the water intermingled with his blood. Nearby, Snaith's bamboo cane floated among the raindrops, dipping and bowing forlornly alongside Walter's limp body.

Yards from his corpse, A Company were caught out in the open by a torrent of shells that burst amongst them. Archie Higgins and Bill Thomson disappeared in a blinding explosion, leaving nothing but pulped flesh and scraps of uniforms. An arm lay pale-white on the ground, its fingers clenched in a tight fist. On its wrist the shattered glass of an expensive German watch had stopped the hands at precisely eight forty-nine.

Urging his men on, Sergeant Bill Clark had a leg ripped from him in another direct hit and was flung into a fresh shell hole where he bled to death in under a minute. A machine-gun surgically excised those men who clustered round the wire in great groups, the bodies jerking and stumbling under the impacts at close range before dropping limply to the ground like rag dolls.

'Oh God! Oh God!' Charlie Horsfall ran as he'd never run before, gasping hard, legs pumping desperately as he skirted a fresh shell hole and aimed at a gap in the enemy wire ahead. He reached the gap and the grin on his face as he did so turned to startled fear as he saw, too late, the muzzle of the machine-gun turning his way. 'Nooo!' he cried, but his words were lost in the staccato sound of the burst that cut him down at point-blank range.

Their bloodlust up, some defenders jumped up onto the parapet and fired at the men advancing towards them, heedless of the dangers of being caught in the open. Roaring wildly as each shot struck home, they fired exultantly. The machine-gunners expended belt after belt, the runners scurrying backwards and forwards for fresh supplies as the guns voraciously worked their way through the boxes of stock-piled ammunition. Gun after gun had to be stopped to clear blockages as they over-heated, but once cooled down their songs of death chattered out again and fresh bunches of men dropped under the weight of their renewed fire.

Charteris and Reggie Pilling arrived at the wire having painfully picked their way through the quagmire of shell holes and clumps of inert bodies. Shells fell around them unceasingly and bullets hissing past exposed them to the full horrors of the battlefield. Bodies lay everywhere, draped in undignified forms over the barbed wire or simply lying in swathes on the ground where they had been caught in the open. Reggie tried to avert his face as he recognised with horror, in some of the contorted, agonised bodies, faces of the men he had laughed and served with. The sight of them became too much and he sank to his knees vomiting, a great outpouring of rank, yellowish-green bile.

Charteris bent down and grabbed Pilling by the lapel.

'Get up, Pilling, we've got to get on. C'mon, quickly!'

'Sorry, sir,' Reggie murmured weakly, 'it's all me mates. Gone. They've all copped it. It's just like Loos all over again, sir, just you and me left!'

'Forget them for now, we'll catch it too if we don't get on.' Charteris tried to move off through a gap he could see in the wire, stumbled, and would have fallen if Pilling hadn't caught him. Together they wrenched their way through the wire and looked desperately round for any sign of the rest of the company. A hand waved frantically from a hollow in the ground and Pilling pushed Charteris towards it. Flopping down into the relative shelter it afforded, Charteris gasped as his wounded side took the full impact of the fall, knocking the breath out of him in a painful grunt. A hand grabbed his shoulder and he refocused on the mud-caked face of his CSM, Frank Mason.

'Welcome to hell, sir, or what passes remarkably close to it!' Mason remarked dryly. 'Are you all right?'

Charteris wriggled round painfully onto his good side and raised himself into a crouching position. He looked round and counted the prone, scared-looking figures lying next to him in the hollow. Five, not counting him and Pilling. He looked back unbelievingly at the CSM. 'Is this what's left of the company? Where are the rest of them?'

Mason jerked his thumb over his shoulder in the direction they'd just come from. 'Lying out there I reckon, sir. Dead, or most of them I should think. So much for the perfect plan.'

Charteris thought quickly. It was obvious they couldn't continue, not with this amount of men left. 'Are you sure there are no other officers left?'

'None that I know of, sir. We never saw Mr Elliot come out of the trenches. As for the others, I passed several officers lying dead back there but I couldn't tell you who they were on account of the fact I was trying to keep on my feet myself at the time.'

A fresh burst of firing distracted Charteris. Gazing past the CSM he saw a dim figure in field-grey standing on the parapet of the trench beyond the hollow. Frantically he lifted his revolver and fired twice. The soldier dropped out of sight but as he fell, the German threw an object which landed in the hollow amongst them. The stick grenade exploded with a deafening roar and Charteris was flung with great force into the earth on the far side.

Groaning, he came to and looked round. Reggie Pilling lay next to him, his face blood-streaked, eyes wide open in the fixed, blank stare of the dead. Next to him, Frank Mason lay face down but as he watched, the CSM's body shook and he stirred then sat up. The rest of the men who had inhabited their shelter with them lay silent in twisted, grotesque attitudes, the air rank with the coppery tang of freshly-spilled blood. Shaking his head and ignoring the blood running down his face and out of his ears, Frank Mason crawled over to Charteris and peered closely at him.

'Christ, sir, you haven't half copped a packet! Can you hear me?'

Charteris tried to answer but his mouth felt exceedingly dry and all that escaped his lips was a low moan. He tried to stand but his leg collapsed from under him and he fell back again as an agonising pain shot up his right leg. Looking down he saw that his leg from the knee down was covered in blood, with great strips of flesh and what looked like bone bulging out from under the scraps that remained of his trousers. The sight made him feel sick and he fell back onto the wet, greasy earth and passed out.

He came to, disorientated, as his body being jerked up and down, his head bumping against something hard. It took a moment or two for him to realise that he was hanging upside down over someone's shoulder and the hard object his head kept striking was an army-issue water-bottle. Above the noise of exploding shells and the sound of continuous firing he could hear the laboured panting of the man carrying him. He tried to form the words, 'Put me down,' but his lips steadfastly refused to work and he drifted in and out of consciousness as the man beneath him staggered on.

The impact of a bullet striking flesh was the next sound he heard and he felt rather than heard the exhalation of breath as his rescuer collapsed with a cry of agony. Both men landed hard, rolled over and lay inert in the mud. Charteris recognised the face of Frank Mason, screwed up with pain as he clutched his shattered shoulder. Crouching on all fours, Mason spat a great wad of blood from between his lips before crawling over to where Charteris lay.

'Don't worry, sir, we'll be on our way in no time,' he gasped. 'If you'll just give me a minute to catch my breath I'll get going again.'

'Leave me, for God's sake, man! Leave me and save yourself,' Charteris gasped, but Frank Mason grinned weakly and shook his head.

'No fear, sir. What? And catch it from that lovely lady we all know you've been seeing! My missus would never forgive me if I interfered with the course of true love. Now, hold still and let me work this out.' He bent over Charteris and grunted with pain as he helped him to his feet, keeping a tight hold as the officer threatened to collapse again. Ignoring the red-hot poker being pushed into his injured shoulder the CSM sank down and then straightened up with the limp body over his other shoulder.

'Hang on, sir,' he whispered through waves of pain, 'this is going to get a bit bumpy!'

He started off again, stumbling repeatedly as he tried to pick a way through the bodies and shell holes. The mud stuck to his boots causing him to slide and slither in all directions but grimly he carried on, the weight on his shoulder feeling heavier with every stride. Above the din he heard a voice and raised his head with an effort. In front of him two figures were clinging to each other as they, too, stumbled painfully back towards the safety of their own trenches, both oblivious to the bullets striking the ground all around them or the shells whining overhead

'C'mon, Titch, old man, hang on, don't dare let go, you hear!' The cooing voice belonged to Archie Parkes and as Frank Mason drew level he could see a blood-stained bandage wrapped round the other man's head, covering his eyes. Becoming aware of him, Parkes raised his good arm in greeting.

'What-ho, sir, me an' Titch have had enough of this lark.' He gestured at his chum, talking as if to a child. "E's been shot through the forehead, poor beggar, says 'e can't see so I'm taking 'im to see Mr Hughes. Get 'im sorted, like'

Frank Mason said nothing, the effort of carrying his officer had robbed him of the power of speech, but he looked at the blood running from under Parkes's tunic sleeve. Following his gaze Parkes looked down.

'Oh that, just a scratch. Copped a bullet, maybe two, in my elbow. Nice cushy Blighty one for me. Ta-ta, then!' He tried to raise that arm as the CSM moved away from him but it flopped uselessly at his side.

'Right, mate, now don't you give me any more grief, Titch, and no more stupid questions or you can find yer own way back. Course I knows where the fuck we're headed! It's you that's bleedin' blind, remember?'

Behind them the firing continued unabated. Shells screamed over and exploded, and the continuous stutter of Mauser rifles and machine-guns was every-where, raking each part of the devastated, churned-up ground over which the 19th had so valiantly advanced. It had been a slaughter. Some men, a futile few, had gained the German trenches only to be cut off and exterminated.

Arwyn Jones, Harry Sheldon and their company commander, Major Giles Redford, died together. Standing over their officer's dying body, Harry and Arwyn roared defiance as they fought off the enemy troops trying to dislodge them from the firebay they had gained in the midst of the German trenches. They had made the furthest gains into the Osnabrucker Stellung but without support they were quickly doomed. Both men soon fell, riddled at close range. Giles Redford tried to stand, weakly, but a pistol shot to the head felled him and he landed heavily across the very bodies of the two men who had tried to save him.

On both flanks the other two regiments suffered the same fate as the 19th. Rolling waves of khaki broke against the stout walls of the German defences. The Cheshires were caught leaving their trenches and cut down in bunches, only a few men making it to the opposite side where they were swiftly dealt with. The West Kents fared slightly better as the Germans opposite them were slow in manning their defence lines, allowing the British troops to close with them before they were discovered. A fierce fight took place at close hand but as the German reserves poured in, their superior numbers began to tell and slowly the West Kents were forced to retreat. Relentlessly, the Germans pursued them, ruthlessly cutting down all in their path. Small groups formed and fought their way back to the safety of the trenches they had left earlier, but behind them the ground was littered with their dead and dying.

Around the Osnabrucker Stellung the vast majority of the men who had sailed from Folkestone six months previously lay thick on the ground in front of the defenders' trenches. Here and there a man moved, slowly, blindly, as he crawled aimlessly in the thick mud. After a while, even the most hardened of the Germans stopped, sickened, as they leant on their rifles on the firestep and looked out on the spectacle before them. From the huddled masses sprawled in great heaps out in front came a low, moaning noise, like cattle in labour. The rain stopped abruptly and in the growing light a vivid rainbow appeared, throwing the bunched lines of corpses into sharp relief.

Charteris passed out for a third time as he was bounced along. When he came to he was lying on the firestep of a trench, next to a shaking, tearful Frank Mason. The CSM was gratefully swigging deeply from a mug and Charteris's senses caught the aromatic smell of whisky. The smell brought back his queasiness and he retched, dry-mouthed. Nothing passed his lips and he writhed in pain as a bloodied figure bent over him undoing the makeshift tourniquet around his lower leg. From a distance he heard the hiss of a sharp intake of breath and struggled briefly until he recognised the muddied, blood-filled face as that of Bevan Hughes.

'Hello, Neville, old chap. Well done, you've made it back. Now lie still and let me have a look at this leg, would you?'

Charteris tried to tell him about the wound in his side and the blood he could feel washing down his right leg but the darkness that had been at his side from the moment the grenade exploded enveloped him and his head fell limply back. The last sound he heard as he slid into the blackness was Bevan Hughes bellowing in his ear, 'Neville, hold on! Hold on man!'

* * * * *

Major David Roberts appeared before the MO, tears coursing down his face.

'Oh God, Bevan, its a slaughter. Simply murder. Twenty minutes and we've been wiped out. Can you s—?'

The MO spoke sharply.

'David, if that's all you've come to say at a time like this, I'd rather you left here now. We're overwhelmed with casualties, can't you see? Now take a handful of bandages from over there and do something positive or just get out of the way. You standing there mourning is a luxury we simply can't afford.'

Roberts shuffled over to the box containing the bandages and began stuffing them into his pockets. He moved to Bevan Hughes's side and peered down. 'Great Scott! It's Neville Charteris!'

'Shut up and hand me those bandages, I think we're losing him. Get out of the way!' The MO pushed him violently and Roberts fell backwards into the mud. He stood up painfully and stepped back to watch as Bevan Hughes frantically applied fresh dressings to Charteris's mangled leg and then gestured to the two waiting men holding a mud-stained, bloodied stretcher.

'Off you two go! Get this man down to where I told you the French ambulances should be waiting and pray that you do find them there. Quickly!' They needed no further bidding. The limp body was gently, tenderly lowered down onto the stretcher and they made off quickly down the trench, staggering under the weight of their load.

He turned back to the adjutant who was standing helplessly, his hands full of fresh bandages. 'Thank you, David. It's in God's hands for that young man now. I just hope to Christ that the French have at least kept their promise to provide advanced medical care for those involved in this attack, otherwise we're going to lose a lot more. All I can do is to provide the most basic of care, try to stop the bleeding and bandage the men up before sending them further down the line to whatever it is the French will provide.'

Both of them waded down the trench to where a tidal wave of staggering, stumbling unrecognisable figures was steadily appearing. They were joined by Bob Findlay, his face a grim mask, clutching a medical bag of dressings. Bevan Hughes tramped on, followed by David Roberts and the RSM.

Two exhausted men approached, one with a bloodied arm hanging uselessly as he guided his friend wearing a blood-stained wound dressing over his eyes, and the MO grabbed roughly at the man's good arm.

'The colonel. Colonel Snaith? Did you see him out there?'

His answer was a weary shrug. The soldier jerked his head back in the direction he'd came and looked the MO squarely in the face for several seconds, almost accusingly. Before Hughes could speak, the soldier spat at his feet and pushed past as he lurched down the trench, supporting his friend. A medical attendant caught up with them and bent over the first man while Hughes and Roberts wended their way further down the trench towards the other shuffling, stumbling figures.

As they made their way towards the flood of wounded men, Bevan Hughes recognised the two battalion chaplains bending over a fallen body. He touched Roger Dundas on the shoulder as he and Roberts squeezed past.

'I'd appreciate it if you two would follow me, Roger,' he said softly. 'I fear there's more than enough work here for us all today.' The chaplain looked up at his stricken face and nodded. Grabbing his bag he straightened up and together the small group of men went to meet the shattered bodies moving towards them. In the distance was an eerie silence as the firing slackened and finally died away.

The last entry in the war diary read:

Saturday 1st March 1916

The battalion attacked the position known as the Osnabrucker Stellung yesterday morning along with two other British regiments. The promised artillery preparation failed to materialise fully, as did the promised participation of further British and French troops. We were forced to go in unsupported. Despite great heroism shown by all ranks we were unable to gain a foothold in the enemy position and were thrown back with lamentable casualties. Preliminary figures indicate a total of 17 officers out of 23 and 629 other ranks dead, wounded or missing. Our Commanding Officer, Lt. Col. J.C. Snaith DSO is known to have been killed, along with his second in command, Major Walter Ramsbottom and three out of four Company Commanders. Captain Charteris DSO MC was rescued with commendable gallantry by CSM Mason and lies near death, gravely wounded. The heart of the battalion has been torn out. A full copy of the battalion orders detailing today's attack can be found in the annexe attached to this entry.

Major D. Roberts, Adjutant, 19th Service Battalion, King's Own Lancashire Rifles

4th March 1916. Tuesday.

'Come along ladies, follow me. This way now.' The speaker, a well-dressed matronly-looking woman of a mature age, beamed solicitously as she regarded her charges as they stood around, nervously glancing down the railway platform at Victoria. The long silent shape of the train waiting there, its carriages emblazoned with red crosses, told of it being an ambulance train newly-arrived from Folkestone. Already the walking wounded were being helped down and Lady Juliet Oliver turned brightly to the young women, clad in their new VAD uniforms, who anxiously awaited her orders.

'Right ladies, walk down the platform and sort yourselves into pairs. See the RAMC men helping our boys down? Attach yourselves to one of them and ask what you can do to assist.'

'No Sarah,' she reached out and gently touched the young girl who had started towards the foremost carriage on the arm. 'No dear, don't bother. That carriage is for the hopeless cases, those poor boys who are not expected to survive. Don't distress yourself, walk further down to the next carriages. Matilda, would you accompany Sarah? Good girl!'

Tillie Fairley started guiltily at the mention of her name. She took a quick glance at the front carriage then moved over to where Sarah stood and together they began to walk hesitantly down the platform towards the burgeoning throng of bandaged men appearing in growing numbers. Behind her the door of the tightly-shuttered carriage opened and the first stretcher appeared, shaking under the attentions of the medical orderlies trying to manoeuvre it through the narrow aperture.

Neville Charteris hissed with pain as the motion of the stretcher jarred the broken ends of his shattered leg. A wave of agony washed over him and he fell back weakly onto the stretcher, his hands fluttering as he tried to make sense of his surroundings. From below his waist, a rank smell of putrefaction wafted upwards and he mentally shrank from its import. Dim shapes appeared in his peripheral vision. Women? He tried to focus on them but his leg moved abruptly, the bones grating, and he sank down once more into a black abyss.

EPILOGUE

I closed the book and sat back with it clasped to my chest. It seemed to me that within these dirty, mud-streaked entries lay the story of a tragedy of the Great War, one easily found in any regimental museum or on the bookshelves of any major bookstore you care to visit. I opened the diary anew and looked at it again. At the back I re-read the appendices with the names of the men who had served in the battalion and the dates of the actions in which they had become casualties. Grouped into their companies and various sub-sections within the battalion, their names jumped out from the pages: Snaith, Colonel, Simpson, Corporal, Sprightly, Major.

Their names and regimental numbers filled the pages and alongside many of the names was a simple: 'killed', 'wounded' or 'missing'. By far the largest group of entries had the date 28/1/16 written in a neat, orderly hand. More confusingly, some names had a number, or series of numbers, or even no number, alongside the words that told of their fate. Colonel Snaith seemed to have the most but why, I had no idea. I looked at these numbers for a while but nothing sprang to mind and I gave up. Someone, a code expert perhaps, might be able to enlighten me, but for the time being their meaning left me in the dark as to the writer's intentions.

The next morning I took myself off to work. All day, though, I kept seeing those entries in my mind and going over the happenings of all those years ago. The weekend couldn't come round quickly enough and I almost ran down the street and into Phil's shop.

He saw me enter and ducked quickly back into his cubby-hole. Not quick enough.

'Oi, Phil, get yourself out here. I saw you!'

A silence, then, reluctantly, he edged out. 'Now what, what d'you want this time?' he almost snarled at me. I took a deep breath and smiled.

'Remember that book you sold me the other day, the war diary? Can you remember where it came from?' I asked sweetly.

'Oh, that one, the one you stole from me!' he replied.

'Okay! Okay! Let's beg to differ on that for the moment. Now, go back a week or so, Phil. Please! Where did the book come from?'

His face took on a pensive look and I waited. And waited. Just when I had decided to leave, his face changed. Sort of brightened. Not pretty.

'I told you before didn't I? It came from some bleedin' house clearance. The geezer, or was it a lady, I forget, brought a box of books in that day. It was stuck in there, wasn't it.'

'Do you still have the box of books, then?' I asked, as noncommittally as I could, so as not to arouse his suspicion.

His eyes narrowed. 'Why, what's so special about the box?' He could smell a big payday coming.

'Look Phil, no more beating about the bush. Do you have the box or not?'

'All right, all right. Keep yer bleedin' hair on. I was only asking that's all. Christ, you can't ask a decent question these days without...' Grumbling, he disappeared out of view and reappeared with a Jaffa orange cardboard box. He heaved it onto the counter and stood back, panting.

'Go on then.' He pointed at the box. 'Go on, take a look. There's nothing of any value in there. You'll see. All this argey-bargey for nothing!'

I delved into the box. He was right. A few musty-smelling Reader's Digest three-in-one books, some ancient *National Geographics* and a host of the usual mix of novels and gardening books were all it contained. Disappointed, I made to turn away.

'Oh, I forgot to mention, there was a few other books in there. Nothing much, but you never know. I put them on the odds-and-sods shelf. The sort of thing that brings a few bob in. Take a look, be my guest.'

It was all part of his funny games. I kept my temper and wandered down the shop, following his pointing finger. At first glance the shelf didn't contain anything out of the ordinary but I stooped and read the titles of each book as I walked along the shelf. At the far end of the middle row a title caught my eye and I pulled the book from its place in the row. Edmund Blunden – *Undertones of War*. One of the classic tales of the First World War, I had my own copy in the house.

My interest aroused, I turned the book over and over in my hands before opening its rather tatty cover. There, inscribed on the inside of the cover, was a message:

To
Captain Neville Charteris, DSO. MC
Merry Christmas to my dearest husband
From your loving wife and son,
Tillie and Arthur.
Xxxxxxxxxxx
PS And Gilbert and Bertha.

Christmas 1929

Bingo! I turned to Phil again, ready for a fight but surprisingly he wasn't interested. His interest was taken up by some good-looking blonde who had just wandered in. I sauntered over.

'How much did you say you wanted for this?' I asked as casually as I could.

His eyes never left the blonde. 'Er, oh I dunno, I was... Well, um. Hows about a quid, how does that sound?'

Done! I slapped the pound coin in his hand. He never looked at me once. He was right, though, the book meant nothing to him but for me it was special. It was linked to the diary in some way and though I'd read the diary from cover to cover, it didn't tell all the story.

I did, however, make a start at looking up some of the names on the Commonwealth War Graves Commission Register. Thank goodness for computers. There's so much information available out there. There were scant references to the attack by the 19th and the other regiments that day, it was just another doomed idea of Haig's High Command that never got off the ground. The casualties suffered that day paled into insignificance when compared with the utter carnage in the Somme just over four months later, when the British Army suffered its worst day in history on July 1st. Mention the Somme to anyone and they automatically think of the July attack, the sideshow that the 19th undertook just never enters their minds.

＊ ＊ ＊ ＊ ＊

I did, try, fruitlessly it must be said, to find out as much as I could. I scoured all the local libraries for any scraps from their First World War sections and my pay-as-you-go 'Googling' began to take on figures resembling the National Debt. All to no avail.

The numbers written in the back of the diary confused and perplexed me. I sat for hours reading and re-reading them, trying and failing to put their significance into the context of the diary entries. It was some sort of simple code but it defeated all my efforts to understand or crack it.

I had better luck with the men's names. By cross-referring the details of all the names I entered, it told me that the vast majority of the recovered bodies had been buried in Combles Cemetery Extension, a few miles from scene of the ill-fated attack.

The majority of the men of the 19th had lain for months, unrecovered, throughout the bloody affair of the Somme until late August. Most were unrecognisable when found by the Chinese labour battalions tasked with the unpleasant job of recovering the dead, their identity only being confirmed by personal items found on the bodies or by the tags the men carried. The names of those whose bodies were never found or recovered are to be found on the huge memorial to the Somme missing, at Thiepval. Other websites such as 'The Long Trail Winding' and 'The Great War Forum' gave sketchy details of the 19th but none that satisfied the hunger within me to find out more.

There the matter might have rested, but one Saturday, a month or so later, the front door bell rang. I was deep into my *Saturday Telegraph* at the time .

'Dawn? Get the door could you? I'm busy!' There was no answer and a second or two later the doorbell went again. I answered its impatient summons and peered frostily at the person standing there who'd disturbed my peace. A man, forty-ish, quite well-dressed in clean chinos and a smart shirt and tie under a dark jacket. Jehovah's witnesses! My anger rose.

'Look, I don't mean to be rude but whatever it is you're trying to sell, I don't want any. Now if you'll excuse me...'

I made to push the door closed but he leant forward with a puzzled expression.

'Mr Barrett? Phil said I'd find you here. Could I speak to you for a moment?'

Phil? How did he know Phil? He didn't look like the sort of person that rummages round Phil's shop on a Saturday, or any other day for that matter. I stopped trying to close the door and stared at him inquisitively.

He put out a hand. 'Sorry,' he smiled, 'I should have introduced myself first, I think. My name's Christopher Charteris and I hope in some way you'll be able to help me.'

Charteris? My puzzlement must have shown because he continued quickly. 'My father was Arthur Charteris, the son of Neville Charteris, Captain Neville Charteris. I believe you bought a diary from Phil's bookshop, and that's what I'm here about, if you don't mind.'

I stepped back and ushered him in. We sat in the front room and after looking slightly uncomfortable for a few seconds or so, he relaxed and began to tell me his story.

'My father died a few months ago and I was in Romford cleaning out the house, getting rid of some old stuff, you understand. There was a heap of boxes I'd put out for the charity shops and to my horror, when I came back two weeks ago, my father's neighbour had let the lady from the charity shop in and she'd taken the boxes. Unfortunately, including the one I'd put aside. That one contained the war diary of the regiment my grandfather, Neville, had served in during the Great War and a book my grandmother had given him as a Christmas present years after the war. Neither book has any real worth other than the obvious sentimental value they have for me, but you can imagine how I felt when I discovered they were gone.

I've been going round the shops frantically these past few weekends. The charity shop woman said she'd passed on the box of books to someone in one of the second-hand bookshops in Romford but couldn't for the life of her remember which one. It was a matter of going through them one by one and as luck would have it, the last one I came to was this chap called Phil. He remembered the books immediately and gave me your name. A quick trawl through the phone book led me here. He said a queer thing, though, as I was leaving. He said, "Remember to tell Mr Barrett, revenge is sweet." What did he mean?'

I lowered my head and ground my teeth. I owe you one, Phil, I said mentally, and motioned for the man sitting on my sofa to carry on talking.

'My grandfather was a war hero, did you know?' he said proudly. 'He was badly wounded in the futile attack that led to the slaughter of his regiment in 1916 and was evacuated from France to a hospital in London after having his right leg amputated from the knee down. God knows why they didn't keep him in France a while longer before evacuating him to England as the infection he caught there nearly killed him. Luckily he had a good doctor in London, the guy did a great job and saved granddad's life. Pity he had to lose the leg, though it never seemed to bother him and he built up a successful career as an insurance specialist after the war, coming here to live in Romford with my grandmother, Tillie and their young son, Arthur, who was my father.

A Belgian refugee my grandmother had taken in during the war, a Mrs Humboldt, stayed with them too. Her husband came over to Britain on his release from a German prisoner of war camp and they settled here.'

'But how did your grandfather come to get hold of the diary?' I interrupted, puzzled.

'Oh, that? A Mr Findlay, I believe. He was the regimental sergeant major of the regiment my grandfather served in and came to visit him after the war to present him with it. He said the regiment had never been re-formed after the final attack they took part in so he had appropriated the book to stop it from becoming lost. When he heard my grandfather had survived the war he sought him out as he said he deserved to keep it more than any other man he knew.

Mr Findlay found my grandfather through another person, a Frank Mason, who had also survived the war. He won the highest award there is, the Victoria Cross, for carrying my grandfather back across the battlefield to safety even though he was badly wounded himself. He was commissioned and ended the war as a major.

Dad was so proud of his father. I have Neville's medals, and my father's from his service in the Second World War. He won a Military Cross at Arnhem. The books were all part of that, our family's military history, so you can imagine how devastated I was to find they were missing. Now I've found them, but it depends on what you want to do. After all, you did buy them legitimately.'

He stopped speaking and looked at me earnestly.

What could I do? Say, 'Thanks for a great story,' and show him the door? He was right. They were *my* books, but I like to think that I have some shred of decency in me. Not where Phil was concerned, I grant you, but this was different. I opened my hands expansively.

'Look Christopher, don't worry, the books are yours. I'll go and get them for you in a minute. You can have them with my blessing, I'm only too glad I'm able to give them back to their rightful owner. No, no, there's no need to thank me,' I said as he made to rise. 'This is a great story and I'd love to hear more of it. Do you have the time to tell me more about your grandfather and the 19th?'

'Why, yes, if you're sure you want to hear it'

'Good God! Of course I want to hear your story, I have so many questions. Such as why are there numbers after the names at the back of the diary? Who wrote them? What happened to...'

He laughed at my reaction to his words as the questions spilled from my lips.

'The number thing is quite easy, Mr Findlay used it as a sort of reminder of the pages in the diary where these people featured, or so my father told me. He simply wrote a page number alongside their names, starting from the beginning of the diary. Easy if you know the secret, unbreakable if you don't.'

I mentally kicked myself. Hard.

'And the survivors, what happened to them, did your grandfather ever know of them?'

He frowned, the laughter gone from his face. 'He did find out some news of those who survived that bloody affair, on the battalion's last day. Major Roberts, the adjutant, was killed later that year, on the Somme. I know a Corporal Simpson survived the war because he used to write to my grandfather for several years after. Christmas cards used to appear every year as far as I can remember. The name Magilton comes to mind too, as does the name Bevan Hughes. He was the battalion MO. I dimly remember him coming to see us once, when I was quite young. He must have been some age even then. Smoked a foul-smelling pipe. Frank Mason was a great guy, my grandfather had a real affection for him and he was a regular visitor for years until he died in Burnley. As to the others...'

He stopped, as if unsure how to continue

'Go on' I urged him. 'Don't stop, this is fascinating stuff and I want to hear as much as possible from you.'

He nodded, then continued.

'My grandfather never fully recovered mentally, I think, from the events of that day. The physical wounds soon healed but he carried the mental scars with him for the rest of his life. He was very bitter that a decision was made not to breathe new life into the survivors of the attack by drafting new men into the battalion. It was as if by allowing such a monumental loss of life by their sterile tactics and lack of proper preparation that the High Command decided to obliterate all acknowledgement of the battalion's existence. The 19th's name disappeared into history, forgotten until the appearance of this diary.'

He burst out. 'It was such a futile waste! The attack was all for nothing, so many good men died because of some staff wallah's hare-brained scheme to assist the French. The 19th's attack was meant to distract the German reserves travelling south. It failed miserably, not a single event of what happened that day diverted the Germans in any way, they still attacked Verdun.

The Somme attack on July 1st was to be a mainly French affair, did you know that, with British participation. Verdun changed all that and the British took on a greater part of the planned assault. Haig's lot were unprepared, the battleground was more or less forced on them by the French and the Germans could hardly believe their luck. The one place on the Western front the Allies did not want to mount an attack was on the Somme. It was too well defended and the result of such poor muddled thinking was the decimation of the British New Armies, the "Kitchener" battalions. I sometimes think that had they not been thrown into the misguided attack on that January morning, the 19th would have been slaughtered along with so many other young men a few months later.

Perhaps that was the saving of my grandfather though, for if he had been involved in the July attack, along with the 19th, he probably would not have survived. Officer casualties that day were simply horrendous. The awful thing was, they failed to learn from their mistakes. The attacks continued throughout the summer and autumn, into November, until Haig called a halt to the offensive. It cost both sides hundreds of thousands of casualties and for what?' He stopped abruptly, a look of embarrassment on his face. ' I'm sorry, there I go, on my soapbox again. It doesn't take much to start me off on the one subject that is so dear to my heart.'

I smiled back at him to show I wasn't offended in the slightest. Here was a man after my own heart, after all. 'Don't give it a second thought, Christopher, I could sit here and listen to you all day. Carry on please.'

He laughed, nervously. "You must excuse me, it's just that the subject of the 19th is one that I heard from a very young age. By the time I was twelve, the name of nearly everyone who served in the battalion was inscribed in my memory and I knew every last detail of the short months they served in France. The men, their lives, their families and their hopes. Everything. Bless him, my grandfather spoke of very little else. In a way it was his whole life and over time it became mine too.

I backed up his knowledge with some detailed research of my own at the National Archives and various other sources so you could say I'm a walking encyclopaedia on the 19th, their unofficial historian. Look, I have here a copy of the orders for the attack. They formed an annexe in the diary but my father kept them apart from the book. I'll just read you a few of those entries if you like."

I felt a momentary twinge. I'd promised Dawn a trip to Asda. It soon passed. To hell with the shopping, I settled back comfortably in my chair and waited expectantly for him to speak again.

OTHER SOURCE MATERIAL

I never set out to write a novel on the First World War that espoused any particular cause. My story tells the simple tale of a New Army battalion, raised in 1914 as a result of the outpourings of patriotism that swept Great Britain in August of that year, and their service in France in 1915-16.

For those readers who might wish to further their knowledge of The Great War there is so much to choose from but the books and other media sources mentioned below may well be of some assistance. The reason for so many references to the Somme battles is that it was upon that anvil that the young enthusiastic men who rushed to join up in their thousands at the start of the war were broken.

Books

The Somme – A new panoramic perspective. Peter Barton.
Published in 2006 by Constable. ISBN-13:978-1-845-399-4.

Somme. Lyn Macdonald.
Published in 1983 by Penguin Books. ISBN 0-14-017867-8.

The First day on the Somme by Martin Middlebrook.
Published in 1971 by Penguin Books. ISBN 0-14-017134-7.

Tommy by Richard Holmes.
Published in 2004 by Harper Collins.ISBN 0-00-713751-6.

Mud, Blood and Poppycock by Gordon Corrigan.
Published in 2003 by Cassell. ISBN 0-304-36559-5.

Blindfold and Alone. British Military Executions in the Great War.
By Cathryn Corns and John Hughes-Wilson.
Published in 2001 by Cassell. ISBN 0-304-36449-5

For the Sake of Example – Capital Courts Martial 1914-20 by Anthony Babington. First published in 1983 by Penguin Books. ISBN 0-141-39100-6

Internet-based material

www.firstworldwar.com
www.fylde.demon.co.uk (Hellfire Corner website)
www.1914-1918.net.   (The Long, Long Trail website)
www.westernfrontassociation.com
www.iwm.org.uk   (The Imperial War Museum)
www.cwgc.org (The Commonwealth War Graves Commission)